## Griffin's head turned at her arrival.

He was sitting on the edge of his desk, dressed in a white shirt, dark plum waistcoat, black ... His hair looked mussed, ... hands through it. He ... etty woman about Finley's ... refined in a silky grey g... had to be family because she ... the same eyes—like a spring sky about to be taken over by storm clouds. When she turned her head, Finley saw the fine chains that ran from her nose to ear. But it wasn't until those stormy eyes met hers and she felt a strange sensation in her head that Finley knew this woman was anything but ordinary.

The thing inside her reared up like a giant hand and came crashing down on the buzzing in her brain, squashing it like a bug.

The woman flinched.

"I beg your pardon," Finley said, a little shaken at having been protected by that shadow of herself—at needing to be protected, "but isn't it a little rude to crawl about in someone's mind without permission?"

**Books by *Kady Cross*
from MIRA Ink**

**The Steampunk Chronicles**
(in reading order)

THE STRANGE CASE OF FINLEY JAYNE

THE GIRL IN THE STEEL CORSET

THE GIRL IN THE CLOCKWORK COLLAR

To find out more visit www.miraink.co.uk and find us
on Twitter @MIRAInk

# THE GIRL IN THE STEEL CORSET

## Kady Cross

With novella prequel *The Strange Case of Finley Jayne*

Mira Ink is a registered trademark of Harlequin Enterprises Limited, used under licence.

Published in Great Britain 2012
MIRA Books, an imprint of Harlequin (UK) Limited,
Eton House, 18-24 Paradise Road,
Richmond, Surrey, TW9 1SR

*The Girl in the Steel Corset* © Kady Cross 2011
*The Strange Case of Finley Jayne* © Kady Cross 2011

ISBN 978 1 848 45112 4

47-0612

MIRA's policy is to use papers that are natural, renewable and recyclable products and made from wood grown in sustainable forests. The logging and manufacturing processes conform to the legal environmental regulations of the country of origin.

Printed and bound by
CPI Group (UK) Ltd, Croydon, CR0 4YY

# CONTENTS

# THE STRANGE CASE
# OF FINLEY JAYNE

This book is for all the girls who provided inspiration:
Elsa, Katlyn, Emma, Madeline, Roxi and Rosie.

Also, for Steve, who not only inspired me, but helped
with research, helped me brainstorm, took care of meals
and never complained about all the take-out he had to
eat while I worked. Thanks, hon—not only for the
support, but for going to see *Twilight* with me.
You so rock.

Hugs to Krista and Nancy and Miriam for believing in
this project, and in me—even when I had my doubts.

And lastly, this book is for me. Because, after
writing 20+, I deserve one. :-)

# Chapter 1

*London, The Age of Invention, late April 1897*

"You're the very spawn of Satan and I'll not have you darken this door ever again."

Finley Jayne jumped as the door was slammed in her face, leaving her standing alone in the small, damp flagstone square that acted as the servants' entrance to the town house.

She'd been fired—well and good—by Mrs. Brown, the housekeeper. Normally being called the spawn of Satan would upset Finley, but lately she'd begun to wonder if the sentiment wasn't true. This was, after all, the second job she'd been let go from.

At least the old crone could have let her collect her things.

Just like in a stage-comedy, the back door opened once more and Finley's carpetbag sailed out of the dim interior. She caught it before it could strike her in the face.

"Oy!" she cried, but the door slammed shut again—and

this time Mrs. Brown locked it from the inside. She heard the tumblers fall into place as the bitter old woman turned the wheel engaging the mechanism which could only be opened once again by a punch card.

Mrs. Brown had taken Finley's punch card from her room before firing her.

Of all the bloody rotten luck. Tossed out without a reference for something that wasn't even her fault. She hadn't been the one to slap young master Fenton hard enough to make him cry when he tried to take a fourth biscuit from the tea tray. That had been the governess—Miss Clarke—who had a particular habit of striking small children.

Miss Clarke slapped the boy, and then Finley punched Miss Clarke.

How was she to know the woman's teeth were so brittle that they'd fall out? They'd certainly been healthy enough to cut Finley's knuckles. And not having much experience with violence, how was she to know that "normal" girls weren't supposed to have the strength to send a full-grown woman, three stone heavier than herself, flying backward several feet?

As she lowered her bag to her side and walked toward the stairs to the street, Finley had to be serious long enough to realize that she hadn't been fired for striking the governess— Mrs. Brown struck the maids all the time. She'd been fired because there was something wrong with her.

She wasn't *right*. Was it the work of the devil? She didn't feel evil. Even when that darkness came over her and made her do the things she shouldn't do, it didn't feel wrong or bad. And she wasn't going to apologize for knocking Miss Clarke on her fat behind when the older woman had brought a child to tears.

The memory of it made her grit her teeth as she climbed

the cracked and crumbling stairs. Even the smells and sounds of Mayfair didn't dent her anger. And now she had to walk through Grosvenor Square with hair frizzy from working a steam press all morning. If she'd known she'd get sacked she would have hit the cow harder.

She stopped two steps from the street. This was exactly what was wrong with her. She'd be thinking—could be about nothing in particular—and she'd have a dark thought, like hitting someone, or saying something true, but cruel. But unlike regular people, sometimes she couldn't help but give in to temptation.

Perhaps it was the devil, after all.

Just like that, her anger receded, leaving a ball of fear and dread in her belly so cold and hard it felt like lead. She was unemployed in a city where good jobs for a girl were scarce, and without a reference.

She was, as her stepfather would often say when he thought she couldn't hear, "buggered."

The thought of her parents only brought her mood down lower. How was she going to explain to them that she'd lost her position because she couldn't control herself? They didn't know about these strange incidents. When she was younger they were so infrequent she barely gave them a thought, but they started getting worse shortly after she got her first monthly, and now happened regularly enough—and without warning—that oftentimes she wasn't even aware anything had happened until it was far too late.

She couldn't tell her parents the complete truth, but she had to tell them something. As of today she had no place to stay, and proud as she was, even she wasn't foolish enough to spend the night on the street.

There were things far more dangerous than her in London.

★ ★ ★

Her mother made hot chocolate.

Finley smiled guiltily at the steaming mug. She knew it would taste like heaven, even when the toast she dunked in it left a buttery haze on top. "You didn't have to do that."

"Nonsense," her mother, Mary, countered, taking a seat at the table. She had her own mug, as well. "We haven't done this for a long time."

It really hadn't been that long, but sometimes it felt like years since she'd left home. "I'm sorry to intrude upon you like this."

Her mother's warm hand closed over one of hers. "Dearest, this is your home, and it always will be. You could never intrude upon Silas and me."

Finley stared down at the scarred, yet polished tabletop. Her mother and Silas weren't poor, but they weren't wealthy, either. The bookshop they ran did a solid business, but life would be easier for both of them without the burden of an extra body to clothe and feed.

If only she hadn't hit Miss Clarke. If only she could bring herself to feel badly for it. She didn't. She felt badly for being here, leeching off her parents, but she didn't feel one ounce of remorse for what she had done—only the consequences of it.

"You'll find a new position," her mother added, giving her hand a squeeze. "And they'll be glad to have you. Only next time, try to keep your mouth closed."

Finley glanced up in time to catch her mother's smile. She hadn't been completely honest, nor had she lied precisely. She told her parents that she had lost her job because of an altercation with the governess who was favored by the mistress of the house. That was all true. She simply left out the part about causing that same servant to swallow her own teeth.

"I will, Mama," she promised, trying to force her own lips to curve.

Slowly, her mother's smile faded away, replaced by an expression of concern that tightened the corners of her pale blue eyes. Finley had often wished her eyes could be that color, but as she grew up she began to appreciate that she had something of Thomas Jayne about her.

"Has something else happened?" her mother asked. "Is there something you want to talk about?"

Words teetered on the tip of her tongue, just waiting to spill out and confess everything, but Finley bit them back. "No. I'm just disappointed in myself."

"Learn from it and then let it go. Dwelling never helped anyone." A strange expression crossed her face. "You must believe me in this."

For a moment Finley wondered, as she often did when her mother was particularly cryptic, if she referred to Finley's father. She had never known her real father, and though Silas had been as good to her as any father could, she often wondered about the man.

She wondered if she looked like him—her mother said she did. She wondered how many things that she enjoyed or disliked had come from him. And she wondered, of course, if he might have been a little mad. Her mother never came out and said such a thing, but there were secrets where her father was concerned. Finley had never even been to his grave. Her mother claimed she wouldn't know where to find it in the graveyard, she'd been so grief stricken, but Finley sometimes thought that was a lie.

Perhaps it was better that she didn't know the truth.

"I will try not to dwell on things, Mama," she promised. "And I will begin to look for a new position first thing tomorrow morning."

Her mother gave her fingers a light squeeze. "I know you will, but I want you to find something that suits you, so don't rush in to the first employment you find. You may stay here as long as you want, and take time to find a post where they will treat you well." A slight smile curved her lips. "One where they hopefully do not employ a governess."

Finley laughed. Laughing made it seem like everything was going to be all right. She would find a new job and there was nothing wrong with her. If only she could keep laughing, she might just believe it.

# Chapter 2

Fate, it seemed, also had an odd sense of humor, because Finley didn't have to go looking for new employment the next morning; new employment came looking for her.

She was in the small parlor in their apartments above the bookshop, taking tea with her mother and mending a tear in one of her best dresses with the small steam-powered sewing engine, when Silas came up from the shop, his lean cheeks pale.

"Silas," her mother began in a concerned tone. "Whatever is the matter?"

"There's a Lady Morton in the shop," he told them. "She says she's here to see Finley."

Finley's hand froze on the lever that operated the machine's engine. She looked from her mother's surprised face to Silas's and then back to her mother. They knew of Lady Morton, of course; she was frequently mentioned in the society pages. "What could she want with me?"

"She didn't say," Silas replied. "And I'm embarrassed to say I didn't know how to ask."

Slowly, on knees that trembled ever so slightly, Finley rose to her feet. Lady Morton was a friend to Lady Gattersleigh—mother of little Fenton, whose governess she had jobbed in the mouth just the day before.

Was the lady there to make her life even more unpleasant? Tell her mother and Silas that she was unnatural? Perhaps she was being overly pessimistic, but she didn't see how this visit could possibly end on a positive note.

"Should I bring her up?" Silas asked, turning now to his wife, who looked horrified at the prospect of entertaining an aristocrat in her humble home.

"No," Finley answered, partially because she didn't want to embarrass her mother, but mostly because whatever Lady Morton had to say, her parents didn't need to hear it. "I'll attend to her ladyship downstairs. Excuse me."

She didn't look at either her mother or Silas as she made her way to the door that led downstairs to the shop. She held her head high and shoulders back and tried to keep her knees from visibly shaking. She would not be afraid. This woman could do nothing to hurt her any worse than Finley had already done to herself.

When she reached the bottom of the stairs and peered out around the entrance to the shop, she saw the lady standing in front of a shelf of leather-bound volumes of poetry by Byron. Ladies always seemed to enjoy the romantic poet's work. A few feet away from her, Silas's automaton assistant, Fanny, toiled at dusting the packed shelves.

Fanny was a little shorter than Finley, but had arms and legs that could lengthen if needed. She was programmed to do menial tasks around the shop—such as dusting and shelving books. She had no voice box and did not respond when spoken to. Still, Finley felt as though the skeletal machine was part of the family.

Lady Morton was perhaps in her mid- to late-thirties. A handsome woman with dark hair and pale green eyes—or rather, one pale green eye. The other was a curved, smoky lens that fit beneath her top and bottom lid. It was like looking into a storm cloud and seeing your own face reflected. Finley didn't know how it worked, but apparently the lens worked much like an eye did, only better.

She wore a dark plum day gown with a pearl-gray shawl and matching hat. Finley glanced down at her own stockings, boots and short skirt and grimaced. Her clothing was very modern—not the sort of thing one wore to receive polite company.

Nevertheless, she was not going to put this off any longer. Better to just get it over with, like tearing a bandage off a cut.

"Lady Morton?" she inquired as she stepped into the shop.

The woman stopped her browsing and turned. Her strange gaze swept over Finley from the toes of her boots to the tip of the pencil she'd used to hold her hair in place on the back of her head.

"Miss Finley Jayne, I presume?" Her voice was low and crisp.

"Yes, ma'am," Finley replied with a curtsy. "My stepfather says you wished to speak to me?"

"I do. Is there some place where we might speak privately?"

Well, it didn't seem the lady was there to cause trouble for Finley with her parents, so that was a relief. "We could use my stepfather's office if you like."

Lady Morton actually looked relieved, as well. "That would be fine, thank you."

Since she was already close to the back of the shop, it wasn't much of a distance to Silas's office. Finley stood near the threshold and gestured for her ladyship to enter first, as was polite.

Silas's office was normally a chaotic terrain of papers, books and coffee cups, but the woman who came once a week to help her mother with some of the cleaning had been there just that morning, so the office was bright, neat and smelled of lemon furniture polish. There was even a chair for Lady Morton to sit upon without Finley having to remove a pile of books first.

Finley perched on the edge of her stepfather's desk as she couldn't bring herself to actually sit behind it in his chair. Plus, this position gave her a height advantage, and helped her feel less intimidated by her guest, whose foggy eye seemed to peer right through a person.

"Would you like something to drink?" she inquired. Her mother always offered guests refreshment, even if she didn't like them.

Lady Morton smiled. It seemed a genuine expression, not a rude one. "No, thank you. I will get right to the point of my calling upon you, Miss Jayne, because I suspect you are naturally quite curious as to why I am here. I wish to offer you a position within my household."

Finley blinked. "I'm sorry. Did you say you wished to offer me a job?"

The lady nodded. She looked as though she did this sort of thing all the time, sitting there with her matching bag clasped in her lap between her gloved hands. Normally, it was the housekeeper or the butler who took care of the hiring of staff within a large household, so this strange circumstance made Finley leery.

"I wish to hire you as companion to my youngest daughter, Phoebe."

A frown squished Finley's brows together. "Why?" She

wasn't the most intelligent of girls, but even she knew enough of how the world worked to know she was completely unacceptable as a companion. For one thing, she hadn't been born into the right social class. Companions were often poor aristocrats, or at least of good to noble birth. She could claim middle class if she was bragging. She knew nothing of society and how to behave in it, but she'd seen enough of the girls who lived there to know that she'd rather cut her own throat than spend time with one.

Lady Morton's eyebrows rose. "Why? My dear girl, from what I hear, you are hardly in the position to question such an opportunity."

"I know that, my lady," Finley replied. "That's why I have to ask. Why would a lady such as yourself want to hire someone as lowbrow as me to spend time with your daughter? Surely Lady Gattersleigh told you why I was sacked."

"She did." Her tone was strangely chipper and dismissive at the same time. "I have no interest in discussing your previous post, Miss Jayne. Suffice to say that I find the kind of girl who would defend a child at the risk of her own welfare to be *exactly* the sort of person I wish to have in my employ."

How was it possible that this woman seemed insulted that Finley didn't think she was good enough to work for her? Shouldn't she be flattered? And should she really argue with the woman? She needed a job. She wouldn't get too many people who would be as tolerant as Lady Morton after hearing what she did.

"May I inquire as to what my wage will be?"

Lady Morton's shoulders relaxed slightly, as though a large weight had been lifted off them. "You will have food, lodgings and clothing provided for you. In addition to that I am prepared to offer you the sum of twenty-five pounds per annum."

Twenty-five pounds a year? Finley's jaw sagged at the amount. That was more than most ladies' maids earned in a year!

"Fine," the lady said in a clipped tone. "Thirty, but that is my final offer."

How many times had her mother cautioned her that when things seemed too good to be true they often were? "When would you like me to start?" She fought to keep the excitement out of her voice.

Lady Morton smiled. "Is tomorrow morning too soon?"

"No, not at all." She hadn't even fully unpacked.

"Excellent." The older woman rose gracefully to her feet. "My carriage will come by for you at nine o'clock. By the time you are settled Phoebe should be awake. We're off to a charity event hosted by Lady Marsden and her nephew the Duke of Greythorne tonight."

A duke, Finley thought. That was only a step down from prince. She imagined he was a plump, pasty-faced creature with bad teeth. Rarely, from what she'd seen and heard of English nobility, were aristocrats handsome or fit—too much inbreeding. Still, it sounded romantic.

"I shall be ready, ma'am." And all she could think was how wonderful it would be if, as the daughter's companion, she could sleep in past nine some mornings, as well. Perhaps even catch a glimpse of a duke.

"I trust you will be," Lady Morton retorted as they left the office. Finley walked her to the front door of the shop, where the woman paused for a moment. She looked at Finley with a gaze that was both kind and somewhat…shrewd. "Thank you, Miss Jayne." Then, without waiting for a reply, she exited the shop into the overcast morning.

Finley watched after her, still battling her astonishment.

She had never heard an aristocrat say "thank you" before.

★ ★ ★

"I'm not sure I like this," Finley's mother said for what had to be the one hundredth time at quarter of nine the following morning. "This whole situation smells unsavory."

Finley rolled her eyes, taking her gaze off the street in front of their home for a few seconds. She was anxious, nervous and excited. And grateful. She was so unbelievably grateful. "Mama, it will be fine."

Her mother, however, was not so easily convinced. "What do we know of this Lady Morton other than what little mention she's had in the papers? There's an air of desperation about the entire affair."

Finley turned back to the window, feelings stung. "Meaning she'd have to be desperate to hire me?"

"No, dear," her mother replied with forced calm. "I am simply worried for your welfare. She didn't even ask you for references."

"She's friends with Lady Gattersleigh."

"Exactly!" A pale finger was pointed in Finley's direction. "Why would she hire you after that woman no doubt disparaged your character?"

"She couldn't have made me sound too bad, Mama. Lady Morton's hired me to spend time with her daughter."

"Makes me wonder how many other companions this girl has gone through if her mother thinks a girl who punched a governess would be a good match."

"Mother!" Finley stared at the older woman in affront. How did she know she'd actually struck Miss Clarke? Was the woman a bloody mind reader?

"Did you think I wouldn't find out?" her mother asked without anger. "One of the maids brought a few of your belongings that got left behind. She told me."

Finley bowed her head. "I didn't want you to know."

"Know what? That you defended a helpless child? I might not approve of the violence, but I approve of the sentiment, my dear. Though, in the future you may want to exercise better control over your emotions." She sighed. "You're a smart girl, Finley. Surely you wonder why Lady Morton is so adamant to have you."

"Of course I have," Finley replied with more indignation than she ought. "I also know I can't afford to be too picky. Lady Morton has offered me a generous wage and all I have to do is play shadow to her daughter. If the girl is too difficult I can always quit, but I cannot afford to refuse this opportunity, Mama."

A sigh was her only answer. Words were unnecessary, however. The rush of her mother's breath spoke volumes. The woman made guilt-inducing irritation an art form.

"It will be fine," she insisted once more. Perhaps this time it would stick. Perhaps if she repeated it enough times she would believe it herself. Her mother was right; there was something strange about this situation. More than likely, however, Lady Morton's daughter was simply a spoiled brat, as many aristocratic girls were. Nothing she couldn't handle.

The clock was still chiming the hour when a black lacquered carriage pulled up on the street below. White puffs of steam rose from the gleaming brass pipe atop the roof, and the buttons on the driver's uniform sparkled in the sun. It was horseless, operated entirely by engine—she could hear the gentle chug of it.

"Now that's just excessive," Finley's mother remarked, as she glanced outside.

Finley smiled. She didn't know what had brought on her mother's general distrust and suspicion toward the upper class, but she'd always harbored it as far as Finley knew.

"It looks comfortable," she replied, easing away from the

glass and picking up her coat from atop her luggage. "I'll come to call on my first half day, and send a note on before that."

"You'd better," her mother said with a watery smile. She was going to cry, Finley just knew it. A person would think Finley had been home for months instead of a couple of days.

She hugged her mother, patted her on the back when she began to sniffle. Silas came round and took up her trunk, leaving Finley with a carpetbag and valise to carry downstairs.

The driver of the carriage stood on the sidewalk. He immediately came forward to take Finley's bags and the trunk and loaded them onto the back of the vehicle. While he was doing this, Silas turned to Finley and offered her a small, paper-wrapped package.

"What's this?" she asked, plucking at the string tied around the paper. Of course it was a book. Silas always gave her books on what he considered important occasions.

"Just a little something," he replied with a warm smile. "I know how much you like the gothic ones. I reckon you're old enough for this now."

Finley arched a brow. "It must be truly frightening then."

"Your mother certainly thought so when she read it. I found it an interesting and provoking look at human nature."

Her lips curved. "Now you make it sound utterly boring."

Laughing, he patted her shoulder. "You'll like it. Of that I'm certain." His smile faded, but the loving glint in his eye did not. "Take care of yourself, my dear girl. If it's not what you want, you can always come back here and work with me in the shop."

Finley hugged him. "I will, thank you." But they both knew she wouldn't. Silas managed to make a comfortable living for himself and her mother with just the two of them working in the store. It wouldn't impinge upon them much if she did work there and lived at home, but she wanted to support herself. Silas had always been good to her, but there were situations when she was painfully aware that she wasn't really his daughter—this was one of those.

He released her and she turned toward the coachman who had put down the steps and held the carriage door open for her. He assisted her into the carriage and then closed the door.

The vehicle was as fine inside as out, lined with rich, maroon velvet. Finley ran her palms over the fabric. The seat was so soft she sank into it. She'd slept in beds that weren't as comfortable.

As the carriage lurched forward, so did she, peering out the window to wave goodbye—first to Silas, then to her mother, who was still in the upstairs window, a crushed handkerchief in her hand.

*Poor Mama.* Finley wiped at her own eyes, which were inexplicably starting to water, and leaned back to enjoy the drive to Mayfair.

The rhythmic noise of the engine was strangely relaxing. She leaned her head back against the cushions and closed her eyes. She must have dozed because it seemed like she had been in the carriage for only a few minutes before it came to a stop. Jerking upright, she peeked out the window and saw a grand, gray stone mansion looming in front of her.

The carriage door opened. This time there was a footman to lower the steps and assist her to the gravel drive.

"Welcome to Morton Manor, miss," he greeted her cordially. "Mrs. Gale will show you to the parlor where Lady Morton will receive you. I'll see to your belongings."

Mrs. Gale had to be the housekeeper. "Thank you," Finley said. She turned toward the house. It was huge. Stately. Silas's shop could fit dozens of times over into this grand estate—one of many the family probably owned.

Even if Lady Morton's daughter turned out to be a cow, living in a house this fine was definitely a benefit.

Mayfair was like a different world from the bustling area around Silas's shop. That was in Russell Square, where people lived, worked and shopped. Mayfair was where rich people idled through their days, entertained in the evening and let other people clean up after them.

Perhaps she had inherited some of her mother's prejudice, but that didn't make her opinion wrong.

Before she reached the top step leading up to the servants' entrance, the door opened to reveal the kind face of a woman old enough to be Finley's grandmother. She wore a black-and-white dress and a white cap that identified her as the housekeeper.

"Good morning, dear. I trust you had a comfortable journey?"

"Good morning," Finley replied. "I did, yes. Are you Mrs. Gale?"

Apple cheeks lifted in a smile. "I am indeed. Come in, come in."

Finley moved past her, into the foyer. It was small, but clean and smelled of freshly baked bread.

"Kitchen's down below," Mrs. Gale said, nodding at a partially opened door that led down a flight of stairs. Finley could hear the clang of pots and chattering voices.

"Smells wonderful," she commented.

"You go down there when you're settled in and Cook will give you bread and molasses. I declare it's the best thing I've ever eaten. Now, follow me."

Finley trailed after the portly woman. Along the way they ran into various other staff, who nodded and said hello. Mrs. Gale introduced her to all of them, and Finley tried to remember all their names.

"I'll show you to your room, then take you to Lady Morton," Mrs. Gale informed her, her sturdy form moving with surprising speed toward what had to be the servants' staircase. It was fairly wide and well-worn, partially hidden not far from what Mrs. Gale told her was the door to the corridor that led to the laundry building.

"Her ladyship requested that you be given a room on the family floor."

There was no censure in the older woman's voice, but Finley was uncomfortable all the same. At her last job she'd slept on the top floor, in a room she shared with three of the other maids.

"Why?" she asked.

Mrs. Gale lifted her shoulders in a tiny shrug and smiled. "I suppose so you'll be closer for Lady Phoebe. Lord and Lady Morton are good people, Miss Jayne. I've worked for this family for almost thirty years and I've never felt as though I had been treated ill."

Too bad her mother wasn't there to hear that, Finley mused. It might ease her misgivings. "I'm already a little overwhelmed by her ladyship's kindness."

"Rather sad, isn't it? That we're surprised to be treated well."

"Yes," Finley agreed. "I'm a little ashamed of myself for it."

The housekeeper gave her a gentle smile and a pat on the arm as if to ease her mind. A few moments later, they reached a landing on the stairs and turned left into a long, wide corridor with cream walls, delicate plaster scrolls and rich red carpet.

"Your room is here." Mrs. Gale stopped in front of the first door on the right and turned the knob.

Finley walked in first. The room was large—larger than the room she shared with three other girls at the Gattersleigh residence. Decorated in shades of sage and cream, it was bright and airy and smelled of freshly cut grass. They must have aired it earlier, while the gardeners attended to the foliage below. She had a lovely view of the grounds from her window.

She removed her hat, checked her reflection in the mirror and smoothed her hands over her hair and skirt. She should have worn a proper gown instead of her more modern kit of stockings, boots, short ruffled skirt, blouse and leather corset. But there was neither time, nor the privacy to change. Mrs. Gale bustled about showing her the armoire, dressing table and adjoining bath.

"It's been outfitted in the latest innovations," the house-keeper told her. "The tub even has a burner to keep the water hot."

And a fancy commode, too—one that flushed with water.

Two footmen arrived with her luggage as they exited once more.

"If you wish, I can have one of the maids see to your be-longings," Mrs. Gale offered.

"No. Thank you. I'll see to my own unpacking. I'd feel strange letting someone else do it."

For that comment she was rewarded with another smile. Back down the stairs they went, but instead of returning to the kitchen, they turned in the opposite direction.

The main part of the house was just as impressive as the outside, with cathedral ceilings, marble floors and classical statues. Finley paused for a moment to take it all in. She clenched her teeth to keep her jaw from dropping—wouldn't do for her to show her awe. Standing around with one's mouth open made one look like a lowbrow commoner, which she might very well be, but was determined not to look it.

Down another corridor. Mrs. Gale stopped and knocked on a partially open door, and when she was given permission from the lady within, she opened the door the rest of the way. "Miss Jayne has arrived, my lady."

"Send her in."

And then Finley was on her own, wishing she had the sturdy housekeeper to cling to. She crossed the threshold into a small, pretty blue parlor and found herself being stared at by three identically green eyes, and one stormy one.

"Miss Jayne," Lady Morton greeted with a smile. "How lovely to see you again. Allow me to introduce my daughter, Phoebe."

"Hello, Finley," the girl said. She was about the same age as Finley. At the oldest she might be seventeen. She was about the same height, with a similar build, but her hair was auburn and her skin as pale as milk, with just a hint of pink along her cheeks. "How do you do?"

Finley was prevented from curtsying, as she had been brought up to do, by the girl offering her hand. Was she to be treated as an equal then? She closed her fingers around Phoebe's and tried not to squeeze too hard. The girl's grip was firm.

"I'm well, thank you. It's a pleasure to meet you, Lady Phoebe."

"Just Phoebe," she was told. "We're to be friends after all. Please, sit. Tea?"

"Yes, please." Finley sat on the edge of the sofa beside Phoebe and watched as the girl fixed a cup for her. She even placed a couple of biscuits on the saucer.

"We're to a party tonight, Miss Jayne," Lady Morton informed her. "You will accompany us. I assume you haven't an evening gown?"

"You assume right, my lady." Embarrassed, Finley took a sip of tea to hide her flush. Would the lady think twice now about hiring her?

"No worries," Phoebe said with a wave of her hand. "I have plenty. You may borrow mine until we can get you some of your own. We'll go to the dressmaker's tomorrow."

Finley paled. If the cost of gowns came out of her salary she'd still be poor next year.

Phoebe chuckled. "It won't be that horrible, trust me. I'll make certain they don't put you in anything horrendous, and Papa will pay for it. You don't have to do a thing but stand there and hope they don't stick you with a pin."

Any minute she was going to wake up from this amazing dream and find herself in a workhouse or something equally awful.

"You're too generous."

Phoebe laughed again and flashed a smile at her mother, who also looked amused. "You won't think that this evening when you're bored out of your skull."

She'd never been to an aristocratic function before. What if she made a fool of herself? Or worse—of Phoebe? The thought made her biscuit taste like ash in her mouth. "What sort of party is it?"

Was it her imagination or did Phoebe turn even paler? Her smile certainly followed. "I thought Mama would have told you. It's my engagement party."

# Chapter 3

Engaged? The very idea continued to baffle Finley for the remainder of the day, long after she'd unpacked all her belongings and had taken a quiet luncheon in her room reading the book Silas had given her.

It was *Frankenstein* by Mary Shelley, a book Finley hadn't been allowed to read prior to this because her mother thought she was too young. The mention of "evil forebodings" in the first line grabbed her attention and she sat by the window reading until teatime, when she joined Phoebe and Lady Morton for tea, sandwiches and tiny cakes so delicious it took all her willpower not to eat six of them.

They didn't speak any more of the engagement then. In fact, they didn't speak of it at all until that evening, when Phoebe came to Finley's room.

"Am I late?" Finley asked. She was just putting on the earrings Phoebe had loaned her. In fact, everything she wore except for her undergarments was on loan from Phoebe.

"No, I'm early," the girl replied, pearls shining in her thick, upswept hair. "I've been assured by many of my friends that constant punctuality is a failure of the worst kind."

Finley smiled at the humor in her voice. "Are most of your friends constantly late?"

Phoebe returned the grin. "Exactly! You look lovely, by the way."

"Thank you." Finley blushed. She wasn't used to compliments, and she wasn't accustomed to wearing such beautiful gowns as the deep plum silk one she wore now. It made her eyes brighter—like the amber her mother compared them to. The color brought out the honey in her hair, as well, which she had always thought of as plain dark blond.

"You're stunning," she told the other girl. Most debutantes wore pale colors, but Phoebe was dressed in a rich peach that really made her green eyes stand out.

"Thank you. One of the perks to being an engaged woman is that now I don't have to wear pastels all the time."

Finley shuddered at the thought. She adjusted the earring and rose from her dressing table. "Have you been engaged for long?"

"Just a fortnight," Phoebe replied. "Hold on, you've got a loose pin." Finley watched in the mirror as the girl walked behind her and attended to her hair. She didn't even wince when her would-be maid shoved a pin deeper into her coiffure.

"There." The paler girl admired her work with a faint smile. "Now you're gorgeous. All the eligible gentlemen at the party will line up to dance with you."

"Not me," Finley argued. "I'm just a companion."

Phoebe's smile faded, only to come back twice as bright— and a little forced. "Didn't Mama tell you? We're telling everyone that you're my cousin from the country. No one will know you're not filthy rich or connected."

A wave of dizziness washed over Finley. For a moment, she felt that other part of her struggle to come to the surface, but she pushed it back down. "Why would you do that?"

Phoebe frowned. "I'm not certain. It was Mama's idea. I reckon she thought we wouldn't look so pretentious if it seemed that you were family. Since I'm engaged I no longer need constant chaperoning, so perhaps she simply wants someone watching over me at all times. I'm not certain what sort of trouble she thinks I'll get myself into."

Finley almost suggested she ask her mother, but then thought the better of it. Phoebe's relationship with her mama was none of her business.

"I suppose being from the country will provide an excuse for any ignorance I might have for proper social behavior."

Phoebe waved her hand. "You have more manners than most lords and ladies I've met. Trust me."

Finley did, oddly enough. She didn't think Phoebe or her mother were trying to harm her in any way, but the entire situation was very strange. She suspected there was more to it than either she or Phoebe had been told.

"We'd best take ourselves downstairs," Phoebe remarked with a glance at the clock on the mantel. "Mama will be waiting."

Dutifully, Finley followed after the girl, despite the lump in her stomach. How on earth was she to pretend she was of the upper class? To be sure, Silas and her mother had instilled good manners in her, and her vocabulary was such that she could certainly speak properly, but she had no idea what that sort of life was like, outside of observing it. She had more of a "mongrel" look to her than aristocratic features—a fact she was more often happy for than not, as some nobles seemed to have been bred out of having any chin to speak of.

Well, there was no getting out of it. She would just have to do as well as she could and hope for the best.

Phoebe had been right, her mother was indeed waiting for them, along with the butler, whose name Finley couldn't remember, if she'd been told at all. He helped first Lady Morton, then Phoebe and finally Finley into their wraps. Hers was yet another loan from Phoebe.

"Thank you, Tolliver," Lady Morton said with a smile. She wore tinted spectacles that partially concealed her odd eye. "We will be home by four at the latest."

"Yes, ma'am." He bowed. "Have a lovely evening, ladies." Then he opened the door so that the three of them could march out into the cool night air. A footman stood by the carriage to hand them in one by one.

As the carriage gingerly lurched into motion, Finley held her clenched hands in her lap and drew deep, even breaths. She could do this. All she had to do was follow Phoebe's example and behave as she did. It would be easy.

So long as she never left Phoebe's side.

It was a short drive to their destination, which was but a few streets away. The metal horses that pulled them moved faster than their flesh-and-blood counterparts. Finley couldn't remember the last time she'd taken a coach such a short distance when she had two feet perfect for walking.

That was exactly the sort of observation she had to remember to keep to herself. Aristocrats did not walk to social events.

As they stepped from the carriage, Finley took a deep breath. There were familiar scents in the air—the smell of real horses, of heated metal, of steam and grass—that calmed her pounding heart somewhat. Relief flooded through her as the anxiety waned. Intense emotions were not conducive to keeping control of herself. The darkness inside her loved to come out at those times.

The house they entered was huge—an old Gothic structure that had to have been built at least two centuries earlier. The stone had probably once been beige, but it had darkened to black in some places, giving the entire structure a sinister feel.

It instantly made Finley think of *Frankenstein* and the castle where the doctor conducted his scientific experiments.

"It's like something right out of a novel," Finley whispered to Phoebe.

Her companion didn't seem to share her enthusiasm. "Yes. It's rather antiquated on the outside, but the inside has every modern convenience, I assure you."

Finley glanced at her, uncertain as to why the girl sounded almost defensive. "I'm sure it does, not that it matters to me. I don't have to live here."

Was it her imagination or did Phoebe just shudder? Perhaps she shouldn't continue reading Mary Shelley's novel if it was going to make her mind so foolish.

They joined a handful of other guests walking up the stone path to the front door. Flickering torches illuminated the way, but that wonderful gothic feeling was lost as soon as they stepped inside.

The interior was just as Phoebe had promised—modern, which caused a peculiar disappointment in Finley's chest. Had she hoped for a spooky run-down ruin?

Chandeliers sparkled overhead, and wall sconces bathed everyone in a warm glow. She didn't hear the hiss of gas, which meant that the house—or at least the lighting of it— was powered by the "battery" manufactured by the Grey-thorne Corporation. The last house she worked at had been in the process of converting to the power source invented by a previous Duke of Greythorne long before Finley was born. He'd discovered an ore that, once refined and properly treated, could power an entire house for months off one small battery that could then be exchanged for another once it was depleted. Amazing discovery, it was. And somewhat expensive, though she'd heard that the current duke was taking measures to make the batteries more affordable so everyone in Britain could light their homes without worrying about fire—or the whole thing exploding.

There were ladies in all manner of beautiful gowns and jewels. Gentlemen were dressed in black and white, some with brightly colored neck cloths. Human servants and gleaming brass automatons milled around the guests, bearing trays of champagne, lemonade and other refreshments.

Finley had never seen so many automatons under one roof except for an exhibition she'd visited a few years ago with her parents. She had to remind herself not to stare.

"Impressive, aren't they?" came a voice from her left.

She turned as an older man, perhaps a few years older than Silas, walked up to stand beside her. He gestured with his champagne toward one of the smaller machines collecting empty glasses. "This one knows his route. He'll move in a precalculated pattern throughout the room, collecting empty crystal, which he'll then take to the kitchen to be washed."

Finley glanced at the man. He had a nice face, and was probably very handsome when he was younger and his dark hair not touched with gray. "Are you not worried about having so many, given the recent accidents?" There had been two or three mentions in the papers over the past few months of automatons acting against their programming. People had been injured, though not seriously.

He smiled at her. Yes, he must have been handsome as a

young man. He was handsome now. "Of these beauties? Of course not. You see Miss…"

"Bennet," Finley supplied, remembering the name Phoebe told her to use, and her manners. She offered her hand. "Finley Bennet. I'm here with Lady Morton and Lady Phoebe

Blue eyes brightened. "Are you? How lovely. A pleasure to meet you, Miss Bennet. I am Lord Vincent, creator of all the automatons you see around you."

Finley flushed. Of course he wouldn't be nervous of them. "Forgive me, my lord. I am new to town." How easily the lie rolled off her tongue. "Am I to understand then, that this is also your home?"

Lord Vincent nodded as he continued to smile at her. "No need to be embarrassed, dear girl. I am surprised that neither Lady Morton or Lady Phoebe mentioned you to me when last we spoke, and that they seem equally remiss in mentioning me to you."

There was nothing dark in his voice when he spoke, but the base of Finley's spine tingled at his words. Why would Lady Morton neglect to inform their host that she would be bringing an extra guest? And why would either she or her daughter feel the need to tell Finley about his lordship?

Suddenly Lady Morton and Phoebe were there, inserting themselves so Finley was forced to step back from the man.

"Forgive me, Lord Vincent," Lady Morton said, a flush in her cheeks. "I was caught up in conversation with Lady Marsden, else I would have made introductions. I see you've already met our cousin, Miss Finley Bennet."

"Indeed I have," Lord Vincent replied as he bowed over each of their hands. "You are lovely as always, Lady Morton. Lady Phoebe, allow me to say that you are more beautiful each time I see you."

Phoebe blushed at his praise. Finley didn't blame her—it

was a pretty racy thing for him to say to someone who was engaged.

Then Phoebe raised her gaze, and Finley saw something in her bright eyes that she could not identify. Was it fear? Panic?

"Forgive me, cousin," Phoebe said to her, her voice low and a little shaky. She slipped her arm around Lord Vincent's, her face now strangely pale. "I should have been the one to make the introductions. May I present Harris Spencer-White, Earl Vincent, our host for the evening and my fiancé."

# Chapter 4

An hour later, Finley was still reeling. Lord Vincent was Phoebe's fiancé? She knew large age differences weren't uncommon amongst the upper crust—or the lower for that matter—but the man was more than twice Phoebe's age!

She watched them on the dance floor. Lord Vincent had a limp, but that didn't stop him from whirling Phoebe through a waltz. If he were only younger, or she older, they would make a handsome couple.

It was warm in the ballroom—too many bodies in one space. The smell of cologne and perfume mixed with heat and sweat gave Finley a headache. She hadn't been asked to dance the waltz, and her card was blank for the next few selections—thankfully, as she wasn't the best dancer—so she took this time to slip from the loud, stifling room.

She was nosy by nature, but her hurting head and pinched toes—Phoebe's shoes were a titch too small—kept her impulse to look about under control. Rather than remain in the corridor, where she might have to socialize with other guests coming and going, she opened the door of the first room she found and stepped inside.

Finley waited a moment before closing the door behind her. She was in a parlor or a gentleman's study—decorated in rich mahogany and dark blue. She'd read that such rooms were perfect places for a lovers' tryst at these sort of parties, and wanted to make certain she hadn't interrupted one.

"If there's anyone in here, just clear your throat and I'll go back where I came from," she said. Better to feel foolish for talking to an empty room than accidentally spy a gentleman's naked backside. Some things could not be "un-seen."

The lighting in the room was mellow, easing the pressure inside her skull. She went to one of the windows and found it controlled by a strange apparatus. Instead of simply flipping the latch and opening the casement, she had to wind the key set into the window frame. Then, she watched as thin brass "arms" attached to the latch pulled it to the open position, and then slowly drew the glass toward her. When the breeze was exactly how she wanted, she merely turned the key back to its starting position and the mechanism came to a halt.

Lord Vincent certainly seemed to like his clockwork and automata. The house was positively crawling with scuttling metal creatures designed to do all manner of tasks. There were human servants, as well, but Finley had never seen such an abundance of brass and steel.

She turned her back to the window so the refreshing spring breeze could cool her nape. She rolled her neck, sighing as it popped and snapped, further easing the tension in her head and shoulders. When she opened her eyes she found herself staring at a portrait of Phoebe and Lord Vincent.

No, wait. That wasn't Phoebe. Finley didn't have to move closer to view the portrait in detail, but she did anyway. At this moment she didn't trust her own eyes—which had become uncannily keen over the past few months. The improvement to her sight had been so gradual that she often forgot she could see much better than the average person. She walked toward the large, gilt-framed canvas, her eyes widening with each step.

It was a portrait of a much younger Lord Vincent—she'd been correct, he had been quite handsome in his youth—and the woman with him must have been his first wife, or at least a betrothed. The woman wore a large sapphire ring on her left hand—the same hand that covered one of Lord Vincent's.

She looked so much like Phoebe it was eerie.

Of course, on closer examination it was easy to pick out the differences—Phoebe's eyes were not quite as dark, her hair a bit more red, but the shape of her face was a perfect match, and her features so close they could have been twins, or at least sisters.

It was unsettling. Disturbing. And Finley wondered if Phoebe knew. She was also overwhelmed by the need to find out just what had happened to this woman.

"Robert, I said no!"

The cry came from outside, carried to her keen ears by the breeze through the open window. It was Phoebe's voice.

Portrait forgotten, Finley quickly crossed to the window. From there she could see into the garden below. Flickering torches cast soft golden light over Phoebe and her companion—a young gentleman. Neither of them looked very pleased.

"I have to go," Phoebe said. "Mama and Finley will be looking for me."

The young man grabbed her by the arm. "You can't leave. Not yet."

Perhaps it was guilt that she hadn't been doing her duty that flicked the switch inside Finley, or perhaps it was the way he grabbed Phoebe like he had a right to. Maybe it was a little of both. Regardless, one moment she was watching them from the window and the next she vaulted over the sill and dropped two floors to the grass below.

The two gaped at her as though she had just fallen from the sky—which she supposed she had.

"Let her go," she told the young gentleman. He was tall and slim with thick dark hair and rosy cheeks.

He scowled, his amazement clearly faded. "This is none of your business."

"Wrong." Finley clapped her fingers around the wrist of his hand holding Phoebe. "My friend wants to leave and you won't let her. Not very mannerly, Robert." As she spoke she tightened her grip, stopping when his handsome face began to contort in pain. She let go as soon as she felt his fingers release Phoebe.

Robert cradled his arm close to his chest. Phoebe immediately brushed past Finley to stop at his side. Her hands touched him as though he were precious or fragile. "Robert, dearest. Are you all right?"

Dearest? Finley scowled. She'd been *this* close to giving Robert the thrashing she thought he deserved when he'd let go. She had seen Phoebe try to pull free of his grip, and now the girl was all over him wondering if he was all right?

"What did you do to him?" Phoebe demanded, glaring at her.

Finley raised her brows. "I heard you tell him no and then I saw him grab you. I thought he was trying to do you harm."

"I would never hurt Phoebe," Robert informed her indignantly. "I love her."

"Love her?" Finley repeated dumbly, before pressing a hand to her head—which had started to ache again. This job was beginning to take on more twists and turns than one of those "sensation" novels.

Lips tight, she looked from Robert to Phoebe. "Someone had better explain to me just what exactly is going on here."

The explanation was truly the stuff worthy of Mr. Dickens—simple, but oddly convoluted. Phoebe loved Robert, and Robert loved Phoebe, but Robert had yet to reach the age of majority so they couldn't marry without their parents' consent. Robert's parents might have been persuaded to allow it, but Lord Vincent had gone to Phoebe's father and asked Lord Morton for her hand. Her father said yes.

Finley's gaze slid back and forth between the two as she struggled to regain her composure. Did this young buck know just how close he'd come to having her fist down his throat? The thought of it made her stomach twist and roll. She'd thought he was hurting Phoebe, and in return that dark part of her had wanted to hurt him. It still wanted to hurt him, even if just a very little.

"So why don't you break the engagement?" she asked Phoebe. "Seems a simple enough solution."

Phoebe glanced away, and even in the murky darkness Finley could tell that her cheeks were red. "I cannot do that."

All right. She could accept that weak-arsed explanation for now, but the other girl would have to explain in detail the next time they were alone.

"You could elope," she suggested.

This time Robert shook his head. "That would bring shame down on both our houses, dishonor me and ruin Phoebe's reputation." The look he directed at the girl embarrassed Finley—it was so warm. "I couldn't do that to her."

Finley grimaced. "So if I'm to understand you, the two of

you are desperate to be together, but are unwilling to make the necessary sacrifices?"

Robert frowned at her. "You mock us with your ignorance."

She probably should have pleaded the contrary, but Finley didn't like being called ignorant, especially when she would do whatever necessary to be with the boy she loved—if there was such a creature. "Yes," she replied honestly. "I do. I would mock anyone who whines about their situation yet can't summon the bollocks to fight for who and what they want."

"Finley," Phoebe began.

Robert cut her off, looking down his nose at Finley. "Of course you would say something so coarse. You know nothing of the ways of our world."

He made it sound like that was a bad thing. Finley shrugged. "You're right, and I don't want to know them if this foolishness is any indication of what your world is like. Now, you have two choices—we return to the ball now before someone starts to wonder where the two of you have made off to, or I can run inside and tell all the wrong people that I found you together in the garden and the scandal will ensure you have to marry each other. What will it be?"

The hopeful glint in Robert's eye almost won Finley over—almost. She still thought he was more of a prat than Phoebe deserved. Then Phoebe said, "You can't do that!"

Poor Robert. He looked as though she'd broken his heart. Of course he had to know rationally that such a scandal would bring about the dishonor he so wished to avoid, but it was nice to know that he truly cared for Phoebe.

Finley didn't question it. She arched a brow at the other girl, who looked away, not only from her, but from Robert, as well. "Then we'd best get inside."

The three of them returning to the ballroom together

would attract little interest. They would simply be a group of young people returning from catching some air out-of-doors. Never mind that they could have been up to all manner of mischief while out there.

"Phoebe," Robert murmured as they crossed the threshold. "I…"

She barely turned her head to look at him. "I think it's better if we don't speak again, Robert." Her voice was so cold, Finley thought she might get frostbite. "It will be better for both of us that way. Goodbye."

Robert's face drained of all color. Finley was glad no one paid them any attention, because if they did they would all see the exact moment that Phoebe broke his heart, and that would entertain a few gossips just as much as if they had been caught kissing.

"Come along, Finley," Phoebe instructed and began to walk away. Finley shrugged—in what she hoped was a sympathetic manner—to Robert, who in her mind was now not nearly as poncey as she first thought, and hurried after Phoebe. Her opinion of the girl had dropped a little right then. There was no need to be mean, and yet, another part of her—the dark part that sometimes seemed smarter than her or rather possessed of a better sense of intuition—wondered if perhaps Phoebe hadn't broken her own heart at the same time.

Finley didn't see much of Phoebe for the remainder of the evening. Lord Vincent took up much of her time—especially after the announcement of their engagement was officially made.

Maybe she was naive in her thinking that love was more important than honor and family and all that nonsense, but any envy she might have felt toward Phoebe and other girls of her class was greatly diminished.

Wasn't living your life based around what people thought and expected of you a little…well, stupid?

*Hypocrite*, a voice whispered inside her head. *You always worry about what people think of you.*

But that wasn't quite the same thing, Finley told herself firmly, and that was the end of the conversation, because everyone knew only mad girls talked to themselves.

She danced another two times before the evening finally came to an end. She couldn't remember the young men's names, but they had been pleasant and polite enough. She was fairly certain they only danced with her because they thought she was Phoebe's cousin and their mothers told them to.

"Did you have a good time tonight, Finley?" Lady Morton asked in the carriage on the way home. She had removed her spectacles and her "odd" eye glowed a little in the dim light—like a cat's.

Finley stifled a yawn. "Yes, my lady." She could hardly admit that her feet hurt and that she'd spent the last hour of the party praying for it to end.

Lady Morton seemed pleased. "Excellent. The Duke of Greythorne was in attendance. Did either of you happen to notice him?"

Finley shook her head. Phoebe yawned delicately behind her gloved hand. "I did not. I'm sure it was because His Grace was surrounded by frenzied young ladies vying for his attention."

One of Finley's brows rose. "Is he that handsome?"

Phoebe grinned. "And that rich. He's only a little older than us, so I doubt he'll be eager to marry anytime soon. They're wasting their energies trying to catch him."

This was an odd concept to Finley, girls trying to "catch" a husband. Her mother always made it sound as though it was the man's duty to woo the lady. Perhaps it was something introduced by the Suffrage movement.

She was about to ask how old Robert was, but caught her tongue just in time. That was not something to discuss in front of Lady Morton. Besides, Phoebe had laid her head back against the cushions and closed her eyes, almost instantly falling asleep.

Lady Morton shot Finley an amused glance. "She's been able to do that since she was a baby. It seems you and I are left to amuse each other as we contend with the crush of traffic, Finley."

And what traffic! The carriage would roll a few feet and then stop, caught up in the steady throng departing the party, clogging the narrow street.

"Lord Vincent has a very lovely home," Finley offered awkwardly. At least it was safe conversation.

"Yes," her ladyship agreed. "All the modern conveniences, as well. The earl is very interested in progress. He's always supported the scientific arts."

"What happened to his leg?"

Lady Morton's expression sobered. "A carriage accident. He and his wife were on their way back from holiday in Scotland. His leg was destroyed and she was killed."

"That's terrible." Finley felt awful for asking.

"Yes. He made himself an automaton limb—one that moves and behaves just as a proper limb would. Is that not amazing?"

Finley murmured in agreement. "I saw a portrait of his wife earlier this evening."

"You did?" A wrinkle appeared between Lady Morton's brows. "How did you happen to see that?"

"I had a headache and needed quiet. I slipped into an empty

room and saw it hanging on the wall." She had said this much, she might as well press on, "She looks like Phoebe."

"Yes." The older woman clasped her hands in her lap—tightly, as though to keep from fidgeting. "Cassandra and I were cousins."

So that meant that Lord Vincent intended to marry his wife's cousin. There was something…icky about that.

One glance at her ladyship and Finley suspected she shared the feeling. She also looked like she dared Finley to cast judgment in a strangely fragile manner.

"It's a good match," Finley said instead.

"Yes." There was an element of relief in the word. "It is." Then she turned her attention to the window, and all conversation came to an end.

The carriage jerked into motion and picked up speed. They were home within a few minutes. Phoebe woke up so quickly and brightly that Finley wondered if the girl had been asleep at all.

# Chapter 5

The next few days were filled with shopping as Lady Morton and Phoebe were determined to see Finley well dressed. She refused to allow them to buy her extravagant clothing, and instead set her mind to simple, well-made garments.

"I'm supposed to be from the country," she argued. "Country fashion is much more practical than City dress." She was right, of course, so they gave in. The result was a modest wardrobe of good, modern pieces—nothing too fine or fussy, but nothing so drab that they'd be ashamed to be seen with her in public.

If she needed something superfine, it was agreed that she could borrow something that Phoebe had already worn and alter it. Being raised by a seamstress had its advantages.

But all this shopping and stopping for tea, more shopping, stopping for luncheon and visiting, and then more tea, followed by dinner and an evening at the theater—in Lord Vincent's box—meant that it was days before Finley had the chance to talk privately with Phoebe, and quite late at night at that.

Before changing into her nightclothes, Finley went to the other girl's room. She dismissed the young maid for the night, so that she could help Phoebe get ready for bed.

Finley felt as though they had become quite close over the past few days. Perhaps not the best of friends, but at least confidantes. She hadn't told Phoebe her secret, and the girl hadn't asked, but Finley definitely felt comfortable around her.

They made small talk for a few moments, talking about the play they'd seen—a production of Oscar Wilde's *The Ideal Husband,* which had been equally hilarious and surprisingly serious. Finley had quite enjoyed it.

"May I ask you a question?" Finley asked, as she loosened the laces of Phoebe's damask corset.

"Only if I may ask one of you," the girl replied, holding on to one of the posters of her bed. "Good lord, Finley, you're going to lift me clean off the floor!"

"Sorry." Sheepishly, Finley gentled her actions. Sometimes she forgot her own strength.

Phoebe smiled over her shoulder. "What is it you wished to ask?"

"Why are you marrying Lord Vincent?"

"How is it you can leap from a second-floor window and not even twist an ankle?"

"Usually how this sort of thing works is that you answer my question before asking your own."

Phoebe shrugged. "I will answer yours after you answer mine."

Oh, for pity's sake. Finley sighed. "I don't know how I'm able to leap out a window and remain unharmed, only that I can." It was an honest answer, if a poor one.

Dark eyes narrow, Phoebe turned to face her, popping the

hooks in the front of her corset, beneath which her chemise was stuck to her skin. "What else can you do?"

"I agreed to one question," Finley dodged. "Now you must answer mine. Why are you marrying Lord Vincent? You obviously don't want to, so why?"

Phoebe glanced away, clenching her jaw in an almost petulant manner.

"Are you going back on our agreement?" Finley demanded.

"I agreed that you could ask me a question. I did not promise to answer it."

"Oh, that's honorable of you." She should keep her mouth shut. This girl was not her social equal. One word to her mother and Finley would be out on the street—again. But she was hurt, insulted and a little pissed. "I tell you something I've never told anyone else and you won't extend the same courtesy. That's just lovely. Good night."

She made it perhaps two steps before Phoebe reached out and seized her by the wrist. For a second, Finley was in a poor enough temper that she was tempted to catch the girl's wrist in her own hand and squeeze until the delicate bones rubbed together.

"Finley, wait." An expression of real distress crossed her face. "Don't go. Please."

With a mulish set to her jaw, Finley turned, relaxing her posture enough that Phoebe dropped her arm. "I'll stay."

Phoebe's thin shoulders sagged. "Good. Why don't we sit down?"

They sat beside one another on the edge of the bed. Phoebe had slipped into a robe to protect her bare arms from the slight spring chill in the air. Finley waited patiently for her to begin.

Licking her lips, Phoebe tangled her fingers in her lap, thumbs rubbing together nervously. "Surely you noticed that Papa did not attend the theater with us this evening?"

"I hadn't given it much thought to be honest."

"No," Phoebe said softly. "I suppose you wouldn't. And it's not as though it's unusual for an engaged girl and her mother to attend the theater with the girl's fiancé."

Finley wouldn't know what was unusual and what wasn't with the upper classes—not really. "Did your father's absence upset you?"

Phoebe's pale cheeks flushed a deep rose. "No. You asked me why I'm marrying Lord Vincent?"

It took a second for Finley to realize that her companion was waiting for her confirmation before she replied. Raising both brows, she gave a small nod. "Yes. I did."

"My father…" Phoebe frowned, tucking in her lips. "My father prefers to spend his evenings at his club or with his cronies."

Finley shrugged. "All right." What the devil did this have to do with Lord Vincent?

"He enjoys horse racing and cards." Dark eyes darted away from hers. "Perhaps too much."

She could have smacked herself in the forehead with the heel of her hand. Lord, but she could be dense at times! She should have already made this assumption—because it made the most sense.

"Lord Vincent paid off your father's debts in return for marrying you."

More pink flooded Phoebe's cheeks. She was quite flushed now. "Yes. So you see now why I cannot simply break the engagement to be with Robert."

Finley nodded. "I assume that Vincent has also agreed to continue covering any debts your father racks up?"

"Yes. It is very good of Lord Vincent to do this."

Who was she trying to convince? Finley or herself?

"No matter how much your father owes, it's not what you are worth," Finley remarked.

The dark-haired girl turned to her. There were tears in her green eyes. "Thank you," she whispered before dissolving into sobs.

What the devil was she to do now? Finley didn't have a lot of experience with crying—her own or that of others. Slowly—and a bit awkwardly if she was truthful—she slid her arm around Phoebe's shoulders and patted her back a bit.

The sobs subsided after a few moments, and Phoebe reared up and off the bed in search of a handkerchief for her eyes and nose. When she turned to face Finley again it was with puffy eyes and a red nose. "Forgive me."

"Whatever for? For being upset over a situation that rots? I think you have every right."

"Lord Vincent has been nothing but gentlemanly and kind to me through the entire process, and I know that I am extremely fortunate to make such a match. I'll be a countess."

"But?" Finley prodded, sensing there was more.

Twisting the crumpled linen handkerchief in her hands, Phoebe's shoulders slumped. "Perhaps you'll think me naive, but I always thought I'd marry for love. Lord Vincent doesn't love me. In fact, I think he only wants me because I look like his dead wife. I know you saw her portrait."

So she hadn't been asleep the entire carriage drive. "So your father makes a mess and you get to clean it up. You're a better person than I, Phoebe. I don't think I could do it."

"I'm not doing it for my father," came the firm reply. She sounded a little angry, but she didn't rush to her father's defense. "I'm doing it for Mama—and for myself—so neither of us has to suffer through the whispers and stares, the social downfall that happens when one's debtors come calling. I would save us both that humiliation. This way if Father ruins himself, I will be in a position to care for my mother."

Wanting to protect her mother was something Finley could relate to, though she still had no idea what role she was to play in all of this. Had Lady Morton hired her to make certain Phoebe went through with the marriage and didn't run away with Robert? Or had she been hired because Lady Morton was uncomfortable putting her daughter in the hands of a man old enough to be her father?

One thing for certain, she was beginning to like Phoebe, and she didn't want to see anything happen to her. That meant she was going to have to find out all she could about Lord Vincent. Lord Morton, as well.

"I should let you get to bed," she said, rising to her feet. "Thank you for confiding in me. I want you to know that I'll do whatever I can to help you."

A shaky smile curved Phoebe's lips. "Thank you, but I'm not sure that there's anything you can do. Although, you never did tell me just what else you are capable of doing."

It was meant as a lighthearted comment, and Finley tried to react as such, but it struck just a little too close to home for her to find it funny. She turned her head to meet Phoebe's gaze past the corner of the door. "I'm not sure either of us wants to find out," she replied. "Good night, Phoebe." And then closed the door behind her.

Finley woke to utter darkness and a sense of determined purpose, which could mean only one thing, though it never occurred to her—her other self was awake, as well, and in control.

It wasn't fair that Phoebe had to marry Lord Vincent, though Finley was aware that life was full of things that weren't fair. That wasn't the issue crowding her head right now. What she wanted to know was why a man Vincent's age wanted to marry such a young girl—other than the obvious, of course. Old men always leered at younger women, always wanted someone new and fresh to give them an heir and make them feel young again.

If the old earl had nefarious plans for her new friend, he was in for a rude awakening. Friendship was a rare thing, and Finley liked Phoebe, she really did.

As much as she could like a girl without much of a backbone. Honestly, she didn't even like herself all that much at times.

She tossed back the blankets and swung her legs over the side of the bed. Ten minutes later she was dressed in a short skirt, striped stockings, heavy boots, black shirt and serviceable leather corset that tied in the front. She pulled on a long black coat, secured her hair on top of her head and opened a window.

It was quite a drop to the grass below, but luck was on her side in the form of a trellis a few feet over. All she had to do was ease her body out of the window and stretch an arm and a leg toward the trellis, while maintaining her balance with her remaining limbs. When she had a solid hold on the trellis, she let go of the window casing and swung as gracefully as a monkey.

Quickly, she clambered down the side of the house and dropped to the soft grass. She glanced around to make certain no one had seen her before jogging toward the garden wall. It was better to keep to the shadows than the street—and faster.

She ran toward the wall, pushed up against the moss-covered stone with the toe of her boot and vaulted herself up to grip the top edge. She pulled herself up easily, and crouched there a moment before jumping down into the neighboring garden. When nothing came at her, she took off running, the thick soles of her boots a blur over the grass. She vaulted another wall, and then another, working her way toward Lord Vincent's estate through a shortcut of back gardens and shadows.

When she reached the top of the wall around his lordship's garden, she paused, barely winded. Every instinct warned her not to charge in like a bull chasing a red flag. Lord Vincent was a technologically minded man. He had automatons for servants, and automatons never slept.

Just as the thought crossed her mind, her sensitive ears picked up a faint grinding sound that seemed to grow louder and louder. A small light shone through the darkness, and then she saw that the light came from a bulb implanted in the chest of an automaton. The bright beam swelled to illuminate the garden like a torch, sweeping a radius of perhaps seven feet in front of the graceful machine.

A sentry. It had pistols mounted on its shoulders and pincers on the end of its humanoid hands. It was made to maim, perhaps even kill intruders. Finley frowned. She understood that Lord Vincent was a rich and powerful man, and that his house was full of things thieves would love to steal, but the Watch kept an eye on this area, and Lord Vincent already had iron grates over his lower windows and top-notch locks on all the doors—she had noticed them the night of the ball.

Which begged the question: what was Lord Vincent trying to protect? Or better yet, what was he trying to hide?

Finley stayed where she was until the automaton had navigated around the side of the house; it gave her time to figure out a way in. She jumped down from the wall, thighs slightly tight from crouching so long, and bolted toward the house. She didn't have much time. The automaton would eventually make its way back, and if her estimation of Lord Vincent's secrecy and intelligence was even half of what it should be, the metal would sense her from a distance.

She was strong and fast, but a bullet could kill her just as easily as it killed anyone else.

Speed gave her momentum and she leaped up at the house, fingers clutching at the top of a window casing. Toes and fingers dug in as she pulled herself up. Was she getting stronger? She felt even stronger than she had before punching that idiot governess.

That silly part of her that worried too much was not going to be happy about that, but *she* was! Quickly, she scampered up the side of the house, sometimes using nothing more than breaks in the mortar for purchase. Past the ground floor, then the first. She stopped at a second-floor window—one without shutters—and pushed.

There was a slight popping noise as the latch broke, bits of it hitting the floor. The window swung open and she pulled herself over the sill just as the automaton approached far below.

As a precaution, she closed the window once more. It gaped slightly without its latch, but as far as she was concerned that wasn't her dilemma.

She was in a bedroom. As she surveyed her surroundings in the dark, with nothing but moonlight and her keen eyesight to guide her, she saw that she was in what must have been the late countess's bedchamber. Either the earl had never closed the room up after she died, or he was in the midst of preparing it for his new bride.

She picked a brush up from the vanity. Auburn hair clung to some of the bristles, answering her question. He had never closed the room up after his last wife's death.

Did he plan to move Phoebe in here without changing a thing? Or would he put her elsewhere, so this room might remain a museum of sorts? Whichever he chose, it was still…

creepy. Marrying a girl who looked that much like your dead wife was just unsettling. Surely society thought the same way? But no one would dare tell an earl that he was clearly on the short list for Bedlam, the lunatic asylum.

Flesh prickling with goose bumps, Finley made for the door. She couldn't stay in this room any longer, cryptlike as it was. Why, her overactive mind could almost imagine the husk of the former Lady Vincent beneath the bedcovers.

Her heart was pounding as she slipped out into the corridor. It was dark and quiet here—not a mechanized servant to be seen, nor a human one. The only light was what peeked from beneath a door at the end of the hall.

Finley crept toward that light, wincing when the floorboards creaked beneath her feet. She froze, scarcely daring to breathe. Nothing. No metal guards, no weapons flying out of the walls, no trip wires designed to maim or kill. Lord Vincent put all of his energy into keeping people out of his house rather than taking precautions against a stranger romancing the inside—thankfully.

At the end of the corridor, she crouched down and put her eye to the keyhole.

*Please, don't let him be naked*, she prayed. She might have to gouge out her own eyes if Lord Vincent was prancing about in his flesh pajamas on the other side of the door.

She needn't have worried, she soon realized. This wasn't a bedroom—or at least it wasn't anymore. It might have been at one time, but now it appeared to be a laboratory of some sort. Lord Vincent stood with his back to her—fully clothed. He seemed to be fiddling with some sort of cabinet with a glass top. She couldn't quite see it all because he was in the way.

The room was brightly lit, and the odor seeping from underneath the door smelled vaguely of chemicals and smoke, and was moist with steam. Jars and beakers sat on shelves and workbenches. Strange tools that looked like things a dentist or surgeon might use hung ominously from hooks in the walls. If it wasn't so clean and bright, she might think she was spying on Dr. Frankenstein himself.

Lord Vincent was probably building a new automaton, or working on one of his inventions. She'd been foolish to be overly suspicious of him. At worst he was an eccentric, dirty old man eager to marry someone almost a third his age.

Finley was just about to move away from the door and go home when Lord Vincent moved away from the cabinet. Sitting on top of the wooden base was a large glass tank filled with a viscous pink liquid. Coils of wires ran from various apparatus and switches into the tank, bobbing as whatever it was they were attached to moved—or rather *twitched*—in the fluid. The movement brought the thing flush against the glass....

Finley barely covered her mouth in time. Swallowing her cry, she rocked back on her heels, gripping the wall for support as prickles of heat swarmed her mind. She did not shock or surprise easily, especially not when the weaker side of herself was asleep, but what she had seen horrified her.

She peeked through the keyhole again despite her better judgment. She had to know if her eyes had deceived her. Her heart hammered as she turned her attention to the tank.

It was still. The wires leading into it did not move, nor did the jellylike contents. There was nothing bobbing like an apple in a barrel of water, only stillness—like a jar of jam.

Could she have imagined it? She wondered as she rose to her feet. Her limbs trembled and her heart continued its throbbing rhythm, even as she doubted her own eyes.

The sound of footsteps grew louder on the other side of the door, spurring her into motion. She had barely ducked into the eerie bedroom at the end of the hall when she heard the door of the laboratory open. Through the crack, she spied Lord Vincent walking down the polished floor toward that room. Whirling on her heel, she raced toward the window and squeezed out onto the ledge, closing the glass behind her. She quickly climbed down to the grass and sprinted toward the wall, narrowly avoiding the patrol automaton.

The vision of that tank haunted her all the way back to Lord and Lady Morton's, and continued to plague her as she lay in bed, wishing for a fast and dreamless sleep. She could not forget the image no matter how hard she tried. Not for the first time she doubted her own sanity, because she couldn't have seen what she thought she had seen. But still…

She had seen something similar in an anatomy book Silas had in the store, and though the thought made her stomach churn, she could have sworn that what she had seen in the tank at Lord Vincent's was a human brain.

# Chapter 6

The bright light of day made everything so much clearer.

When Finley woke up the next morning, mortified that the other part of herself had taken over and broken into Lord Vincent's home, she told herself of course there hadn't been a brain in that tank. It had only looked like one—not that she had any experience with brain examination. It had probably been something his lordship was working on—something machine related, and not human at all.

That was what she told herself, and part of her believed it enough to decide not to give it any more thought. Even when she went down to breakfast and found herself alone with Lady Morton, she said nothing.

"You look tired this morning, Finley, my dear," the lady commented, her tone sincerely concerned. "Are you quite all right?"

"I'm fine, thank you. I didn't sleep well last night."

Lady Morton concentrated on spreading jam on her toast

and did not look at Finley. "I thought I heard you come in quite late last night."

Finley froze. "I… I went for a walk in the garden. I'm sorry to have disturbed you."

"You didn't. I thought perhaps you might have gone out." Now she raised her pointed and somewhat unsettling gaze.

Frowning, Finley could only stare back. Was she correct in suspecting that her ladyship had hoped she had gone somewhere, or was the woman merely trying to control her anger? It was difficult to tell, but a little voice in her head—a voice she recognized as her "other" self, urged her to trust her instinct. Against her better judgment, she listened to the voice.

"Where do you suppose I might have gotten myself off to? Had I gone out, that is."

The lady smiled and poured hot coffee into the delicate china cup in front of Finley before topping up her own. "Oh, I don't know. Perhaps around the neighborhood? Perhaps you might take a walk around Lord Vincent's?"

Finley swallowed. Hard. Had Lady Morton spied on her? She hadn't seen anyone follow her—not that she could remember. Sometimes when her darker half took over the details were fuzzy. "Why ever would I go to Lord Vincent's?"

This time her ladyship lost all pretense. She set aside her coffee and her toast, and leaned in. "Because you have become a friend to my daughter, and because, like me, you have an unsettling feeling about Lord Vincent."

This was unexpected. Finley's fingers trembled as she picked a piece of bacon from her plate and lifted it to her mouth. She took a bite of the salty, crispy goodness and chewed thoughtfully before answering. "He wants Phoebe to replace his dead wife."

"Yes." The older woman looked relieved to hear it said aloud. "But there is more. There is something in the way he looks at her, something that makes me shiver. It's as though he has plans for her, Finley. Like she's just another one of his inventions."

This was obviously something that had been bothering Lady Morton for some time. "What does Lord Morton say about it?" It was impertinent for her to ask, but she didn't think the lady would mind.

Lady Morton rubbed the back of her neck. She looked tired. "He says I'm being foolish, but he would sell Phoebe to a gypsy caravan if they offered to pay his debts." She pressed her fingers to her mouth, a horrified expression on her face. "I should not have said that."

But she had, and now Finley had a better idea of what the woman thought of her husband. And what Phoebe's father thought of her. Poor thing. Finley might not have grown up in a fine house with servants and pretty gowns, but at least she'd always known that her mother and Silas would do anything for her—including lay down their own lives. Silas would never sell her off to protect himself.

"Why did you hire me, Lady Morton?" An unsettling suspicion had begun to form in Finley's stomach. "It wasn't merely to be a companion to Phoebe, was it?"

The lady wrapped her fingers around her cup of coffee, as though trying to warm them. "No. I heard from Lady Gattersleigh about your…altercation with that dreadful governess of hers. I knew you would protect anyone you cared about, and how could you not care about my Phoebe?"

That was true. "She's easy to like, ma'am."

"Yes." She smiled faintly, but proudly. "She's a good girl. Lady Gattersleigh also told me that she thought you were *unnatural* in regards to your strength. Is that true?"

Finley swallowed the rest of her bacon. Since she'd begun to change she'd had to hide what she was, because people always reviled or feared her for it. Now, someone actually wanted her to be different. "Yes. I am unusual, but Phoebe is not in any danger from me. I want you to know that."

"I have seen enough to know you would never hurt my daughter. Your excursion last night proves to me that you are exactly as I hoped." She reached across the table and took Finley's hand. "You will protect her, won't you? If his intentions are nefarious, you will find out before the wedding?"

The wedding was to take place closer to the end of the Season, in late June. "I'll do everything I can," Finley promised with a solemn nod.

The older woman squeezed her hand once more before releasing it. "Thank you. I want you to know you have my permission to come and go at all hours. So long as you do not neglect Phoebe or raise her suspicions, I will gladly make excuses for your absence."

Finley thanked her. She didn't know what she could do against someone as powerful as an earl, but maybe she could find a reason for Phoebe not to marry him. That would please everyone.

"Three evenings from now we are expecting Lord Vincent to dine with us," Lady Morton informed her, returning to her toast. "If you should happen to develop a headache immediately after the meal and need to lie down, I shouldn't hold it against you."

One of Finley's brows rose. The woman was actually encouraging her to lie in order to sneak away from the house and break into Lord Vincent's! Why, it was enough intrigue to make a girl's heart race. And yet...and yet that dark part of her relished the opportunity. Even underneath all her misgivings, Finley wanted to do this.

"That's good to know," she replied. "I believe I am due for a headache that evening."

They shared a conspiratorial smile, but it was the relief and thankfulness on the woman's face that meant more to Finley than anything else.

"What are the two of you talking so quietly about?" Phoebe asked as she came into the dining room looking brighter than anyone had the right to when just out of bed.

Her mother smiled at her. "You, of course."

The girl laughed. "Because I'm such a fascinating topic."

Finley smiled, as well, and when Phoebe joined them at the table, the conversation turned to happier, lighter subjects, which suited her just fine. She felt almost like a normal girl sitting there with Phoebe, discussing parties and dresses and who was caught doing what in the scandal sheets.

But the part of her that wasn't normal kept thinking about Lord Vincent and how something just wasn't right with him. After all, it took a monster to know one.

That afternoon Lord Vincent came calling to take Phoebe for a ride in Hyde Park. It was a fashionable pastime, though one Finley thought ridiculous. Imagine, a bunch of rich people all swarming the park at five o'clock just so they could be seen there? Why not go when it was less busy? At least then a body could enjoy themselves.

Finley was *not* enjoying herself. While Phoebe and his lordship rode in a comfortable open carriage pulled by gleaming brass automaton horses, she was forced to follow behind on an actual smelly horse.

She had only ever been on a horse twice in her entire life, and the first time she had cried until her mother took her down from the saddle. Horseback was a long way up when you're five and city-raised.

At least she was able to ride astride. It wasn't terribly fashionable, but it wasn't considered as scandalous as it had been years ago. A famous horsewoman from Astley's Amphitheatre had started a trend for it and it had only taken a few noble-women to follow suit for the rest of society to catch on. It was supposedly much safer than riding sidesaddle, for which Finley was greatly thankful.

She wore a black split skirt—wide-legged trousers that had a panel that could be brought about in front to make it more resemble a skirt—and a purple riding jacket with matching hat. She felt like a great eggplant atop the chestnut mare, despite Phoebe's assurances that she looked "smashing." The ostrich plume in her hat kept bobbing in her face no matter how many times she blew it out of the way.

She followed behind the carriage at a discreet distance, ob-viously a chaperone for the couple. If that wasn't bad enough, many of the young men she had danced with at the engage-ment party tipped their hats and said hello to her as they rode past in their modern vehicles, calling even more attention to her eggplantishness.

Still, she could hear whatever Phoebe and her fiancé said to one another. No "usual" person would be able to at this distance, but since she was unusual the same rules didn't apply.

"I have something for you, my dear," Lord Vincent said.

"Oh, you shouldn't have, my lord," came Phoebe's pleased reply. She might not want to marry the old man, but who didn't like presents?

There was a space of silence, probably the time it took Phoebe to unwrap or open the gift. "Oh, they're beautiful!"

"Champagne pearls," Lord Vincent explained. "They'll look lovely with your skin. They were Cassandra's favorite."

The dead wife. Finley winced. Not the sort of thing you wanted to say to your future bride. *Oh, I bought you this gift that my dead wife loved.*

"I can see why," Phoebe replied politely, but Finley could

hear the stiffness in her voice, the disappointment. No one wanted to be compared to someone else.

"I thought you might wear them on our wedding day."

"I should be delighted to, my lord."

And that was it for the conversation. Personally, Finley thought Phoebe handled it very well. For a man who was a genius with machines, his lordship didn't know much about women.

The silence gave Finley a chance to look around—and to enjoy the ride. It was easier now. Her body seemed to adapt to the mare's natural rhythm. She was comfortable enough to notice how beautiful the day was as the sun began its slow descent. The grass was green, birds were singing. Voices carried on the breeze, the sounds of conversation and laughter mixing with the smells of grass and horses and machine oil.

Occasionally a young man or woman would pass by on a penny farthing, the large front wheel so funny when compared to the tiny back one. Others rode mechanical horses much like Lord Vincent's, only their metal had been dulled so it didn't glare so under the sun. Finley preferred these to his lordship's. Some of them had fancy scrollwork on them, as well, unlike Lord Vincent's hammered and embossed plates.

Given a choice, Finley would rather ride one of those new velocycles—a two-wheeled vehicle better balanced than the penny farthing, and much faster as each was powered by an engine. They weren't allowed in Hyde Park however, because they scared the horses—the real ones, that is.

The carriage came to a halt in front of her, so she rode up alongside it. Lord Vincent had just climbed down when she reached Phoebe's side.

"A gentleman from the Scientific Academy," the girl explained, tipping back her head so Finley might see her face beneath the wide brim of her hat. "Lord Vincent wished to say hello."

Finley nodded. She didn't care and didn't need to know about his lordship's social life. "What's that?" she asked, knowing the answer as she nodded at the box in the other girl's lap.

Phoebe glanced down, a flush spreading through her cheeks. "A gift. Pearls."

Finley waited for her to continue, but she didn't. Perhaps she was too embarrassed, for which Finley couldn't blame her.

One of the mechanical horses attached to the carriage began to make an odd whirring noise. Frowning, Finley glanced at it, then Phoebe. "Is that normal?"

Phoebe frowned, as well. "I have no idea." She turned her head—presumably to ask Lord Vincent if the horse was going to explode—and then was gone.

It took Finley a split second to realize that the carriage had taken off, with Phoebe still inside.

Lord Vincent looked horrified—which he should. "How do I stop them?" she demanded.

White-faced he turned to her, obviously in shock. "There are foot controls on the floor of the carriage, and a stick brake on the right."

That was all she needed to hear. She dug her heels into her horse and fell low over its neck. The animal shot forward at breakneck speed. Finley was a fast runner, but not this fast.

"Come on, darling," she urged the mare. "Just a little faster."

People cried out as she sped past. Some had already stopped to watch the runaway carriage as it careened out of control with Phoebe screaming inside it. Did the girl not think to try the controls? She must have seen Lord Vincent use them. Perhaps she was too frightened to think.

Odd, but Finley found that fear always made her mind that much clearer. Her horse picked up the pace as though she realized what was at stake. As she closed the distance between Phoebe and herself, she pulled her feet free of the stirrups and began to lean to the left.

She came up on the carriage on the right side. As soon as she was convinced her horse could keep pace, she reached out and grabbed the side of the vehicle. Phoebe's cries of panic grated her nerves and urged her on. She would stop this carriage if for no other reason than to shut the girl up. She refused to think of what might happen if she failed.

Up ahead there was a curve in the track. The carriage would run off the gravel, onto the grass and head straight for the Serpentine. The weight of Phoebe's skirts would be enough to drown her if she wasn't tossed from the carriage and crushed by the metal horses before that.

Finley let herself be pulled free of the saddle and swung her legs toward the shiny lacquered vehicle. Narrowly she managed to avoid getting her foot caught in a wheel. She would not think about how badly her leg could have been broken if not for her reflexes.

She heaved herself over the side, onto the padded seat. Phoebe screamed hysterically beside her.

Righting herself, Finley slammed her foot down on the first pedal. Nothing. Then the second. Nothing. She seized the steering mechanism and tried to turn it so the carriage would stay on the track. Nothing. She pulled the brake.

Nothing. It was like pulling on a ribbon hanging by a thread. No resistance.

They were, she realized, buggered.

They were going too fast to jump, and her horse had given up the chase shortly after she leaped from its back. The turn in the track was closer now.

And Phoebe still screamed.

Finley whirled around and slapped her. Instantly the girl stopped screaming and stared at her in shocked indignity.

"Pull it together!" Finley shouted at her. "I'm going to see if I can disengage the horses. I need you to see if you can get the brake to work. Can you do that?"

Her cheek had turned an angry red, but Phoebe nodded. She was still terrified, but at least she wasn't screaming.

Finley crawled over the other seat, legs dangling over the side as the ground rushed by below. If she fell now, the best she could hope for would be to live. More than likely she would be caught beneath the frame and dragged to her death. Lovely.

She took a breath and cautiously extended a foot toward the bar that connected the two metal horses to one another. At least she'd have a perch. She pushed forward, wavered for a heart-pounding second, and then found her balance despite the terrible bouncing and swaying of the vehicle.

The horses' exteriors were made of plates, so she dug her fingers beneath one and pulled. It resisted, having been welded in place, but she ground her teeth and yanked.

The plate flew into the air and spun backward. Phoebe ducked just in time to avoid being brained by it. Finley didn't take the time to even consider how bad that could have been.

"Duck!" she shouted this time, and repeated the maneuver with the other horse. She didn't check to make sure Phoebe did as she bade. They were almost at the turn.

Inside each horse she could see pistons and gears pumping and spinning. If she grabbed the bar that seemed to be the part that drove the legs...if she broke that, the horses should stop.

But it was a solid metal bar. No, wait! It had a rotating piece attached at the end for the back legs. She could jam it if she had a tool....

Each horse had a metal tail—more for appearance than any real use. She snapped the tail from each horse and, holding each like a spear in either hand, drove them into the open drive works. Sparks flew up, but she didn't flinch, even when the molten metal landed on her clothes and skin.

The carriage lurched as the horses made the most horrific noises—grinding that sounded almost like a woman screaming. Steam rose all around them as the metal beasts staggered and stumbled. They were coming apart.

At the last second, Finley realized she was in the wrong spot. She turned and dived toward the carriage, taking Phoebe to the floor with her as the horses came apart. She sheltered the other girl with her body as they slammed to a standstill, pieces of metal raining down around them. Something hard slammed her in the back of the head. She saw stars but didn't pass out. Warmth ran down her scalp and neck. Drops of crimson plopped onto Phoebe's pale green jacket.

There was a heaviness on her back as everything finally stilled. As Finley pushed up, she realized it was the head of one of the horses. It must weigh a good three and a half stone. Hopefully none of the people racing toward them saw her toss it aside like it was no more substantial than a jug of milk.

She offered Phoebe a hand. "Are you all right?"

The girl nodded, face so white she might be a ghost. "You're bleeding."

Finley nodded. "I'll heal." And she would—quicker than she ought.

Suddenly they were surrounded. Voices demanded to know if they were all right. Finley tried to reassure them all, but the sight of her blood only added to the frenzy.

Lord Vincent appeared, his face almost as white as Phoebe's. His relief to find her whole and unharmed might have been touching if he hadn't then turned to look at his precious horses. His brow furrowed when he saw the damage. Something strange flickered in his eyes when he spied the tails sticking out of the open sides. He turned his gaze to Finley, and what she saw there sent a shiver down her spine.

He knew what she had done. It was there for everyone to see, but only Lord Vincent knew just how impossible it should have been for her to get those panels off, let alone rip off the tails and jam up the works.

Suspicion, and the understanding that she was not as she ought to be, turned his eyes flinty and dangerous—just like the villagers turned against Dr. Frankenstein when they realized what a monster he had created. Lord Vincent looked at her like she was that monster.

So Finley did what so many rich girls did when confronted with a situation they did not want to face. She rolled her eyes back into her head and pretended to faint.

# Chapter 7

"It's almost completely healed."

Finley shrugged at the awe in Phoebe's voice as the girl examined her scalp where she'd been injured during the carriage accident. "I know."

She pointed at her cheek where Finley had slapped her. There was a red mark on her cheek with faint bruising. "But I'm stuck with this."

"I'm sorry, but I couldn't think of any other way to calm you down." Finley really did feel bad about it.

Phoebe waved a dismissive and impatient hand. "That's not what I meant. Of course you were right to strike me. I was an absolute hysterical mess. A little powder will cover it. What I meant is that you should have more than a fading scar."

Shoulders sagging, Finley sat down on her bed. "I should, but I don't." Was this the moment that Phoebe finally turned on her? "I'm not normal."

The other girl laughed. "No, you most certainly are not."

She plopped down beside her, dark eyes wide. "You are extraordinary, and you saved my life. Thank you."

Finley stared at her, jaw loose. "You're not afraid of me?"

More laughter. "Of course not, silly! I might be a little nervous around mechanical horses for a while, but I could never be afraid of you."

Heat pricked the back of Finley's eyes. She blinked away the sting. "Thank you."

"You're welcome. Now—" she gave Finley's leg a slap "—why don't we get Mama and go out for a bit? I've a craving for chocolate from that little shop on Bond Street."

Chocolate was good, and getting out of the house would be good, as well. If she was distracted, perhaps she wouldn't think of the look Lord Vincent had given her. It scared her and angered her at the same time. Part of her was afraid of him now, while another part of her wanted to grab him by the throat and thrash him until he cried like a baby.

But it wasn't really herself she was worried about. She was worried about Phoebe. Phoebe was more breakable than she was.

They found Lady Morton downstairs. She agreed that an outing sounded delightful, and insisted that Finley allow her to treat—a thank-you for saving her daughter's life.

"You don't need to thank me, Lady Morton," Finley told her.

The lady put her arm about Finley's shoulders and squeezed. "When you are a mother, my dear girl, you will realize that I will be beholden to you for the rest of my days."

That was a strange concept for Finley to wrap her head around—that someone might feel indebted to her for so long.

They called for the carriage and collected their coats. The day was slightly overcast and a little cool, but still pleasant. The city bustled with activity. Vehicles filled the cobblestone streets with pedestrians threading in and out of traffic. The steam-moistened air was filled with the scents and sounds of London as ladies in bright walking gowns mingled with the drably garbed lower classes.

Bond Street was one of the most fashionable locations in the West End. A place Finley rarely ever haunted before coming to the Morton household. There were many fine shops catering to any number of tastes, and little coffeehouses and tearooms where ladies might stop to rest their shopping-weary feet.

Their destination was a small shop with a bright blue awning and sign that read Chocolatier. As soon as Finley crossed the threshold, her stomach growled in appreciation. Here, there was nothing but the smell of chocolate—warm and delicious.

They sat at a table near the window and ordered a pot of hot chocolate along with a selection of sweets, such as chocolate-filled croissants and tiny, decadent cakes.

Finley glanced out the window and spied two men on the opposite side of the street. They were a little rough looking—not normally the type that one saw in this part of the city—and they seemed to be looking directly at her. Her heart gave a nervous kick at their intent gazes, and she quickly turned her head.

"He's so handsome," Phoebe commented just as Finley directed her attention at her.

"Who?" she demanded.

"The Duke of Greythorne," came the reply. "He just left."

She glanced out the window, but all she saw was a tall gentleman with reddish-brown hair and wearing very fashionable clothing as he walked away from her. "Well, he has a tolerable back," she commented drily.

Phoebe snickered. "Looking at his back*side* are you, Finley?"

Lady Morton chuckled, as well. A slight heat crept up Finley's cheeks. Why she was embarrassed escaped her. It wasn't as though she could actually see his derriere with his coat in the way.

"He'll make a fine catch for a debutante one day," Lady Morton commented. She wore her dark spectacles, but Finley could see a twinkle in one eye. "Rich as the devil, handsome and polite."

"Not much for society, though," Phoebe rebuked. "Whoever marries him will have to be content to go to balls alone, or stay at home for the most part. He's not out and about very much."

Her mother raised her cup of chocolate to her lips. "He may grow into enjoying society."

"Well, it hardly matters to me. It's not as though I'll have a chance of ever marrying him." Phoebe's tone was surprisingly sharp, and drained the color from her mother's face.

"I don't have a chance with him, either," Finley jumped in, hating that guilty look on her employer's face. "All I'll ever have is the memory of his backside."

Phoebe's smile broke first, then she chuckled. Her mother followed suit, and the tension at their table lessoned. By the time they'd finished their treats—the croissants were to die for—they had been in the shop for more than an hour, talking, laughing and indulging in more chocolate than was wise.

They bought croissants to take home with them for breakfast the next morning. Personally, Finley thought they'd be lucky if the pastries made it to midnight. They were to attend a musicale that evening, and might be in need of a snack when they returned home.

As they left the shop, Finley glanced across the street. The men she'd spied earlier were gone, much to her relief.

They barely made it half a block before an arm snaked out of the alley they were passing and grabbed Lady Morton, snatching her into the narrow space. She cried out, but her abductor slapped a hand over her mouth and pointed a pistol at Finley and Phoebe.

It was the ruffians. She'd been right to be suspicious of them.

Phoebe gasped, and looked as though she was about to scream. The second man pointed a knife at her. "Make a sound and I'll slit yer mum's throat."

The color drained from Phoebe's face, but Finley was most concerned with Lady Morton. The woman was terrified—to the point where she might pass out.

"What do you want?" Finley asked, a strange calm settling over her. The other part of her had come to call, and she was glad of it.

Both men looked at her. "Yer money and yer valuables," the larger of the two—the one with the knife—informed her. "You come over here and take off Lady Posh's glittery bobs."

Slowly, Finley advanced toward them. How dare they terrify Lady Morton so. How dare they be so brazen as to accost them in broad daylight on Bond Street!

She stopped directly in front of her employer, and gave her what she hoped was a reassuring glance before turning her attention to the man with an arm around her shoulders. He had yet to pull back the hammer, so that gave her a little room to play.

"You ought to be ashamed of yourselves," she told both men. "Picking on harmless, defenseless women."

"Gotta eat, girly," Lady Morton's captor replied with a sneer.

Finley's lips twisted. "That's going to be difficult for you from now on."

Before he could ask or utter a sound, her first flew into his mouth with all her strength. Blood and teeth sprayed the air as he screamed in pain. She snatched the pistol from his hand and pointed it at the man with the knife. Then, she gently nudged Lady Morton behind her, pushing her toward Phoebe.

The bully with the blade gaped at her. He barely glanced at his friend, who was laid out cold on the ground, blood dripping from his slack mouth.

"It's not loaded," knife man announced just as he lunged for her.

Finley didn't think; she simply acted. She caught him hard across the jaw with the pistol and dodged out of the way of the knife he swung at her. The tip of the blade sliced through the fine wool of her coat, but did not touch her flesh. She caught his arm before he could swing again, and gave his wrist a sharp twist. He dropped the knife, crying out as his friend had as she snapped the bones in his arm like they were as brittle as matches.

Finley let him go when his knees buckled. He fell to the ground, clutching his wrist, calling her names that she had never heard of before.

"Maybe I am all those things." She sneered at him, pocketing the knife. "But I'm still the girl that kicked both your arses."

She turned then, toward the two women near the mouth of the alley. Both of them rushed to her, crushing her in their fierce embrace. Lady Morton might have actually been crying.

"There, there," Finley consoled them. "Enough of that. Let's get out of here before we attract attention, shall we?" The last thing she needed was some nosy Peeler—the nickname given to those on the London police force—coming by asking how a girl like her managed to debilitate two very large, full-grown men at least eight stone heavier than her.

She bustled them out of the alley and then down the street to where their carriage and driver waited.

"Home, please," Finley said as the man helped them inside. She sat on the back-facing bench, giving the two of them the front-facing one just in case either of them felt ill.

"You deserve a raise," Lady Morton murmured, her voice oddly high.

"I'll settle for a handkerchief," Finley replied, holding up her bloodstained hand.

Immediately her ladyship pulled a square of linen from her reticule and gave it to her. Finley wiped as much blood away as she could, but some had already dried, and she wasn't about to spit on herself in front of her companions.

"Can you teach me to do the things you can do?" Phoebe inquired.

Finley's head snapped up. She frowned. "You don't want to be like me."

"Oh, I assure you I do."

She shrugged. "I suppose I can teach you how to throw a punch, but the other stuff I can do…that's just me."

"Extraordinary." Lady Morton practically sighed the word. "What's your favorite food, Finley? I'm going to demand Cook make it for you."

Finley grinned. They didn't hate her. They liked her. They thought this part of her was wonderful. Wouldn't her goody-goody half choke on this?

"I'm partial to chocolate croissants," she replied.

Her companions chuckled, and Phoebe offered her the paper bag that held their purchase from the chocolate shop. She reached in with her clean hand and took one out.

This being extraordinary really worked up an appetite.

★ ★ ★

Lord Vincent glared at the men who sat across from him in the cab. One had blood all around his mouth and down his front, and the other held his wrist, moaning like an imbecile.

"You mean to tell me that a slip of a girl managed to incapacitate you both?"

"She weren't no ordinary girl," the moaner replied. "Slip or not, she weren't natural. Snapped me wrist like a chicken bone."

*Chicken,* Lord Vincent thought, sounded like the appropriate term. He took out his purse and tossed them each several coins. "Get out. I don't want to see or hear from either of you again, and if I hear that you've mentioned this little task to anyone, I'll have your guts for garters. Am I understood?"

The men nodded and fled the cab as quickly as their bulk would allow. Lord Vincent knocked on the ceiling with his cane and the carriage lurched into motion. He almost groaned. Flesh-and-blood horses were so damn slow.

He drew a deep breath and pushed it out, trying to free himself of this frustration and rage. He never used to be an angry man. Never used to be a violent man. Before Cassandra's death he never would have dreamed of hiring ruffians to accost a young girl, but he had to know what he was up against. He hadn't been able to believe what she'd done to his beautiful automaton horses. He'd been too relieved that she saved Phoebe's life, but afterward, when he'd had time to really examine the damage…well, it had been an astounding revelation.

Finley Bennet was not normal. In fact, the only thing he'd ever seen able to wreak so much damage was an automaton—a large one at that. No, she was not usual, and he'd wager his entire fortune that she was not a cousin to Lady Morton and the lovely Phoebe. He'd seen the way his future mother-in-law looked at him when she thought he wouldn't notice. She knew his intentions were not as pure as he pretended. Not that it mattered. Lord Morton had sold the girl and signed a contract. She was his, and he would marry her, whether her mother liked it or not.

And no one was going to stop him now that he was so close to having his hopes and dreams realized, especially not a freakish little girl.

# Chapter 8

Dinner with Lord Vincent was one of the most uncomfortable situations Finley ever found herself in.

First of all, she was wearing one of the gowns that Lady Morton had insisted on buying for her. It was lovely and a gorgeous shade of plum satin, but the little sleeves were snug and didn't allow for much movement, and Phoebe had laced her into her corset so tightly she thought her lungs might come out her nose.

Secondly, there was the fact that Lord Morton was there, as well, and he was about as pompous and self-important as she could stand. He practically ignored his wife and daughter, and had the table manners of a Newfoundland dog.

Most obviously, there was Lord Vincent himself. Oh, he was all manners and decorum, but Finley caught him looking at her several times with a gaze that was anything but polite. He looked at her like she was an insect he would like to pin to a board and dissect.

"I heard you ladies were set upon by ruffians the other day," he remarked—rather casually.

Lady Morton's head snapped up. "Oh? Where did you hear that, pray tell?"

The earl smiled gently. "Lord Morton informed me when he called upon me this morning."

Finley didn't miss the flush that crept into Lady Morton's fair cheeks. It was obvious from the way that she looked at her husband she suspected he had called on Lord Vincent for more money.

"My valet told me," Lord Morton explained with a sniff. "Damn fine kettle when a man has to hear about his wife being accosted from the servants."

The most caustic and bitter smile Finley had ever seen curved the lady's lips. "I knew how you'd worry if I told you."

A similar expression crossed her husband's face. "You're always so considerate, my dear."

Good lord, these two despised one another! Finley glanced down at her plate. Aristocrats were a queer lot—marrying for money, staying with spouses they couldn't stand, living by all manner of foolish rules.

Selling their daughters to save their own hides.

"I also heard," Lord Vincent continued, as though the tension between Lord and Lady Morton didn't exist, "that it was Miss Bennet who fought the bounders off."

Finley lifted her head and met his cool gaze. "You shouldn't believe everything you hear, my lord. I'm hardly a heroine."

"So you didn't return home with bruised and bloody knuckles from striking one of them?"

She glanced at Lord Morton, but he had gone back to his plate and paid her no attention. The man certainly liked to talk—at least when he was begging for money.

She held up her hands, palms toward herself, so that he

could examine them. "Not a bruise nor a cut." There wasn't either. They had disappeared earlier that day.

Lord Vincent's lips pursed. "I see I was mistaken." He didn't cast an accusatory glance at Lord Morton, but still he seemed perturbed. Perhaps it was a reach, but the thought flittered across Finley's mind that perhaps he hadn't heard details of the altercation from Lord Morton. What if he had gotten his information from a more reliable source, such as the thugs themselves?

No, that was too much. Wasn't it?

"Although it would be extraordinary if I had fought them off, wouldn't it?" she asked with a cheeky smile. "They'd write novels about me then—stopping runaway automaton horses, fending off ruffians. I'd be a sensation."

Lady Morton and Phoebe chuckled—and sounded almost genuine, though Finley didn't miss the look Lady Morton shot her. It was a look that demanded to know if she had lost her mind.

"Indeed," Lord Vincent replied, then he dismissed her and turned to Phoebe. "You look lovely in the pearls, my dear."

Phoebe had worn his gift to dinner. He was right; she did look lovely. She also, Finley imagined, looked like a younger version of his dead wife. It was enough to make a body shiver as though an icy hand trailed down her spine.

"I'm afraid I've developed a terrible headache," Finley announced suddenly, pressing her fingers to her forehead. "It's been brewing all day. I think I might lie down for a bit. Will you all excuse me?"

The gentlemen rose as she did—Mr. Morton looked rather put out about it. He also had beef in his moustache, but Finley didn't point it out. Let him wear it for a while. Hopefully it would still be there when he went to his club later.

"I hope you feel better soon, Miss Bennet." Lord Vincent sounded sincere, but she didn't trust it.

"Thank you, my lord."

Both Lady Morton and Phoebe wished her a quick recovery. As far as Phoebe was concerned the excuse was legitimate. Only Lady Morton and Finley knew exactly what she was truly about to get up to.

And she got up to it quickly. As soon as she entered her room she squirmed out of the gown, corset and underclothes. Then, she redressed in fresh bloomers, short skirt, blouse and leather corset. She laced up her sturdy black boots and shrugged into a black sweater to ward off the slight chill of the evening.

Then she repeated the same maneuver she had a few nights before when she last ventured to Lord Vincent's estate, even entering the house through the same window.

This time, however, she did not linger in the countess's old room. It was simply too disturbing. She opened the door a crack and peeked out into the corridor. It was dimly lit, but there was not a servant in sight, which only added to her suspicion that he had something he didn't want others to see up here. Quickly, she slipped into the hall, closing the door behind her. This time she avoided the places where the boards had creaked beneath her feet. It wasn't the middle of the night, and there were people and machines in the house that might hear her mincing about.

Her heart thumped hard and heavily against her ribs as she turned the knob on the door at the end of the hall. She pushed. Locked.

Bloody hell. What now? She couldn't very well kick the door in—that would cause a bit of a ruckus. She knew nothing about picking locks, although it seemed it shouldn't be *that* difficult.

She turned and glanced down the corridor in the direction from where she'd come. Most grand houses had separate bedrooms for the mistress and master of the house, but those rooms were almost always connected. Down the corridor she went, again taking pains to avoid creaking floorboards. This time she stopped one door before the countess's room—approximately halfway down.

This door was not locked, and she ducked inside the darkened room. There was a lamp on the wall beside the door. She found the switch and flicked it, bringing light to the room. How fortunate she was that Lord Vincent insisted on having his entire house outfitted with modern conveniences.

His room was large and very masculine, the walls cream with lots of wood paneling and trim, the air filled with the scent of Bay Rum and hair pomade. It made him seem a far nicer man than she believed him to be.

She didn't have to look hard. Sitting atop his dressing table was a key attached to a ladies' hair ribbon. The ribbon was dark blue, slightly frayed and creased. It had to have belonged to the former countess. He was still in love with her.

For a second—and only the one—Finley felt sorry for him. Then she remembered that he was marrying Phoebe, and why, and her pity faded. She snatched up the key and crept back to the room at the end of the hall.

Satisfaction blossomed in her chest as the key turned and kicked the tumblers into place. She slid the key into the pocket of her sweater and turned the knob. Tiny beads of sweat formed along her hairline. She was a little scared to go in.

There was nothing that could hurt her on the other side of this door—unless of course Lord Vincent had rigged some sort of trap for people who came spying—like perhaps an automaton with blades for hands, or a pistol set to go off as soon as the door opened.

Perhaps it was just her overactive imagination that made her paranoid, but Finley jumped back after giving the door a push, just in case.

Nothing happened. No blades, no bullets. Cautiously, she peeked around the door frame into the room. Aside from scientific equipment, it was empty. It was a little disappointing, really. As an inventor he could at least have had a hunchback assistant, or perhaps a metal one.

The room was clean to the point of being sterile. The walls were a fresh white, the benches and sideboards a deep walnut. A stack of folders sat at the far end of the counter, near a tray of neatly arranged surgical instruments.

Finley turned her head. There was another workbench on the other side of the room, and near the window, with a large chandelier over it, there was a table—the kind she'd seen at the doctor's office.

Why would a man who built automatons have a surgical table? Surgical equipment? Lady Morton said Lord Vincent had built his own prosthetic leg, but surely he hadn't installed it on himself, as well? Perhaps he had. But why maintain the equipment? Who was he working on now?

As if in reply, there came a gurgling noise from behind her. She froze. Her heart was so far up her throat she could feel its beat on the roof of her mouth. Cold heat prickled her fingers and toes, and spread up to the nape of her neck.

She did *not* want to turn around, but she had no choice.

Slowly, mouth drying out with every movement, Finley turned toward the tank. She had been able to ignore it until now, when the contents had apparently come alive.

The coils of wires running into the tank were mostly concealed by a white cloth draped over the top. Finley's fingers trembled as she reached for that cloth. Once she removed it she would not be able to put it back, not without seeing what lurked beneath.

She clutched the linen and pulled. Lord, was it possible for someone her age to die of heart failure? Surely the poor thing could not continue this furious beating for much longer.

The cloth fell away, revealing the bubbling pink goo beneath. Revealing what lurked there.

She had been right. It was a brain. Her stomach twisted, threatening to expel her dinner. It was awful and fascinating at the same time, floating there in the goo, wires attached to it. The wires had to be what kept it "alive"—some sort of electrical current? The goo had to be similar to human tissue, perhaps the lining of the skull. She had no medical knowledge, so she could only assume these things, but it made sense to her shocked mind.

What sort of madman kept a brain in a tank?

She turned away, unable to stare at it any longer. It bobbed in the liquid, as though begging for her help, which she had no idea how to give. It had been inside a human once. Did it maintain memories, feelings? Was it suffering?

It was too much.

On the opposite wall there was a large metal door. Finley turned her attention to it instead of the brain. She wanted to run away, but she couldn't. Not until she'd uncovered every secret Lord Vincent had.

It was at that moment that she felt a calm settle over her. She knew at once that her darker nature was taking over, and she let it. It always seemed to come during times of high emotion or stress, and since it was better equipped to handle this sort of situation, she didn't put up a fight.

A couple of deep breaths later and her nerves settled. Fear was replaced with determination, and a healthy dose of righteous anger. Instead of feeling sorry for the thing in the vat, she was angry for it. Instead of being afraid she was determined.

She turned the wheel on the front of the large metal door. There was a hissing sound, the release of steam. As she turned, gears clicked into place until finally there was a loud thud as the locking mechanism slid free. She pulled the lever to the side and the door slowly swung open.

A wave of cold struck her, fogging the air as it clashed with the warmth of the room. For a moment she couldn't see, the stuff was so thick.

When it cleared she wished she hadn't opened the door. This was obviously an ice chest, and standing in the middle of it, strapped to a board was the late Lady Vincent. She wore a simple robe—which her husband had obviously dressed her in out of a sense of modesty rather than warmth. This poor lady wasn't in any condition to mind the cold.

Finley stared at the corpse, mouth grim. There was a large, unhealed slash across Lady Vincent's forehead. She didn't have to be a genius to know it went all the way around.

At least she knew now who the brain in the tank belonged to.

"You're a very nosy girl, Miss Bennet."

# Chapter 9

Finley swore under her breath—the kind of swearing that would have made her mother wash her mouth out with soap.

How could she not have heard him coming? He'd sneaked up on her like a cat on a deaf mouse.

She turned, and met the glittering gaze of Lord Vincent.

"So, what's the plan?" she asked. "Are you going to attempt reanimating your wife?"

He arched a brow, gazing down that big nose of his at her. "That might cause some issue, considering the world knows her to be dead."

Frowning, Finley glanced at the brain in the tank. It was bobbing furiously now. He kept the brain alive, so he must be planning on using it for something....

It was as though a giant hand of ice reached inside her and seized her heart. "Oh my God," she rasped. "You're going to put her brain in Phoebe's head."

It was a horrible assumption, one she hoped was wrong, but

the second the accusation left her lips, Lord Vincent smiled an awful smile. "Nosy and smart. Never a good combination, my girl."

Rage swelled up inside her. Who did he think he was, God? "I can't let you do this. I won't." She clenched her fists at her sides.

More of that self-satisfied smirk. "And I won't allow you to stop me." Suddenly he had a pistol in his hand, pointed at her head. It was one of those six-shooters like the cowboys in America used. It was deadly, but at least it wasn't one of his fancy inventions. "I know you're fast, and much stronger than you ought to be, but even you aren't faster than a bullet."

Hadn't she thought the same thing the other day? "You don't know anything about me."

"I know you destroyed my precious horses in a way even a circus strong man would not have been able to. I know you single-handedly fought off men armed with a pistol and knife."

How did he know exactly what weapons they had? Neither she nor the other women involved had mentioned that—hadn't wanted to bring more attention to her than necessary.

"You hired them to attack us." Disbelief dripped from her words. "You could have killed your own fiancée."

"They had strict orders not to harm Phoebe, but you and Lady Morton, not so much. Don't look at me like that. I had to know what you were capable of. I had to know what I was up against so I could protect what I've worked so hard to achieve."

"You're bloody mad."

"Perhaps. Have you ever been in love, Miss Bennet? No, of course not. You're but a child. What do you know of love?" He sneered at her, but there was pity in his eyes, as well. "I loved my wife. I love her still. And now I have been given a chance to make everything right. I can make her forgive me."

"You think she's going to thank you for shoving her brain in someone else's body?" He really was insane.

"It will be like having her own body back. Phoebe is the spitting image of Cassandra when she was young. Once I give life back to her, she'll forgive me for taking it away from her in the first place."

That was a surprise. Had he killed her? "Lady Morton said it was a carriage accident."

"It was, much like the one you and Phoebe almost had. We were driving home in the snow, and the horses I'd built malfunctioned. We went over a small ravine. I survived. Cassandra did not."

"That still sounds like an accident to me." Not that she felt sorry for the lunatic, but he hadn't been in control of the situation.

"If I had been more intelligent..." His voice cracked. "If I had done a better job, the horses would not have malfunctioned."

She shrugged. "They malfunctioned at the park, too. What did you do wrong there?"

He shook his head, scowling. "I don't know."

"So, if you're not 'intelligent' enough to make metal horses work, do you really think you can make a brain transfer work?"

Lord Vincent stilled, all of the frustration in his expression melting away to pure, determined rage. "I will bring Cassandra back." He raised the pistol once more, so that it was pointed right at her forehead. "I will have my wife's forgiveness, and you will not stop me."

Some deep instinct told Finley to duck even before he pulled the trigger. As it was, she felt the bullet as it whizzed above her, just inches from her head. She hid behind the metal door of Lady Vincent's frozen tomb.

"How are you going to explain my death, Lord Vincent? Lady Morton knows where I am."

"Let her go to the police. They will think she's mad. And they wouldn't dare search my house. Even if they did, I could have all of this easily concealed. No one will care about you, Miss Bennet. Or should I say, Miss Jayne?"

Finley didn't react to the sound of her real name. It didn't matter how he had found out. All that mattered was getting out of this alive. She shrugged. "Whichever you prefer, my lord."

His smug expression mixed with irritation. "It's not as though you are really of noble blood, are you? You're just some freakish little girl Lady Morton hired because she doesn't like me."

"That might have something to do with the fact that you plan to give her daughter a new brain!" Finley shouted.

Another shot. This one bounced off the door. She bolted from behind it and dived behind the surgical table. She had to get to him, overpower him.

He fired off three more shots, each of which ricocheted off equipment. One grazed Finley's shoulder, drawing blood. She cried out.

"Got you, did I?" came Lord Vincent's pleased tone. "Come on out, dear girl, and I'll make your death quick."

*One more bullet*, Finley thought. *That's all he has.* There was a spindly sort of stand next to her that looked like a skeletal coatrack on wheels. She kicked the base of it and it went flying across the room. Startled, Lord Vincent fired another shot at it.

Six. That was it. He was out of bullets.

Before he could reload, Finley lunged to her feet and threw

herself at him. He looked up from shoving more bullets into the pistol with a horrified expression.

She hit him hard, sending both of them crashing into the workbench. The tank shuddered. Lady Vincent's brain bobbed wildly. Suddenly, Finley knew what to do. There was only one way to end this without either she or Lord Vincent dying.

Grabbing him by the coat with one hand, she hauled him close and punched him twice in the face, hard. He fell back with a groan, the pistol falling to the floor.

Finley didn't waste any time, she grabbed a handful of wires leading into the tank and yanked. There was a squishing sound as they pulled free of the brain, and she winced. Then she seized the tank with both hands.

"No!" Lord Vincent screamed.

Finley pulled. He grabbed her just as the tank crashed to the floor, splattering its gruesome contents all over the lab.

Everything went eerily quiet—even Lord Vincent. He clung to Finley for a moment, like a child clinging to its mother, before slowly sinking to the floor, sobbing. When he crawled toward the destroyed grayish-pink mass in the middle of all the glass and goo, Finley made her escape. Lord Vincent's plaintive wails rang in her ears as she ran. "No," he cried. "Cassanda, no."

It was heartbreaking—or it would have been had he not tried to kill her, had he not been prepared to kill Phoebe for some mad experiment that probably wouldn't have worked.

Finley shuddered as she burst through the door of the countess's bedroom. She hoped it wouldn't have worked.

She crawled out the window just as servants clamored up the stairs—about time they came to investigate all the shots. When she hit the grass, there was another shot, and she froze. Had Vincent shot one of his servants?

There was screaming from inside the house—lots of it.

Lights began to come on in the upstairs windows, and one man shouted for someone to fetch the Watch. That's when Finley broke into a run. She did not want to be there when the police arrived.

Lady Morton and Phoebe were waiting for her when she returned. The relief on the older woman's face touched Finley.

"I was so worried when Lord Vincent decided to leave early," she explained. "I had no way to warn you."

"She was so distraught I made her tell me what the two of you had been up to," Phoebe added, with a stern glance at her mother. "Finley, that you would do that for me is humbling, but I would never have forgiven myself if you had been harmed."

"He tried," Finley replied. "He had a gun and shot at me, but he wasn't very good at it." The spot where he'd grazed her shoulder was already healing, and her dark clothing concealed the blood stain.

"Thank Heaven," Lady Morton whispered, hand pressed to her chest. Her artificial eye gleamed, as though expressing its own relief.

Finley flopped against the back of the settee. She was exhausted.

"What was he up to anyway?" Phoebe demanded, sitting on a nearby chair. Her posture was much better than Finley's.

Staring at her, Finley wondered how much to tell. If the police had taken Lord Vincent into custody, how much would be in tomorrow's papers? Would it be worse for Phoebe to read about it and have people whisper about her? Or would it be better to know the truth?

"He wanted to use you to bring his dead wife back to life," she explained. In such cases, the truth had to be the best course of action.

Phoebe's normally smooth brow furrowed. "How did he plan to manage that?"

Finley glanced at Lady Morton, who was suitably horrified, and drew a deep breath. "He was going to put her brain in your head."

"But that—" All the color drained from Phoebe's face. She swayed a little on her chair, and Finley moved closer to catch her in case she swooned. "He planned to kill me?"

Grimly, Finley nodded. Phoebe's reaction to the news was unexpected. She threw herself at Finley and wrapped her arms around her so tight Finley could scarce draw breath. "Thank you, Finley. Thank you so much."

They were still sitting like that a few minutes later when Lord Morton stumbled in, drunk. He took one look at the embracing girls and his pale wife, and said, "You've already heard then."

"Heard what?" Lady Morton inquired.

The portly earl swayed on his feet, face flushed and his eyes glassy. "About Vincent. Seems shortly after he left here he went home and killed himself."

A collective gasp rose from his audience. Finley's heart stopped for a second. The shot she heard before all the screams broke out. That had been Lord Vincent taking his own life. When he realized he would never resurrect his wife, he decided to join her in death. It was almost romantic, in a mad-inventor sort of way.

She looked at Phoebe, who was staring at her, big green eyes filled with tears and shock.

"You're free," she whispered to her. Tears streamed down the girl's face, and Finley hugged her close once more. Lady Morton joined them on the settee and wrapped her arms around them both.

"Women," Lord Morton muttered. "Well, at least there's a

debt I won't have to pay back." With that profoundly sensitive remark, he staggered out of the room, leaving the three of them alone once more.

He wasn't missed.

Finley stayed on long enough to attend the funeral, as was proper. As Lord Vincent's fiancée, Phoebe was socially obligated to observe mourning protocols, but she was determined to spend the shortest amount of time possible at it. Since she wasn't going to be out and about much for the next few months, Finley didn't see much point in continuing on as her companion.

Besides, every time the girl looked at her, Finley knew she was a reminder of all that had happened. Aside from Lady Morton, Finley alone knew what Vincent had planned to do to her, and that was the last thing the poor girl needed.

"Are you sure you won't stay?" Lady Morton asked her, pen poised over her checkbook.

Finley nodded. "I'm sure. Thank you, though. And thank you for the letter of reference."

The lady smiled. "Thank you for saving my daughter's life." A tear glistened on her lashes and she wiped it away. "Here are your wages."

The check was generous—more than Finley was due, but she took it regardless. It would be an insult to Lady Morton if she argued. "You're very kind."

Lady Morton set aside her pen and straightened her spine. "A friend of mine's daughter is returning from Paris tomorrow and is in need of a lady's maid. It doesn't require much in the way of social appearances, but it does pay well and affords more freedom than most domestic posts. I told her about you. Should you like, you can stop by on Wednesday morning for an interview. Here is her address."

Stunned, Finley took the card she offered. "Lady August-Raynes," she read aloud.

Lady Morton nodded. "I know nothing of the daughter, but she had a son with a bit of a reputation as a rogue. If you accept the position, you keep an eye out for him. Swat him about a bit if he steps out of line."

Finley grinned. "I'm sure I can handle him." She thanked the lady again. Then she went and said goodbye to Phoebe, which was more difficult than she thought it would be.

"I hope it works out with you and Robert," she said.

Phoebe nodded. "Me, too. Thank you, Finley. For everything." She grabbed her then, in a tight embrace that robbed her of breath and threatened to bring big fat tears to her eyes. Finley let it continue for as long as she dared, and then she pulled away.

"Take care," she murmured before walking away.

And that was it. A few weeks spending more time together than sisters, and it was over just like that. Who knew if the two of them would ever see each other again. It made Finley a little sad.

She climbed into the carriage that would return her to her mother's house, check tucked into her glove. Lady Morton and Phoebe waved to her from the step as the vehicle pulled away. Finley waved back, and then turned away before either of them could see her wipe a tear from her cheek.

She'd go home and spend a few days with her mother and Silas, have her faith in love and human beings in general restored. She'd buy her mother something nice with the extra money she'd been paid—maybe even treat herself to a new pair of boots. And maybe she'd tell Silas that she'd prefer something by Jane Austen next time he gave her something to read. She'd had her fill of monsters for a while.

She gazed out the window at the passing city and hoped

that Lady August-Raynes offered her the position within her household. She could use long-term employment.

And hopefully the darkness inside her would be content with that, as well. She wasn't too worried. In fact, she was looking forward to it. How much trouble could she get into as a lady's maid?

★ ★ ★ ★ ★

*How much trouble can Finley get into as a lady's maid?*
*Find out in THE GIRL IN THE STEEL CORSET,*
*the first story in Kady Cross's exciting new miniseries*
THE STEAMPUNK CHRONICLES.

# THE GIRL IN THE
# STEEL CORSET

# Chapter 1

*London, 1897*

The moment she saw the young man walking down the darkened hall toward her, twirling his walking stick, Finley Jayne knew she'd be unemployed before the sun rose. Her third dismissal in as many months.

She tensed and slowed her steps, but she did not stop. She kept her head down, but was smart enough not to take her gaze off him. Perhaps he would walk right by her, as though she were as invisible as servants were supposed to be.

Felix August-Raynes was the son of her employer. At one and twenty years of age, he was tall and lean with curly blond hair and bright blue eyes. Every woman who saw him called him an angel. Most who knew him thought him the very devil.

The other maids in service had warned her about Lord Felix her first day in the house. A mere fortnight ago. He belonged to a gang of privileged ruffians known for their facial piercings and lack of respect for anyone else, especially females. She had been hired to replace the previous girl hurt by the young lord. Rumor had it that the maid had required serious medical attention.

Finley didn't court trouble, but part of her—that part that was going to keep her safe, yet get her fired—hoped he'd try something. It was horribly delighted at the prospect of the violence to come.

The rest of her was terrified. Were it not for the steel boning of her leather work-corset, she fancied her heart might slam through her ribs it was pounding so hard.

Lord Felix smiled, teeth flashing in the dim light as he stopped just a few feet in front of her, blocking the only route to the servants' quarters where she slept. The tiny brass bar that bisected his left eyebrow—and proclaimed him a member of the Dandies—glinted. "Hello, my lovely. I had hoped to run into you."

Finley hesitated. Maybe he'd move out of her way and let her pass.

*Or,* a voice in her head whispered—her voice—*you could kick his teeth in.* She lowered her gaze, not wanting him to see the bloodlust there. Silently, she willed him to let her pass. For his own safety.

Instead, he closed the scant distance between them.

"You're new, aren't you?" he inquired, moving closer. He was already much too close for propriety and there was no one around to make sure he didn't overstep his bounds. The light on the wall above them flickered as though attuned to the fluttering in Finley's chest. This close, she could smell stale ale, cologne and the undeniable oily scent of mech-boxing on his fine suit. Lord Felix was a great patron of the sport.

Though why anyone would want to watch automatons pound the gears out of each other was beyond her.

"Please, my lord," she said softly, wincing at the pleading in her tone. *Please don't make me hurt you.* "I wish to retire. It's late."

It was after three in the morning, to be exact. She would have been in bed hours ago were it not for the fact that the darling debutante of the house had demanded her pink riding habit be laundered for the morning. As Lady Alyss's maid, it was Finley's job to take the ensemble down to the laundry where the air was thick with hot steam and the smell of overheated gears. She had washed the clothing and set it to dry. Right now her blouse and short skirts were damp, and her feet were sweating inside her high, thick-soled boots. She wanted nothing more than to unfasten the many buckles and take them off, along with her corset. She was going to be up early to collect the habit for Lady Alyss to wear.

And now this annoying *twit* stood in her way. Finley didn't like it. The thing inside her *truly* didn't like it. She used to think of it as an imp on her shoulder, urging her to be naughty, but lately she'd come to think of it as less mischievous and more dangerous.

Dangerous to whoever threatened her.

Lord Felix propped a palm against the plaster by her head, turning so that he pinned her against the wall with his own body. "What's the hurry?" he asked, beer breath hot on her face. "Don't you like me?"

Finley held her tongue. If she opened her mouth she'd tell him exactly what she thought of him, and she needed to keep this employment. She needed to get out of this situation without either of them getting hurt.

He slid his other hand behind her, down her back to her

backside and squeezed. "Don't you want to make me happy? Smart little girls want to make me happy."

Finley turned her head as his face came down toward hers, and narrowly escaped being kissed. His wet mouth landed on her ear instead. She shuddered. "Please, my lord. Let me go." *For your own sake.*

His lips fastened on her neck instead. Nausea rolled through her stomach and then suddenly stopped as she felt his palm against the striped stockings that covered her thigh. He wasn't going to cease. He wasn't going to let her go. He was going to take what he wanted, because that's what rich young men did to girls under their control.

But she wasn't under anybody's control. Not even her own. She could feel it fracturing as something deep inside fought to get out.

Finley brought both hands up and pushed hard against his chest. He flew backward, hitting the opposite wall with enough force to crack the plaster.

Lord Felix stared at her, in both shock and outrage. "You nasty tart," he snarled as he brushed dust from his sleeves. "Like a bit of the rough, do you?"

"You've no idea," Finley heard herself reply coolly. "But make no mistake, my lord, I do *not* like you, so keep those damn hands of yours to yourself."

The young man's face reddened and his eyes shone with anger. "Bitch. No guttersnipe servant talks to *me* that way." He straightened and took a step toward her, shrugging out of his purple velvet frock-coat. "Someone needs to teach you a lesson."

She didn't see the blow coming, but she certainly felt it when it hit. Her head jolted back under the force of his fist, striking the wall. Lights danced in the darkness of her eyes as pain shot through her skull. But she did not pass out.

It would have been so much better for Lord Felix if she had.

She could feel blood trickling from her mouth and she wiped at it with the back of her hand. Vision finally clear, she saw that Lord Felix had also removed his waistcoat and was now rolling up his sleeves. The excited glint in his eye told Finley exactly what kind of lesson he intended her to "learn."

Something inside her stretched and pulled—still fighting to get out. There was no point in denying it anymore. She had been raised in a loving home with her mother and stepfather—a kind and honest man who doted on them both. He would never dream of such violence—no good man would.

But Lord Felix August-Raynes was not a good man. And it was time someone taught him a lesson.

The warm rush of familiar power brought a slight smile to her battered lips. She gave up all attempts to keep it reined in. It was the only way she'd survive this night with her virtue and bones intact. It was as though she was watching herself from a perch on the ceiling—all she could do was observe as her other self took over. Her boots shifted on the bare floor, right foot forward, left foot back and pointed out. She raised her fists.

"Coming back for more, eh?" Felix grinned at her. "I like a little fight in my girls."

She grinned at him, causing blood to dribble down her chin. "Then you're going to love me." The voice was hers, but deeper and throatier than she'd ever heard before. It was a dangerous voice, and even Felix paused at the sound of it.

Finley, however, did not pause. She drove her fist right into her attacker's throat. He staggered backward, eyes wide with shock as he coughed and choked and struggled for breath.

She bounced on her feet, waiting for him to recover. She

should run and hide. She should be gasping in fear, lungs constrained by the tight lacing of her corset. But she wasn't afraid anymore and she wasn't about to run. She was going to *fight*.

But first, a little fun. She hadn't hit the bully as hard as she could have. She was going to let him think he stood a chance first.

When Felix recovered enough to come at her again, she was ready for him. He swung and she ducked, landing another punch to his kidneys. When he doubled over, she grabbed his head and brought her knee up fast. Unfortunately, the layers of skirts she wore softened the blow. He struck her in the stomach, knocking the breath from her, and then hit her in the face again. She fell to the floor, rolling just in time to avoid being kicked by one of his boots.

She'd never been struck before—not like this. She'd never felt as though someone meant to kill her—or didn't care if they did. She gasped for breath against the polished wood floor, rolling again when he struck out with his foot once more. She moved faster than she should have, the pain from his blows already easing.

He called her all kinds of horrible names—guttural and nasty sounding. But instead of making her feel awful or frightening her, they only made her want to hit him all the harder.

She pulled herself to her feet. Her stomach and face ached, but not like it should have. It never hurt like it should.

Her hands grabbed Lord Felix by the front of his shirt. She pulled him toward her, hard, and smashed her forehead against the bridge of his nose. There was a snapping sound just before he screamed. Finley thrust him backward, satisfaction tickling her when she saw the blood coursing down his face.

He was good and mad now. He raised a hand to his nose,

and when he saw the blood on his fingers, he made a growling sound in his throat. She'd ruined his pretty face and now he was going to make her pay for it. She smiled. Or rather, he was going to *try* to make her pay for it.

He came at her again, like a bull. Finley didn't think, she simply reacted and took two quick steps forward. With that slight momentum, she lifted her right boot to the wall and pushed up, grabbing the scrolled brass of the wall sconce for support and whipped her left leg out.

She kicked him in the face.

He keeled over like a milk bottle knocked off a step, hitting the floor with a solid thump. He lay there, motionless, an imprint of the heel of her boot smack in the middle of his forehead, blood trickling from his already swelling nose.

She hopped down from the wall and went to stand over him, victorious and self-satisfied. Adrenaline rushed through her veins, making her practically dance in her boots. Lord Felix had promised to teach her a lesson, but he was the one who had been schooled. He'd think twice before laying a hand on another girl.

But Finley's satisfaction was short-lived. In fact, it was over at almost the precise moment when she looked at Lord Felix's face. He was so still, so pale except for the blood. What if he was dead? All the fight whooshed out of her, leaving her trembling and cold in its wake.

"What have I done?" she whispered.

*What you had to.*

She felt his neck for a pulse, relief engulfing her as she found it. She hadn't killed him. At least she wouldn't hang. But she had still attacked the son of a peer of the realm and there would be consequences.

Three jobs in three months and they'd all ended with an experience like this one, although this was by far the worst.

She'd been let go from each position because of her behavior, something that had released this *thing* inside her. Urges to act in a way that was far from civilized, far beyond what she as a young woman should be capable of.

They'd bring the law down on her for this. They'd lock her up. Or worse, use her for scientific experiments in New Bethlehem Asylum—Bedlam. And they *would* experiment on her once they realized she was abnormal.

*Run,* the voice inside her whispered. *Run away.*

Listening to the voice had gotten her into this mess, perhaps this time it would get her out. There was no way Lord Felix wouldn't exact retribution upon her for harming him—either by finishing what he'd started or by bringing the authorities down upon her. There was no way she was going to let him do what he wanted to her. No way she'd risk having her brain dissected for giving him less than what he really deserved.

So Finley listened to the voice and ran.

Bent low over the gleaming steering bars of his velocycle as he sped through the rainy darkness of Hyde Park, Griffin King felt a faint ripple of warning in the Aether a split second before the girl ran right out in front of him. The rune tattoos he had to heighten his senses and abilities blazed with heat, calling out the danger just in time.

He swerved, jerking hard on the bars to avoid her, but it was too late. The glare of the headlamp slashed across her surprised face and then she was thrown through the air as he struggled to maintain control of the machine and failed. The notched wheels tore into the ground as the cycle tipped to the side, tossing him to the path before skidding to a halt several feet away.

The leather duster he wore protected him from being torn

up by gravel as he slid and rolled on the rough ground. When he finally came to a stop, he lay sprawled on the wet grass just for a moment to catch his breath and spit out the dirt that had flown into his mouth.

"Is she all right?" he called out as he gingerly rose to his feet, flicking mud and grass from his leather gloves. Nothing was broken, but he still felt as though he'd been slammed into a brick wall, and tomorrow he'd have bruises to match.

In the glow of the light from the second cycle—this one upright and braced on its support bar—he saw his friend, Sam Morgan, kneel over the prone body of the girl. From this angle, all Griff could see around Sam's large frame was a pair of long legs encased in tall, thick-soled leather boots and orange-and-black-striped stockings. Servant's garb.

At eighteen, Griff was at an age when all he should be concerned with was ensuring his allowance lasted a full term at Oxford. His parents' death had made him the Duke of Greythorne at age fifteen, subsequently making him all too familiar with what servants wore, since he'd recently had to hire new staff. There were some chores machines couldn't do—or weren't wanted to do—and those demanded a host of human employees, all of whom were designated by the uniforms they wore. Orange and black made her a ladies' maid. Too exalted a position for this girl to be out alone at this time of night.

"Sam?" he questioned, favoring his left leg as he moved closer to the pair. "Is she all right?"

"Got a pulse." His friend's low, laconic voice came from beneath the dripping brim of his hat as Griff crouched beside him. "It's steady, but she's bleeding. So are you."

Pulling his smudged goggles down so they hung around his neck, Griff glanced down. His blood, coming through the shredded left knee of his trousers, glistened bright red in the light. "I'll be fine. I'm more concerned about her."

"Did you see her face?" Sam demanded, taking a handkerchief from his jacket pocket. "She looked almost wild."

Griff had seen her face—just before he hit her. There had been something untamed in her features. Something fierce and beautiful, as well.

"What was she running from?" Sam asked, as he pressed the linen against the wound on her forehead. It was bleeding heavily. "Or *who?*"

Griff glanced at the girl whose head was cradled in his friend's large hand and saw the red mark on her rain-soaked cheek, the blood at her mouth. Injuries from the accident? Or something intentional?

Regardless, until he was certain she was unharmed, she was his responsibility.

"We'll take her with us," he decided, lifting the limp body into his arms. A glint of steel peeked through where the leather of her corset had torn.

"You reckon that's wise?" Sam, Griff knew, wasn't being cold, he was being practical. They already had enough to worry about with the recent robbery at the British Museum and tension within their own little group. Adding this girl and her troubles into the mix could only make things worse. Strangers were always an issue in his house. Always the fear of someone uncovering too much.

"We can't leave her." It was as simple as that. Although, they could take her to a hospital, but Griff's honor wouldn't allow that. Besides, something told him not to let this girl out of his sight, and he'd learned to trust his instincts. The times he hadn't always ended badly.

Sam swung one leg over the seat of his cycle and took the

girl from Griff's embrace into his own. "Do you want me to send word ahead?"

Griff shook his head, rain running down his face, seeping below his jacket collar to dampen his shirt and skin. "I'll do that. Just get her to the house—don't leave her unattended." As he spoke, he slipped a battered leather case from his pocket. Inside was a flat machine smaller than a deck of playing cards. It was a personal telegraph machine—all the rage now for fast communication. His machine and the ones belonging to his friends were a little "faster" than those available to the general public as not only were they based on Mr. Tesla's "wireless" design, they'd been augmented to transmit through the Aether by the amazingly brilliant Emily, whom Griffin had hired over her less-capable brothers a year ago.

Griffin flipped the case open at the same time as Sam started up his velocycle. He punched a few of the keys and hit the transmit button. A few seconds later, as Sam drove away, the heavily treaded wheels of his cycle kicking up dirt, a reply appeared on the grainy screen. He squinted to read it in the dark and rain. He needn't have bothered. He knew Emily would do as he asked and make preparations for their guest, and that was exactly what her response said.

He limped harder now, his leg already beginning to stiffen. He clenched his jaw against the discomfort and set about righting his own cycle. The heavy metal frame looked relatively unscathed, but he'd give it a thorough going-over in the morning. It started up immediately and Griff slipped his goggles back over his eyes before following in the direction Sam had gone.

He'd deal with the museum robbery in the morning. Nothing terribly valuable seemed to have been stolen, and that was what puzzled him. Special Branch would want answers, but they would have to wait. Right now, the girl was his first priority. An aura of danger clung to her like an oil slick. Unfortunately, he couldn't tell if she was in danger, or if she *was* danger.

That was what he intended to find out.

# Chapter 2

Greythorne House was a sprawling neoclassical mansion situated in London's Mayfair district—where the *important* people lived. Important, of course, meaning that you were from an old family and rich. That said, you didn't have to be incredibly rich, you just had to give the appearance of it.

Fortunately for Griff, he was very rich. His family was very old. And until a few years ago, when his parents died, his family had been very secretive. It wasn't until almost a year after their murder that he discovered the extent of the secret rooms and laboratories below this house and the main estate in Devon. And just as long since he realized just how much Great Britain owed his family for keeping it safe. He reminded himself of that debt on the few occasions when Her Majesty Victoria suggested that it was Griff who owed something to the Crown instead.

Almost twenty years ago, his parents had taken it upon themselves to continue the work started by his grandfather, the fourteenth Duke of Greythorne, and journeyed to the center of the earth. There they discovered the Cradle of Life—the place where creation began. What they'd found there had been astounding, but would never see the light of day, at least not in the foreseeable future. The world wasn't ready for it. Helena and Edward King had dedicated their lives to Crown and country, and they'd been killed because of it.

In return, Queen V sent a lovely arrangement of roses to the funeral.

So when Griff dedicated himself to the protection of his homeland, it wasn't for any monarch or out of a sense of duty. He did it to honor his parents, and one day he would find the person responsible for their deaths, and he would have justice.

Right now, that justice was far in the back of his mind, though it never really left entirely. He stood at the foot of a large four-poster bed in one of the many bedrooms available in his home and watched with his arms folded across his chest as Emily O'Brien, one of the most intelligent people he knew, tended to their unconscious guest, whom the maids had relieved of her soaked clothing and put to bed.

"She doesn't look scary," Emily commented in her soft Irish brogue as she applied the tip of what had once been a perfume atomizer but was now a pretty glass bottle with a brass syringe tip attached, to the wound on the unconscious girl's brow. As she squeezed the bulb, a fine mist from the glass reservoir sprayed through the syringe onto the broken skin. The mist was made up of the life-giving material Griff's parents had found at the earth's core—tiny little creatures that could mimic the body's own cellular behavior. The Organites—or "beasties" as Emily called them—attached themselves to the human tissue and copied its composition, so that when applied to the wound, they worked to rebuild the flesh and heal the injury. By morning, the girl would be completely healed, without even the tiniest scar. A similar brew had been used on Griff's torn knee and he could already feel an improvement.

This existence of these Organites was one secret Griff kept to himself. The queen hadn't wanted to know about it when his parents first discovered it. She liked the ore that his grandfather had mined—a wondrous substance made by the Organites that emitted energy that could be used to power anything from one machine to an entire household—but the rest of it came too close to proving Mr. Darwin's radical theories of evolution correct. Victoria thought the church might take offense to such a discovery, or worse, that man might be corrupted by it and start playing God. In fact, she'd ordered the Organites destroyed, or at least returned to the earth's core.

Griff thought she was just a scared old woman, but no one asked his opinion.

Thankfully, Griff's parents hadn't obeyed their sovereign and kept a small batch of the primordial goo on hand. The Organites thrived in a small grottolike vault far beneath the mansion, replicating and producing the fantastic blue-green substance that Griffin used as his personal supply. While the rest of the world benefitted from a diluted version of the ore, Griff had the purest samples at his disposal for Emily to use in her inventions—such as the velocycles, which moved faster than those available to even the wealthiest consumer.

They were their own "Special Branch."

"There's something not right about her," Griff said finally, frowning as he studied the sleeping girl.

"She's come to the right place then," the redhead replied with a touch of a smile as she pushed her ropey hair out of her face. "There's not one 'right' amongst the lot of us." And then, "She must have jumped out of your way and struck her head on the ground. If you had hit her, she'd be more seriously injured."

Griff kept frowning. "I did hit her. That's part of what's not right." The girl had practically leaped onto his cycle, hadn't she? He shook his head, uncertain whether his memories were real or imaginings.

Other than remaining unconscious and the gash on her head, there was nothing wrong with the girl. Nothing at all—except for the bruising on her face, which he could now see bore the imprint of a signet ring.

"Someone beat her," Emily remarked. "You probably saved her."

"Or saved whoever was after her," Sam commented from the doorway.

Griff flashed a quick glance in his friend's direction. He practically filled the door frame with his broad shoulders and height. His longish black hair was damp, but he'd changed into dry clothing. His dark gaze was intense as it fell on Emily. Angry but admiring.

Griffin shook his head. "You should have seen her, Em, like something out of one of those gothic novels you're always reading."

Finished with her patient, Emily tucked a chunk of bright red hair behind her ear, revealing a line of golden hoops that stemmed from lobe to high on the cartilage, and rose to her feet, atomizer in her hand. "Are you implying she's a monster, then, Griffin King?"

He arched a brow at her challenging tone. "No, but she could have escaped from someone's attic. I'm told these things happen more often than you might think."

She actually smiled at that. Emily's love of gothic novels was no secret, and she took a lot of teasing for it, being the only girl in the house. The only girl until now. There was Aunt Cordelia, but she was away more than she was home. He looked again at the sleeping young woman—who couldn't be any older than Emily's own sixteen years—before motioning them both out of the room. When the door closed behind them, Emily asked, "What happened at the museum?"

Sam caught Griff's eye with a questioning look. Griff shrugged, indicating that he didn't care what information he shared. Sam seemed to have this old-fashioned notion that women needed to be protected. Some of the most devious people Griff had ever encountered had been female. He didn't share the sentiment.

Sam's lips tightened. "Griff found a small glob of oil."

"Oil?" Emily shot him a frown. "What kind of oil?"

Sam shook his head. Griffin said what he could not. "We took a sample. It's in your lab. Em…" He ran a hand through his hair. "It looks like the kind of oil used to lubricate exposed automaton joints."

The implication of that froze Emily on the spot. "An *automaton* robbed the museum?" Her crystalline blue eyes were wide as they turned to Griff. "Was it The Machinist?"

"It looks that way," he replied, seeing Sam continue on without them. Recently there had been a few crimes around town seemingly perpetrated by automatons acting against their programming engines, none of them particularly dangerous. Except for one. That one had been enough. It had almost cost them one of their own. The authorities suspected a criminal calling himself The Machinist was behind the incidents.

The thought called to mind a vision of blood and smoke. Of a broken body close to death, held in the clutches of a metal man. Griff remembered leaping onto the machine's back, tearing open its panel to reach the controls inside. He knew Sam must be reliving a few memories of his own. After all, he had been the one the thing almost killed.

They'd been chasing similar, though less violent, incidents for almost a year. Griffin figured they were looking for a man with superior mechanical knowledge, particularly that of automatons. Thus far, Emily had found nothing in the programming of the two specimens they had to even suggest they'd been tampered with.

The automatons' power sources were the same as all standard androids—the same compound that powered most of London. Griff was a bit of an expert in this, since the compound was derived from the ore discovered by his grandfather. He owned the patent on it, owned the rights, too. So Griff knew that the small nugget inside each machine was just as it should be.

So how did the villain make the automatons act against their programming?

"We should assume that any mech involved was accompanied by a human master until we know otherwise." He fought the fear coiling around his heart. Machines that could think for themselves. Surely it was impossible?

Emily was paler than usual, and Griff knew she was thinking of what had happened to Sam, as well. He should comfort her, but he didn't know how. Give him a problem to solve and he would jump in with both feet, but he didn't know how to give comfort, and he hated it.

Sam was waiting for them as they entered the library, where they took all their group meetings. As his gaze fell upon his friend, whom he had known for almost the entirety of his life, Griff couldn't help but feel surprised that anything had ever managed to hurt him. Sam was so strong. He was a little taller than Griff and certainly more powerfully built. His rugged features only added to his intimidating demeanor. He hadn't always looked so fierce. Less than a year ago, he'd been quick with a grin or a naughty joke.

Six months ago, an automaton had attacked him in the middle of a routine assignment and tore Sam apart. It had been brutal, a shock for them all to see their strongest member taken down like that. It had been Emily who'd saved him. Emily who'd put him back together. And sometimes when he looked at her, Griff suspected Sam had never quite forgiven her for it. In fact, when he looked at her now, the fingers of his right hand—the hand she'd repaired—twitched.

Emily saw it, too. Griff could tell because she quickly looked away, purposefully focusing on anything but Sam.

"We should have taken the girl to the hospital," Sam muttered, leaning against the corner of a sofa. He rubbed the back of his neck with his left hand. "Bringing her here puts us all at risk. What if she's a wanted criminal?"

Griff tilted his head. "I don't think it would have been safe to take her to the hospital, for her or the staff."

His friend raised a heavy brow, sarcasm written all over his face. "So you decided, 'hell, why not bring her home with me?' Well done."

His doubt irked Griff, who wasn't accustomed to being questioned. Still, he could understand Sam's misgivings. "You said so yourself—she was scared of something, or someone," he replied. "I'm certain that's the August-Raynes crest on her corset." It was common now for domestic servants to wear their master's crests on their clothing, like the livery worn by footmen.

"He's one of the richest men in England!" Sam's tone was incredulous. "Are you sure he's someone you want to cross?"

Griff smiled. "Don't you read the scandal sheets, Sam? Supposedly *I* am the richest man in England. Surely that makes me more formidable? Besides, I've a notion it's not the father I'd be crossing."

"Who, then?"

Griff's own blue gaze locked with pitch-black. "Remember that girl in Whitechapel last winter? The one who had been raped by her employer and tossed out when he discovered she was pregnant with his child?"

Sam nodded, jaw clenched.

Griff inclined his head. "Lord Felix August-Rayne, his lordship's youngest. He's gotten in with the Dandies and seems to have developed a habit of abusing his servants, and anyone else he considers beneath him."

"Do you...?" Emily paused, face white as she glanced toward the door, as though afraid the girl upstairs could hear. "Do you think he hurt her?"

Griff shot her a sympathetic glance. He didn't know much about Emily's past, but guessed that she'd had her share of unpleasantness. She had been quick to accept his offer of employment, as though she couldn't wait to leave her old life behind. "I don't know."

"It's not safe having her here," Sam insisted, trying to bash Griff with his will once more. "For her, or for us. We can't afford to call attention to ourselves. Not with those...things out there." His voice cracked on *things*. They all heard it. They all ignored it.

He meant the machines. Most were perfectly harmless, but there was nothing quite as frightening as metal out of control. That was why Griff had the remains of Sam's mechanical attacker in Emily's workshop, so they could figure out what had happened to turn an uncomplicated underground railway digger into a murderer. It had attacked five people—only Sam survived.

"What would you have me do, Sam?" Griff ran a hand through the thick mass of his hair. "Toss her out like rubbish?"

Sam's mouth opened and Griff knew he was going to suggest just that.

Emily jumped in, "You know we can't keep her for long, lad. She isn't...one of us."

Griff's mouth lifted on one side, a half grin he always got when he thought he was right. "I'm not so sure about that."

"What does that mean?" Sam scowled. "Why do you have to be so damn cryptic all the time?"

Sam's frustration was so strong Griff could almost taste it. He'd known the big lad long enough to know when he was spoiling for a fight, and he also knew that, physically, he was no match. Sam was the strongest person in Britain, perhaps the world. But Griffin had his own powers that didn't require brute strength.

He could become one with the Aether, that mysterious indiscernible force that was everywhere and in everything. It was also the realm of the dead—where ghosts existed. It was like another dimension hidden within the normal world. He didn't know why, but he could feel it in his veins, and when he called it, the most terrific power came forth to serve him. All that universal energy filled him, making him feel as though he was part of everything and somehow everywhere. Sometimes it scared him. So much so, that he hadn't confided any of it to his friends.

Nor had he confided just how much he believed the terrible power took from him.

Instead of giving Sam the fight he wanted, Griff turned to Emily, which just annoyed the bigger boy all the more. Wisely though, Sam held his tongue. Emily had been silent all this time, watching and listening. She nodded at him—on his side as he believed she would be.

"Did you see how she ran through the park?" he asked Sam, finally looking at his friend.

The large boy scowled. "No. I didn't notice her at all until we were upon her."

"Exactly." Griff's gaze traveled to each of them as he continued. "One second all was well and the next she was in front of us. I had barely sensed a disturbance in the Aether before I hit her. No normal human could move that fast."

"What the hell is she, then?" Sam demanded, his fists clenched tight at his sides.

Griff shrugged. "I have no idea. But the three of us should find out, shouldn't we?"

"Cordelia isn't going to like this," Emily reminded them. Griff's aunt wasn't due back from Yorkshire until the day after tomorrow. She was up there investigating strange circles that had appeared in a farmer's field.

"It's not her house, nor her decision," Griff reminded her.

Emily held his gaze. He'd always admired her backbone. "If she is different, then it's our duty to help her."

Sam shot her a dark look, then one at Griff, as well. "The two of you are too bloody trusting. Being different doesn't make her good any more than being metal makes one of those monsters a toaster."

Normally Griff would have laughed at such an absurd comment, but the door to the library burst open at that exact moment. It was the housekeeper, Mrs. Dodsworth.

"What is it?" Griff asked, stepping forward with a frown. The woman was positively white in the face. Had one of the few automated servants left in the house turned on them? After Sam's attack, Griff had decommissioned many of the machines out of consideration for his friend and for the safety of every living creature under his responsibility.

"It's the girl you brung home, Your Grace. I think you should come right away. It's as if she's got the very devil in her!"

Griff took off running. Emily and Sam followed, chasing him up the stairs to the room where the girl had been left sleeping just a short time ago. A man came flying out of the open door frame like a child's toy tossed aside. Sam caught him before he could hit the wall.

"Thank you, Master Samuel," the footman said in a shaking voice as Sam set him on his feet. "I thought she was going to kill me. She's like a demon, she is!"

Sam's mouth tightened as he lifted his gaze to Griff's. "I told you so."

# Chapter 3

Griff ignored his best friend's taunt and turned his back on his friends. What in the name of all that was holy had he brought into his house? What kind of girl could hurl a full-grown man?

From the sounds of it, she was definitely angry. He couldn't quite make out all the words, but the ones he could were… colorful.

"I've met dockside trollops with cleaner mouths," Sam snarled.

"Met many of those, have you?" Emily's tone was sharp.

Griff shot both of them an annoyed glance and turned to the open doorway once more. He wasn't offended by her vocabulary, just surprised by it. It made him all the more curious about her.

Taking a deep breath, he walked into the room, confident without having to look that his friends were with him. Out of habit, he tugged on his waistcoat, straightening it. He should have put on a coat and tried to look more lordly, but he'd never been very good at that. His real strength wasn't in intimidation. It was in subtlety and confidence. And in the fact that people tended to know who he was.

He didn't bother to knock. Quite frankly, he thought better of announcing his arrival. The less time she had to prepare, the better. As it was, he narrowly missed being brained by a candlestick. It whipped past his head to embed itself in the opposite wall.

"Oy," he said roughly. "Is that any way to act when you're a guest in someone's home?"

"Guest? You mean, prisoner," came the growled reply.

The girl stood in the center of the large four-poster bed. She wore a nightgown and robe that Cordelia had generously, and unknowingly, donated. Anything of Emily's would have been far too short and too small. Her honey-colored hair fell over her shoulders in messy waves and her similarly colored eyes were almost black with wildness, her pupils unnaturally dilated.

Fear. He felt it roll off her in great waves. It shimmered around her in a rich red aura Griff knew he alone could see, as it was viewable only on the Aetheric plane. She was afraid of them and, like a trapped animal, her answer to fear was to fight rather than flee. Interesting.

She was certainly a sight to behold. Normally she was probably quite pretty, but right now she was…she was…

She was bloody *magnificent*. That's what she was. Except for the blood, of course. She'd opened the wound on her forehead and blood was trickling down toward her nose.

"What have you done to me?" Blood covered her hands as she held them out to him, not in supplication, but to make him acknowledge the mess. "Why do I feel like maggots are crawling beneath my skin?"

"The Organites," Griffin whispered to Emily. She had come to stand on his left. "Is it possible for her to feel them?"

"I don't know," Emily replied in a hushed voice, her gaze glued to the girl on the bed. "She shouldn't."

"Organites?" the girl snarled. She looked at her hands, the sticky crimson fingers. "You mean, this excrement you smeared on me?"

She'd heard? Griff tilted his head in silent contemplation. So not only was she fast and strong, but she had heightened hearing, as well. It made him wonder if all of her senses were so acute.

"It's to help you heal," he informed her softly. "And now you've made it worse."

She mocked him by jerking her head to the side, mirroring how he regarded her. Then, she straightened and took a step forward on the bed. She was like a cat inching toward a mouse.

It happened quickly. Sam, as he always did, stepped between Griffin and what he perceived to be a threat. Did he think Griff incapable of defending himself, like a weakling?

The girl only smiled that off-kilter smile and then lunged. Her hands came down on Sam's head and she neatly leap-frogged over him, landing right in front of Griff.

The others instantly went into combat mode, especially Sam, who whirled around with fists raised. Brave little Emily had produced a wicked-looking dagger from somewhere on her person. Griff held up his hand. "Stand down."

They did as he commanded, but only to the extent that they didn't intervene. He knew that if this girl so much as sneezed on him, she would be sorry.

"So you're the leader of this lot, Rich Boy?" She sneered as her gaze raked over the others before returning to him—she was clearly unimpressed. "You don't look so special."

"You're looking in the wrong place," he replied with a hint of a smile. "Look into my eyes."

And she did. They always did. It never occurred to anyone that looking into his eyes was the last thing they should do. He let his guard down, letting the Aether take him a little bit deeper into its realm. The girl's aura poured around him and he seized it—not with his hands, but with that part of him that could bend this strange element to his will. Quickly, he forced the color to change from anger to peacefulness and finally to the tranquil glow of restfulness. His power flowed around her just before her mental defenses slammed shut. Whatever she was, her instincts were fast.

But not fast enough in this case.

She swayed. Staggered a little. One thin, bloody hand grabbed his shoulder. "What...? What have you done to me?"

"You need to relax," he told her in a low voice. "I'm going to help you do that."

She stared at him, eyes wide now, the fear pouring off her like water from a spout. It left a bitter taste in his mouth. "Don't take me back. Please! I don't know what he'll do to me."

So his suspicions were correct. She had been a victim.

"I won't," he promised, all the while gently forcing his own calm into her. "You're safe here." Her defenses faltered, and he slipped inside once more.

She staggered again and seized his other shoulder, as well. He supported much of her weight now, but she wasn't that heavy. Besides, the Aether gave him strength. He watched as her eyes changed—pupils shrinking until all that was left was warm gold. Much of the wildness left her features, and as her knees gave out she actually smiled at him.

"Thank you," she whispered. And then her eyes rolled back into their sockets.

Griff caught her before she hit the floor. "Help me get her back into bed," he commanded.

Sam gave him a glance, brow raised. "You can't be serious? That scary little girl needs to go. Now."

"No," Griff argued, and he smiled when Emily came forward to help him, just as he knew she would. He placed the girl on the mattress as the little redhead pulled back the sheets and paused just for a moment to study the blood on her face and the dark circles beneath her eyes. "As frightening as we may think her, I believe she finds herself even more so."

When Finley woke again, she felt more like herself than she had in some time. She felt rested and not nearly as battered as she ought. More important, she felt safe. The why of it was a mystery, because she rarely felt safe anywhere.

She sat up against the great mound of soft down-filled pillows and glanced around the room. It was a large bedroom, decorated in shades of cinnamon and cream. The bed was so big she could lie sideways on it and still her toes would not dangle over the edge. Beside her on the nightstand was a lamp and a small brass box with buttons on it labeled with titles such as *kitchen, butler* and *maid*. If she pressed one of them, would someone come? Or would they be too afraid?

Large windows to her right treated her to a view of the most lush and beautiful garden she had ever seen. Were it not for the dirigible marked *L'air France* high in the surprisingly blue sky, she might have thought herself in the country, it was so peaceful. She had never experienced true silence in London before. A house like this could only stand in Mayfair.

This was what it felt like to be a lady waking up in the morning. Quiet and snug.

On the desk there was one of the new candlestick-style telephones, its brass gleaming. She could call someone to come get her, but who? Her mother? No. She didn't want to involve her mother or her stepfather in this mess.

Above the desk on the wall was a portrait of a lady from Henry VIII's time, its frame heavy and gold-gilt. Beside it, a silver candlestick lodged in the plaster. Had she done that? Oh, Lord, she had! The events of the previous evening came rushing back at her with sickening violence. She remembered an all-too-familiar feeling—that someone else had taken over her body, leaving her an observer in her own skin. She could remember all the things she said and did, but she couldn't begin to find reason or excuse.

Was she going mad? These spells had been coming upon her more often as of late. They'd started right around the same time she'd "become a woman" by biological standards. That had been three years ago, but never had she had an experience like these past few. She'd never lost herself so completely.

And yet…when she was in the midst of madness, it didn't feel like madness at all. It felt right, like that awful part of her was as natural as breathing. But it could *not* be natural. It was something dark and wrong and—evil.

Was there anything that could save her? Anything short of death that could stop it from happening again? Felix had deserved the wallop she gave him, but the young man with the striking blue eyes and the thick red-brown hair, he didn't deserve what she might have done to him when she leaped over the giant one to get to him.

She hadn't wanted to hurt him, not really. Something had drawn her to him, and when she looked up into those amazing eyes, doing him harm had been the last thing on her mind. She had actually wondered what it might be like to kiss him.

It had to have been some kind of sorcery. What else could it have been? He had drained all of the fight out of her without lifting a hand. One glance had filled her with such peace and lethargy that all she had wanted to do was curl up and sleep. Which she had.

Had he—or any of them—done something to her while she slept? She couldn't tell, as she was still somewhat tender from the tussle with Lord Felix. She didn't want to believe the pretty gentleman capable of such violence, but she had learned the hard way that pretty gentlemen were often the worst of the lot.

But now what? She couldn't stay here forever, and she had no idea if she could trust these people. It was obvious the others didn't want her around. What if they turned her over to the police? Or worse, what if "Rich Boy" was a friend of Lord Felix?

A knock at the door made her heart jump. The knob turned and the door opened before she could call for whoever it was to enter.

The redheaded girl walked in. Her bright, ropey hair was pinned haphazardly on the back of her head, with thick coils hanging around her pretty face. She wore trousers tucked into high black boots, a white shirt and a tight leather vest. It had become fashionable for young women of independent thought to emulate the masculine fashion, but Finley hadn't the nerve to do it herself. She much preferred the "Oriental" look that had come over from China. She hadn't the nerve to copy that, either.

The girl glanced at her with large, intense blue eyes as she entered the room. Finley's fingers went to her forehead where she'd been injured. The skin there was soft and smooth, not even a lump or slightest scab, even though she remembered tearing at it the night before. In fact, her cheek and lip felt better, as well. But then, she'd always been a fast healer.

"You...fixed me." She couldn't keep the awe from her voice.

The young woman's expression was puzzled as she dipped a cloth in the washbasin on the stand near the dresser. Of course she would be expecting Finley to act as beastly as she had last night. "Yes. I did. I'm glad you left it alone this time."

Finley smiled, hoping she looked friendly rather than demented. This girl was no threat to her and so that dark part of her was peaceful. "Thank you."

"I've brought you breakfast." She gestured to the doorway, where the large young man with longish black hair and rugged features stood holding a tray. Her dark self raised its head, but didn't make a fuss. "And I would like to examine you, if that's all right."

So young and a doctor? It was impossible, of course, but that didn't mean the Irish girl didn't have a proper knowledge of medicine. After all, she had healed her wound. "Of course. Thank you for breakfast."

"I'll clean you up and we can talk while you eat."

Finley's smile was stronger now. She kept her attention focused on the girl while watching her companion from the corner of her eye. "I'd like that." She felt something of a kinship with this girl. Girls didn't normally like her, and young men tended to like her in ways she didn't want. She didn't understand why because it wasn't as though she was uncommonly beautiful or anything.

The girl didn't look like she was convinced of her sincerity, but she came closer all the same. "If you try to hurt me, he'll stop you. Understand?"

The smile melted from Finley's lips and slipped down her throat to form a hard knot. She nodded, not daring to glance at the grim-looking young man.

She sat still while her companion wiped her forehead and face, trying not to notice how much blood stained the cloth, turning it rusty. She was given another warm, wet length of linen to wash her hands. They were stained, as well.

Finley swallowed. "I must apologize for my behavior last night. I was not myself."

"No?" A high, red brow arched against the girl's pale forehead as she took both cloths away. "Who were you, then? A Changeling perhaps?" She had a beautiful, lyrical Irish accent.

"I'm not sure," Finley replied with a frown, watching her walk away. Was she teasing her, or did she honestly believe she might be a Faerie trying to pass as human?

The girl dropped the soiled cloths back into the basin, turned and walked to the dresser. She rummaged through a small leather kit and pulled out something that looked like a perfume bottle. "I'm going to give you another treatment, just to make sure you continue to heal. I promise it won't annoy you like it did last night. You can eat, as well."

Finley blushed, unable to contain a rush of humiliation. "Of course." She pushed herself up farther on the pillows to be more accommodating and so she would be able to eat. The movement apparently startled the girl because she jerked back and dropped the bottle. It landed on the floor with a loud thump.

"Ah, blast! It went beneath the dresser."

Before the girl could bend down to stick her hand underneath the piece of furniture, the dark-haired young man was there. He set the tray on the bed and then went to the dresser, bending down. How he expected to find the mechanism with those big hands of his, Finley didn't know. But then she realized he had only reached underneath to get a good hold. When he straightened, the large, heavy piece came with him, held between his two hands with ease.

No man was that strong. Even in her "altered" state she couldn't come close to that kind of easy strength.

"Astounding," Finley whispered, staring at him in open awe.

The other girl smiled then, as though she couldn't help herself. "This coming from a girl who tossed a footman like a sack of potatoes." Quickly, she bent down and retrieved the item. "Thank you, Sam."

He said nothing, merely glanced at her before setting the furniture back in its proper place. The girl made a point of not looking at him, but her pale cheeks turned red.

"My name is Finley," she said when once again her nurse-maid attended her. "Who are you?"

The girl hesitated, her fingers wrapped around the depression bulb of the atomizer. Whatever the reservoir contained, it smelled of rosemary and something earthy—like dirt. She didn't quite meet Finley's gaze as she applied a light, cool layer of mist to her forehead. She was still wary of her. "Emily."

Finley held out her hand. "Pleased to meet you, Emily. Thank you for being kind when I was such a wretch."

Emily looked down. For a moment, Finley thought maybe she'd reject the offer of friendship and she held her breath. But just when she was about to drop her hand, Emily switched the contraption to her left and accepted the handshake. The Irish girl's hands weren't smooth like a lady's. They had a little roughness to them, like Finley's own. They were the hands of someone used to working, and it made Finley like her even more.

More so, it made her want to trust this small girl with her strange red hair and old eyes.

"You're welcome…Finley." Emily gestured over her shoulder. "That's Sam."

Finley managed to smile at the large young man. Him she wasn't so eager to trust, nor, from the stony expression on his face, was he about to trust her. "Hello, Sam. My apologies for leaping over you as I did last night."

"You're fast," he allowed grudgingly, lifting the breakfast tray and setting it across her lap. "But I caught the footman when you threw him, and next time I'll catch you." It wasn't said in a threatening manner but Finley knew beyond a doubt that he would crush her like a bug if he caught her.

"There won't be a next time," she said hoarsely.

The brute actually grinned. He had big, white teeth and he would have been handsome if he wasn't so bloody frightening. "Good." Then to Emily, "We should go. Griff will want to see us."

"Griff?" Finley froze in the middle of reaching for a slice of toast. They spoke of him like he was their leader, and she knew exactly who Griff was. *Rich Boy.*

Emily nodded. "This is his house. He would like you to come down to the library when you've finished breakfast. Just push the maid button and someone will come and help you dress."

He wanted to see her. Suddenly Finley didn't have much of an appetite, not when her fate would be so soon decided.

To her surprise, Emily reached out and squeezed her hand. "Don't worry yourself, lass. All will work out as it ought. Now, eat. You need to put some meat on your bones."

The backs of Finley's eyes burned. That sounded just like something her mother would say. Oh, how she wished she had her mother! "Thank you," she rasped.

Emily gave her another squeeze, and dipped her head to look her in the eye. "I mean it. You needn't worry."

Finley nodded, not trusting herself to speak. She might burst into tears and she had already humiliated herself enough in front of these people. She managed to hold out until they had left, closing the door behind them. Only then did she allow a tear to run down her cheek.

She had attacked her employer. She would rather live on

the streets than let her mother know how she had shamed herself. She would never work for any decent family again once word got out. She would have to find some other kind of employment without reference and hope that word of her disgrace didn't spread to the shops. And she was either going mad or was possessed by a demon.

What did she possibly have to worry about?

The brick wall shuddered under the force of Sam's left fist. It crumbled under the force of his right.

Bricks broke loose of their mortar. Those that weren't smashed into dust toppled to pile at his feet. He choked and stumbled backward, coughing, eyes watering. "Bloody hell!"

He was in the ballroom of Greythorne House. Since the death of Griff's parents, the large space had become less and less for entertaining and more and more of a training ground for the lot of them.

He'd started spending more time in here over the past couple of months. As soon as Emily said he could start training again. Well, maybe a little before. Emily didn't know everything, even if it seemed like she did.

Once his vision and the cloud of dust cleared, Sam lifted his arms, putting his forearms side by side in front so he could study them. There was no discernable difference between the limbs. They were the same relative size and tone. When he flexed his fingers, he could see tendons moving beneath the skin.

But the two were not the same. Sometimes he fancied he could hear a faint squeaking or creaking sound coming from his right arm. It was rubbish, of course—his arm never made any noise at all.

He'd probably feel better if the damn thing did squeak, if it felt somehow different from the left. At least then he could properly resent it. Hate it. Emily had saved his life and turned him into some kind of freak. He hated her almost as much as he was grateful to be alive.

He'd been born different, just like Griff. They'd grown up together, as Sam's father had been the old duke's steward, and had discovered early on that they had abilities other boys did not. Over the years Griff developed different theories as to why that was. Maybe it was something in the water. Maybe they'd been exposed to some kind of toxin. Or maybe, as Mr. Darwin apparently once predicted to both Griff's grandfather and father, they were simply examples of man's natural evolution into something *more*.

Whatever they were, there had been no denying they were more than human. Anyone who had ever witnessed one of Griff's "fits," when his eyes did that terrifying thing, would call him anything but normal.

As for Sam, he had realized his own differences around the age of six when a cart lost a wheel and toppled onto his father, pinning him to the ground. Instead of running for help as he was told, Sam lifted the cart enough for his father to crawl out. His father didn't say a word, but later that night he went up to the big house to talk to the duke, and after that, Sam and Griff were raised almost as brothers, enjoying the same education and many of the same benefits. Many of the same trials, too, because it was very important to find out what Sam was capable of doing.

While he had learned to hone his abilities, he also learned to conceal them. That was the one rule—to never reveal your true nature. There were people out there who wouldn't understand, who would be afraid. For some reason that made Sam think of the book their tutor had made them read. *Frankenstein* or something. It had been about a man who created a monster who was feared and hated despite his desire to be part of the human race.

It hadn't been intentional, but that was the day that Sam secretly began to think of himself as something of a monster.

And now Emily—the one person he never wanted to see him as such—had turned him into even more of an abomination. Rationally, he understood that she had saved him. In some ways she had even improved him. He was certainly stronger now, but at what cost? Underneath the flesh rebuilt by her little "beasties" were fingers, wrist and other bones no longer made of bone. He was metal there.

"It's your flesh, Sam," Emily had said, touching his new arm lightly with her clever fingers. "The Organites copied your cellular design. The skeleton might be metal, but the rest of it is all you." Her eyes had pleaded for him to understand, to forgive, but he hadn't been able to do that then and he couldn't do it now—not entirely. Not like she wanted.

Just like Victor Frankenstein's monster, he wasn't one complete human body. Some of his humanity had been lost. But as much as it scared and angered him, part of him liked being even stronger. He liked knowing that the next time he went up against one of those damn machines he could give it a little taste of its own.

Something was happening in the mechanized world. Something that enabled metal and gears to revolt against humans. The machine that ripped his arm off hadn't been the first to go against its engineering. It had simply been the worst.

And now its remains lurked deep beneath the house, in a vault for which only Emily and Griff knew the combination. He hated her being so close to the abomination, but he couldn't stand to be there with it—or Emily.

His cowardice was why Griff had replaced much of the

mechanized staff with flesh and blood, because his friend knew how much metal terrified him now.

What if the machine hadn't been destroyed? Griff claimed its power supply had been removed, but what if there was something else? He had Emily working on the thing, and even though Griff often worked with her, he wasn't little and fragile. Griff had his magic to protect him. Emily was brilliant, but she would be as delicate and as easily broken as china in the hands of a machine like the one that had nearly killed him.

Rage. Despair. Joy at still being alive. These emotions and more warred within him, filling him with restless energy, so much that he thought he might explode. He had to get it out. He had to stop thinking.

He smashed what was left of the wall. Bricks exploded as the wall itself actually lifted off its foundation. A slab of stone and mortar flew up and struck him in the face before he could dodge out of the way. It hit hard across his cheekbone. A clanging sound reverberated in his brain as the projectile shattered.

Stunned, Sam lifted his hand—his real hand—to his face. There was some blood—he could feel the warm wetness, but there was little pain. It should have hurt more, even though pain didn't affect him like it did others.

What if...? No, it couldn't be. But the idea was already taking hold in his stunned brain as he crossed the room to a wall of mirrors they often used to analyze fighting techniques.

Sam came up to one of the mirrors, putting his face close. He lifted both hands to the wound on his cheek. He ignored the blood as he pried his skin apart, digging his fingers into the bleeding gash. His stomach rolled at the sight, but he kept going, widening the wound, digging until he found the hard ridge beneath. He peered through the blood. *Please, let it be bone.*

It wasn't.

He dropped his bloody hands from the gore that was his cheek, stumbling backward as shock overtook him. He trembled, felt as though the world had been ripped out from beneath him.

Pain pierced his chest. What was this feeling? This hollow burning? *Betrayal.* It fed the rage within him, driving him from the room with great strides. He ran down the great staircase, ignoring the startled servants who gasped in horror at his appearance. He tore down the corridor to the door that led to the cellar, nearly taking it right off its hinges as he yanked it open.

The lift was too bloody slow. It was all he could do not to punch through the floor of it and jump clear to the bottom like the freak he was. Making himself wait for this damn box to take him underground was the only thing keeping him human at the moment.

Emily was alone, as she usually was, blindly believing this was her haven—her safe place. There was barely a foot of empty space anywhere. A clockwork monkey, its gears exposed, sat on a shelf next to a model rocket and a stack of punch cards. On the workbench there were designs for a gun—something for Jasper Renn no doubt. She was always making new weapons for the American, a fact that annoyed Sam. It wasn't as though Renn was one of them, regardless of how chummy he was with Griffin.

Emily stood at another bench on the opposite side of the room. Electric lights flickered on the walls and from supports hanging from the ceiling, illuminating her workspace. She was working on her pet project—something that had been her goal for almost a year now—her cat. A mechanized beast she could control.

She looked up from her project, lifting the magnifying goggles that allowed her to do delicate work. For a second, her pretty eyes looked as big as silver dollars behind the lenses.

"Oh, my God, Sam!" She slid off the stool with an expression of horror. "What happened?"

He took a step forward before stopping himself, but he couldn't stop her. She foolishly, trustingly, came toward him, worry etched in her every feature.

"How much?" he demanded as she approached, fists clenching at his sides.

She actually frowned—like she didn't know what he was talking about. "What do you mean? What did you do to yourself?"

He grabbed the hand she raised to his face. Her wrist felt so tiny inside his fingers. He could snap it so easily, but he didn't want to hurt her. It didn't matter what she had done to him. He would never hurt Emily.

Still, she gasped at the pressure of his grasp. He shook her, on the edge of madness. "How much of me is bloody machine?"

She went white—even more than usual—but she was not afraid. He didn't know if she was stupid, or if she truly knew him better than anyone else, but she wasn't afraid of him. For him, but never *of* him.

"Your right arm," she whispered, blue eyes locked with his. Was that shame he saw there? And relief. She was relieved to finally reveal all to him. Whose idea had it been to lie? Hers or Griff's? "The left side of your skull and most of your ribs have been reinforced because the bones were severely shattered."

Sam's grip on her wrist eased as nausea blossomed in his

stomach. He started to step back but her voice stopped him. "Your left shin and your right femur were both grafted and plated. And your right clavicle."

He stared at her in horror. All of that? The machine had done all of that? How had he survived? And then he looked deep into her eyes and he saw the truth there. He hadn't.

He hadn't survived.

"What else, Em?" His voice was a ragged whisper. "What else did you replace?"

She lifted her chin, not the least bit sorry for what she had done to him. "I'd do it again, Sam. I don't regret savin' you, no matter how you might hate me for it. I'd do it again."

*"What else did you replace?"* His shout reverberated through the room, seeming to shake the very foundations of the house. Emily winced, but she did not cringe. She straightened her shoulders and looked him dead in the eye.

"Your heart," came the unapologetic reply. "I replaced your heart."

# Chapter 4

Finley was tying the sash on the embroidered red-silk kimono a maid had brought her when there was a loud bang and the entire house seemed to quiver. A quick peek out the window showed the big fellow—Sam—stomping across the garden toward the path leading toward the stables. A few moments later as she slipped her feet into matching slippers whilst simultaneously shoving pins into her hair, she heard a loud rumbling. Another glance out the window revealed Sam charging out of the stables on one of those heavy two-wheeled contraptions that he and Griffin had been driving last night.

What had happened to make him so angry? And just how strong was he that he could make a house this size tremble by slamming a door? She wouldn't stand a chance against him, even if her darker self took over.

The thought made her uneasy. This house, these people and this situation were just too good to be true. In her experience, no one was ever kind for no reason. They always wanted something.

But she couldn't hide in this room forever. And since someone had absconded with her own clothing, she would have to play along. At least for now. Better she play along and find out what they wanted from her than sit around and wait. Although a naive part of her wanted to think the best of the handsome Rich Boy. Griffin, that was what Emily called him.

He intrigued her, this young man who managed to calm her beast with nothing more than a few words and his heavy-lidded eyes. He had helped her last night and, that she could tell, no liberties had been taken with her person. And the door to her room was unlocked from the outside. Surely that was a good sign?

As she left her room, she was struck by the grandeur of the house, seeing it in the full light of day. He must be very rich indeed.

A small sweeper automaton the size of a toddler cleaned the Axminster carpet that lined the corridor and staircase, its thick brushes scooping up debris and depositing it in the removal dust tray. It was one of the few machines she'd seen since her arrival—not that she had seen much of the house. Still, there seemed to be more human servants employed than mechanical ones—a fact proven by the chambermaids she spied farther down the corridor.

Portraits ranging from centuries ago to present day lined the stairs as she slowly made her way down, trying not to gawk at the white-washed walls and incredibly high ceilings. This place made the August-Rayneses' house seem a shack.

"May I help you, miss?" asked an older lady, when she reached the bottom. The woman's black-and-white uniform and mobcap gave her away as the housekeeper. She seemed somewhat…wary.

Someone else who was afraid of her. Lovely. "I'm supposed to go to the library," she explained.

"Ah, yes," the housekeeper replied. "His Grace no doubt wants to speak with you. Down the south corridor, second door on the right."

Finley muttered her thanks and started off in the direction given on rubbery knees. His Grace? Rich Boy's father was a duke? Bugger it. She was certain he had to know the August-Raynes family. Would he send her back? Or worse, call the Peelers—the police force named after Robert Peel—and have her arrested?

At the thought, that *other* part of her rose up in defiance. She'd break Rich Boy's daddy's pretty neck before she'd let the Peelers carry her off to Newgate or Bedlam.

She shook her head, trying to rid it of the darkness. What was this...this *thing* inside her? It made her think such horrible things at times. It also kept her from becoming a victim. Made her strong when others thought her weak. She hated it and yet, shamefully, she liked it.

One thing she knew for certain—it wasn't right.

The library door was open, but she knocked lightly before entering. She wasn't accustomed to walking about freely in a house like this. Generally she kept to her rooms if she hadn't work to do. Servants weren't supposed to flutter about where someone important might see them.

But she wasn't a servant here. She was a guest. Or perhaps a prisoner.

And what a prison! Finley's jaw dropped as her gaze fell upon floor-to-ceiling shelves filled wall-to-wall with books. So many books—more than she'd ever seen in one place.

"Hello?" Not so cocky now, she moved cautiously into the room. "Is anyone here?"

"Hello."

She looked up. There, on the balcony that wrapped around the entire room, was Rich Boy. His forearms rested on the railing as he smiled down at her, thick reddish hair falling over his forehead. He wore black trousers and a white shirt with the sleeves rolled up and collar open underneath a black leather waistcoat. She watched as he walked around to come down the narrow, curving staircase, his thick-soled boots clomping slightly on the wooden steps. He moved with loose-limbed grace, like someone who knew exactly who he was and didn't care if anyone liked it or not.

Lucky bugger.

He came right up to her and offered his hand. "Griffin King."

Finley's head jerked up. Griffin King. The Duke of Greythorne. She had overheard Lady Alyss discussing him with several of her friends just last week. They said he was handsome, rich beyond understanding and had a nice bottom. At this moment Finley couldn't give an opinion on the last, but he certainly was lovely to look at and gave the impression of being filthy rich.

No daddy then. Just him. They had something in common it seemed, despite the vast social chasm between them.

Hesitantly, she put her hand into his before slipping into a deep curtsy. "Finley Jayne, Your Grace." She lowered her gaze.

"Don't do that," he replied in a low, stern tone. "We're equals in this house."

She glanced at him in surprise, and quickly rose to her feet. "How's that?" she asked.

His smile was crooked, but it did little to ease the wariness in Finley's chest. "I've seen what you can do, Finley. Would you be surprised if I told you I had some *talents* of my own?"

"What I have is hardly a talent," she replied. A curse, perhaps. More than likely a demon. What she needed was a good exorcism.

He cocked his head to one side, still holding her hand. His gray-blue gaze narrowed slightly, as though he was looking right into her. "How would you describe it?"

She pulled away, suddenly unsure of herself, but sure enough not to say aloud what she'd thought to herself. "What happened with Sam? The whole house shook when he stormed out."

"It could be any number of things." There was that lopsided grin again. "Nice attempt at changing the subject, by the way." Then he gestured toward the sofa. "Have a seat."

Part of her wanted to run, but a stronger part wanted to stay. She wasn't certain which was the smarter choice, but she crossed the carpet and sat down on the violet brocade sofa. She stiffened when Griffin seated himself on the opposite end, scarcely two feet away.

"Relax," he said. "I'm not going to hurt you. I doubt I could anyway. I suspect you could trounce me with one hand behind your back."

As he spoke, some of the rigidity left Finley's spine. She was indeed relaxing—at his command. "And I suspect you're not as powerless as you would like me to believe," she commented, turning so that she could face him directly.

He seemed amused, and she was very much aware that he wasn't the least bit afraid of her. "You think I pretend weakness?"

She nodded. "Not weakness, but you like to let others think they're in control, when really it's you." What she said was true. Of course she could defeat him physically, but then what? She could run, but she was wearing nothing but a nightgown and a kimono with flimsy slippers. Where could she go that his influence could not reach? She was in enough trouble as it was, there was no need to run into more. Not yet.

"Interesting." His pale eyes sparkled for a second before becoming serious. "What if I told you I could help you become the one in control?"

She frowned. "In control of what?"

"Of the wildness that overtakes you." He said it so matter-of-factly, as though it were nothing more than a cold or a silly notion.

"It only comes on when I'm threatened, or scared," she heard herself divulge. She shouldn't have said anything. Should have put her thumb in one of those pretty eyes... Finley pushed that thought back down deep where it belonged.

"Is that why you were in Hyde Park last night? Someone threatened you?"

She glanced away, but nodded.

"Felix August-Raynes?" His voice was soft.

Finley closed her eyes as dread washed over her. Of course he knew. He would have seen the crest on her corset.

"There was nothing in the papers this morning so I assume the blackguard is still very much alive?"

Her chin came up defiantly. "Do I look like a murderer to you?"

Griffin smiled. "Jack the Ripper had a very gentle countenance."

"But they never caught..." Something in his expression prevented her from completing the protest. "Lord Felix was very much alive the last time I saw him, though I reckon he has a bit of a headache this morning."

"Rightly earned, no doubt." Griffin leaned back into the corner of the sofa and brought one booted foot up to rest across his knee. The smooth black leather looked soft and the silver buckles gleamed in the light. "Like the rest of Jack Dandy's bunch, Lord Felix has an overinflated sense of self."

"Who?"

He propped his elbow on the back of the sofa and leaned his head against his hand. So open and trusting with her. Even though he knew what she could do, he wasn't the least bit afraid. It made her wonder what kind of monster lived inside of him.

"The Dandies. They fancy themselves street thugs, but they're just a bunch of spoiled whelps with metal in their faces. Dandy, on the other hand, is precisely what he claims to be."

Finley wondered what that was exactly. "What do you want from me?" She was tired of this pointless small talk.

He didn't look the least bit surprised or offended. "Nothing. Not yet."

"But you do want something eventually." Oddly enough, having him live down to her expectations was disappointing, to say the least.

"Eventually, if I'm right and you're willing, I'd like for you to join us."

"As what?" For all she knew, Emily was a concubine for the rest of them. They could be getting up to all kinds of perverse things in this house.

Griffin smiled again—it was as though he could read her mind. "Who do you think keeps this country safe so you can sleep at night?"

"I don't sleep most nights. And to be honest, Your Grace, I don't feel all that safe."

He tilted his head. "I can change that."

And in that instant, Finley believed him. Not only that, but she knew he believed what he said. It made her want to trust him. When was the last time she'd trusted anyone of the male gender?

"First," he began, abruptly rising to his feet, "we need to get you some new clothes. A seamstress will be here any moment to fit you."

"But I don't have any money."

He looked incredulous at her protest. "You needn't worry about that. I have enough for both of us, I assure you." His eyes were twinkling again—laughing at her, but not maliciously.

Slowly, Finley rose from the sofa, tilted her head back and looked him dead in the eye. "I have no desire to be any more in your debt than I already am."

He looked thoughtful for a moment. "Would it make you more comfortable if I demanded something in return? Would that put you at ease?"

When he put it like that, it made her sound like an awful sort of person for thinking the worst. "It would, yes. At least that would be honest."

It might have been laughter that came scoffing from his throat, but there was little humor in it. He shook his head, the light reflecting glints of russet in his hair. "I'd like to meet whomever it was who made you so distrusting and pull his teeth out one by one."

The vehemence in his tone startled her, yet was strangely warming. "'Twas more than just one."

His face darkened, like clouds overtaking the sun. Suddenly, this was no longer just some seemingly kind, bored aristocrat standing before her, but a young man capable of many dangerous things.

*Interesting,* she thought, borrowing his own term.

"What I want from you," he said, and Finley braced herself, "is your trust. Irrevocable and unshakable. I want you to put your life in my hands, and I want to be able to do the same without hesitation."

Disturbed to her very soul, Finley could only shake her head. "You ask too much." Put his life in her hands? He was deranged! A bedlamite for certain.

A crooked grin curved his mouth. "Too much? You strange and wonderful girl, that is the *least* I'll ask of you."

Anyone who got within fifteen feet of Sam Morgan could tell the young man was spoiling for a fight. Unfortunately for Sam, everyone in the tavern was either sober enough to give him a wide berth or too drunk to bother indulging him.

He sat at a table in a corner as dark as his mood and as far away from the automated barkeep as he could get. Just the sight of the gleaming brass android caused his left eye to twitch. Thankfully, a human—a young girl—came to his table. She wore a white blouse off her round shoulders, a tight corset that made her waist incredibly tiny and called even more attention to her abundant chest and a short, flouncy skirt that showed off shapely calves in dark stockings.

"Right," she said, rolling the *r* in a thick Welsh accent. "What can I gets ye, then?"

"A pint," he replied brusquely, pushing a half-crown across the scarred tabletop. It was a generous payment. She snatched it up with a grin and hurried off to fetch his drink. Across the gin- and ale-soaked, sawdust-littered floor, a shabbily dressed man dropped a coin into the slot of the automated "Victoria Victrola." There was a slight clinking sound as the coin hit bottom, followed by a gentle whirring as the torso in the top glass half of the machine stirred. "Victoria" had thick auburn hair and a lovely papier-mâché face with bright blue eyes and painted crimson lips, the bottom of which was designed to open and close, as though she was actually flesh and blood singing a song and not a cheap wind-up doll designed to mime in time to the music. Victoria didn't bother Sam as much as the shiny creature behind the bar. She was confined to her glass prison, half a woman with no chance of escape.

No, it was the metal behind the bar that set his teeth on edge. Did these people not realize the danger they put themselves in simply being in the same room as that…that *thing?*

At least he was better equipped to fight them now. Emily had seen to that. He flexed the fingers on his right hand. It felt completely normal. How was that possible when it wasn't? He couldn't even discern a difference in weight between his arms, but surely the metal one had to be weightier?

The waitress returned to set a frothy pint of ale in front of him. Some of the foam ran down the outside the mug to pool on the dirty tabletop. "*Wanting* anythin' else, will ye be?"

Sam wasn't dumb. Maybe he wasn't as smart as Emily and Griff, or even as witty as Jasper, but he wasn't stupid. He understood things they didn't, and he understood what the girl offered him. He also knew that no one liked being rejected.

"Not right now," he replied with a slight smile. It felt forced and false on his lips, but she didn't notice. She returned the smile, flashing a pretty dimple in her cheek.

"If you change yer mind, let me know."

"I will," he promised, knowing full well he wouldn't.

As she swished away, Sam lifted the mug. Warm ale flooded his mouth, awakening his tongue with its rich flavor. He could swallow three gallons of the stuff and still not be drunk enough to get Emily's soft brogue out of his head.

*"I replaced your heart."*

What did that mean? It wasn't being kept alive that gnawed at him, or that a machine pushed the blood through his veins. How did this affect him as a human being? Would he live longer? Was it a lie when he saw Emily and the thing in his chest began to beat a little faster? What did a machine know of feelings? Would there ever be a time when he could honestly say that he felt something to be true in his heart and trust in it?

Making it all more confusing was his undeniable thankfulness at simply being alive, no matter what his present form.

The Victoria Victrola was singing a song about lost love, adding to his melancholy. He drained the pint and signaled his waitress for another, watching warily as she gave the order to the automaton barkeep. He imagined those metal hands suddenly dropping the heavy mug and grabbing the waitress around the throat, squeezing the life from her as ale spilled to the floor. He saw himself trying to rescue her, and suddenly his own hand, by no volition of his own, joined in crushing the girl to death....

"You look as though you could use some company."

Sam jerked, barely glancing at the man standing beside his table as the charming blonde bird delivered his second ale. "How's that?"

"You look miserable," the man replied in strangely accented English. "It loves company, does it not?"

Oddly enough, the lame attempt at a joke made Sam chuckle. He gestured at the chair on the other side of the table. "If that fires your furnace, have a seat."

The man did, setting his own full mug on the table before flipping out the tails of his coat. He began stripping off his fine leather gloves. He was fancy-dressed like a gentleman, in a russet coat and gold-striped waistcoat. He wore a chocolate-colored bowler hat and a pristine white cravat tied around his neck. He had a foreign look about him—a kind of sophisticated swarthiness with his dark hair and eyes.

"Leon Adamo," the man said, offering his hand.

"Sam Morg—" Sam froze, unable to take his eyes off the...

*thing* in front of him. It was long and slender, and looked as much like a hand as any other he'd seen, except for one major exception.

It was metal. Dull silver in color, it was fully jointed, notched where every knuckle should be. It even had fingernails etched into its surface, and the top was decorated with an elaborate swirling pattern that extended along each finger, as well. On the inside of the wrist was a small clear panel, through which the delicate gears could be accessed.

His companion chuckled, and withdrew his hand. "My apologies. I forget how startling it can be."

"No," Sam replied, somewhat distracted, his gaze still riveted on that strange limb. "I've just never met…" *Someone else who was part machine.* "Forgive me. I meant no offense."

"None taken, Mr…Morgan, was it?"

Sam nodded, and this time he offered his own hand. "Nice to meet you."

The gentleman smiled and accepted the handshake. The smooth metal was cool against Sam's palm, but the fingers were strong. It felt like holding the gauntlet of a suit of armor. Nothing frightening or repulsive about it. Certainly Leon Adamo didn't seem the least bit ashamed of it.

Sam returned his companion's smile. "You know, I find I'm in the mood for company after all."

King House was quiet, still as a church when Finley opened her eyes in the wee hours. The moon cast long shadows through her room, illuminating her bed and part of the wall in fingers of silver.

She felt restless, agitated. It had been brewing all day, ever since her strange conversation with Griffin.

Did he mean her harm or not? She didn't think so, but she couldn't be certain. And then there was that cryptic remark he'd left her with. What did he mean absolute trust would be the *least* he asked of her? Arrogant toff. What made him think she'd fancy his skinny arse worth saving?

Inside her, that frightened, cautious part of her squealed in protest as it always did. The "good girl" didn't like conflict, shied away from violence and danger. Poor little mite. She had no idea that confrontation was the basest form of self-protection. She was just doing what was best for both of them. And she wanted to know if Lord Felix's friend Dandy was a threat to her.

She slipped out of bed and padded barefoot across the carpet to the wardrobe. Griffin had made good on his promise of new clothes and she now had a few ready-made items to do her until the rest were made. She slipped into soft black stockings and hooked them onto the new garter belt round her hips. Then she put on the snug, black leather "knicks"—black pants that covered her from her waist to the tops of her thighs—and a soft plum velvet corset. She laced up her tall, sturdy black leather boots and slipped on a long, black velvet frock coat that hung almost to her ankles. Then she coiled her hair into a messy bun and shoved a pencil through it to secure it on the back of her head. Pencils were excellent for hairstyling. They also made very effective weapons if the need arose.

Ready, Finley crept to the window, lifted the latch and pushed out. She sat on the ledge and swung one leg out. Then, holding on to the top of the window, she brought her other leg out, as well. She climbed down the side of the house by digging her fingertips and toes into the shallow crevices between the stones, agile as a spider.

A few feet from the bottom, she let go and dropped silently to the grass. The night smelled of coming rain, freshly dug soil and summer heat. Her eyesight was good, but always so much more acute when this side of her was free. Every sense was heightened, just a little more than human.

A quick glance around ascertained that she was alone, and she sprinted toward the stables where she'd seen Sam go earlier that day. He still hadn't returned and the little redhead—Emily—was worried about him. Finley had heard her say so to Griffin over dinner. He'd assured her that Sam was fine, but he was worried, too. Finley could tell.

Finley didn't care where the gargantuan went. This part of her felt safer without him around.

The stables were dimly lit with a soft golden glow. Finley was surprised to see that there were actually horses there along with several strange-looking mechanical contraptions like the one Griff had been driving when their paths happened to cross the night before.

She moved toward the hay-covered wood floor toward a smaller, sleeker machine with thickly notched tires and gently curved steering bars. It looked like one of the modern bicycles, only much heavier, fancier—faster. She ran her hand over the chrome front, enjoying the cool metal beneath her fingers.

"Going out?"

She jerked back and whirled around. Kneeling on the bare floor was Emily. She appeared to be doing some work on one of the smaller machines—a red one that had three wheels instead of two. She had a smear of something dark on her pale cheek and her hair was up in a thick, haphazard bun on top of her head.

"Yes," Finley replied, lifting her chin.

The other girl looked up from her work, an oily rag in one hand. She seemed surprised that she was still there. She pointed at the machine beside Finley. "Take that one. It's lighter and easier to handle."

She wasn't going to try to stop her? She truly wasn't a prisoner, then. Didn't she think Finley might steal the vehicle and never come back?

"Don't you want to know where I'm going?"

The smaller girl wiped her forehead with the back of her hand, leaving a smudge behind. "If that was my business, you'd tell me."

Finley smiled at that. She was strong enough to seriously hurt this girl, but she acted cool and calm. It made her wonder what secret defense the girl possessed; if Emily had abilities as interesting as Griffin and Sam. It made her wary of the girl.

She respected that.

"What are you doing?" she asked, suddenly not quite so eager to go out.

Emily removed a dull-looking piece of the cycle and replaced it with a shinier, newer-looking one. "Just replacing the velocity control."

Finley crouched beside her, watching as she secured the device in place. "What does it do?"

The redhead smiled crookedly. "Makes it go fast."

"*Very* fast?" Finley asked, returning the smile.

Emily chuckled. "Very fast, yes."

"How did you learn to do this?" It was fascinating and strange to her, a girl knowing how to fix machines. What wonderful knowledge to have.

"I've been interested in how things work since I was but a lass. My father and brothers are all inventors or mechanically inclined. I'm the only girl, and my mother died when I was young, so I grew up watching them. It just seemed to make sense that I start tinkering myself."

"Fascinating," Finley murmured, watching the girl's dirty, nimble fingers move like a virtuoso playing an instrument. Then, "I'm sorry about your mum."

"Thanks. I don't remember her."

"My parents are still alive. Well, my mum is. She lives with my stepfather. My father—my real father—died when I was a baby."

"I'm sorry."

Those simple words surprised Finley, touched her. For a moment she entertained the notion of ignoring her need to get out into the night and staying here. Maybe she could help Emily with her repairs.

But this girl wasn't her friend, and wasn't likely to be her friend because Finley couldn't stay here forever. She didn't belong in that fancy house with these smart and privileged people. This wasn't her world.

"Right." She slapped her palms against her thighs. "I'll be off then."

Emily watched her as she stood. "Be careful."

Finley grinned at her as she swung her leg over the cycle she'd chosen and sat down. "Careful? Where's the fun in that?"

And then she found the mechanism to make the beast move and she tore out of the stables without a backward glance.

# Chapter 5

If the city of London was a body, Whitechapel would be the groin; a great unwashed area that only showed itself under the cover of darkness, and only for the most salacious of entertainments. No one of "proper" birth ever admitted to going there, but they all did at one time or another—or at least they wanted to. Slumming was very popular these days.

A perpetual mist seemed to hang over the streets like the stench of a drunkard's breath. It was a dismal place, where the "unfortunate" ladies sold themselves and "three penny uprights" were often conducted where anyone might stumble upon them. Gin was cheap, too, and if you knew what doors to knock on you could buy a bit of oblivion in an opium den, or time with a lost loved one from an Aether monger. The mechs in this part of town were rough and awkward, tarnished.

In short, it was a poor, pathetic place that the modern world seemed to have forgotten, or conveniently ignored. Here, the streetlights still ran on gas and flickered with a watery yellow glow. Coal was used instead of the more expensive teal ore sold by King Industries because coal was easier to steal. Dentistry was a pair of dirty tongs, and bathing was thought to make a body susceptible to all manner of illness. And any vice ever dreamed by the mind of man was available for a cheaper price in Whitechapel than anywhere else in all of London.

Of course, you got what you paid for.

So a pretty girl with a full set of teeth and not a pockmark to be seen, all toffed out in the latest style, stood out like a rose in a pile of steaming offal. She was spotted near Princess Alice pub in the Commercial Street area, not far from where Saucy Jack, or "The Ripper" as many called him, had done some of his "work" nine years earlier. And word spread quickly that she was looking for Jack Dandy, prince of this abysmal kingdom.

Finley tried not to smile as heads turned to watch her walk. Whispers followed her, as did the odd ragged man. The weaker half of her would be afraid of this part of the city. She'd think it foolish to flaunt herself this way, but why shouldn't she go wherever she wanted? There was very little here that could hurt her. Even if they descended upon her in a pack like wolves after a deer, she'd still prove herself more of a predator than all of them put together.

Rich Boy's earlier remark about Lord Felix being a member of the Dandies had stuck with her. Lord Felix was a bully and liked being in control, so if he actually followed this Jack Dandy, then Finley wanted to meet the man. Have a little chat with him, perhaps, and take his measure for herself.

Dandy might prove to be a handy person to know.

She'd left her transportation on top of an old but sturdy shed a few streets back. She didn't trust Dandy not to steal it from her and she'd rather have a means of escape should it come to that. Besides, being on foot would make it that much easier for Dandy to find *her,* which is what she was counting on him to do.

She looked forward to meeting the infamous criminal, now that she'd heard some of the rumors about him during this evening's search. She just had to meet the man that had half the young bucks in London putting bits of metal in their faces and committing all kinds of mischief. And, yes, she wanted to make a little trouble for Lord Felix.

She turned a corner onto a darker side street. It was quieter here in an eerie sort of way, but that didn't stop a ragged man from following her. He wasn't what anyone would call stealthy by any stretch of the word. He sniffed and chuckled and hawked up phlegm as though wanting the entire city to hear. Finally, she'd had enough and turned to tell him to bugger off.

Only…only the ragged man wasn't there. No one was. Frowning, Finley turned on her heel.

And found herself staring at a full, unsmiling mouth. She didn't jump back; she was too stunned—and impressed. How had he managed to sneak up on her? *No one* ever snuck up on her. Raising her gaze, she discovered two of the darkest eyes she'd ever seen, framed by thick, long eyelashes that no fellow should ever be allowed to own.

"Hullo, darling." He grinned, revealing teeth that were startling straight and white in the moonlight. "I 'eard you was lookin' for me."

He was tall and slim, dressed in the height of fashion in solid black, so as to blend with the shadows on the street. His hair was dark, as well, and fell about his pale face in tousled waves. A Cockney gentleman—the strangest oxymoron. He was handsome—in a Lucifer kind of way. He was cool night to Griffin King's warm light of day, though why she would even bother to compare the two was a mystery.

"I was," she replied.

He held his arms out to the side, displaying himself in a vulnerable pose that on him didn't seem vulnerable at all, but rather like a taunt. "And now that you 'ave?"

She shrugged. "I thought you'd be more impressive." In truth, she rather liked the sight of Jack Dandy—and there was no one else he could be but the fellow she was looking for.

He laughed, throwing his head back so the sound echoed through the night. A shiver slithered down Finley's spine. Anticipation, mixed with a rare taste of fear, fluttered in her stomach. She liked it. She liked *him*.

Done laughing, but still smiling, he offered her his arm. "Care to take a turn, Treasure?"

Finley slipped her arm through his. The black wool of his frock coat was soft and warm beneath her hand. He walked her into the moonlight as though escorting her into a ball. Even though she knew she could snap his neck in an instant, she felt slightly off center—somewhat as her other half had with Griffin. Dandy had power, and that gave him confidence. She might have the strength to harm him, but he wouldn't go down easily, and she might not survive the altercation.

And as with Griffin, this elevated Dandy in her estimation.

As they walked, the subtle lamplight of a dirigible washed over them. Finley glanced up, watching the light grow closer, slowly descending from the sky in a whirl of propellers as the ship made its way into the London air dock just a few miles away. How amazing it must be to float so high, to travel so quickly.

Dandy followed her gaze, but they didn't stop walking. "I was up in one of them flyers once," he told her. "I climbed over the rail and hung on to one of the ropes. Freeing it was. I almost let go."

She whipped her head around to gape at him. "The fall would kill you."

He smiled ever so slightly. "Not afore I flew. Worse ways to go."

Falling to one's death was in no way pleasant, but Finley thought for a moment—of what it would feel like to fall from that great height, to feel the wind through her hair, taste the clouds. Yes, it would be like flying. And she *could* think of worse ways to die.

He drew her up the shallow stone step to a stone row house. There was nothing special or welcoming about it. The windows were grimy, the paint peeling off the front door, and Finley had to question the intelligence of stepping over the threshold. It could be a trap. He could have men with weapons inside, and trained thugs would be harder to fight than common men.

Still, she wasn't about to be afraid, not in front of this young man, who was just wolfish enough she reckoned he could smell fear. He was exactly the type to take advantage of a weakness when he found it. It was what she would do. And, honestly—vainly—she was a girl of little weakness.

She entered the dim interior ahead of Dandy. Inside, the house looked nothing like it did on the exterior. The hardwood floor was buffed and polished to a high shine. Paintings hung on the wine-colored foyer walls, and just beyond that she saw an inviting parlor. That was where Dandy took her.

She gave a low, appreciative whistle. "You live here?" she asked, relieved that there wasn't a thug in sight. Obviously she and Dandy shared an enjoyment of the finer things in life, judging from the rich colors and fabrics that swathed the room.

Dandy chuckled. "Too many people would like to kill me in my sleep, right? So I never sleep where I conduct me business."

She glanced at him out of the corner of her eye as she crossed the richly patterned rug that covered most of the parlor floor. "Are you truly that wicked, Mr. Dandy?" she inquired, running her fingers over the plush velvet cushions on the sofa as she watched him from beneath lowered lashes.

Leaning against the door frame, he arched a dark brow at her mildly flirtatious tone. In the brighter light, she could better ascertain his age. She guessed him to be one and twenty at the oldest. Young to have such a reputation. "I can be, Miss Jayne."

Fingers of ice closed around Finley's heart. For the first time, her confidence was genuinely shaken, and for a moment, that weak side of her threatened to take over. She sank down onto the sofa. "You...you know my name. How?"

He grinned—a baring of those perfect teeth—and stepped away from the door frame. "Wouldn't be much of a villainous mystery if I told you that, would I?"

She wasn't quite sure how to respond, nor could she be confident that her voice wouldn't shake, so she remained silent. She simply sat there and watched him cross to a polished oak sideboard where an array of crystal bottles sat. A deep breath set her nerves to rights. Dandy was no threat to her. She knew this because she was no threat to him. They were alike, they were. Both predators, both dangerous and both vain. And they each found the other fascinating.

"Care for a little of the Green Fairy, Treasure?"

Absinthe. She'd never had it before, but she'd heard others talk about. Artists drank it. It was something improper people indulged in. That alone was reason enough for Finley—given her current personality—to say yes.

"How do I know you won't slip laudanum in it?" The medicine didn't have as much of an effect on her as it did on "normal" people, but it would still make her groggy for a bit—less sharp.

He smiled over his shoulder at her. "I've a sneakin' suspicion you're much more entertainin' awake than asleep."

Now who was being a flirt? Satisfaction curved Finley's lips, but she watched him like a hawk regardless. They were similar enough that she knew better than to trust him completely. He might not try to hurt her, but he'd take the upper hand however he could.

Slotted silver spoons topped with absinthe-soaked sugar cubes lay across the rim of each small glass. Dandy produced a box of safety matches and struck one, igniting the tip in a strong-smelling blaze, which he then applied to the cubes of sugar. They burned for but a second before he tipped them each into their respective glass. The absinthe went up in a beautiful flame, which Finley thought was sure to set his cuffs ablaze, but Dandy calmly emptied a measure of water into both drinks, dousing the flames. He stirred each, and handed one of the glasses to Finley. She stared at it in wonder.

"Blimey, if you ain't a rare one," said Dandy, seating himself on the crimson loveseat opposite her.

"What do you mean?" She raised her glass to her lips and drank. The now milky liquor tasted like licorice, vaguely sweet on her tongue.

"Come in 'ere, bold as brass, but you ain't got none of the street stink on you. I bet right now your mum's wonderin' what you've got up to. Wouldn't she be disappointed to discover you 'aving a drink wiv me?"

"My mother doesn't know I'm here." As she said it, guilt tugged at her conscience. She buried it with a coy smile. "You're not going to tell on me, are you?"

Her attempt at flirting only seemed to amuse rather than intrigue him. "Why are you 'ere?" he asked, looking like a pale, night-clad creature on that bloodred velvet. He reclined as though he hadn't a care in the world, long legs splayed. His boots were as perfectly polished as Rich Boy's. "We don't get many girls like you in these parts."

She snorted. "No, I bet you don't." There weren't any other girls like her, were there?

Dandy just sat there, watching her as he took a swallow from his glass. Waiting.

"I've got a message for Felix August-Raynes," she told him, finally getting down to business. "He's one of yours, is he not?"

"One of my what?"

She waved a dismissive hand and took another sip of lovely absinthe. "Followers, lackeys. Disciples."

Both dark brows went up as teeth flashed again. "Disciples. I likes that one, luv, 'onest to God I do." The smile gave way to a vaguely mocking frown. "But I fink you're a tad misguided in your information. I don't have that kind of power over no one. I has associates and that's it."

Obviously it was a familiar spiel he gave to disengage himself from criminal activity committed by his cohorts. Finley rolled her eyes. "Do you know Lord Felix or not?"

He regarded her for a moment and made her wait while he decided to answer. He even went so far as to take another swallow from his glass. She enjoyed watching him as he did so. "I know 'im."

Finley inched forward on the cushions until she was perched on the edge of her seat. She forced herself to meet his gaze and not look away, not even to blink. "Then perhaps you'd tell him that if he ever tries to force himself upon another girl, I'll kill him."

She'd wager Dandy didn't often look as surprised as he did right at that moment. But it wasn't for the reason she thought. Her threat of violence bounced right off him. "Did he try to force himself upon you?" His voice was oddly calm—the Cockney he affected absent.

"Yes."

Watching his expression change was like watching thunderclouds suddenly blot out the entire sky. In that moment, she saw the truly dangerous side of Jack Dandy and it was as glorious as it was terrifying. This was why entitled brats like Lord Felix followed him; because they wanted a little bit of that danger for their own. Only, Dandy didn't give his power away to anyone.

And then, as suddenly as it appeared, it was gone again. She might have thought she'd imagined it were it not so emblazed upon her memory.

"I'll pass on the message if I see his lordship, rest assured."

"Thank you." She took another sip of absinthe. She liked it, but it wasn't something she'd want to drink vast quantities of. "I'll take my leave of you now."

He didn't try to talk her out of it. He simply raised his lanky frame from the cushions and followed her to the door.

"Thank you for seeing me, Mr. Dandy." She wished she could be there the next time Lord Felix came 'round and heard her message. He'd probably suffer an apoplexy.

"My door is always open," he replied, but his tone was lacking its previous joviality. "You know how to find it."

Finley arched a brow at him, not liking at all this new seriousness. She had just gotten accustomed to his flippancy, and his tone was just a little too sincere for her to discredit. "That sounds an awful lot like an offer of friendship, sir."

Jack Dandy reached out the long fingers of his right hand and gently touched her cheek. "Don't mistake me, Treasure.

I can offer you many things, but friendship ain't one of them. Now, for once in your life, be a sensible girl and run away."

And surprisingly, Finley did.

By the time his aunt Cordelia arrived, Griff had already had the morning from hell. First, he awoke a few hours before dawn to the sound of a velocycle pulling into the drive. It was Finley. He hadn't known she was gone. And a note from Emily told him that before Finley left last night she'd been very much unlike the timid sweet girl she'd been earlier that day. She'd seemed almost like a completely different person.

Awake and irritable, he took a shower, wishing he were on his estate in Devon where he might have gone for a swim in the pond instead. Once dressed, he went downstairs for an early breakfast and found a letter waiting for him from Sam's father, steward of that Devon estate. It was brief, but annoying. It seemed the new groundskeeper had left his post without any warning over a week ago and now Morgan was left trying to hire someone new. Knowing Morgan's dislike of modern technology, Griff tried not to be too irritated that the man had written rather than telephoned or even telegraphed the information.

There was also a similar missive from the museum curator who had sent on a list of things taken the night of the robbery. Amongst the various innocuous items was a hairbrush on loan from Queen Victoria for an upcoming Jubilee exhibition.

Bloody marvelous, now he'd have to deal with the Buckingham set.

He was just pouring a cup of coffee when a bleary eyed Emily emerged from her workshop/laboratory in the cellar. He avoided the lab if at all possible, riding the lift down there made him feel as though he couldn't draw a deep enough breath.

"Have you been up all night?" he demanded, incredulous. He'd been the only one in bed the night before, and now he felt foolish for it. He was supposed to be the leader, shouldn't he have had *something* to at least keep him up late?

Emily nodded, obviously almost asleep on her feet. Her ropey hair was mussed and her shirt wrinkled and stained beneath her open smock. There was a smudge of something thick and oily on her pale cheek. "I had to replace the velocity control in my cycle and then I wanted to go over two of the automatons we recovered again. I know the explanation for these crimes is in them somewhere."

Griffin smiled at her and brought his hand up to squeeze her shoulder. "I won't have you exhausting yourself, you wonderful, foolish girl. Off to bed with you now. Get some rest."

Nodding wearily, she turned on her heel and walked away as though she were already asleep.

Griffin went on to the dining room where breakfast waited. He filled a plate and sat down at the head of the table and opened the newspaper sitting there.

As he read, he finished his coddled eggs, sausage and toast and then poured a second cup of coffee before making his way to his study.

With dark paneled walls, huge oak desk and large leather chair, the study was Griff's refuge from the rest of the world. It looked exactly as it had his entire life, right down to the books on the shelves, though he had added a few of his own. Oh, and of course the Aether engine in the corner.

The room had belonged to his father up until his untimely death three years ago. Edward and Helena King had been killed in a steam-carriage accident. Only, it hadn't been an accident at all. He knew this because his father told him. Shortly after the event, deep in grief, Griffin had accessed the Aetheric plane and tried to contact his parents. He had wanted only to see them one last time, but when his father appeared he told him that almost everyone involved with their journey to the earth's center twenty years earlier was dead, as well—quite possibly murdered.

Since then, Griff made it his personal mission to give his parents peace. The fact that he had yet to find the culprit was a deep and private disappointment, but he refused to give up, even when his aunt Cordelia told him she worried about him.

Even Cordelia didn't know just how deep Griff's connection with the Aether went. He'd always been able to access it, even as a child. Back then he'd been something of a medium and could contact the dead. Now…it was difficult to explain, especially when no one truly understood what the Aether was. To many, it was the Fifth Element. To others, it had to do with the propagation of light. For some, it was another dimension. And to scholars of the classics, Aether was the anthropomorphic representation of sky, space and even Heaven.

But to Griff, it was much simpler and terribly more complex than any of that. The Aether was the thread that bound everything—humanity, the world and the cosmos—together. It was energy. It was *everything*—and he was a conduit for it.

If not for the control he cultivated, it would kill him. Man was not meant to know what lurked beyond the veil. The living were not meant to traverse the world of the dead. There was always a price to be paid for tapping that kind of power— a loss of self. And yet, lately he'd felt more at peace with it, even though he knew his connection to the Aether had grown inexplicably. As his connection deepened, so did his understanding and control of it. Still, he had to be careful. It was too easy to become addicted to accessing the plane. Talking to the dead, seeing old friends and relatives—even old pets—was what drove so many to the Aether dens. But the Aetheric was for the dead, and every time a human accessed it, they lost a little of themselves. He had seen it for himself, and had been cautioned by his parents. The more time spent there, the less appeal real life held.

He had tried to use the Aether to find his parents' killer and found nothing. His parents couldn't tell him because in life they hadn't known the answer.

Though, he was not entirely without hope. As he searched for the person responsible for destroying his family, he dedicated himself to hunting down other villains, as well. Eventually, he would find the one he sought.

As always, being in this room made him feel connected to his father, to whom he had been very close, especially as the only child and heir. That bond eased the tension in his shoulders and the pounding that threatened in his skull. When he sat down in front of the Aether engine, he was relaxed but with purpose.

He turned the key on the side of the mahogany box that also housed the auditory speaker. There was a slight thumping noise as the engine came to life, followed by a gentle hum. Next he flipped a small brass lever on the upper casing to illuminate the viewing screen. Those who traversed in the Aether knew that a reflective surface was the best medium for transmission. When the engine wasn't in use the screen appeared to be nothing more than a simple mirror, but when illuminated from within it became the perfect receptacle for Aetheric images.

Emily had put the monstrosity together using different items she found around the mansion. It was a godsend because it meant he didn't have to tap into the Aether directly and open himself up to the barrage of spirits and suffocating power.

The machine also doubled as an analytical engine and,

like those belonging to governments and police organizations across the globe, was connected through telegraph and telephone lines, sharing important and often coded political information. The information was carefully encrypted to keep people like him from understanding, but Emily's great big brain had also devised what she called a "cryptex"—a code breaker.

To begin his search, Griffin spoke into the "phonic accelerator" Emily had made from a candlestick phone base. "Lord Felix August-Raynes."

The engine kicked into motion, filling the room with its gentle chugging. He didn't expect to find much as August-Raynes was still alive. Only the dead lurked in the Aether.

The engine instantly chugged faster, going from a slow, steady beat to a heart-pounding rhythm in mere seconds. He peered at the screen—nothing but a newspaper article. He slipped a piece of paper into the typewriting machine's rollers and hit the spacer bar. Immediately the article began to print.

"I do hope you're using that thing to look at photographs of Moulin Rouge ladies as a young man your age should, and not hunting down another bothersome criminal."

The sound of aunt Cordelia's voice was enough to put a grin on Griff's face. Though she was technically his guardian until he turned one and twenty, she was more a friend to him than an authority figure. They were the only family either of them had left.

He met her in the center of the room for a hug. A tall, blonde woman with the same gray eyes as his, she was handsome and dressed in the height of fashion. Delicate strands of six silver chains ran from a piercing on the right side of her nose to one in the same ear—one chain for every year without her husband, the Marquess of Marsden, who had gone missing during a mission. It was a blatant symbol to any man who might approach her that she was not available, no matter what the gossips might say.

"It's good to have you home," Griff told her when he finally released her. "What of the mysterious crop circles?"

She shot him a slightly chastising look, but it was softened by her smile. "You know I can't tell you any of that."

"Not even if you had a good trip? Found a being from another world?" He was only half teasing. Her work for the Crown was often a sore spot between them.

"The trip was what it was. No Mars men, either," she replied lightly, stripping off her gloves as she moved toward the analytical engine. "Not Moulin Rouge, but at least it's a pretty girl. Well done, Goose."

Griffin rolled his eyes at the unfortunate moniker given to him as a child because of how he waddled when he walked. He had grown out of the waddle but not the name. He glanced at the article, which had a photograph attached. "It's not like that. She was a servant who worked at the August-Raynes household." He tore the paper from the rollers so he could better read it. "She disappeared after accusing Lord Felix of rape."

"I always despised that boy, but what does this have to do with you?"

"I've found a girl in Hyde Park two nights ago. She'd been hurt and she had the August-Raynes crest on her corset."

Cordelia clucked her tongue, still looking at the image. "Taking in strays again? You don't have to save everyone, you know."

Griff chuckled. "She can take care of herself. I find her intriguing. It's as if Finley—Miss Jayne—is two people in one body."

Cordelia stiffened and suddenly straightened like a marionette with its strings yanked. "What did you say?"

Bewildered, Griff frowned. "I said it was as though Miss Jayne was two people in the same body."

When his aunt turned to face him, she was pale. "I would like to meet this guest of yours. I think I might know her."

"Really?" Griffin couldn't believe the luck! "How extraordinary."

His aunt clasped him by the shoulder. "Don't get your hopes up, dearest. In fact, I've never hoped to be more mistaken in all my life. If she is who I think she is, then we may all be in very grave danger indeed."

Chapter 6

Finley was still half-asleep when she was "summoned" to Griffin's study late that morning. Her memories of the night before were somewhat foggy—as they always were when the darker side of her nature took over. She vaguely remembered Whitechapel and the enigmatic Jack Dandy—the thought of his dark eyes sent a tremor to the base of her spine. What had she been thinking going to such a place to see such a man?

She had to get this under control or someday her other half would get them—*her*—killed.

So it was with some trepidation that she entered the study, wearing an embroidered silver-silk dress of Oriental design— one of the more sedate clothing selections in her closet. It was sleeveless and had knee-high slits on either side. Over it she wore a cherry-red corset with little silver dragons stitched on. The clothing felt appropriate—like armor for going into battle.

Where had the clothing come from? More hand-me-downs

from the absent aunt? Or had the duke actually purchased the items for her? She hoped it was the former. She couldn't afford to repay the latter.

Had he heard of her adventure and decided to turn her out? She'd been cast into the street before, so there was no need for this sudden chill of fear—except that Griffin had made her think he could help her and she desperately wanted that help.

She didn't want to live like this—as though something crawled beneath her skin wanting out. It was getting worse. Last night, she'd had no control over herself and she'd walked boldly into very dangerous territory. Fortunately, the "other her" seemed to be right at home with danger and had managed to escape in one piece.

Griffin's head turned at her arrival. He was sitting on the edge of his desk, dressed in a white shirt, dark plum waistcoat, black trousers and boots. His hair looked mussed, as though he'd been running his hands through it. He had a woman beside him. A pretty woman about Finley's size but older, and much more refined in a silky gray gown in the latest fashion. She had to be family because she and Griff had the same eyes—like a spring sky about to be taken over by storm clouds. When she turned her head, Finley saw the fine chains that ran from her nose to ear. But it wasn't until those stormy eyes met hers and she felt a strange sensation in her head that Finley knew this woman was anything but ordinary.

The thing inside her reared up like a giant hand and came crashing down on the buzzing in her brain, squashing it like a bug.

The woman flinched.

"I beg your pardon," Finley said, a little shaken at having been protected by that shadow of herself—at needing to be protected, "but isn't it a little rude to crawl about in someone's mind without permission?"

Griffin's expression was all surprise and censure as he glanced at his companion. "Aunt Delia, you didn't."

The woman rubbed two fingers against her temple. "I did, but I was promptly shut out." She looked at Finley in a manner that was both distrusting and respectful. "Well done."

Finley didn't know what to say to that, and since there was no way to explain it, she kept silent. Griffin spoke instead, introducing her to the woman, who was his aunt Cordelia, Lady Marsden, recently returned to London.

"Cordelia is a telepath," Griff explained. "And telekinetic. That is to say—"

"She has a very powerful mind," Finley interrupted. "I've noticed." Not only because the woman had tried to intrude upon her thoughts, but because she'd held out her arm toward one of the bookcases and a leather-bound journal had flown off the shelf into her hand.

"That must make you very entertaining at parties," Finley said to the woman, a tad snidely.

"And at court," Lady Marsden replied with equal bite. She passed the book to Griffin. "Tell me, Miss Jayne, is your mother's name Mary by any chance?"

"It is," Finley replied, trying not to look too shocked. "What else did you see inside my mind?"

"The only thing I saw in your head, my girl, was my nephew's visage next to that of Jack Dandy. Might I say what interesting company you keep."

Finley flushed as Griff stared at her, but she held the older woman's gaze. It was obvious that Griff's aunt neither liked nor trusted her. "Who I see is none of your concern, ma'am."

The woman stiffened. "While you're in this house—"

"She's my concern," Griffin interjected. "Not yours, Aunt, and this conversation is getting way off track. Why don't you enlighten both Miss Jayne and me as to how you knew her mother's name?"

Lady Marsden looked both mollified and embarrassed. She no doubt was not accustomed to her nephew speaking to her in such a manner in front of others. "It's in the book," she said with a lift of her chin. The book in Griff's hands opened, the pages seeming to flip on their own, though Finley knew it was the power of his aunt's mind that moved them. Finally, they lay still, open to a page of photographs.

Finley moved closer, drawn by her own curiosity. She stood beside Griff and peered at one of the tea-colored images adhered to the page. It depicted a small group of people standing next to a strange vehicle that looked like a metal carriage with a large drill on the front of it. The man standing closest to it with his hand on the vehicle looked so much like Griff he could only be his father, the late duke. Next to him was a beautiful woman she took to be the duchess. There were other people, as well, but Finley gave them little notice as her gaze fell upon the man and the woman farthest away. The man she didn't recognize, but the woman she did. Though this photograph had to have been taken almost twenty years ago, she knew her mother's face.

Astonished, she looked up and saw Griff's aunt watching her warily. "This is my mother," she said unnecessarily.

Lady Marsden inclined her head. "Yes."

"Who's the man with her?" Griffin asked.

His aunt smiled tightly. "That would be Thomas Sheppard. He was a great scientist." Her gaze cut to Finley. "And Mary's husband."

The bottom of Finley's stomach felt as though it had dropped to the floor. "But that would mean…"

Lady Marsden nodded. "Your father, yes."

Finley had always despised those girls who fainted anytime

something fantastic or surprising happened, but at that moment she felt as though her knees might give way. Her head spun and she clutched at Griff's arm for support.

She had never seen a photo of her father before this day. He mother said she hadn't any.

"My father's name was Thomas Jayne, not Thomas Sheppard." Even if she said the words, they tasted like a lie. There was enough of her own looks in Thomas Sheppard's face to prove his indentity.

"Then perhaps we should call upon your mother," Lady Marsden suggested, a note of challenge in her voice. "I had heard that Thomas and Mary had a daughter they named Finley *Jane* Sheppard. What a coincidence you made your way here after all these years, your parents having been so closely tied to my brother and his wife."

Finley stared at her and finally understood. Her ladyship thought she'd machinated all of this to get into Griffin's household. She believed Finley to be capable of throwing herself in front of a moving vehicle, risking injury to capture His Grace's attention. Seeing Jack Dandy in her thoughts only solidified what Cordelia King-Ashworth already believed— that Finley was a liar, possibly a criminal and not to be trusted. That her being in that house was simply too much of a coincidence.

To be honest, Finley thought exactly the same thing. She'd never been much for believing in destiny or fate, but it certainly seemed as though she and Griffin had been connected long before they'd ever met.

"Yes," she agreed, obviously surprising Lady Marsden. "We should visit my mother." In truth, she'd rather stick pins in her eye. She didn't want to hear what her mother had to say about the photograph and Thomas Sheppard, not because she thought her mother would lie, but because she was very much afraid of the truth.

Sam was sitting at the dining-room table, reading the paper and eating his usual breakfast of oatmeal, sausage, ham, eggs, fried potatoes, toast and coffee when Griffin walked in.

"Hello, Samuel," Griff said, going to the sideboard and pouring himself a cup of coffee.

Sam's spine went rigid. Had Emily put metal in his back, too? he wondered bitterly, waiting for his friend to make some remark about it being closer to luncheon than breakfast time, or to ask what hour Sam had returned home. It was none of Griff's business, and it wasn't as though *he* ever felt the need to explain himself. Sam could come and go as he pleased, as well, but that didn't change the little worm of guilt swimming uneasily in his stomach.

"Morning," Sam replied somewhat gruffly.

"Did you sleep well?" the other boy inquired.

Here it came, thought Sam. An interrogation. "Yes."

Griff nodded. "Excellent. Listen, Aunt Delia is back. She and I are taking Finley to visit her mother. Seems there may be a connection between Finley's father and my parents."

This was what he'd missed by being out late and sleeping the morning away. He knew there was more to Finley than they first thought, and now it seemed they were about to find out just what. Though he ought to thank her for taking Griffin's attention off him.

"Do you need me to come along?"

"No need. Although, if Emily comes down, let her know what's going on, will you?"

Emily. The thought of seeing her again filled him with a mix of eagerness and dread. He'd been so angry at her, so hurt and…well, he didn't know what else. He was still angry, still hurt, but he knew he should apologize.

"I'll tell her," he said, noticing that Griff had been watching him, waiting for a reply.

His old friend smiled. To Sam, Griffin looked relieved. "Thank you. And, Sam?"

He had lifted his fork in an attempt to resume his rapidly cooling breakfast, and gritted his teeth as he raised his head once more. "What?"

The smile, and the relief were gone. All that he saw was Griff's unapologetic face. "I told Emily to do whatever necessary to save your life. If you're going to be mad at anyone, it should be me."

Too stunned to say anything, Sam just sat there in stupefied silence. Coffee in hand, Griff left the room without a backward glance and all Sam could do was watch him go as betrayal and anger ignited in his gut and slowly set him ablaze.

Were he not so bloody hungry, he would have thrown his plate, but someone would have to clean that up. Instead, he finished his breakfast. Then, he got up and went to Griff's study. He stood there, in the room he'd spent so much time in during the course of his life, and looked for something to destroy that hadn't belonged to the former duke, that was solely Griffin's.

His gaze fell upon the Aether engine Emily had built so Griffin could access the Aether without becoming part of it. It was a testament to Emily's brilliance and Griff's power. If he ruined it, both of them would be hurt by it. Both of them would feel as he did at that very moment—betrayed, bewildered.

It would be so easy. The engine was right in front of him now. His mechanical arm would reduce the entire rig to rubble in seconds. All he had to do was make a fist and swing.

*"I replaced your heart."* The words rang in his head as his fingers curled into his palm. *"If you're going to be mad at anyone, it should be me."* The voices of Emily and Griff overlapped in his mind, creating a cacophony of misery he couldn't silence.

They had ruined him out of love. Ruining this thing the two of them had built might ease his anger, but he wouldn't feel good about it. He would want to apologize later. Neither Griff nor Emily would ever apologize for what they'd done to him because it had saved his life. To them that was all that mattered. Even now, knowing how angry he was and how much he despised the metal parts of himself, they would do it all over again because they would rather have him as a mess than not have him at all.

It wouldn't even matter that he loathed them for it.

Sam lowered his fist and left the study. He wrote a note for Emily telling her where Griffin had gone and slipped it under her door. Then he went to his own room. He tossed some clothes and a few personal items into a bag before heading to the stables and climbing on his velocycle. He needed to get away. He needed to think.

Most of all, he needed to put as much space as he could between himself and the people who loved him.

Finley's mother and her husband lived in Chelsea, which was just enough of a distance to make being stuck in a steam carriage with Griffin and his aunt uncomfortable.

Finley had never been in a carriage this fine before. The outside was a glossy black, the driver perched up high in a padded seat. Plumes of white steam rose from the shiny exhaust pipe that ran from the steam engine up the side of the carriage. The interior was all soft velvet, so dark a blue it was almost black. Though there were lamps on either wall for nighttime travel, it was dim inside the coach with the shades drawn.

They didn't speak. There were a hundred and one questions she wanted to ask, but there wasn't any point until they met with her mother. If what Lady Marsden said was true, then her mother had lied to her when she was a child and continued to lie until this very day. Why?

She sat next to the lady on the carriage seat. Griffin sat across from them, looking every inch the haughty duke in his pristine cravat, black jacket and dark gray trousers. He wore a long black greatcoat of soft leather over the ensemble, and carried a silver-topped walking stick. She had heard of gentlemen carrying swords concealed in their canes. She wondered if Griffin was such a gentleman.

Every once in a while she caught him watching her with absolutely no expression on his face or in his eyes. He must be a very good card player. It made her nervous. It made that other part of her nervous, too—nervous and indignant. Part of her wanted to slap him, even though she didn't blame him for thinking the worst of her.

Finley opened the shade on her window just enough so that she could peek out at the passing scenery. She leaned her temple against the velvet-covered wall and watched hackney coaches, still pulled by horses, lumber past. Omnibuses, run by coal-fed engines cast grime-laden soot—like dark thunderclouds—into the damp air. Public transportation was nowhere near as luxurious as this vehicle. She doubted the Duke of Greythorne or his snooty aunt had ever seen the inside of an omnibus, or the third-class seating section in a dirigible—nor the second-class section, for that matter. They took this opulence for granted.

She didn't know whether she envied them or pitied them.

What must it be like to have all these fine things and not truly appreciate just how fine they were?

The rhythmic chugging of the carriage's engine lulled her into a false sense of relaxation despite the questions gnawing at her mind. The rain had stopped but the day was still overcast and gray, making her long for a fire and warm bed to hide in. She would pull the covers up over her head and sleep until this nightmare was all over.

She was almost asleep, just drifting in that weightless, careless world between waking and dreaming, when she felt a push inside her head. It was ever so faint, like the brush of a butterfly's wing, but she felt it.

Lady Marsden was trying to get inside her head again.

This time Finley didn't immediately terminate the telepath's rude intrusion. Instead, it was as though some part of her mind got up off a sofa, walked calmly across the room and slowly, but firmly, closed a door to shut her out.

Out of the corner of her eye, she saw Griffin's aunt turn her head toward her, so Finley angled her own head, still resting near the window, to meet the older woman's gaze.

"What *are* you?" Lady Marsden asked, not bothering to hide her surprise. Obviously the lady was not accustomed to being caught snooping, let alone shut down twice.

"I have no idea," Finley replied honestly. She started to turn back to the window but Griff was staring at her with a glint in his eye she found hard to ignore. He watched her as though she was some kind of exotic animal—one he thought might bite him, even as he was sticking his hand into the cage.

Why had he been able to soothe her so easily before? Why hadn't she felt him in her head as she felt his aunt? Or was his "magic" something different?

What did he think of her now? More importantly how could her parents possibly have known his? They were from two different worlds. He was rich and Finley and her mother had been anything but before her mother's remarriage. Even still, Finley had decided to go out on her own and support herself rather than be a burden.

Silas Burke's bookstore was located in Russell Square. He and Finley's mother lived in a set of comfortable rooms above the shop. Finley had lived there, as well, until eight months ago when she moved out to go work as a nanny. That post had lasted a little longer than the others, but once her mercurial moods began to frighten the children, she was let go. At least they gave her a good reference.

There were a few curious stares as they stepped out of the carriage, first Griffin who then stood to assist both his aunt and Finley. Silas Burke, Bookseller, did a good business and books were something only people with money could afford to purchase, but dukes were rare in the peerage and seeing one was always something of an event. Seeing someone they recognized as one of their own—in this case, Finley—in the company of a duke was even more exciting. More gossip worthy.

But as soon as Finley stepped inside the shop, her ire and anxiety eased as negative feelings always did when she caught the smell of paper, ink and leather mixed with her stepfather's sweet pipe tobacco.

Fanny, the spindly automaton that assisted around the store, was at the shelves, placing a volume on the top of one of the many ceiling-high cases, her long arm extending even farther with a series of clicks and pops until it had the desired reach. The book slid easily onto the shelf and then Fanny's arm retracted. The automaton needed a good oiling judging by the grinding sound that accompanied the movement.

"Hullo, Fanny," Finley greeted with a smile, not expecting to hear a reply—Fanny didn't have a voice box as some new metal did, nor was she programmed to respond. Still, Finley had always talked to the ancient android, and it seemed wrong not to do the same now.

She didn't see either Silas or her mother, but it was luncheon time for working folk. Griffin and his aunt wouldn't take their repast for another two hours, and they would still be enjoying their supper when Finley's mother readied for bed. She didn't feel any resentment for these differences, but they did make her wonder just what the devil she was doing in their company when it was so obvious she didn't belong.

The bell over the door had chimed when they entered. By now, her stepfather would be on his way back down here. Finley blocked out all other sounds and listened. She heard Silas's voice, and the opening of a door.

"My stepfather is on his way," she told her companions, a bit of her nervousness returning.

Lady Marsden regarded her closely. "You can hear him." It was a statement, not a question, so Finley didn't bother to respond. It was almost as though the marchioness was accusing her of something nasty. She felt guilty just standing there in what was essentially her own home.

When the door that led upstairs opened at the back of the shop, Finley ran to greet her stepfather and was met with a pair of open arms.

Silas Burke was of moderate height and build. In fact, everything about him was moderate—his temperament, his income, his appearance. He was nothing extraordinary except to his wife and stepdaughter.

"Oh, ho!" he cried, practically sweeping off her feet. "Look who we have here! Mary, see who's come for a visit!"

Smiling, Finley looked up into his warm brown eyes, framed by deep grooves that proved his good nature. When she heard her mother's footsteps on the stairs, she stepped out from around Silas to greet her, as well. More hugging and laughing followed. It wasn't until her mother stepped into the store for introductions that Finley remembered she wasn't there for a pleasant visit. Her mother's pale face as she stared at Lady Marsden made Finley's stomach drop.

"What are you doing here?" her mother demanded of Lady Marsden, drawing a shocked glance from her husband.

"Mary!" he exclaimed, his face flushing. It was terribly rude to speak to a lady of rank in such a tone, but Finley's mother wasn't about to apologize.

"I told you people to leave us alone." Her mother practically trembled with rage. "Edward said we were safe—that we would never be bothered again."

"You know each other?" Not that Finley needed an acknowledgment, but she wanted to hear it all the same.

It was Lady Marsden who answered. "We used to. Although, Mrs. Burke and I haven't seen each other since I was but a girl. Edward was my late brother. How are you, Mary?"

Finley frowned. For Griffin's aunt to refer to her mother by her Christian name, or for her mother to refer to the late duke in a similar manner, they must have known each other very well indeed at one time. Her only consolation in this confusion was that Griffin didn't seem any more aware of what was going on than she was.

Her mother, back stiff as a board, replied, "I was very well until a few moments ago."

There could be no mistaking the insult this time. "Mama, we need to talk to you," Finley said, taking control before her mother did something foolish like toss the marchioness out of the shop. "May we go upstairs where it's more private?"

Her mother looked as though she'd rather swallow rat poison than go anywhere with Lady Marsden, but the gentle slump of her shoulders signaled defeat. That innocent gesture formed a cannonball of dread in Finley's gut. She wasn't sure she wanted to have this conversation anymore, no matter how much she wanted to discover how to fix what was wrong with her.

The lot of them climbed the stairs in single file, Finley's mother leading the way and Silas at the rear. He'd even gone so far as to flip the Closed sign over and lock the door so they wouldn't be disturbed.

Burke's home was a comfortable space—certainly not as grand as the Duke of Greythorne's mansion, but welcoming and warm. Fitzhugh, the family cat, trotted over to Finley and twined himself between her ankles before rubbing his head against Griffin's calf. To his credit, the duke bent down with a smile to pet the fluffy orange tom.

"I apologize for the intrusion," he spoke, rising to offer Silas his hand. "It's just that I discovered a strange connection between our families and I'd like to learn more. I'm sure Finley would, as well."

Mary's eyebrow rose at the familiar use of her daughter's name, and Finley blushed a little. She straightened her shoulders. "Mama, how is it possible that you and my father knew His Grace's parents?" She couldn't help but sound incredulous. It was too strange to fathom. "Is it true that my father was Thomas Sheppard, not Thomas Jayne?"

Her mother looked as though she might be ill. Surprisingly, Lady Marsden came to the rescue. "Perhaps we should sit?"

Mary nodded. Her face was pale, but she led the way to the small parlor where Finley had often lain about and read on a Sunday afternoon.

They seated themselves almost as if preparing for battle— The Burkes on one sofa, Griffin and his aunt on the other. This left Finley to sit by herself in a high-backed chair. How appropriate that she be odd man out, as that was actually how she felt.

"I'm not certain where to start," her mother remarked, a hint of anxiety in her voice.

Silas reached over and took her hand in his own. "The beginning is often a good place."

Mary smiled at him. For the first time in her short life, Finley was jealous of their relationship. She wanted someone to look at her like that—like she hung the moon and stars.

"Thomas Sheppard—your father—and I met the previous Duke of Greythorne more than twenty years ago. It was at a scientific lecture your father was giving on the dual nature of man. The two immediately struck up a friendship despite the difference in social stature. The duke became something of a patron to Thomas, funding many of his experiments." As she spoke, a faint smile curved her lips.

Finley stared at her mother. How could she not have heard any of this before? Why had Mama lied about her true surname? Her father must have been a brilliant man, an important man, and yet her mother rarely spoke of him. She didn't ask this, however, but allowed her mother to reveal what she would.

"Thomas often experimented on himself when no other subject was available. He believed man's evil side the result of an imbalance in the humors. Purity was the balance of the four—sanguine, melancholy, phlegmatic and choleric. By creating an imbalance in any number of the four, he believed he would discover a way to treat not only criminal behavior, but madness, as well." Mary shot a pointed look at Lady Marsden. "Greythorne agreed and sanctioned further research. He even gave Thomas compounds to work with. One night, I watched as he took one of the new potions himself." She stopped, but no one made a sound. Even Lady Marsden was watching with noticeable sympathy in her eyes.

Finley stared at her mother, who had dropped her gaze to her own trembling fingers. "That night I watched as my husband became…" She pressed her fingers to her mouth as her voice broke. Her other hand still held tightly to Silas's. "He became a different man, in every way. His appearance changed and he became like a wild thing, base and crass. I didn't know what to do so I sent for the duke. He made Thomas drink another potion that turned him back to his former self. The two of them laughed and celebrated—congratulating each other as though my husband's turning into a monster was a good thing!" At this point, Mary's attention jerked to Griffin, as though pleading with him to understand.

And Griffin, it seemed, did. "They continued with the experiments, didn't they?"

Mary nodded. "Thomas continued to use himself as a subject oftentimes, with varying degrees of results. There were nights that I left the house altogether for fear of what he might become."

Finley made a small sound low in her throat. Things were becoming all too clear now. "Did he… Was he conducting these experiments before I was born?"

Her mother could barely look at her, hesitated, then nodded. A hot, prickly sensation raced from the top of Finley's head straight to her stomach. For a moment, she thought she might actually swoon.

She was the way she was because her father had been experimenting on himself when he impregnated her mother. He had made her this way. How could she ever fix what was wrong with her when it was in her blood?

She looked at Griffin, who had an almost apologetic expression on his face. Of course he would look that way—his father had encouraged hers to become a monster. But Lady Marsden's expression was almost triumphant, satisfied—as though she'd forced Finley to own up to a lie.

She believed Finley had known this all along. That Finley had been using Griffin to get revenge.

Rage washed over her with the swiftness of a sudden wind, tearing down the delicate walls she'd built inside herself to protect what she considered the "good" side of herself from the bad. In an instant Finley went from sitting demurely in her chair to seizing Lady Marsden by the throat, lifting her, the fingers of her right hand like claws, itching to tear out those damnable mocking eyes.

Behind her, her mother and stepfather cried out, but neither made a move to stop her.

"Would you like to know what I'm thinking now?" Finley asked, almost fully controlled by her darker nature. She could snap this woman's frail neck.

Lady Marsden's eyes widened, but she made no other move. Finley felt a slight push against her mind—a sweet voice cajoling her to let go. Mentally, she squashed it like a bug beneath her boot. Crunchy.

The marchioness winced. One would think the silly woman would know better by now.

Finley smiled. "You annoy me, your ladyship. In a most vexing manner."

And then a strong hand gripped her arm—the one poised to strike above her ladyship's face. "She's not the one you want to hurt," Griffin said in that melodic voice of his.

Finley turned her head, but she didn't let go. "No? Because I have to tell you, this feels pretty good right now."

He reached over and took hold of her other wrist, as well. Gently, but firmly, he pulled her hand from his aunt's neck. Finley let him do it. She knew she was physically stronger than he was, but there was something about his voice and the way he spoke to her that took the anger out of her and made her want to do what he said. That terrified her even as the darkness eased from her soul. What else could he make her do if he wanted?

She whirled on him, but he kept his hold on one of her wrists. His other hand, instead of coming up to defend himself as she thought it would, circled her waist, pulling her against him. He hugged her. Letting go of her wrist, he cupped the back of her head, holding her so her face was in the crook of his neck. He smelled warm and spicy—like cinnamon and cloves. Safe, and comforting. As he held her, he murmured soft words. She wasn't even sure if any of them made sense, but she listened all the same, too shocked by this display of concern—of trust. It would take little effort for her to hurt him right now. She could hurt him badly.

But Griffin King could hurt her, as well, and he hadn't. Instead of using force or violence against her, he used patience and understanding. She had no defense against that.

When he let her go, she was shaking. Tears filled her eyes as she turned to her mother who stood staring at her in horror.

"My sweet little girl," her mother whispered. "I didn't know. I would never…" Her words faded into a choked sob. Finley crossed the short distance between them on quivering legs and wrapped her arms around the shorter woman. She didn't care if Griffin or his nasty aunt saw her tears. If anything was worth crying over, the discovery that her father had made her a monster had to be one.

# Chapter 7

You owe Finley an apology." Griffin and Cordelia were alone now, having sent Finley to her room for rest—something the poor girl no doubt needed, along with time to process everything they'd learned that day.

Cordelia shot him a sharp look. "For trying to kill me? I think not."

"For believing that she'd lied about her father," Griff retorted, closing the study door. "She had no idea of what the man was up to."

She picked up the chunk of teal ore he used as a paperweight and pretended to study it. "So she claims."

"Cordelia, not even you are good enough an actress to put forth such a performance." He folded his arms over his chest. "Finley Jayne is a victim in all of this, not our enemy. If anything, it's my responsibility to help her."

"For something that happened before you were born? Rubbish."

"Why? You were content to blame her on the same criteria."

His aunt pursed her lips and Griffin knew she couldn't argue. "Our fathers made a mistake and now Finley's paying for it. I think she deserves our help, don't you?"

Cordelia shrugged somewhat sullenly. Times like this reminded Griffin that she wasn't even ten years his senior.

Griffin sighed and pushed a button on the box atop his desk. "I'm going to have some coffee, during which I'm going to read Father's notes on Thomas Sheppard. Then, I'm going to sit down with Finley. I can't image how she feels knowing her father was the inspiration for Jekyll and Hyde." That had been a tidbit that came out earlier in the afternoon—courtesy of Cordelia, of course.

His aunt set the ore on the desk once more. "Sheppard was careless. There was gossip. Of course he provoked Stevenson's interest. Finley will do the same if she's not careful, which she won't be. She could call undue attention to all of us."

And by that she meant Griffin most of all. He shook his head. "And that gives you the right to be mean to her?"

His aunt turned to stare at him, as though she could not believe he'd question her. "She pushed me out of her mind, not once but three times. Do you know the number of people who have ever been able to do that? None! Whether or not you want to admit it, that girl's dangerous—and you treat her like a houseguest!"

"She *is* a guest."

"Until she snaps someone's neck. What if she attacks Emily?"

"She won't." If only he felt as certain as he sounded.

"You have no way of knowing that. Mrs. Dodsworth told me how she threw the footman as though he was nothing more than a toy. You put everyone in this house in danger by having her here. I cannot allow it."

Griff stiffened. He met his aunt's gaze carefully, fighting to keep his anger under control. "You have no say. It's my house."

Cordelia scowled, fists on her hips. "I am your guardian."

"Do you really want to fight me, Delia? Because I'm certain the family solicitors will side with me." Of course they would, they knew it was Griff's fortune that paid their bills, that Cordelia ran things in name only. It was Griff who made estate decisions.

His aunt looked at him as though he'd slapped her. "She's that important to you?"

He nodded. "She is. I can't explain why, but I know she belongs here, with the rest of us."

"She'll never be able to be part of something while she's two halves of a broken whole."

Griff smiled slightly, knowing he'd won without driving too much of a wedge between himself and his aunt. "Then we'll just have to put her back together."

Cordelia arched a brow. "We?" But Griff knew she would help him. She always did. Sooner or later, she would see that he was right about Finley.

His coffee arrived—an entire silver pot full, piping hot and smelling like heaven. He poured some into the china cup and added cream and sugar. When it was the perfect color and sweetness, he took a drink. It was good.

Cordelia took her leave—she had plans for tea and had to change first. Griffin sat down at his desk after finding a journal of his father's marked "Thomas Sheppard." His father had kept copious notes on all aspects of his life—a habit Griffin did not share.

His father's notes only backed up what Finley's mother had

told them—that Thomas Sheppard had been conducting experiments with his father on the dark vs. pure side of human nature. Sheppard took to experimenting on himself, unsure of what his potions might do to others. What he'd done had enabled his darker nature to totally obliterate his good, and vice versa. He split himself into two opposite halves. Apparently he tried to stop the experiments once he found out Mary was expecting Finley, but by then it was too late—the metamorphosis was happening on its own without the aid of chemistry. The damage had already been done. Though Sheppard hadn't known it at the time, he had passed his affliction onto his unborn daughter.

Sadly, Thomas Sheppard was killed shortly before Finley's first birthday. He'd been overtaken by a seizure away from home, metamorphosing into his dark self. He hurt someone who got in his way and that set the Peelers after him. In his quest to escape, Sheppard had tried to steal a carriage and was shot by the owner. The officers who took the wounded man to Scotland Yard were shocked when he changed from his almost bestial form into that of a soft-spoken scholar. Thomas Sheppard died before the surgeon could attend him.

His father's notes went on to express a sense of responsibility for Mary Sheppard and her daughter, but the woman disappeared, refusing the duke's help. There was also regret. Griffin's father wrote, *"If only I had not provided the catalyst for Sheppard's drastic transformation. It makes me fear for my own family."*

What had his father given Sheppard? Was it the same mysterious "catalyst" as that which had caused both Griffin and Sam to develop their abilities? If so, why hadn't they been driven mad like Sheppard? Why were they not affected in a similar fashion?

He turned his attention to the final notes on the page. His

father was worried about Mary and her child, worried what effects their experiments might have had upon Sheppard's daughter.

Poor Finley. Not only had she discovered the tragic truth about her father, but she must be terrified that the same fate awaited her.

Despite her violence against Cordelia earlier, he believed it was possible for Finley to control her darker side. In fact, he believed that uniting the two sides of her nature was the only answer. No person was entirely good or entirely evil—one side could not exist without the other. He just had to figure out how to make Finley whole again.

He poured another cup of coffee—his third since sitting down—and rose from his desk. He wanted to research Thomas Sheppard on the Aether engine, as well, but before that he wanted to check in on Finley. He needed to go down into Emily's laboratory and talk to her about the defective automatons—and about Sam, who was notably absent once again.

He also wanted to contact an acquaintance of his who ran in a different circle than he did. Jasper Renn was an American he'd met late last year. In fact, the cowboy had saved him from having his head coshed in by a band of ruffians intent on robbing a fancy toff. If not for Jasper, Griffin would have been forced to use his abilities in public, and that wouldn't have been a good thing. Afterward, Griffin had brought Jasper back to the house for a drink and a little of Emily's medical attention for his wounds. Since then, the two of them enjoyed a mutually beneficial friendship—helping each other out of trouble and occasionally attending a mech-boxing match together.

Jasper spent a lot of time in the gaming hells and clubs around Covent Garden and other east-end establishments. If there was talk about these automatons and their maker on the street, then he would know of it.

Griffin had to get to the bottom of these automaton attacks. He couldn't ignore them just because Finley Jayne posed such an intriguing problem in such a pretty package.

And she was pretty—even when off her rocker. In that respect, she was every bit as dangerous as Aunt Cordelia seemed to think.

It was a good thing, then, that he enjoyed a little danger now and again.

"You look like a man in need of a drink."

Sam looked up from his empty tankard. Leon, his friend with the mechanical hand, stood beside his table. "If I have another, I'm likely to fall asleep in a puddle of drool on this table."

"Would that be such a bad thing?" Leon asked in his melodic accent—Italian, he'd said he was—as he sat down.

Sam smiled. "It's a dirty table."

His companion chuckled. "This is the second time I've found you here, my friend. You're obviously troubled. Perhaps I can help."

It was on the tip of Sam's tongue to declare that an impossibility—that no one could possibly help him—but then his gaze fell upon Leon's etched, metal hand.

"Do you ever regret that?"

Leon, who had at this point raised his other hand to signal for a waitress, glanced at the metallic appendage. "What, this? No. It's not quite as good as the real thing, but you would be surprised at just how much I am able to do because of this marvel of modern science."

Sam almost snorted, but didn't. "You don't mind being part machine then?"

The older man frowned—just as two tankards of ale were set on the table between them by a round-faced, ginger-haired girl. "Of course not. Does it bother you? I can wear a glove."

"No." Sam shook his head. Making the man wear a glove just because he couldn't stand himself seemed stupid. "Don't do that. It doesn't bother me."

Leon smiled. "You are just curious, yes? I get a lot of that. People wanting to know how I came about to have it. You have yet to ask me."

Sam shrugged. "None of my business. I figure you'll tell me if you want me to know."

His companion lifted his tankard to his mouth. His dark eyes shone with something that looked like amusement. "It was an accident. I was working on a burrower automaton and my hand got caught in the gears."

"A burrower?" Sam's mouth went dry as he fought back memories of his own experience with a large machine. Diggers were larger as they dug into the earth rather than drilling into it as burrowers did. Still, a burrower could do a lot of damage to a man. "That's awful."

Leon inclined his head. "It was, but I survived. Now, I'm more careful when I work on any machine, automaton or no."

"You still work with them? Aren't...aren't you afraid?"

"I was, for a bit, but the automaton did not hurt me on purpose. It was my fault, not the machine's. I wasn't as careful as I should have been."

Sam lifted his tankard to his lips. He was starting to sober up. "Kind of a slap in the face, though, them giving you a metal hand." He couldn't help but think of all the metal in his own body.

Leon looked surprised. "My dear sir, this work of art was *my* choice."

His tankard hit the table with more force than intended.

"Why the devil would you choose to be partially metal when that's what took your hand in the first place?" There were other options—wood and wax for two.

Leon flexed the shiny appendage. Sam watched, entranced as the jointed fingers gracefully opened and closed. "I chose it because I made it. There's not an artificial limb anywhere that can compare to this one. I can do everything a whole man can do—perhaps more, because I can do work so fine and intricate it would make your eyes cross."

But Sam hardly heard him. "You built it." Emily would find this man fascinating.

"Yes. I told you it was my choice."

"Wish I'd had a choice," Sam grumbled into his ale.

Leon frowned, leaning across the table. "What do you mean?"

Sam met his gaze. There was nothing but sincerity and confusion there. He made up his mind right then that Leon was someone he could trust—someone who just might relate to what he was going through. Who might understand.

"I mean, I wasn't given a choice when an automaton tore my arm off. It was replaced with metal."

The older man's perplexed gaze immediately dropped to Sam's hands. "But…but you are flesh!"

Sam took another drink, smiling for the first time all day. "It's a long story."

Leon signaled for the waitress again before turning and leaning his forearms on the table. "My friend, I have all night."

"I need to talk to you."

Griffin glanced up from his desk. He'd been sitting there for hours, and Emily was a welcome intrusion. Now he needn't go looking for her. He smiled as he looked at her, noticing she was paler than usual. "Come talk, then."

He left the desk as his friend came deeper into the room. He'd been poring over Thomas Sheppard's notes—which he'd found in his father's safe there in the study—trying to better understand Finley and how to help her. But Sheppard had been all about isolating parts of man's personality, rather than bringing them together. He did have some research on reha- bilitating the criminal and the insane, but Griff wasn't about to try these methods on Finley.

At least he knew now what it was his father gave him to experiment with—the ore and a sample of Organites. He just couldn't quite figure out how these things could have brought about the changes Sheppard mentioned. The answer was so close he could taste it, and it vexed him to the point where he was ready to break something.

"Have you found something in the automatons?" Griff asked, rubbing his eyes as he sat down on the sofa.

Emily shook her head. "Not yet." She cast a nervous glance around the room, as though making certain they were alone. "That's not why I'm here, lad."

"Is it Sam?" It wasn't like his friend to stay gone this long— though he had to be angry knowing what Griff had allowed Emily to do.

Wrapping her arms around herself, Emily shook her head. It was obvious she felt Sam's absence, as well—and that she felt just as responsible as Griffin did for it. "No. It's not about Sam. It's about me."

Griffin's eyebrows shot up. Emily rarely talked about herself or her past. He wasn't certain he was ready to hear whatever it was she was about to share. "What is it?"

"I've noticed lately I've been goin' through some peculiar… changes."

Oh, lord. Had no one ever talked to her about these things? Her mother? "What sort of changes?"

Her fingers tangled together in her lap. She had black beneath her nails from working in her laboratory. "Remember when you told me about how you first learned about your abilities?"

He nodded. "I told you about the first ghost I saw."

"Three months ago, you told me you sometimes felt as though the Aether might swallow you whole if you let it."

Griff closed his eyes. He shouldn't have told her that. "I believe I said I thought my talents were increasing."

She scooted closer, perching on the edge of her seat. "I think… I reckon something's happening to me, lad. Something strange."

Caught between curiosity, concern and irritation, Griffin frowned. "What is it, Em?"

"It might be better if I showed you."

"Show me then."

The girl got up from where she sat and hesitantly walked over to the phonograph in the corner. Instead of operating by setting a needle into a flat disc, Emily had moderated it to work with metal punch cards of her design. They wouldn't "warp" like discs or scratch so easily. And instead of winding it, there was a tiny steam engine built in so it could play for longer periods of time, punch card after punch card.

Emily, looking tiny in her knee-length ruffled trousers, billowy shirt and grungy leather corset, tugged absently on one of the ropes of her bright red hair as she reached a pale hand toward the machine. Griff watched in amazement as the phonograph whirred to life at her touch. Emily closed her eyes, an expression of concentration on her face. The phonograph shuffled through the punch cards until it found a harpsichord piece Griff knew to be one of Emily's favorites.

As the song began to play, the volume increased, as well—all without Emily even turning the key to start the machine's engine. Technically, the phonograph wasn't even *on*.

The music played for a few brief moments, but ended abruptly when Emily removed her hand. She looked at Griff over her shoulder. He couldn't tell if she was proud or terrified.

"I can tell them what to do," she said. "Machines. And sometimes, I think I understand them, too."

"Incredible," Griffin remarked, awestruck. He had risen to his feet during the amazing demonstration and now leaned against the sofa. He ran a hand through his hair. Words eluded him.

Emily didn't look so convinced. "What's wrong with me?"

It hadn't occurred to Griffin, who'd had "abnormal" abilities from a very young age, that these new talents would scare his friend. He supposed they felt the same way he would if suddenly he wasn't able to consult the Aether.

"Dormant abilities?" It was a guess at best. Then he thought about it. Hadn't he noticed changes in himself over the past six months to a year? Subtle changes, but the fact remained that his own powers had increased significantly. To the point where he fought for control at times.

"We're evolving," he murmured. He knew it sounded preposterous but what other explanation was there? "I don't know why or how, but we are."

"What about Sam?" Emily asked. "Has he mentioned any new abilities?"

"He might not be aware of any changes, or attributes them to his automatonic enhancements. Besides, I don't think he'd tell any of us right now even if he had."

"It's not as though we can ask him," Emily commented. "He's off somewhere again."

Griffin noticed how Emily's face fell as she spoke. "Em, Sam's behavior is not your fault. It's not anyone's fault. You did what you did to save him and I told you to do it. If he wants to be angry about it, fine, but eventually he has to get his head out of his arse and be thankful he's alive."

Emily's aqua eyes widened at that.

"Right now I'm more concerned as to the catalyst for these changes in us," Griff went on. "There has to be something causing it, but what? There hasn't been anything new in our lives."

"I'll run some tests," Emily offered. "Check our water and our food—anything that gets brought into the house and used by all of us. There has to be somethin'. Changes like this don't happen over a few months, they take years."

"Hundreds of them," Griff added. "Evolution is a slow and steady process. This is anything but. If something in this house is responsible for these changes, I know you'll find it, Em."

She blushed slightly. "I hope I'm as smart as you seem to think I am."

"I know it's a lot." Griffin ran a hand through his hair. "You already have your hands full with the automatons. You tell me what you need and I'll make sure you have it."

Emily thanked him and Griff smiled. "Don't thank me. You're going to have me underfoot in the lab for the next couple of days. I want to do some tests on Finley's blood." Briefly he filled her in on what they'd discovered earlier that day. He left out the part about Finley threatening Cordelia.

Emily frowned. "Doesn't it seem odd to you that everyone who has had ties with your family is either dead or some sort of meta-human?"

Griffin hadn't thought of that. He'd always been different, so these things sometimes escaped him when he was too caught up in particulars.

Emily jumped on that thought and took it further. "You and Sam grew up together, and both of you have had your abilities from a young age. Finley's father made sure she was born with hers, but they didn't manifest until she entered puberty. I've been around for a short time and now I'm changing, too. Lad, I think this has to do with you—rather than something we've been exposed to in this house."

The answer smacked Griffin hard, like a slap to the face. "The Organites. Finley's father was experimenting with them. Sam and I grew up around them, and you've been exposed to them since you first came here." The answer he'd been searching for finally came. "My father said they were the wellspring of life, and that Sam and I had 'evolved natural abilities.' Finley's father didn't make himself a monster, the Organites simply evolved aspects of his nature to the highest degree."

Emily's eyes were wide with excitement. Griff could almost see the gears of her mind working. "We should test blood from all of us, not just Finley. I can compare it to samples I've taken in the past. If the Organites have changed us on a cellular level, I'll find it."

Griffin had no doubt that she would. Never had he been so glad that he had chosen her over one of her brothers to work for him as he was right then. Sometimes Emily's intelligence scared him, while his own lack of perspective was sometimes so narrow he wanted to slap himself. "We'll start tonight. I'll send for Finley and you can take a sample from her, as well."

"She's not here," Emily informed him, looking a little uneasy. "I saw her leave about an hour ago."

"Leave?" She hadn't said a word. He hadn't even heard her. That could mean only one thing. Her dark side had taken over. He should have known this might happen given the stress of the day. How could he have been so careless?

"You want me to go look for her?" Emily asked.

Griff shook his head. He wouldn't dream of letting Emily roam around at this time of night by herself. "You won't find her if she doesn't want to be found. No, get what you need to take my blood and your own. I'll worry about Finley."

And worry he would. The last time she'd gone out, she'd visited Jack Dandy, according to the quick glimpse Cordelia had seen into Finley's mind. God only knew what kind of trouble she'd be getting up to tonight. Right now he had more important things to do than chase after her. Too many people were depending upon him.

He just hoped Finley didn't get hurt. More importantly, he hoped she didn't hurt anyone else.

Chapter 8

Finley woke the next morning still in her clothes. What had she done the night before? Where had she gone? No memory came to her as she sat up, mind blank.

She looked down at her boots—no dirt. At her hands—no blood. Surely that was a good sign? Her knuckles were tender and slightly bruised, but that didn't mean she'd hurt anyone. She could have hit anything. That didn't stop dread from pooling in her stomach.

This had to stop. She couldn't go on like this, turning into her own version of Mr. Hyde. Her darker self had taken over completely—something that had never happened before.

Griffin had offered to help her, but in the few days she'd been in this house nothing had happened that made her think there was any cure for this madness. In fact, the "switches" between her two sides seemed to have worsened. What if Griffin couldn't help her? Was she doomed to lose herself as Jekyll had and end up a monster?

The thought made her stomach roll and tears burn the back of her eyes. Had her father felt this way, helpless and sick?

Well, she wasn't helpless, not completely. It was obvious that Griffin had some kind of sway over her darker half. Twice now he had calmed her as that chaos had tried to take her. If anyone could figure out how to make this all stop, it was him.

Feeling slightly less sorry for herself and a tad bit optimistic, Finley swung her legs over the side of the bed. She rose and removed her slept-in clothes, bathed and slipped into fresh black-and-white-striped stockings, black skirt, white shirt and a pretty pink corset with black velvet trim. Everything was brand-new, part of the new wardrobe Griffin had bought her.

His generosity still made her uneasy. She wasn't accustomed to people, especially young men, being nice just to be nice. That was one thing she and her dark nature had in common—there was always a price. Still, she was willing to try trusting him. He'd been genuinely upset to learn that his father had been involved with her father's downfall. Maybe he felt as though he owed it to her to do what he could to keep her from suffering the same fate.

Dressed, she put her hair up in two messy buns on either side of her head. She squinted and leaned toward the cheval glass. Was that a streak of black in her hair? It was. It began right at the roots and continued down a bit before stopping abruptly. It was as though someone had started to paint this one-inch-wide section of her hair and then thought the better of it. Curious. It looked somewhat nice, she thought, but it would look better if it went all the way to the ends of her nondescript locks.

Finley left her room and hurried down the stairs to the great hall. It was there that she met up with Emily, who was carrying a small metal tray with what looked like medical instruments on it. The smaller girl looked tired and worried, her eyes rimmed with red. Finley slowed her steps.

"Are you all right?" she asked.

Emily glanced up, as though she hadn't even noticed Finley's approach. "Oh," she said. "It's you. I was just coming to see you."

Finley arched a brow as the Irish girl fell silent with a small frown, obviously distracted.

"What did you want to see me about?" she asked, noticing that what she thought was a headband was really a pair of strange goggles with interposing lenses on tiny brass arms.

Ropey red hair swung as Emily's head shook. "Lord, I'm a dunderhead this morning. I need a wee bit of your blood. Griffin wants me to do some tests, see if I can't figure out what's going on with these abilities we all seem to have."

"What's wrong with you?" It didn't come out as Finley intended. She didn't mean to make it sound like Emily had a disease or something. She was just surprised that they had something in common. So surprised that she wasn't even alarmed that Emily wanted her blood.

Pale cheeks turned light pink. "I can talk to machines."

"Do they...talk...back?" It was all she could think to ask.

Emily actually laughed. "Not with words, no. But I can sometimes tell what's wrong with them, how to fix them."

"How very extraordinary." Finley smiled. "Much more useful than tossing footmen through doorways."

"I don't know about that," Emily replied. "I've often wished I could toss a particular fellow around."

"Sam. He's what's got you so distracted, isn't he?" Too late she realized it was really none of her business.

Emily blushed again, but she nodded. "Yes. He's been spending as much time as possible away from here lately."

Away from her—that was what she didn't say and didn't have to. Emily was as easy to read as an open book.

"He'll come 'round," Finley assured her, even though she had no way of knowing for certain. "You just wait. I wager he'll be home tonight."

Emily didn't look convinced, but she didn't look quite so down in the mouth anymore, either. "Perhaps. I suppose it's out of my control, so I shouldn't worry about it."

"That doesn't mean you can't be concerned for a friend."

The red-haired girl smiled at her then, and Finley was struck by how pretty she was when she was happy. "Thank you, Finley. It's properly pleasant to have another lass in the house. The lads are lovely, but they're rubbish at trying to make one feel less morose."

Warmth filled Finley from the inside out. So this was what it was like to have a friend.

"I really should get a sample of your blood," Emily remarked. "Then you can go on and have your breakfast. I'm sure I'm keeping you."

Finley protested that she wasn't doing any such thing, and they went to one of the parlors regardless, where Emily swabbed the crook of her elbow with a strong smelling liquid and then expertly pierced the flesh with a sharp needle. A few seconds later and she was done, placing a bandage on the spot and wrapping it in place. She could have told the little redhead not to bother—her blood clotted fairly quickly—but she liked having the company a little longer.

"I wonder if my blood looks like everyone else's," Finley thought aloud. "Or if it looks as different as I feel."

"Everyone's pretty much the same under the skin," the other girl replied, putting her needle away. "Except for Sam, of course."

"Why, what does he look like?"

Emily blinked, then smiled. "Sorry. I'd forgotten that you'd only been with us a short time. Sam's what I term a man-droid—part man, part machine."

Finley's eyes widened and her jaw dropped. "How?"

The smaller girl's smile faded. "I couldn't let him die. Now he hates me for it."

What was she supposed to say to that? She couldn't argue it because she didn't know Sam, but he had seemed like an angry young man the few times she saw him. If he blamed Emily like she blamed her father for making her what she was, then there was nothing she could say to make the girl feel better.

"I don't think he *hates* you," Finley remarked, thinking back on how Sam had looked at Emily. "But I would think he's very confused right now. It's not easy discovering that someone close to you has made you into something...abnormal."

She and Emily locked gazes. The other girl said nothing, so Finley had no idea if she was upset or not.

"I'll let you know if your blood looks any different," Emily said, smiling slightly. She gathered up her gear. "You should go get breakfast."

Finley stood, feeling like a student being sent away by the headmistress at school. She went to the dining room, hoping she hadn't offended the girl she looked at as her one chance to have a friend.

The dining room was empty when she walked in, but the serving dishes were still on the sideboard, the top of which was like a radiator, circulating hot steam to keep the food warm. She helped herself to coddled eggs, ham, tomatoes and toast, then poured a cup of coffee and took the mouthwatering bounty back to the table.

She was just finishing her last piece of toast and jam when

Mrs. Dodsworth came bustling in, high color in her round cheeks.

"Begging your pardon, miss, but His Grace requests your presence in his study immediately."

The harried look on the older woman's face and the nervous twisting of her hands had Finley instantly on her feet. "Did he say why?"

"No, miss. Just that you should come right away."

Finley stood and followed after the round little woman. She had to hurry to keep up despite the housekeeper's much shorter legs. When they reached Griffin's study, Mrs. Dodsworth announced Finley and then walked away, leaving Finley to face the room alone.

Griffin sat behind the massive desk, looking every inch the lord of the manor. His gray-blue gaze flickered briefly to hers, lingering just long enough for her to know that everything was going to be all right.

"Sit down and let Griffin do most of the talking," whispered a voice in her head. It wasn't her own, but sounded very much like Lady Marsden, who she noticed was also in the room, along with a tall thin man with thinning brown hair and a pleasant face punctuated by an unfortunate nose.

Obviously it was easier for the lady to put thoughts in her head rather than take them out. Regardless, the man had the look of authority about him, so Finley reckoned she'd take Lady Marsden's advice, just this once.

"Miss Jayne," Griffin said, rising to his feet as did the other gentleman. "I'm sorry to have interrupted your breakfast, but Constable Jones would like to speak to you."

How had he known she was having breakfast? And...constable? Dizziness teased the edges of Finley's mind and she felt that familiar surge that often precipitated the arrival of her darker side. She pushed it down. The last thing she wanted was to reveal her other nature to Scotland Yard, or worse, throw a police officer across the room.

She moved cautiously closer, enough of her other self coming to the surface that she felt calmer. She even managed a smile for the Peeler. "Good day, Constable Jones. What is it you wish to ask me?"

The officer waited until she'd sat down before returning to his own chair. They sat together in front of Griffin's desk.

"My apologies, Miss Jayne," said Constable Jones in a melodic, slightly Liverpudlian accent. "But I understand that you worked for Lord August-Raynes until recently?"

"I did, yes." She had to bite her tongue not to offer more information.

"You left that household in a bit of a hurry I'm told."

"Yes."

"And why was that?"

Do not lie, a voice in her head—her own this time—whispered. More sound advice. Better to omit facts than tell a bold-faced lie. "Because I no longer felt safe under that roof, sir."

The constable was writing all of this down in a little notebook. He looked up from it now. "Why did you not feel safe?" He asked it in much the same way one might ask a child why they hadn't eaten all their turnip.

Finley glanced at Griffin, who sat there with a perfectly serene expression on his face. Either he was terribly adept at hiding his feelings, or he simply didn't care what happened to her. His aunt had said to let him do the talking but so far he hadn't made much of an effort. "Because Lord Felix August-Raynes made unwanted advances toward me."

"Advances?"

Finley sighed, part of her wanting to reach out and slap the man for being so dense. "He tried to force himself upon me.

Apparently he made quite a habit of it amongst the younger servant girls."

Constable Jones frowned. "Why did you not report this injury, Miss Jayne?"

She snorted, drawing a censorious look from Lady Marsden. "Begging your pardon, Constable Jones, but you and I both know that the police would have done nothing against a peer of the realm and I would have been turned out without so much as a reference."

"I doubt very much running away will serve you well, either, miss."

Finley smiled at him. "It got me here, didn't it?" Dear God, what was she saying? She felt perfectly normal and yet her other self was awake—and talking.

The constable looked so surprised by her statement that he was momentarily speechless. This was when Griffin finally joined the conversation. And it was about bloody time. "Really, Constable. I respect that you have a job to do, but surely you can see that Miss Jayne has no knowledge of your reason for calling upon her today. A girl her size would be no match for Lord Felix, I'm sure you would agree."

The officer seemed to mull this as he watched Finley. Finley looked away from him for a moment to stare at Griffin, who now had a strange glint in his eye. She wondered just how far he would go to protect her—and why he would bother. Then she returned her gaze to Jones. "What is your reason for calling upon me, sir?"

Constable Jones sighed. "It will be in all the papers by tomorrow. Lord Felix August-Raynes was found dead this morning. He was murdered."

Griffin watched as the color drained completely from Finley's face. For a moment he'd feared that her "other" self might make an appearance given the earlier change in her demeanor, but now she just looked shocked.

"How?" she asked.

Constable Jones didn't look surprised that she asked, which meant that he didn't really consider her a suspect—at least he didn't anymore. There was no faking such terrible surprise as Finley's. "He was strangled," the Peeler replied.

Finley pressed a hand to her mouth. It was a good thing she was a girl, and that Jones knew nothing about her past, otherwise he might not be so quick to scratch her—and her bruised knuckles—off his list of possible culprits.

Griffin didn't know whether to scratch her off his list, either. Oh, he believed her shock, but that didn't mean she was completely innocent. She might have been so completely taken over by her darker nature that she didn't remember. She had been out late last night and he had no idea where she'd been or what she'd been doing. He didn't want to believe her capable of such violence, but the simple truth was that she was not a normal girl and she was very capable of killing a full-grown man should she put her mind to it.

Regardless, he had made up his mind to help her as best he could, and that meant protecting her as he would any of his friends. If she had harmed Lord Felix, it wasn't her fault.

It was his father's, and—by primogeniture—his, as well. The reminder drove him to action. He rose to his feet, officially put an end to the interview. "Constable, if you're done I think Miss Jayne needs time to recover from this terrible news."

The officer gave Griffin a bland glance, obviously accustomed to being brushed aside by rich and powerful men who rose and dismissed him before he was ready. "Of course, Your Grace." He tucked his notebook inside his coat and stood.

"Thank you for your time, Your Grace, Lady Marsden, Miss Jayne." Jones bowed. "I'll show myself out."

Griffin remained by the desk for a few minutes, watching Finley, waiting until he knew the three of them were truly alone before crossing the plush rugs to close the study door.

The police had only been in his home twice, once after the death of his parents and now. He didn't like his home or his people being looked at by Scotland Yard. Not even Sam's attack had brought the law into this house. Part of him was a little angry at Finley for calling attention to him. People would talk about this. Society would be abuzz, wondering what the Peelers were doing at the Duke of Greythorne's.

He turned and looked at the girl sitting in front of him. This wasn't about him. He was a bloody duke and could tell the world to go to the devil if he wanted. In fact, he was above the law in most circles. He had nothing to fear except a few whispers, which would blow over when another scandal erupted.

"Finley," he said. "Are you all right?"

"Isn't there another question you should ask her?" Aunt Cordelia prompted from the sofa where she'd been sitting quietly up until now. "Such as whether or not she killed that boy?"

Finley's head lifted. Wide eyes turned to his. "I don't know what I did last night. I don't remember anything."

*Bloody hell.* Griff ran a hand through his hair. It was as he feared. "Nothing?"

She shook her head, little tendrils of hair brushing her cheeks. Had she always had that bit of black in her hair? "Nothing."

"Wonderful," Cordelia muttered.

Griff shot his aunt a sharp look. "She didn't do it." He believed it. He had to.

Cordelia returned the expression, mouth tight. "She's capable of it. You thought so yourself."

Finley flinched and Griff swore under his breath. "She is physically strong enough to do it. That's a far cry from having the moral flexibility to snuff out a life. And stay the hell out of my head."

His aunt rose from the sofa. "Enough of this debate. If you won't take control of this situation, I will."

Griff wasn't sure what she meant until he heard Finley make a low noise. His head whipped around. She was sitting in the chair in front of his desk, her head in her hands, an expression of pain on her face.

"Stop it," she pleaded. "Please stop."

His attention jerked to his aunt, who was staring at Finley with such intensity she looked positively frightening. A trickle of blood slowly slipped from her right nostril.

"Cordelia."

Finley moaned. Her eyes were squeezed shut now as she leaned forward. She was on the edge of the chair, looking as though she might slump to the floor at any moment.

"Delia!" He grabbed his aunt's arm, but she didn't seem to notice. She kept her gaze fastened on Finley. Blood trickled from her nose, and slowly ran down her chin to drip on the front of her gown. She was too deep into Finley's head—determined to get past the girl's barriers even at the cost of her own well-being.

Any force against Cordelia might do real damage to his aunt's mind. The connection had to be broken at the focal point, which was Finley, who was on the floor now, kneeling in a silent scream.

Griff swore again. He knelt beside Finley and put his hand around the back of her neck. She didn't even seem to notice his touch, she simply continued to suffer, in so much distress not even her other nature could overcome this attack. All of her energy was directed at keeping Cordelia out as instinct demanded, when it could all be over so quickly if she just let his aunt in.

"Finley?" he said softly. "Sweetheart, can you hear me?"

Nothing.

He took a deep breath and focused inward. Summoning up his determination, Griffin concentrated very carefully. He had never done this before, but it was the only solution he could think of with both of them so far beyond his reach in this realm.

It was like opening a window and letting the wind in. The Aether welcomed him with the spiritual equivalent of open arms. Power rushed to meet him, so potent he could taste it. He resisted the urge to let it fill him completely, closing his eyes and allowing himself to see Finley with his inner sight. On the Aetheric plane she was awash in pain, but the strength of her soul was undeniable. Her power glowed around her in a dual aura—one for each separate side of her personality. Those auras would have to merge into one for her to ever have any peace. At this moment the darker aura was the more powerful, pulsating under the strength of Cordelia's psychic attack. His aunt was a powerful telepath—and determined. She would not give up until Finley let her in—a moment that very well might come too late for either of them. She wouldn't give up because she thought Finley was a threat to him, and despite being cocky about her abilities, Aunt Cordelia would give her life to protect him. As much as he loved her for it, it was bloody inconvenient at the moment.

Fortunately, mediums, spiritualists and telepaths like his aunt operated within the Aether. He could see and sense them in the Aether—like the ghosts they sought. Only, they pulsed with life, while ghosts did not.

But ghosts weren't what he needed to think about right now, and he ignored those who "tugged" at his sleeve in this strange world behind the world.

Griffin turned his attention to the connection between the two women, fixating on the stream of undulating power between his aunt and Finley. It bathed them both in an iridescent light, covering them, joining them. He reached out, concentrating on the Aetheric stream. His free arm went around Finley as he tried to bend the energy to his will. Cordelia's power didn't want to let go, and if it was forced, his aunt would be struck by Finley's. There was only one other solution.

His heart skipped a beat—just one—before he recaptured his calm. If he lost control now there was no telling what the Aether would do to him. Once, it had sucked him in and kept him for a full day. It had taken him three to recover from the experience. And left him with several white hairs, which he'd promptly plucked from his head. That was when he'd learned there was a price to pay for being able to touch the Aether.

He moved the chair so he could kneel beside Finley and wrap both arms around her. She was warm against his chest, trembling as her mind fought against Cordelia's intrusion. His concentration deepened as he drew the energy pushing against her—and emanating from her—into himself. Slowly, he took control of the Aether, pulling it away from Finley to focus instead on him. Once he had it, all he had to do was hold it. It tried to dance away from him but he held fast. The energy whirled around him, filling him. It was so much.

When Cordelia's mind seemed to realize the connection between it and Finley had been broken, it stopped pushing. Like an elastic band pulled so taut it snapped, the energy flew into him, hitting him with a force that sent both him and Finley to the floor.

Griffin barely managed to catch the girl, still bombarded by Aetheric energy. With his guard now so lowered, the Aether rushed at him. Spirits—that's how the strange beings here had always seemed to him—crowded around him, a million voices talking at once. Some were crying, others shouting—some were just whispers.

The energy filled him, like a crashing tide. Cordelia and

Finley had exchanged so much energy that it was in constant motion. He had drained the power, but without direction it blew around inside him with hurricane force, trapped in one body rather than cycling between two. To the Aetheric plane he was a doorway, not just a mere window. And it wanted out.

He struggled to his feet, barely aware of the two females lying unconscious on the floor. He had to get out of the house.

French doors at the back of the room led out into the garden and he ran toward them. Power arced from his hands as he reached for the handle, sending the doors flying open without a touch.

He leaped down the shallow stone steps to the garden, the frantic pounding inside him pushing him to run at full speed across the freshly cut grass. He stumbled but kept running, his vision beginning to blur. He could feel his scalp starting to stretch under the pressure.

The Aether was tearing him apart.

There was a pool in the garden—picturesque with statues and perfectly groomed topiaries surrounding it. That was his destination. Just another forty feet—water would fix this.

He almost stumbled again. He was running out of time. His skull felt as though it was about to crack.

Almost there.

His feet ate up the distance. He could see the edge of the pool now, blurred and multiplied. Colors danced before his eyes.

As his boots hit the stone edge, Griffin launched himself. He flew through the air, falling now. God, he hoped he'd calculated correctly. If he hit the ground…

He hit the water, the shock of it hitting him like a cold boot to the chest. His mouth opened, water drowning his shout as the Aether forced its way out. He let it go.

Then everything went black.

# Chapter 9

It was the explosion that woke Finley up.

Groggily, she used the desk to pull herself to her knees and then to her feet. Her head felt as though it had been kicked repeatedly, such was the pounding in it. A few feet away, Lady Marsden was also coming around. Blood covered the older woman's face. Slowly, she began to sit up, her gaze quickly scanning the room as she dabbed her nose with the back of her hand. She looked at Finley, her eyes wide.

"Griffin."

Finley didn't think, she simply reacted. She knew the ferocious noise she'd heard had to do with Griffin, just as she knew he'd run out through the garden doors. The shattered glass from the panes in the doors lay scattered across the wet stone steps.

The entire garden looked as though it had been heavily rained on, despite the sun shining in the sky. Fog clung to the ground at the far end of the lawn, where the pool was.

That's where Finley ran, despite that every time her feet struck ground the pain in her head made her want to vomit.

As she reached the pool, she realized it wasn't fog curling around the wet grass. Fog wasn't hot—steam was. It burned her as she walked through it to stand on the stone edge.

There was no more than two inches of water left in the entire pool, and there, lying in the middle of it, was a sopping-wet Griffin, steam pouring off him like a teakettle at full boil.

"Griffin!"

Heedless of her boots or her own safety, Finley jumped into the pool, hot water splashing her legs, burning her skin through her stockings. She hissed in pain, but ran to Griffin's side.

"Griffin?" She crouched next to him, tentatively reached out and touched his dripping hair as he pushed himself to his knees.

He didn't lift his head, but his mouth curved into a smile. "Finley." His voice was a raw rasp, as though the heat that emanated from him had burned his throat, as well. "You're all right."

Realization hit her hard—he had stopped his aunt's intrusion into her mind, and this was the result of whatever he'd done. For her. She could have kissed him right then, if she hadn't thought his lips might blister hers.

Lifting his arm, she placed it over her shoulders, gritting her teeth against the fiery sting as water seeped through her clothes. Her other self rose up just a bit and she allowed it, taking the edge off the pain.

"Can you stand?" she asked, putting her arm around his waist.

He nodded. Together they stood. Finley could feel the tremor in Griff's body as he stood. He couldn't support his own weight at all, the stubborn liar. She bent down and put her other arm beneath his knees, sweeping him off his feet into her arms, carrying him like a child toward the top side of the pool.

"Finley," he said.

"Yes, Griffin?"

"Put me down, please." There was laughter in his voice.

She looked at him. Their faces were so close she really could kiss him if she wanted. He had quite nice lips, and right now they were smiling at her. "Please," he said again. "As nice as this is, I refuse to be carried into my own home by a girl who weighs a good three stone less than I."

Heat that had nothing to do with the steam filled her cheeks. "Sorry." But she didn't set him on his feet until they were out of the pool, then she let his legs down, but she continued to support him with an arm around his waist, his over her shoulders. His male pride obviously did not mind *leaning* on a girl three stone lighter than he.

"What happened?" she asked as they moved slowly toward the house. The steam seemed to be lessening, no longer rolling along the grass.

He sighed. "Simply, I went into the Aetheric plane and absorbed the energy flowing between you and Aunt Cordelia to disconnect your psychic connection. The water helps to disperse the excess, so I jumped in the pool." He glanced over his shoulder. "I shall have to refill it."

"You pay people to do that for you," she reminded him a little sharply. "And you shouldn't have put yourself in that kind of danger for me."

He glanced at her out of the corner of his eye—she knew this because she was doing the same to him. "If not for you, then for whom?" he asked softly.

Finley looked away. "Thank you," she mumbled. Of course

he might have done it to save his aunt, but he had done it for her, as well. No one had ever done anything like that for her.

"This might not be the best time to bring this up," he remarked as they neared the house. "But did you happen to notice when you picked me up whether or not your 'other' side was in attendance?"

Finley stopped, forcing him to, as well. She was so astounded that she could neither move nor speak for a good few seconds. Then she turned to him. "I don't know. I felt it earlier. I let it take away the pain, but then..." She stared at him. "But I couldn't have been so strong without it."

Griffin grinned, flashing straight white teeth as water trickled down his face from his hair. His cheeks were flushed, making his eyes seem all the brighter. "You controlled it."

She stood there, looking at him with wonder. She *had* controlled it. Not simply fought it until it went away, but honest to goodness used it and made it work for her! She didn't know how she'd done it—only that her thoughts had been on Griffin not herself. But if she could do it once, surely she could do it again?

They began walking again. Griffin's steps were stronger now, though he didn't remove his arm from her shoulders, nor did she take hers away from his waist. Despite the discomfort from the burns, she liked this contact.

"Griffin!" cried a voice from the terrace. It was Lady Marsden. Emily and Sam were with her. Her ladyship had wiped most of the blood from her face, although there was still a bit of red around her nose and chin.

Sam—barefoot and clad only in a loose shirt and trousers—came forward as they approached the terrace. Griffin lifted his arm from Finley's shoulders, so she dropped hers, as well. He climbed the stone steps by himself, holding up his hand when the large, dark-haired boy tried to help him. "I'm all right, Sam."

Was it her imagination or had Sam flinched? Griffin's rejection struck him on a personal level. A guilty conscience for not being there when his friend needed him? Good. Finley didn't know all the details of the strife between them, but she could commiserate with Sam to an extent. She also wanted to kick the behemoth's backside for feeling so sorry for himself, because she knew how that felt, as well.

Lady Marsden rushed forward to hug her nephew. Over his shoulder, her gaze met Finley's. Finley wanted to look away, but she didn't. The contrition she saw there surprised her. Once her ladyship released Griffin, she walked over to Finley and offered her hand.

"I want to apologize to you, Miss Jayne, for being so reckless with both of our health. I've been a harridan to you since my arrival and you do not deserve it."

Finley hesitated a second before accepting the handshake. "What changed your mind?"

"Yours," the lady replied. "You may be fractured, but you are not evil. I know now that you are not a threat to my family."

Finley's heart sped up. "You mean, I didn't... Lord Felix...?" She couldn't come right out and ask if she was a murderer.

Still holding her hand, Lady Marsden patted it with her left. "No. You did not. I saw that much."

Her relief was so great that Finley's shoulders sagged. "Oh, thank you." It didn't matter how ruthless the lady had been in getting the information out of her mind, she had gotten the truth and now Finley could stop worrying, stop being afraid that she might have taken a life.

Lady Marsden released her with a strained smile and then

turned her attention to her nephew. She put her arms around Griffin and drew him in to the house. As Finley approached the doors, she saw just how completely the terrace doors had been decimated. Had Griffin's power broken them, or had he dove through them? She hadn't seen any cuts on him, so she could only assume it had been the former.

Emily linked her arm through Finley's and smiled. "Come with me, lassie. I'll get you something for those burns."

The burns would heal quickly, but Finley said nothing. She felt as though she actually belonged in this house with these people. It was the first time since being a child that she felt that way. Accepted. Wanted.

How long would it last?

Later that day, after a bath, food and some sleep, Griffin came downstairs with the intention of using the Aether engine to search for clues into Lord Felix's demise. It wasn't enough that Cordelia had seen Finley's innocence in her mind. Scotland Yard tended to need more "physical" evidence. If Griffin could find a lead, then he could at least give Constable Jones a direction to look in other than Finley.

Of course, it was convenient that Scotland Yard also wouldn't believe that a girl weighing eight stone plus change—not much more than a baby horse—had the strength to strangle a young man the size of Lord Felix.

Unfortunately, his men were still repairing the French doors in his study, so using the engine was out of the question for the time being. He didn't want any prying eyes. Servants knew the strange machine was there, but no one had ever seen him use it and that was the way he wanted to keep it.

It was close to teatime, so he went to the blue parlor instead. He was surprised to find Finley there alone.

She looked up as he entered. Odd, but she looked almost

nervous to see him, as though what had happened that afternoon pushed them apart rather than brought them closer together.

"Emily said she'd be here, she just has to get changed. She's been in her laboratory," Finley explained unnecessarily. "Sam is going to come, as well, after he's done training. Your aunt was resting last I heard."

Griffin smiled in what he hoped was a soothing manner. "And here we are, being idle."

Her wide lips curved slightly at that. "Yes, lazy bones that we are."

He hadn't bothered to wear a jacket, so he had no tails to flip out as he seated himself on the blue brocade sofa beside her. Oddly enough, he wished he'd taken more time in getting dressed, but Finley was hardly the type of girl to be impressed with the knot in his cravat, though she seemed to like looking at his throat. Still, he felt somewhat common in nothing but trousers, shirt and braces.

Finley herself was wearing one of the Oriental-style dresses he'd bought for her. Her honey-colored hair was up in a messy bun held in place with what appeared to be a pencil. He made a mental note to make sure she had hairpins and all those other gewgaws young ladies needed.

"Where did the black come from?" He nodded at the streak in her hair. Oddly enough it looked longer than it had earlier that day.

She raised a self-conscious hand to her hair. "I don't know. It was there when I woke up this morning. I suppose it might have been there before, but I didn't notice it. It's not artificial."

"Curious." He smiled. "It suits you. Makes you look very mysterious."

He thought she blushed a little at his teasing.

"I've neglected you," he said. "And I'm sorry for it. Tomorrow morning we're going to meet in the library and get started on helping you learn to control this better."

She started. "Control it? You mean…I'm going to be like this forever?"

It wasn't appropriate, but he reached over and took her hand in his regardless. They'd been through too much for him to stand on ceremony now. "Your father's alchemy essentially made you two halves of one whole, fracturing your personality. I believe that's why you're having so much trouble with your other nature now. You're imbalanced. The two halves must be brought together into one personality."

She didn't look pleased. "What if that shadow-me takes over?"

"It won't, but even if it did, it wouldn't be long before this side of you started to come through. Wouldn't you rather have control over both sides rather than constantly worrying about it?"

Finley thought for a moment, chewing absently on her thumbnail. She lowered her hand and tucked her thumb into her fist. "Yes. I would."

Griffin grinned, pleased to hear the determination in her voice. "That's my girl." He hadn't meant it to sound so proprietary, but it did. He looked away so she wouldn't see his embarrassment, so he wouldn't see hers.

A few moments later, he turned back to her. "I want to apologize for what Aunt Cordelia did to you."

"Don't. She already asked for my forgiveness and I gave it to her."

"That was very good of you."

She snorted. "Good had nothing to do with it. If she hadn't done it, I'd still be wondering if I'd killed Lord Felix." Her bluntness took him back a bit, even though it amused him.

"I suppose something good came out of all of this, then.

How are your burns?" He hated the idea of her putting herself in harm's way to help him. Since the death of his parents, few people had come to his aid so selflessly and they all lived under this roof.

She raised a hand—but not the one still beneath his on the sofa—to the back of her neck. "Almost gone. Emily gave me some ointment for them, and it seems that my father's work also gave me the ability to heal rapidly."

"Not to mention the ability to lift twelve stone with little effort," he reminded her with a teasing grin.

"Twelve?" Her eyebrows shot up. "A bit more than that soaking wet—and fully clothed." A flush crept up her cheeks to her hairline and Griffin bit the inside of his cheek to keep from chuckling at her expense. He didn't have to have Cordelia's abilities to know that her own remark had then turned her thoughts to him without clothes.

"I did ask you to put me down, if you remember correctly," he reminded her, steering the conversation in a less embarrassing—for her—direction. He turned serious. "I'm going to find out all I can about Lord Felix's murder."

Finley's finely arched brows lowered into a frown. "Why? We know I didn't do it."

"Scotland Yard doesn't know that. If I can give them evidence to lead them elsewhere, I'll feel much better knowing you're permanently off their suspect list."

Her gaze locked with his. "Thank you. For everything."

No one had ever looked at him as though he were the answer to all their prayers. It was humbling. It was startling. It was…*attractive*. He leaned closer, dangerously close to giving in to the temptation that had provoked him since the first time he saw her.

He was going to kiss Finley Jayne. Wouldn't that complicate things?

Fortunately, Finley didn't notice his sudden nearness, or if she did, she misinterpreted it. She leaned her head against the back of the sofa and turned her gaze toward him.

"Is it awful of me to be relieved that he's dead?"

The question was like a bucket of cold water in the face. The shock wore off immediately, leaving Griff feeling slightly guilty. The poor girl. She must have put herself through hell thinking she'd killed that waste of breath Lord Felix and now she felt guilty for not mourning him.

"No," he told her honestly. "It's not wrong. I wager you're not alone in your feeling."

Her lips twisted wryly. "No, I reckon not. He hurt a lot of people." Her gaze met his again. "I know it's awful to be glad that someone is dead, but I think of what might have happened if he was allowed to go on..."

"How many other people he might have gone on to hurt," Griffin offered softly. Gads, how he wished he had August-Raynes at hand so that he could knock the bounder's teeth loose.

Finley nodded. "I don't blame him for what he did to me. Well, I did for a bit, but he wasn't himself. He didn't know what he was doing."

A burst of harsh, humorless laughter escaped Griffin. "You are too forgiving."

"Am I?" She sounded dubious at best. "When it was that vile drink responsible?"

"I admire you for looking for good in the man, but the fact remains that he was a good-for-nothing wastrel who indulged in drink and took delight in hurting people he believed weaker than himself."

Her gaze was wide and...angry as it locked with his. "Surely you don't mean to imply that he was that much of a villain?"

He didn't understand her vehemence. "I certainly do. I've heard accounts the length of my arm that testify to just how much of a scoundrel he was. You are the last person I would expect to defend him."

"How can I condemn a man I didn't even know?" She looked as though she might cry. "A man my mother thought of with such high regard and love? Dear God, I might be glad he is gone and his suffering over, but I could never despise him!"

Griffin blinked. "Wait a moment. About whom are we talking?"

Finley froze. Slowly, her mouth opened. "My father?"

He didn't know whether to laugh or swear. "I referred to Lord Felix. Damn my eyes, Finley, I would never speak so lowly of your father. My own thought him the very best of men, and I am certain he was right."

Pink filled her cheeks. "And I must be awful for being partially glad he is gone."

"Never. You said so yourself, his suffering is at an end. Lord, you must have thought I was thoroughly heartless, believing I spoke of your father."

She chuckled. "A little, yes. I am glad to be wrong. To be honest, I am not sorry to be done of Lord Felix, but I am even happier to know that his end did not come at my hands."

Something happened then—a subtle shift in her expression that made him jump to the logical conclusion. "You think Dandy did it."

"No," she insisted. "He wouldn't."

One eyebrow rose as Griffin fought to keep his expression neutral, but inside he despised Dandy for inspiring such hope in a short period of time. Would she be so quick to defend him were he and Dandy reversed?

"Probably not," he reluctantly agreed. Then he couldn't

help adding, "Dandy wouldn't get his hands bloody. He'd get someone else to do it."

"Not if it was personal he wouldn't."

Griffin didn't like the idea that she had such insight into Dandy's nature, or that she almost sounded as though she respected the man for it.

"Jack Dandy is a criminal, Finley. No matter how much you might wish it otherwise, he is not a good person."

"Some would say I'm not, either—not completely," she retorted with a stubborn lift of her chin. "You've seen what I'm capable of. That doesn't make me a murderer, and it doesn't make Dandy one, either."

She had him there. He sighed. "No, it doesn't. But he is one of the most infamous crime lords in this city for a reason. Because he *wants* to be one."

And now they were even because she couldn't argue with that, either. She pulled her hand from his. "Why are we arguing about Jack Dandy?"

Griffin reluctantly drew his own hand back, as well. "Because part of you likes him."

Finley smiled that wry smile again. "Part of me also tried to strangle your aunt. I think taking control of this *part* of myself can't happen soon enough."

He was glad to hear it, but it put a lump in his chest, as well. When the two halves of Finley came together, she would no longer be this girl in front of him, nor would she be as dangerous as her other self. She'd be a little of both, and she might not like him so much then. He might not like her quite so well as he did now.

Still, it was a risk he had to take.

The door to the parlor opened and Sam, Emily and Jasper came into the room, followed by two of the maids carrying trays of tea, sandwiches and sweets. Griffin was immediately swept up into other conversation, as was Finley, giving him very little time to regret that he hadn't kissed her when he had the chance.

Later that day, driven by forces she didn't understand, Finley sent a note 'round to a certain house in Whitechapel. It contained one line: *Tell me you didn't do it.*

She waited for a reply. Even though she was off the hook, she knew the truth about her own involvement. And if Dandy had killed Lord Felix because of what she had told him, then she was responsible for the bounder's death, to an extent.

Nothing that night, but the next morning as she sat alone at breakfast, the butler delivered a letter to her on a silver platter. Her name and direction were scrawled upon the envelope in sharp, black ink. The seal on the back was black, as well, the impression in the wax that of a simple gothic *D*.

Her fingers shook as she broke the seal and withdrew the heavy, quality paper. Her one-line request had been acknowledged with a one-line answer:

*Of course I didn't, Treasure.*

She tossed the note on the fire and went off to meet Griffin in the library. She had her answer. That was the end of it.

But part of her wasn't satisfied. It wasn't enough that Jack Dandy had told her he hadn't killed Lord Felix, because that part of her knew Dandy was smart enough not to tell her—or anyone else—even if he had.

# Chapter 10

Chapter 16

The following morning, another delivery arrived for Finley. It was brought to her in the morning as she and the others—even Sam—enjoyed a somewhat amiable breakfast. It seemed that by assisting Griffin she had earned a spot in the good graces of not only Lady Marsden, but the big "mandroid," as well.

"What is it?" Emily inquired, eyes wide as saucers as Finley took possession of the large pink box, tied with an elegant black-and-pink-striped ribbon.

"I don't know," she replied with all sincerity.

Lady Marsden arched a brow. "It's from Madame Cherie's. Whatever it is, it is expensive." When Finley gaped at her, she continued with a smile, "Don't just stand there, girl. Open it!"

Fingers clumsy with anticipation, Finley did just that, draping the ribbon over the back of the empty chair next to her. She removed the lid and set in on the floor, and then parted the delicate blush-pink tissue paper....

She gasped. Inside was a costume for a fancy dress ball—a fairylike gown of iridescent ebony feathers that glowed with deep violet, rich green and bright blue under the light. A matching mask accompanied it.

"It's the loveliest thing I've ever seen," Emily whispered.

Finley was inclined to agree. Certainly she'd never owned anything so fine before. Why, the bodice was the same green as in the feathers—like a vibrant peacock's plumage.

Astounded, she glanced up to see Griffin scowling and his aunt smiling coyly. "It seems you have an admirer, Miss Finley. Very bold of him to send you such an extravagant gift."

"Read the card," Griffin suggested, sounding as though he spoke through clenched teeth. Finley glanced at him. His jaw was tight indeed. Was he jealous? The notion seemed too fantastic to entertain, and yet he was certainly displeased. Either he was jealous or he thought her loose—it was highly improper for a gentleman to send a girl such a personal present. This was the kind of thing men bought their mistresses.

Suddenly, Finley was afraid to open the card. The beautiful costume had been ruined by the scandalous nature of its deliverance. Everyone was watching her, however, so she had little choice but to pick up the small envelope and withdraw the note inside.

Wear this tonight. I will come for you at nine o'clock.
We're going to the Pick-a-Dilly Ball.
Jack

"Who's it from?" Griffin asked in a low voice.

Finley glanced at him, heart pounding hard against her ribs. She cleared her throat. "Jack Dandy." Still it came out a hoarse whisper.

Griffin said nothing, but she could see how white his

knuckles were as he gripped his cup of coffee. His eyes were positively thunderous, his expression as hard as stone.

"You can't go," Sam blurted out. "That's no place for a girl."

Emily scowled. "Oh, but I suppose t'would be all right for you to go, would it, Samuel Morgan?"

The muscular young man flushed. "It's dangerous, Em. Men are better equipped to defend themselves."

"I'm better equipped to defend myself than most men," Finley reminded him tartly. She didn't like being told what to do—and there was a part of her that very much wanted to go to this ball. She'd never been to one before—not as a guest. She'd sat in a stupid room with other ladies maids and tapped her foot to the music while sipping warm lemonade, but never had she been one of the dancers or a debutante in a beautiful gown.

"Of course you should do whatever you want," Griffin said, his voice still that strange, low pitch. "No one would argue that you are more than capable of taking care of yourself should a situation arise."

Finley stared at him. Did he mean that, or was he just saying it? And why did another part of her want him to demand that she not go? Wanted him to act like a tyrant and command that she return the dress to Dandy and never see him again.

"It might be advantageous," Lady Marsden remarked casually—a little too much so. "Much of London's underground attends that ball, along with the upper classes. It would be the perfect spot to gather information on The Machinist and his plans."

The Machinist—Finley had read about him in the papers. He was the one the Peelers thought responsible for the recent automaton malfunctions. She cast a quick glance at Sam out of the corner of her eye. His face was taut and pale, but otherwise impassive. Surely he wanted to find the man believed to be behind the attack that almost cost him his life? She would be doing him something of a favor then, wouldn't she? If she went.

But it was Emily who finally convinced her—not stony Griffin or wounded Sam, not even sly Lady Marsden. Little Emily with her ropey hair, trousers and too-short fingernails. She had gotten up from her chair and come around the table to peer inside the pretty box, her pale hand stroking the exquisite bodice.

"You'll look like a princess," she murmured, her voice trailing off into a sigh.

Yes, Finley thought. She would. She would probably feel like one, too, and at a ball where the seedier side of London mixed with the aristocracy and everything in between, Jack Dandy would be something of a prince, wouldn't he?

She met Griffin's hard gaze with a determined lift of her chin. It wasn't as though he had asked to take her. Everyone would think her his mistress—a prostitute—if he did. But Jack Dandy, he could take her without such foolishness. Jack Dandy was within her sphere; Griffin King was not.

"You're right. I should do what I like," she said, forcing her voice not to tremble. "I'm going to go."

Griffin had never been one for physical violence. His talents made it so that he rarely had to resort to using his fists. Still, part of being a man of rank meant engaging in some degree of physical exertion. Many young men of his acquaintance preferred boxing or fencing, but he engaged in a precept called jujitsu. It was a way of fighting from Japan in which samurai used their hands and bodies as weapons rather than swords or guns.

Recently Jasper Renn shared his knowledge of an art called

kung fu, which he claimed to have learned in San Francisco. They had sparred together, teaching each other various strikes and stances of each method. Griffin liked the physical and mental aspects of each, and one day hoped to travel to China and Japan so that he might learn from true masters.

He was breathing hard and perspiring despite being naked from the waist up. In fact, all he wore were his trousers—even his feet were bare—as he sparred against an invisible partner.

Perhaps he should teach Finley how to fight this way. Perhaps then she'd think him as appealing and dangerous as Jack-swiving-Dandy. Honestly, what was it about those kinds of men that made girls go all weak in the knees and soft in the head?

He'd heard stories about Dandy at school. The criminal was a couple of years older than him and already notorious. Rumor had it that Dandy's father was an aristocrat—perhaps one of the royal dukes, or at least an earl. Whoever sired the blackguard, he had to be of some means and rank, because he could afford to make certain his illegitimate offspring had the best education England had to offer.

"Hardly fair to fight your shadow, is it not?" came Aunt Cordelia's humorous voice. "After all, it's not as though it can defend itself."

Snatching up his shirt, Griffin used it to mop his face and chest before slipping his arms into the sleeves. "It does all right," he countered with forced lightness.

She smiled as she walked toward him. "After the other day I'm surprised you have enough energy to lift a finger let alone train."

Griffin shrugged. "I feel fine." In fact, he felt bloody great, a condition that went against all his theories about the Aether actually draining his life force. Yet, on other occasions, he had felt as though ten years had been sucked from him.

"Excellent. It occurred to me that it might be good for you to attend the Pick-a-Dilly Ball, as well. See what you can find out about The Machinist and his *machinations,* for lack of a better term."

He frowned, seeing something in her expression he didn't quite like, and feeling a gentle nudge in his mind toward agreeing with her. "I intend to, but that's not the only reason you suggested it. Your reason must be important or you wouldn't be in my head as I've asked you repeatedly *not* to do."

Most would have looked away from his sharp tone, but his aunt merely shrugged and met his gaze evenly. He knew she cursed the fact that he, unlike most people, could feel her intrusions. "It might also do you some good to see Miss Jayne with her own kind."

"Her own kind? You make her sound like a commoner."

Her expression spoke volumes—and he knew he'd guessed correctly. "She's not far from it, Griffin. She's a special girl, yes. She's also very pretty and intriguing. I can see why you would be drawn to her, but you will do her more harm than good with your attentions."

He crossed his arms over his chest in a classic defensive posture, but he couldn't help but ask, "How so?"

"Sam and Emily you can pass off as employees, but the way you look at Miss Jayne…well, I can tell you're attracted to her."

Griffin's cheeks heated. "What of it?"

His aunt took a step closer. "Show her attention, and people will talk. They will assume that there is something sordid between you—especially while she lives under your roof. She is in your protection, Griffin. You do not want to take advantage of that, or be seen to do so. Her reputation will be forever damaged." Her expression was one of sympathy. "She's not for you, my dear."

It was one of those times when Griffin wanted to act like a spoiled brat—stomp his foot and declare that he was a duke and he could do whatever he damn well pleased. But that would be too selfish. Of course he could do what he wanted, but it would be Finley who suffered for it.

He hooked his thumbs under the braces hanging loosely around his hips and lifted them over his shoulders over his partially open shirt. "You've never been one for proprieties, Aunt Delia. Why now?"

Her strong features softened with sadness. "Because I want to see you happily settled one day with a normal girl rather than one who might get you killed, or worse—leave you without a trace, wondering what happened to her. If she's alive or dead, safe or in pain."

It was impossible to be angry with her when she spoke so candidly about her own life. She did not want for him the misery she lived every day, wondering if her husband was alive or dead. Holding on to hope when doing so must surely be folly.

Griffin hugged her, suddenly realizing how much taller he was than she, that the woman he'd always thought so amazingly powerful felt small and fragile in his arms. "I promise you I will be careful with my affections, but beyond that I can offer nothing else. I cannot tell my heart what to feel."

Were it but that easy, he would tell his foolish heart to shut out all thoughts of Finley Jayne, because it was painfully obvious that her heart was engaged elsewhere.

She had a little over an hour before Jack Dandy arrived to collect her, and Finley stood in her bedroom in nothing but a short silk shift using curling tongs on her hair. Her time as a lady's maid certainly came in handy for getting ready for an evening. She could have asked one of the housemaids to help her, but why bother when she was more than capable of doing the same job herself?

Besides, she didn't want to give Griffin any more reason to be angry with her. He had barely spoken to her since breakfast.

Since Jack's gift arrived.

Her gaze went to the costume hanging on her wardrobe door. Even in the dim light of her room, the feathers reflected the most beautiful colors.

Propriety told her to send it back and politely refuse Dandy's attentions and invitation, but she wanted to go so very badly. And she wanted Griffin to see her before she left so he could see how she looked in such a beautiful creation. Was that wrong of her? Undoubtedly, but that didn't stop her from silently wishing for it all the same.

Lifting the tongs from the pretty matching heater her mother had given her on her previous birthday, Finley fitted the last uncurled lock of her hair between the barrel and curved clamp and quickly rolled it. She took care to ensure she didn't get it too close to her scalp. She might heal quickly, but that didn't mean a burn wouldn't hurt.

A few moments later, she released her hair from the tongs and a perfect ringlet joined the others she'd made. Then she plucked up her brush to smooth the front and began arranging curls—some still warm—into the style she wanted, pinning them in place. By the time she was done, curls cascaded down her back from high on her head while a few others framed her face in delicate spirals. Perfect—except for that strange patch of black. Was it longer?

Finley was just about to tackle her pretty black lace corset when a knock sounded upon her door.

"Who is it?" she called, quickly reaching for her robe and slipping her arms through the sleeves.

"Emily," came the muffled reply. "I have something for you."

Finley started. Something for her? "Come in."

The door opened and the petite redhead came in, carrying a medium-size box. "Oh, good, you're not yet dressed."

She never expected to hear someone say that to her, let alone a girl. "Do you think you could help me with my corset?"

Emily grinned. "That is exactly why I'm here." She set the box on the bed and removed the lid. "I made this especially for you."

Finley's mouth dropped open as Emily lifted the most wonderfully strange contraption she'd ever seen. "Is that…is that a *corset*?"

Smiling broadly, Emily nodded. "Do you like it?"

She stepped closer, tentatively reaching out to touch the cold metal. A steel corset—thin, shiny bands with embossed flowers and leaves, held together with tiny hinges to allow ease of movement. Little gears and other decorative pieces of steel were soldered over some of the larger gaps between bands. The garment looked like an industrial metal flower garden.

"The spaces are small enough that bullets and most blades won't be able to get through, and if someone hits you the bounder's going to break a knuckle or two."

There was a side of Finley that saw the corset as a little frightening, but it was beautiful. Another side couldn't wait to put it on. It was protection—armor. A normal girl shouldn't need armor, but a girl who often courted trouble, who wanted to protect herself and her friends, loved it.

"I thought you could wear it tonight," Emily said, shooting her an uncertain look. "Do you like it?"

"Oh, Emily!" Finley threw her arms around the girl in a rare burst of affection. "I love it! Forgive me for not saying so earlier—I was too amazed to speak."

The other girl sighed against her. "Oh, good! Now I won't be quite so worried while you're gone."

Finley gave her another quick squeeze for the sentiment. "Then help me put it on."

There were smooth grommets and laces in the back as in a normal corset to adjust the fit. A small panel of metal then closed over the ribbons to protect exposed flesh. The hammered metal molded to Finley's torso as though it was made of supple fabric and not unyielding steel. It was snug but allowed her to bend and move as well or better than regular underclothes. Best of all, it was surprising light and comfortable.

"It's brilliant," she whispered as she looked at herself in the full-length mirror, twisting to the left and right to see how the corset moved.

Emily beamed, clapping her hands together. "Thank you."

"Thank *you*." Finley squeezed her shoulder. "Let's see how it looks with my costume, shall we?"

Her friend—her *friend*—helped her into the beautiful feathered gown, pulling the fabric over her head and shoulders and then tugging it into place as Finley slipped her arms through the little feather sleeves that sat low on her shoulders. Then, small nimble fingers quickly hooked the frogs to close the back of the bodice.

"I was right—you do look like a princess."

Standing in front of the mirror, Finley smoothed her palms over the snug bodice and downy skirt. "I've never seen anything like it."

"Try the mask." Emily handed her the feathery accessory.

It was black, with the same sheen as the gown, trimmed with peacock-green like the bodice and framed with more feathers. It came down over her cheeks to form points and the nose cover protruded slightly and came to a rounded point, so that it looked something like a tiny beak. She tied the ribbons around her head, hiding the bow beneath her hair.

Emily's mouth hung open. "Stay right there," she instructed, before running out of the room. Finley did as she was told, and a few minutes later, the girl was back with a camera and stand. Quickly, she set the stand on the carpet, adjusted the accordion-like camera and pointed it at Finley.

"Smile!"

Finley did and was rewarded with a bright flash that left stars dancing before her eyes. She shook her head as Emily babbled about something having to do with emulsion, light-sensitive something or other and special paper. When the colors cleared, she looked down to see Emily holding a photograph under her face—it was of a beautiful bird lady. Oh! It was *her*.

Emily was truly a genius. Somehow she'd invented a way to develop photographs almost instantly. A way to make Finley look at herself and see not a monster, but something...lovely. It brought tears to her eyes, but she held them back. As much as she liked Emily, she wasn't ready to let the girl see her cry. Not yet.

"So you can remember this night forever," Emily said with a hopeful smile.

Finley thanked her—and hugged her again—and then it was time for her to go downstairs and wait for Jack. She slipped a hooded black cloak over her shoulders and fastened it at the throat, then she left.

When she reached the great hall she was brought up short by the sight of the devil himself. Standing before her was a tall, lean man in head-to-toe black. Glossy dark hair curled about his shoulders and a black mask covered most of his pale face, leaving only his full mouth and dark eyes visible. The top of the mask came up on either side to curve into horns, and a long, barbed tail peeked out from beneath the back of his long coat.

Emily gasped at the sight. The devil grinned, revealing bright white teeth, and bowed formally from the waist.

"Hello, Treasure. Care to introduce me to your friend?"

Pick-a-Dilly Circus was housed in a great domed building near Covent Garden. Colorful banners ran from a pinnacle on the roof to various points along the edge of the building before trailing to an end down the wall. From the street, one could hear music over the busy din of evening traffic and clamoring crowds.

The grounds were filled with those merrymakers who hadn't the fare or inclination to go inside. Inside was where most of the aristocrats would be, so they could avail themselves of all entertainments. Outside there would be small amusements, but food and drink were available to all as were the music and dancing.

Griffin peered from the cutout eyes of his mask—the eyes and nose of a lion—as his carriage approached the chaos. He shouldn't have come. Drunken revelry held no appeal to him for the simple reason that drinking or opiates often made it difficult for him to control his abilities. Therefore he had to remain sober—and being sober made being around people who weren't all the more tedious.

He opened the compartment in the wall beside him and spoke into the voice-amplifying device secured there. "Stop here. I'll walk the rest of the way."

A few moments later, he ambled up the front steps of the

circus, long coat billowing slightly behind him. He'd find out what he could about The Machinist and perhaps track down his American acquaintance Jasper Renn, and then he'd leave. He would not stand about all evening like a fool, watching Finley with that scoundrel Dandy. It would be far too tempting to lay Dandy out flat.

Inside the main building, the theater of the circus was closed off by a round wall that circled the entire ring. Between that wall and the outer structure was a wide corridor that housed various vendors selling ale and punch, toasted nuts and other savory snacks. There were also several stands selling souvenirs of the circus and its performers.

It was this corridor he stuck to for the first quarter hour. He purchased a mug of cider from one of the vendors and planted himself by the south entrance to the main tent. That was where he was to meet Renn, right about...now.

"Howdy, stranger."

Griffin smiled. Punctual as ever. He turned and watched as a young man dressed like an American cowboy, right down to the dusty boots and spurs, approached. He had a black demi-mask covering the upper half of his face.

"Howdy, yourself." The decidedly Western greeting sounded awkward in his English accent.

They shook hands and clapped each other on the shoulder. They made the necessary niceties for a moment before Griffin got down to business.

"The Machinist," he said softly. "What have you heard?"

Renn removed his hat and scratched his head. "There are some folks who reckon that Machinist fella's just playin' with these small-time jobs and random attacks, working his way up to something bigger." He plopped the Stetson back into place.

Griffin considered that theory then shook his head. "If he's working his way up, perhaps the incidents aren't as 'small' and random as one might think. Perhaps he's simply experimenting at perfecting his technique."

"Which is?"

"Deuced if I know. Building a metal assassin? Or perhaps an automaton he can control from a distance to commit crimes for him?"

Renn whistled. "You're right. None of that sounds small-time at all."

No, they certainly did not. "I need your help, Jasper," Griffin spoke, using Renn's Christian name as a show of friendship. "The Machinist is responsible for a friend of mine having been seriously injured. If he's up to something even more dangerous, I want to stop him. And quickly."

The cowboy gave a curt nod. "Understood. I'll do what I can. I'll come by the day after tomorrow and I'll give you all the information I can find."

Griffin almost sagged in relief. "Thank you." Renn wasn't noble-born, but he had honor. His more "common" status, however, allowed him to travel within circles of moral ambiguity that Griffin could not. Griffin could never pass himself off as anything other than what he was, but a genuine American cowboy was an instant celebrity in London—exotic and strange, and not bound by the same rules.

He was just about to say goodbye and head home again when two identically clad ladies approached them. He recognized the amazing cherry-red of their chin-length hair immediately. They were the Cardinal Twins—trapeze performers with the circus. Tonight they wore porcelain-like masks painted with features almost exactly like their own—oddly disconcerting to look upon—and matching crystal-adorned corsets and bloomers with long, white ostrich-feather trains.

"Hello, gents," they chorused in perfect unison. "Care to

accompany us inside? It's much more entertaining than out here."

Griffin could hardly refuse when one of them held out her hand. He had been raised to be a gentleman, and gentlemen did not give ladies the cut. He offered her his arm, which she took in a supple yet strong hold. Her mask was smiling, but if the real lips beneath mirrored her painted ones, he had no idea.

He led the way with his escort, parting the heavy red drapes that served as door to the inner sanctum. In here there was lively music and people dancing as performers moved through the crowd. There would be a grand spectacle later—one that no doubt featured the Cardinal Sisters.

As soon as they were inside, Griffin was struck by how warm it was, crowded and humid with perspiration. Still, the music stirred him and the excitement of the crowd filled the air—and the Aether—with a buoyant energy even he could not discount.

Something drew his gaze. A young woman in a splendid feathered costume that made her look like the most exotic bird. His heart gave one tight thump against his ribs as he recognized her. His senses had found her even when he hadn't been looking.

Finley. And she was holding on to Jack Dandy like a woman in love.

# Chapter 11

Chapter 11

What was she doing there? Finley asked herself as she glanced around the crowded circus.

Oh, her escort was charming enough. He was handsome in a sinister kind of way and had such a beguiling way of both murdering and evoking the English language that she found herself fascinated by every word that came out of his mouth. What she couldn't fathom is why he wanted to bring her, of all people, to such a place.

Of course, it wasn't really her he wanted, was it? It was her darker self that had piqued Jack Dandy's interest, and that side was steadily growing stronger the more time she spent under this roof. She felt it clawing at the walls of the imaginary cage she'd built for it deep inside herself. It would love this place—and the company—but she couldn't let it out. Not completely. She couldn't remember what happened the last time it took over, and she wasn't about to risk *that* again.

"You all right, Treasure?"

She glanced up at the concerned eyes watching her from behind the devil mask and smiled slightly. "A little overwhelmed."

He nodded. "I understand. Crowds put me in a bit of a right old mess sometimes m'self. Dance then?"

Before she could answer, he had whisked her out onto the dance floor, caught her up in his arms and guided her into a waltz. They were entirely too close for propriety, though not quite close enough to be scandalous. Mr. Dandy obviously knew how to skirt the fringes of polite behavior.

"Might I say how deliciously lovely you look tonight?" he said, close to her ear, voice low enough that she could hear.

Finley shivered. "Thank you. It's a beautiful costume. You oughtn't have spent so much. Your generosity humbles me."

He squeezed her hand. "Don't you ever be 'umble. You deserve to be treated like a queen. Certainly by better than the likes of me, but I can't seem to 'elp myself."

She swallowed hard. "Good lord, you certainly know what to say to a girl, don't you?"

He laughed at that—a loud, joyous sound that drowned out the music as he tossed his head back. Finley glanced about to see if anyone was staring. Everyone within a mile had to have heard him.

A tall man in a lion mask stood at the edge of the crowd, dressed in black-and-white evening clothes that had obviously been tailored to fit his lean, broad-shouldered frame. As he watched her, the light of the chandeliers overhead caught the red-gold highlights in his brown hair.

Griffin.

Awareness washed over her, like her entire body just woke from a dream. What was he doing here? And who the devil was the scantily-clad harridan hanging off his arm?

An unpleasant taste rose in the back of her mouth, one that

brought a petty feeling with it. She had no say whatsoever in Griffin King's life, and hardly any room to comment on the sort of company he kept, when her own escort was allegedly a criminal overlord. Still, she did not like seeing him with that girl.

And from the tightness of his mouth, she'd wager he didn't much care for seeing her dancing with Jack.

What would Emily say about all this? Her friend had made her promise to wake her when she returned home and tell her all the details. She had been quite impressed with Jack and his tongue-in-cheek costume, but then again, there weren't too many young women who wouldn't be impressed with some aspect of Jack, just like there would be an equal amount enthralled by Griffin.

But she'd wager her last ha'penny that she was the *only* young woman who found them both equally as fascinating and maddening.

Odd, a few moments ago she wouldn't have thought the preference was equal. Her other self had risen a little bit closer to the surface when she saw Griffin and the girl with the impossibly red hair.

She tore her gaze away and focused her attention on Jack's cravat. It was the safest place to look, except that her gaze inevitably traveled up the part of his neck that was bared, then to his jaw and then to his lovely mouth.

He had a slight cleft in his chin. Had she noticed that before? It was a very nice cleft.

"Committing my magnificence to mem'ry, are you, ducks?"

Her lips tilted in a lopsided smile. "Have you always had such a high opinion of yourself, Mr. Dandy?"

His head titled slightly. "I thought you agreed to call me Jack."

So she had. "Why did you invite me here, Jack? I seem to

remember you telling me to run as far away from you as I could."

He shrugged. "P'rhaps I wanted to see if your will was any stronger than mine. I invited and you came. I think you like me, Treasure."

She blushed, but something told her not to play demure with him. "I think *you* like *me,* sir."

He pulled her closer. "What fellow with all his faculties wouldn't?"

What was she supposed to say to that? His words made her warm—too warm—and made her want to search out Griffin in the crowd. Was he watching?

"Looking for your duke?" Dandy's voice had lost some of its teasing, sounding as though he had to make an effort to sound disinterested.

Finley's gaze jerked to his and saw what she thought was pain in the dark depths of his eyes. Had she actually hurt him? "Jack, I…"

"Don't fret, Treasure. I know how the world works." He whirled her around the floor in so many quick, graceful circles she felt as though she were spinning right off the ground into the air. Then, abruptly he stopped—so suddenly she crashed into him and the only thing keeping her upright were his arms, strong and sure around her.

He looked directly into her eyes as the room seemed to continue to spin around her. "I'll play the game, Finley Jayne, because I think you are worth it, but I won't be trifled with. Do you understand? Someday you're going to have to choose."

She stared at him, a hollow feeling in her stomach. She understood, but was confused at the same time. Did he believe her a flirt? She opened her mouth to offer some kind of argument, or defend herself, but nothing came out. Jack's lips curved caustically beneath his mask. The waltz ended and he led her off the floor, silence stretching between them.

"I'm sorry," Finley said as they stood together.

Jack glanced down at her. "Whatever for, Treasure?"

She winced at the sweetness of his tone. "For whatever it is I've done to hurt you."

"Hurt me? I'm Jack Dandy, love. I'm one of the coldest, darkest bastards in all of London, don't you know? Nothing hurts me, so don't you worry your pretty little head about it."

Finley glanced away, feeling like an awful person. As luck would have it, when she raised her gaze, she found herself looking right into Griffin's eyes.

Griffin told himself to turn away, but he couldn't. He wanted to go to her and take her away from this, but he had an escort of his own to think of, and the night's entertainment was about to begin.

Then he felt it, a disturbance in the Aether. It was like a ripple—a shimmer of something tickling the back of his neck, sending a cold shiver down his spine. He looked around and saw a small, spindly automaton with a serving tray heading toward Finley and Dandy. Its movements were jerky but determined, as though it had never moved that way before. It reached for Finley...

"No!" he cried, leaping into action. All thoughts of rudeness and propriety vanished. He pushed through the crowd, fighting the throng to get to her.

But it was too late. The automaton already had her by the throat.

Time seemed to slow. His vision altered, seeing the people and surroundings through the veil of the Aether, auras blazing. Finley's dual aura flared dark—the color of her other self. Dandy tried to fight the automaton. Jasper had a pistol in hand as he fell into step beside Griffin. The cowboy wouldn't shoot unless he had to, though—too much margin for error. Someone could get hurt—or worse.

And then Finley seized the spindly metal arm attached to her throat. A normal human would have no hope against such strength, but Finley was not normal. She snapped the arm at the elbow joint and then ripped the offending hand from her neck.

Holding the arm by the hand and wrist, she used it to beat the automaton, driving it savagely into the control panel as people screamed and rushed around her. They were scared gazelles, running for an exit, terrified they would be the machine's next victim. Meanwhile Finley beat the thing to death, for lack of a better term, with its own arm. It tried to fend her off, but it wasn't built to sustain damage, only to serve. She snapped off the other arm in a similar fashion and drove both of them into the metal's "neck," severing connections, snapping gears.

Griffin and Jasper stopped a few feet away, finally free of the crowd. They could have rushed in, but there was nothing for them to do. Sparks flew from the automaton's wrecked neck, raining around Finley's smiling face like little fireworks.

Her darker self had fully taken over.

Those who hadn't fled in panic had watched the entire altercation, and now they drew closer, closing in like curious cats, eager for a peek at the girl who had just destroyed a machine literally with her bare hands.

The bodice of Finley's costume was torn, revealing what appeared to be a metal corset beneath. Griffin heard people whispering about it—whispering about her. And Finley looked as though she was ready to take a piece out of the hide of anyone who dared approach. He had to get her out of there. It was a big risk for his own reputation and secrecy, but he

couldn't leave her there to hurt someone, or to let someone
else hurt her.

He moved forward, reaching out to stop Dandy as he tried
to touch her. "Don't. Not unless you want to lose that hand,
Dandy."

Smart fellow that he was, Dandy froze, dark eyes watch-
ful behind his devil mask. Griffin approached Finley like he
might a scared animal. "Finley?"

She looked up at the sound of her name. "Rich boy. And
Mr. Dandy, as well. Aren't I a lucky girl?"

"Let's get you out of here," Griffin said, trying to hold
her gaze and work his Aetheric magic at the same time. If he
could control her aura, he might be able to subdue her, but
then everyone would see that he had done something to her,
even if they didn't know what it was.

Fortunately for him, she seemed to like the idea. "All right.
Where do you want to go?"

"Anywhere you want," he lied. "We'll take my car-riage."

She tossed her head, straightened her spine, calling attention to the rips in her bodice and the metal beneath, so close
to her skin. "No velocycle tonight, Your Grace?"

He smiled. "Not tonight, no."

She stared at the hand he offered for a second before putting
her own in it. Her fingers trembled as their gazes locked once
more. This time he exerted his power toward her aura.

Finley blinked. "Griffin?"

"That's my girl," he murmured in a low tone, so no one
but her could hear. Then, as the crowd drew too close, he
swept her away, Jasper on their heels. Dandy didn't follow, but
Griffin heard him deal with the curious costumed onlookers
who tried to give chase.

Moments later Griffin had Finley in the carriage, and Jasper
sat on the seat across from them.

"What's the matter with her?" he asked Griffin.

Griffin shook his head. "Nothing. She's just two personas struggling for dominance in one body."

The cowboy's eyebrows shot up, but his expression was sympathetic. "Poor little thing."

"Griffin?" came a small voice. He turned toward her. Finley peered at him, eyes huge in her pale face. "I don't want to be like this any longer," she murmured as she sagged against the padded seat. "I hate not being able to control myself. Please. Help me."

Griffin squeezed her hand. "I will. You have my word."

A slight smile curved her lips. "Thank you. I knew I could trust you."

He watched her as she fell asleep, exhausted by her ordeal. He hoped he could hold on to her trust. He hoped he could help her, because the thought of what she might become if he could not was simply too horrifying to entertain.

Chapter 12

The headline in the morning's paper read: Automaton's Reign of Terror Brought to Efficient End by Mysterious Girl in a Steel Corset!

And then in smaller print: Duke of Greythorne Whisks Extraordinary Damsel Out of Arms of Notorious Dandy.

Finley was a topic of conversation all across London. Who was this strange girl everyone wanted to know?

The man known as The Machinist was not impressed. Now Griffin King had another one of his lovelies. It would be only a matter of time before the young duke and his intelligent Miss O'Brien would suss out the truth.

It was time to press forward with his plan. Soon, Britain and the entire world would see what he wanted them to. Would see *him*.

And not even the magnificent Griffin King and his motley bunch of extraordinary strays would be able to stop him.

★ ★ ★

Finley didn't know what was in the potion Griffin gave her to drink, but whatever it was, it was *wonderful*. She felt as though she was floating on a bed of clouds, warm and safe in a summer sky, only without the sun in her eyes.

He said it was to help with the integration of the two sides of personality, but she didn't feel anything like she normally did when her darker self came out. She felt good, relaxed. Peaceful.

"You have lovely eyes," she told Griff with a grin. "All four of them."

She heard him laugh, as though from the other end of a long tunnel. "Thank you. Just lie back a bit. There you go."

"You're not going to take advantage of me, are you?" The cushions felt so nice behind her head. It was so *nice* to lie down. "Novels are always warning young women of the dangers of being taken advantage of by wealthy young men."

"You are perfectly safe. Emily is here to protect your virtue."

"That's too bad." Finley thought she heard Emily chuckle, but it was so far away she couldn't be certain.

"Are you comfortable, Finley?" Griffin asked. He was smiling, she could hear it.

She tried to nod but her head wouldn't move. "Indeed, I am."

After that things became a little fuzzy. She was dimly aware of that dark part of her raising its groggy head, but she hadn't the strength to fight it. Oddly enough, it didn't seem to have much strength, either. Griffin was asking questions, which she answered, but for the life of her she had no idea what she said. She wished she wasn't so sleepy so she could pay better attention.

She drifted off, and when she woke up she discovered that a

little over two hours had gone by since she first drank Griffin's concoction. She was still on the sofa in the library, and Griffin stood not far away, placing what looked like an engraved brass tube into a cardboard storage carton.

"What's that?" she asked.

"There you are," he said, turning to glance at her with a smile. "I thought you might sleep through luncheon. This is a phonograph cylinder. I recorded our session so you could listen to it later if you want."

That he had recorded her without her knowledge bothered her, but he was right, she would like to hear what transpired while she was "gone." Gingerly, she sat up. "Are we done?"

"For today." He crossed the carpet and crouched in front of her to take hold of her hand. His fingers were warmer than hers. "How do you feel?"

Gazing into the faded blue of his eyes, she felt a little light-headed, like when she used to twirl in circles as a child, only to fall in a dizzy heap. "Fine," she replied hoarsely. Lord, she hoped she didn't make a cake of herself in front of him. The last thing he needed was her mooning over him like some infatuated idiot. He had rescued her last night, and for that she would be forever grateful—and sorry for whatever shame or scandal she brought down upon him.

"Excellent." He stood, still holding her hand. "May I escort you to the garden? It's a beautiful day, it would be a shame to miss it."

Slowly, Finley rose from the sofa. Her brain seemed to swing slightly to the right, then to the left before righting itself. Griffin released her hand once she was steady and offered her his arm instead. She took it.

"What happened?" she asked as they crossed the great hall, then down another corridor. She tried to ignore how solid his arm was, how tall he was. How peculiar, but it was as though she was seeing him for the first time, or through different eyes.

He grinned. "Do you want the simple answer, or the long, drawn-out scholarly answer?"

"Let's start simply. My head's still a bit foggy from that awful stuff you made me drink."

"First, I feel I should tell you that I didn't take advantage of you as per your wishes." He chuckled when she blushed. "I gave you a weak relaxant that opens the mind up to mesmerism. While you were in this tranquil state, I was able to bring out your other self without creating the kind of stress that normally precipitates a change. By doing this, and allowing both halves to coexist without opposition, we were able to overlap the personas, easing them onto the path of becoming one rather than two."

Finley didn't say anything. It took a few moments for her to understand what he'd just said through the fog in her brain. "So, is that it?"

"No. We still have work to do, but it went much easier than I expected. I thought I'd walk out of there with a bruised jaw at least, but you didn't hit me, not even once."

What a relief that was! She'd feel terrible if that other part of her had struck him while he was trying to help her. Yet... well, he seemed to accept that it *could* happen.

"Do you feel any different?" he asked.

"A little," she replied, certain the direction of her thoughts seemed unusual. She was more aware of him as the opposite sex, and didn't feel quite so guilty for her "other" nature. She felt calm, but stronger, pleasant, but not timid. It was odd. "I'm still me, but different somehow."

He nodded. "That feeling will intensify as the two personas merge, but once it's done you'll feel more comfortable with it, and you won't have to worry about one side taking over the other anymore."

And that was what made this strange unease in her skin worthwhile. "Good. Griffin…" She stopped, trying to think of the right words to describe all the things she felt. There weren't any. "Thank you. I know I've been a trial for you, and you've been so very good to me despite it all."

His lips curved into a lopsided grin. "I reckon you're worth it."

Finley warmed and tried to conceal her pleased smile as she fell into step beside him once more.

They walked out into the garden via the main exit rather than the newly repaired door in Griffin's study. There, on the back lawn, close to the house, was a canvas shelter on posts. It cast shade on the pristine cloth beneath it, the table loaded down with cold meats, breads, cheeses and fruit. At the sight of the banquet, Finley's stomach growled once again. She placed her hand over it in mortification.

Griffin only chuckled. "I'm starving, as well," he whispered near her ear, sparing her the embarrassment of anyone else overhearing. And anyone could have—Emily, Sam, Cordelia and even Jasper, the cowboy from last night, were all in attendance, the lot of them already gathered around the table.

"It's about time," Sam admonished with a frown. "I'm bloody starving out here." Sam seemed a little moodier than usual. Finley wondered if that had anything to do with the way Jasper Renn looked at Emily.

Griffin arched a brow. "You're always starving." There was no maliciousness in his tone, only the easy teasing Finley had come to expect of him. She wondered if Griffin King, Duke of Greythorne, ever lost his temper.

She'd wager it was spectacular when he did.

Yes, she had changed already. Yesterday the idea of a man's

temper would have unsettled her. But then again, she'd changed a lot since coming to this house. The fragments of her were coming together, like a puzzle long left unfinished.

Griffin led her to the table. As duke, his place was at the head. Lady Marsden was at the foot. Sam sat to the right of Griffin, which put him beside Emily, who looked vastly uncomfortable sitting next to the boy she obviously adored. The big oaf didn't seem to notice, or perhaps, given the tightness of his jaw, he noticed too much. Finley sat in the empty chair to Griffin's left, next to Jasper. The boys had stood at her arrival and now they all sat once more. The American smiled at her. He was very handsome with his sandy hair, strong jaw and quick grin. "You look right fine today, Miss Finley."

She smiled at the compliment, embarrassed that he had seen the other side of her the night before. "Thank you."

"You'll have to excuse Jasper," Griffin said to her. "Flirting's like breathing to him."

Jasper grinned, not at all insulted by the darker boy's barb. His green eyes sparkled. "Yes, it is. And, Miss Finley, might I say that you are a breath of fresh air."

They all laughed at that, even Sam, though Finley thought there was little humor in his dark eyes.

"There was a burglary at Madame Tussaud's last night," Lady Marsden said a few moments later as she nibbled on a piece of cheese.

"What did they take?" Emily asked.

"*Who* did they take?" Jasper echoed, causing a few chuckles, Finley included.

Lady Marsden shot him a droll look. "How very perceptive of you, Mr. Renn. Scotland Yard believes it to be nothing more than a jubilee-inspired prank, but the thieves absconded with the likeness of Victoria."

"*Queen* Victoria?" Finley asked, jaw dropping.

The lady nodded, not quite meeting her gaze. The older woman hadn't been quite so confrontational with her since forcing her way into her mind. "The one and same."

"It must be a prank," Sam commented, stuffing cheese and meat between two slices of bread. "Why would anyone want to steal a wax doll of an old woman?" He shook his head.

Griffin watched his friend for a moment, a smile curving one side of his mouth. Then, he turned to his aunt. "It can't be a coincidence that her likeness would be stolen during celebrations of her diamond jubilee."

"Indeed," Lady Marsden agreed. "Less so when you consider that it was Her Majesty's hairbrush amongst the items stolen from the museum."

Jasper frowned. "A hairbrush?" He made a scoffing noise as he leaned back in his chair, an apple in his hand. "Why would anyone steal that? Was it gold?"

The lady looked down her nose at him, obviously dismayed at his lack of "Britishness." "It was a gift from Prince Albert." When Jasper stared at her, she added, "The queen's late husband. He died thirty-six years ago and she mourns him still."

Jasper's eyebrows rose. "That's an old hairbrush."

Lady Marsden rolled her eyes and Finley hid a smile behind a grape.

Griffin picked up a ripe, red strawberry and seemed to study it before taking a bite. "Does the Yard believe the theft to be the work of The Machinist?"

Cordelia shrugged. "They are uncertain at this time, but it seems probable."

He swallowed and licked juice from his lips. "What does he want? I can't hypothesize the method to this madness."

"What else was taken from the museum?" Emily inquired. "Perhaps if we put together what has been taken, we'll know better what his goal is." Finley understood what the other girl left unsaid—that they might also better understand why The Machinist toyed with the automaton that attacked Sam.

"I don't know," Griffin replied. "The room was left in shambles. The curator was to send me a list once an inventory was able to be completed. I'm sure he's very busy with the collection Franks left the museum upon his death." Finley didn't know much about Sir Augustus Wollaston Franks, but she'd heard that he bequeathed to the museum a collection that included, amongst other things, more than a thousand antique finger rings from various cultures.

"There might very well be a connection," Lady Marsden commented. "You should proceed with caution just in case."

Griffin arched a brow. "Because I'm normally so reckless. I'm not the one who once apprehended a criminal using only my own shoe."

Lady Marsden's cheeks flushed ever so slightly as all attention focused on her. "I suppose not. Forgive me for feeling somewhat protective of you."

"No," Griffin replied firmly, but with a sparkle in his eye. "I refuse to forgive you for caring about me when I do so little to deserve it."

It might have been Finley's imagination, but she thought she saw him shoot a pointed glance at Sam when he finished speaking. Nice way to drive a point home.

Lady Marsden smiled and said nothing more on the topic, obviously placated by her nephew's pretty words.

A little while later, Mrs. Dodsworth came looking for Griffin—apparently he had an urgent call from Sam's father, the steward of his estate in Devon. He rushed into the house to take it, with Cordelia following after him at a more ladylike pace.

Finley smiled nervously at Emily, who sat fidgeting next to a frowning Sam. Only Jasper looked completely at ease. He watched the other two for a moment before swiveling in his chair to address Finley, "Do you know jujitsu or kung fu?"

She shook her head, certain she had not heard him correctly. "Beg pardon?"

"Jujitsu and kung fu." He raised his two fists. "Ancient methods of fighting."

She stared at him. Surely he was somewhat touched in the head to even ask such an absurd question. "No," she replied.

"Huh. Would have thought His Grace would have taught you. Would you like to learn? Might come in handy for a girl like you."

Like her. She thought of how she'd bested Lord Felix and was tempted to tell the American she didn't need to know his mysterious arts, but a part of her agreed with him. She didn't know how to properly fight, and given her predilection for finding trouble, defending herself would be a very good thing for a young woman to know.

"Yes," she said, surprising not only him, but Emily and Sam, as well. "I would like that."

Jasper looked positively gleeful at the prospect. "I ain't never sparred with a girl before."

She smiled at him, not the least bit ashamed that the curve of her lips was a little coy. "I'm not just any girl, though, am I, Mr. Renn?"

"Call me Jasper, Miss Finley. Since you're strong enough to pound me senseless, I hope you don't mind that I plan to use my own abilities."

It wasn't a question, but Finley responded as though it were. "Of course not, although I hope you'll show me the basics first." And just what were his abilities? she wondered. The secret heightened her anticipation.

He grimaced, mildly affronted. "Wouldn't be very gentlemanly of me not to."

"Wait a minute," Sam said, butting in. "This is foolish. You can't fight a girl. I don't care how strong she is." He glanced at Finley. "No offense."

Finley arched her brows, but didn't get a chance to say anything because Emily spoke first. "Samuel Morgan! That is the gackiest thing I've heard you say. What does it matter if she's a girl? She's the strongest person I've ever met other than you, you great dense article."

Sam's cheeks reddened ever so slightly. "When she's like this—" he jabbed a finger in Finley's direction "—she's not that strong. And I am *not* dense."

"Oh, aye, you are," Emily argued. "And she's supposed to be learnin' how to bring the two sides of herself t'gether, so this will be a good exercise."

Finley flushed at Emily's mention of her two selves, but the American didn't seem the least bit perplexed. Either Griffin had already filled him in after last night's debacle, or he didn't care.

"You folks got a place to train 'round here?" he asked.

Emily nodded. "The ballroom."

A slow grin spread over his face. "Thank you, Miss Emily."

The red-haired girl's pale cheeks turned red. She muttered her thanks.

The four of them got up and made their way into the house, Emily and Sam leading the way. Finley could hear them talking heatedly with one another and smiled. There might be hope for them yet.

They entered the ballroom and Jasper immediately leaped into the boxing ring set up near the wall. Finley followed him. He stripped off his waistcoat and shirt, leaving himself naked from the waist up, not the least bit self-conscious in front of their spectators—not that he had any reason to be embarrassed. He was quite fit—like a classical statue—and though

Finley admired his physique, she did not feel the strange flutter in her stomach that she often felt around Griffin.

But she was glad she wore a short skirt with her corset, undershirt and boots. She would have as much freedom of movement as possible.

Jasper leaned against the turnbuckle, as though he did this kind of thing every day. "They have a wager," he whispered conspiratorially, pointing at Emily and Sam.

Finley glanced at them. "Really?" Jasper offered his hand to help her step into the ring, which she gratefully accepted. "I thought this was just a friendly training exercise."

"So did I," the American agreed. "Seems your friends have other ideas."

Finley liked the fact that he thought they were her friends, but she wasn't so naive as to totally believe it. Right now she was little more than a houseguest—a stray Griffin had taken in because he felt responsible for fixing her. She was all right with that for now. She'd rather earn their regard than simply have it handed to her.

Jasper wrapped his hands and then hers with thin strips of gauzy cloth. "It will help protect your knuckles," he said, tearing a strip of material with his teeth. "And it will absorb any sweat."

"Or blood," she added.

Jasper's gaze lifted, locking with hers. Good-natured amusement shone in the hazel depths. "Or blood," he agreed. "Let's hope we don't spill too much of that."

Finley shrugged. "I heal quickly."

Jasper laughed. "I don't."

"Emily can fix you." She nodded at their onlookers.

The cowboy shot a quick, appreciative glance over his shoulder. "I reckon she can do anything she puts her mind to," he said—with the first amount of real seriousness Finley had heard from him. There was also no mistaking that Emily liked the praise, just as there was no ignoring the darkening of Sam's face.

A love triangle, Finley thought. *How very dramatic.* She blinked. Sarcasm wasn't something she usually tended toward. Griffin's experiment must have truly worked. The two sides of her were coming together into one.

Their hands wrapped and ready, Jasper began by teaching Finley the basics of the martial arts. He showed her the proper way to stand and strike. He struck different poses to demonstrate the stances that made one's attack more efficient. He also taught her how to fight so she didn't hurt herself more than her opponent, and explained the importance of being quick on one's feet. That was when he chose to reveal to her that his strange talent was the ability to move *very* quickly. So fast, in fact, that he was a blur.

Finley wasn't afraid; she was excited. She wanted to see what Jasper could do. She wanted to see what *she* could do.

They started out slowly, Jasper alternating between instructing and baiting her as they moved around the ring. When Finley did something right—like a kick that would have struck his jaw—he praised it, and when she did something wrong, he stopped to correct her.

"Keep your guard up," he ordered. "A dirty fighter will go for the places that will put you down the fastest—your head, stomach and groin."

As soon as he pointed the places out to her, Finley felt the most devilish impulse come over her. She took a swing at his stomach—she wasn't so mean as to target his...ahem... *nether regions.* But Jasper must have sensed her plan, because he moved swiftly—very swiftly—out of her way. He grinned at her, though.

"Exactly," he said. "You keep those places in mind if a

fella ever gives you a rough time, but try not to make your intentions so obvious." As if to prove his earlier point, he tapped her on the chin with his knuckles. "Could have got you there."

A few minutes later, both of them were breathing a little harder, but Finley felt she was finally learning the rhythm to this strange art. Her ear stung from a blow she wasn't quite quick enough to avoid, but Jasper's left cheek was red from one she managed to land.

"C'mon, Finley lass!" Emily cried out, bloodlust thickening her accent. "Take him down!"

Finley grinned at her opponent, who flashed his teeth back at her. He moved on her, but instinctively she ducked and came up with a fist into his hard stomach. They weren't using the martial art techniques specifically anymore, and a little pugilism made an appearance.

"Oof!" He doubled over. She got him again with another in the jaw, bouncing on the balls of her feet with barely re-strained energy.

When he straightened, he had a wary but determined ex-pression on his face. "I see your friend has come out to play."

It took a second for her to realize what he meant. Her other self had surfaced but without its usual intensity. She felt like she could fight—or dance—all night. But she was still in control.

"I suppose so," she said.

Jasper smiled. "Good. Now it's my turn."

Before she could figure out what he meant, he came at her so fast she barely had time to react. In fact, she took a fist to the shoulder for her inability to react fast enough.

Her darker self had instincts and reflexes much more sharp than her own, so she reached out for that particular talent, ducking and weaving as the American moved faster than any "normal" man could.

He backed her into a corner and she leaped onto the turnbuckle before neatly somersaulting over his head. Behind him, she landed a sharp jab to his kidneys. Her exaltation was short-lived as he swept one leg out and knocked both of hers out from beneath her.

Emily was shouting for her to get up. Sam was yelling out encouragement to Jasper, but neither she nor the cowboy took their eyes off each other.

Out of the corner of her eye—her sight was much more acute when her darker half was in residence, as well—Finley saw the door to the ballroom open and Griffin walked in. She felt that queer fluttering in her stomach, but she wasn't sure if it was for Griffin or for the dark, almost sinister-looking young man standing beside him. What the devil was Jack Dandy doing here?

She would have asked, but at that second, Jasper took advantage of her dropped guard and struck—fast. He had no way of knowing just how distracted she was, and so his fist connected nicely with her cheek.

Pain shot through her face. Stars danced before her eyes as they rolled back into her head and her knees buckled. Finley fell to the mat. Hard.

# Chapter 13

By the time her vision cleared, Finley was surrounded by a sea of concerned faces—the most worried of which belonged to Jasper. Jack Dandy, she noticed, was also in the ring, but didn't hover like the others. He stood near the ropes, looking grim.

"Are you all right?" Griffin asked, frowning down at her.

Finley nodded. "Except that I might die of embarrassment." To be honest, however, at that moment she felt as though she was actually part of their group—as though their worry made her one of them.

His scowl turned to a smile. "I didn't know you and Jasper were sparring. I should have waited or announced myself before barging in."

She turned her gaze to Jasper. "I should have known better than to take my eye off you." And then, "I'd like to get up now."

Griffin offered her his hand as the others drew back. They

stood clustered together, apart from their dark guest. It was Dandy who had Finley's attention as she stood.

"Mr. Dandy," she said. "Whatever are you doing here?"

"Luvly to see you again, Miss Jayne," the dark, lanky fellow replied in his usual laconic manner. "Apologies for interruptin' your sport, but I wanted to inquire as to your health after last night."

All eyes turned to her, turning her cheeks hot. "I am quite well, thank you. I'm terribly sorry for making a spectacle."

He shrugged. "I likes a bit of spectacle m'self." He held her gaze a moment longer than was proper before turning to Griffin. "And I wanted to bring His Grace a gift."

All attention turned from Finley to Griffin, for which Finley was greatly relieved.

"Mr. Dandy informs me that he had a delivery at his Whitechapel address late last night." Griffin cast a brief glance at his guest. "*Someone* deposited the missing wax likeness of Queen Victoria on his doorstep."

"Poor thing was in her drawers," Dandy added. "I reckon it would have caused quite the stir this mornin' had I not realized I'd left somefink at the property and returned to fetch it."

"There was a note attached to the figure," Griffin told them, opening a folded piece of expensive-looking parchment. "It says: 'A thank you for ingeniously solving our mutual "problem." Yours, F.J.'"

Now everyone stared at Finley. She would have done the same were it possible. Her jaw dropped. "You think *I* stole the queen from Madame Tussaud's and left her half-naked on Mr. Dandy's step?" It was ludicrous—and just plausible enough that it made her fearful.

Griffin handed her the note. "It's written on my personal stationery. See the watermark?"

Finley held the paper up to the light where she saw the image of the Greythorne crest engrained in the weave. "That's not my writing," she told him. It wasn't, either.

"Maybe it's the writing of your *friend,*" Sam suggested through clenched teeth.

Of course he would think the worst of her, Finley realized bleakly. He thought the worst of everyone.

"My handwriting stays the same regardless of who I am," she defended, realizing how preposterous this must all seem to Jack Dandy—and ashamed that she cared what he thought of her.

"Aside from that," Griffin interjected, "there's no possible way she could have had enough time to get to the wax museum, steal the figure, take it to Dandy's and return home. Not without being noticed."

"Sure she could have," Sam argued. "You just don't want to admit bringing her here was a mistake." Emily put her hand on his arm but he shrugged her off and went to stand in one corner of the ring, his back to the rest of them.

"Excuse me," Jack Dandy said, drawing their attention once more. "Don't you agree that it seems a tad bit, I dunno, *suspect* that someone would leave a likeness of Her Nibs on me doorstep with Miss Finley's initials on your stationery?"

Finley stared at him. For a moment she thought he was pointing a finger at her, as well, until Griffin spoke once more. "Yes, I do. Regardless of anything else, Finley wouldn't be foolish enough to leave such blatant evidence against herself with the wax figure. No one would." He directed that piece of logic at a red-faced Sam.

"But, if it wasn't Finley, who?" Emily stepped forward. "No offense, Finley, but who else could have gotten your stationery, lad?"

Finley wasn't offended. She wanted to hear the answer, as well.

Griffin flicked a glance at Dandy, and obviously decided the darker fellow could hear whatever it was he was about to say. "Anyone with access to one of my homes could easily sneak into my study and remove paper from my desk or the guestrooms. You all have similar parchment in your own rooms."

Jasper pushed his hair back from his face. "Someone sure is taking a lot of trouble to make it look like Miss Finley stole the figure, and to make it look as though she's in league with Dandy." He glanced at Jack. "No offense."

Dandy bowed his head. "None taken. And now that I've done me duty, I'll be off. I just wanted to make sure Treasure weren't in no trouble."

Finley's face warmed. She walked across the mat to where the tall, dangerous young man stood. It hadn't escaped her what a favor Jack had done her by coming there. "Thank you," she said.

Dandy grinned rakishly. "No fanks, dove. Someday I'll need a favor and I'll come to you." And then to Jasper, "Oy, Yank. Thursday nights I've a bare-knuckle affair going on. Miss Finley can give you my direction."

Finley flushed even hotter. Jasper told Dandy he'd "think about it." Dandy bid them farewell and gracefully slipped between the ropes to the floor and sauntered out the door. Finley watched him go with a little sadness. She liked Jack.

When she turned back to the others, they were all staring at her. "Why would someone do this?" Emily asked.

Griffin's stormy eyes narrowed. "I don't know, but someone has taken pains to cast doubt in her direction, first with Scotland Yard inquiring into the murder of Felix August-Raynes and now this."

Sam stepped forward. "She was questioned about a murder? Bloody hell, Griffin. Why is she still here?"

Finley didn't flinch. She wondered the same thing.

Griffin scowled at his friend. "She didn't commit either crime, Sam. Someone's trying to make her appear guilty so I'll toss her out. I think The Machinist wants to cause tension in my house so I'll leave him alone. And I believe I have proof."

That stopped conversation. Everyone stared at Griffin, who took a deep breath to calm himself before elaborating. "Earlier, when I spoke to my steward he told me that someone had forced the locks on the entrance to my grandfather's caverns, where the Organites and ore were originally discovered. It seems too coincidental that a groundskeeper from that estate resigned a few weeks ago. I'm fairly certain this 'groundskeeper' stole some of the ore. God knows what else he might have taken. He sent this letter, and he stole the queen's likeness from the wax museum. I'm convinced it's The Machinist."

"To what end?" Jasper asked, bewildered.

"I don't know," Griffin replied. "If he'd only broken into the cavern, I'd think he was simply after ore, but obviously there's more to it. It's personal. And he wants to us to suspect Finley."

"She's done a good job of that herself," Sam growled. Finley forced herself to meet his angry gaze. She'd done nothing wrong.

Griffin ignored him. "What bothers me is that if it is The Machinist he's obviously watching us, otherwise how would he know about Finley's association with Dandy?"

Finley shifted uncomfortably. The idea of someone watching her was unnerving, and almost ludicrous, but the note in Griffin's hand was overwhelming factual evidence.

"Why keep the figure's clothes?" Jasper asked, taking some of the attention from her. "Why take the queen's hairbrush?

None of that will fetch him much of a price, and I've not heard of anyone trying to sell Victoria's belongings."

Finley's head was beginning to spin. None of this made any sense.

"Have you stopped to consider," Sam began in a dark tone, "that maybe Finley is in league with The Machinist? You start investigating The Machinist and all of a sudden she shows up, turning your head."

It was a valid suspicion, Finley had to admit. She didn't like the implication, but she'd think it if the situation were reversed.

Obviously Emily disagreed. She whirled on him. "Samuel Morgan! If you have nothing useful to contribute to the conversation, kindly keep your mouth closed!"

Sam's rugged cheeks flushed bright red. "Fine. Obviously no one here wants to see reason. I knew it was a mistake to come back." He turned on his heel and stormed out of the ring and out of the room.

Finley's eyes narrowed, but she put her arm around Emily's shoulders and gave her a squeeze. She turned to Griffin. "Sam made a good point. You should distrust me."

Griffin stared at her—hard. "No, I shouldn't." Then, "We need to go to Madame Tussaud's. Maybe he left a clue behind. Emily, the wax form of the queen is in your laboratory. See what you can find on it."

Emily chewed thoughtfully on her lower lip. "Griff, if he took some of the Organites along with the ore…"

Griffin's mouth thinned. "He would still have to decipher the uses for them. Let's hope he simply thought they were nothing but ooze, and had more interest in the ore instead. That would power his machines for a long time."

Emily nodded, but Finley could see real worry in her eyes. She knew the Organites could heal—she'd witnessed it first-hand—but there had to be more to it for Emily to look so worried.

"Jasper, you're with me," Griff said, climbing out of the ring. "While Em's in the lab, we're going to go to Madame Tussaud's."

That left Finley lost. "What do you want me to do?"

Griffin's head turned. His gaze locked with hers. "I think it for the best if you stay here, especially since our friend has taken an interest in you. Assist Emily in the lab."

He wasn't trying to brush her aside, but she knew a dismissal when she heard one. He might as well have told her to go sit in her room and try not to get into trouble. She knew he was right, but she felt shut out all the same.

She wasn't one of them after all.


Sam went to the tavern and found Leon sitting at their usual table.

"My boy," the older man said as Sam joined him. "Whatever is the matter? You look as though you just lost your best friend."

"Friends," Sam corrected him grimly as he signaled the waitress for a pint. "They're all so enamored with Finley Jayne they can't see what's right in front of their noses."

Leon's expression was all sympathy as the bar wench set a mug on the table in front of Sam. "The girl you told me about?" he asked. "The one I said sounded like trouble?"

Sam nodded. "She is, with a capital *T.* Only, Griffin's taken with her and refuses to admit that she might not be as wonderful as he thinks."

Leon's countenance was all concern and understanding. Sam knew he would understand. He understood about Emily and Griff and how he felt about what they'd done to him. He understood what it was like to feel as if he was on the outside looking in. "Tell me what has happened, my friend."

After a long swallow of his drink, Sam did.

Griffin and Jasper rode velocycles to Madame Tussaud's waxworks on Marylebone Road. Usually Griffin disliked using the cycles in broad daylight because of the attention they drew. Velocycles were relatively new forms of transportation and were quite costly, hence they immediately singled out the driver as a person of wealth. Not only that, but each cycle in his stable had been customized for the person it was intended for, making them even more eye-catching. People already gossiped about the Duke of Greythorne and the company he kept.

All that aside, however, velocycles were the faster way to get about the city, and that trumped gossip.

They left their cycles behind the long, elegant white building, disabling their engines so they could not produce steam and therefore were useless to anyone who might entertain the idea of stealing one or both of them. Although, unless they had the strength of Finley or Sam, he doubted anyone could successfully make off with one.

"What's going on with Sam?" Jasper asked.

Griffin tossed a startled glance in his direction. "He's angry."

"I got that," the American replied with a chuckle. "He sure doesn't seem to like Miss Finley. No more than you like Jack Dandy."

Griffin didn't respond to that. There was nothing to say that would make Jasper believe he didn't care about Finley and Dandy. "Sam's my best mate," he said. "And I don't know him anymore."

"He'll come 'round," Jasper replied as they approached the door.

"You really believe that?"

The American shrugged. "It might take a good boot to the arse first." He grinned. "I volunteer to do the kickin'."

Griffin laughed, and when Jasper opened the museum door, he walked in first, still smiling.

The wax museum was no longer owned by the Tussaud family, so Griffin asked to speak to the person in charge, and when the gentleman appeared, introduced himself and Jasper. The gentleman, whose name was Mr. White, was quite beside himself at having a duke in his establishment. When Griffin told him they would like to see where the Victoria figure had been taken from, Mr. White didn't hesitate. It was one of the advantages to being the highest rank below a prince—one was rarely, if ever, questioned or denied anything.

The curator led them through the museum to where the "royal" exhibit was. Griffin had been there before and wasn't captivated by the amazing likenesses of modern and historical figures. Jasper on the other hand had a difficult time keeping his head still; his gaze jumped from statue to statue.

Griffin shot him an amused glance. "We can stop by the Chamber of Horrors before we leave if you want."

The cowboy merely nodded, his attention already distracted by another lifelike display.

"Obviously we've had this exhibit closed since the theft," Mr. White informed them. "I don't have to tell you it's been very inconvenient given that it's Her Majesty's diamond jubilee."

"Yes," Griffin agreed. "I assume it would be very inconvenient given all the tourists visiting the city."

"Indeed. Fortunately, there are always those who will pay the admission fee simply to see the site where the figure was when it was stolen. Humanity, I'm sure I do not have to tell Your Grace, is a strange animal."

On that point Griffin couldn't agree more, and he said as much as Mr. White led them directly to the royal display. Prince Albert's likeness stood alone, forever frozen as he looked at the time of his death. It would be odd to see this man, who had been in his prime, standing next to the queen as she looked now.

"Did anyone witness the theft?" Griffin asked Mr. White.

"No. We have a night watchman, but the poor man was knocked unconscious by the thieving wretch. Took a nasty blow that split his head open."

The curator had a strange expression on his face—as though he were working over a puzzle. For a second, Griffin wondered if the watchman had been privy to the theft, but he quickly discarded that theory. Stealing a waxwork figure was hardly worth the loss of a position, and if he'd been paid to let the thief in, it was unlikely he would have sustained such a serious injury, if one at all.

"Was anything else taken?"

"No. That is what led Scotland Yard to believe it was nothing more than a harmless prank."

"I doubt your watchman would agree with that assumption," Griffin remarked. "Could you give us his direction? I'd like to speak to him when we're done."

Another benefit of dukedom was rarely being questioned or told no. Mr. White was obviously curious as to why Griff would want to speak to the man—what Griff's interest was in this whole debacle—but he kept his questions to himself.

"Of course, Your Grace. I will get that for you directly."

The curator didn't hang about once he'd shown them where they wanted to go. He had to man the front, of course, and copy the watchman's address, but he asked Griffin to summon him should he require anything—anything at all. Then he bowed and took his leave.

Jasper waited until the man was gone before asking, "You ever get tired of folks puckerin' up to your backside?"

Griffin faced him with mock gravity. "Yes. It is deuced tiring, people doing whatever I wish. Makes my life so very disagreeable."

With an arched brow and wry smile, Jasper shook his head. "I sure do feel sorry for you."

"Indeed, and for your information, I don't enjoy having people trip all over themselves to please me." Griffin frowned. "They usually want something in return. It makes it very difficult to know who my real friends are."

"You live with them," Jasper reminded him.

That was true, but there was no need of him to say that since Jasper knew it, as well. Griffin ducked under the velvet rope that surrounded the display and crouched beside the spot where the queen's likeness had once stood.

Who would do this? And for what purpose? He scanned the area, seeing nothing, not a hair nor scrap of clothing nor...

There was something. He took glass slides and a small blade from his inside coat pocket.

"Jas, come look at this."

His friend drew closer. "What is it?"

"Oil." He scraped the blade through the globule, taking care not to scratch the floor. He smelled it. "The same texture and scent as that found at the automaton crime sites."

Jasper bent over his shoulder for a better look. "The Machinist?"

Griffin smiled slightly. He had no reason to feel pleased at being correct in his assumptions, but he did. It felt as though they were closing in on the criminal even though they still had no idea where or who he was. "Indeed. Our devious friend has been busy as of late."

"Why the heck would he want to steal a wax dummy when he obviously prefers metal?"

"I don't know." Griffin sandwiched the oil between two glass slides. He'd take it to Emily for further analysis.

Jasper scowled at him. "If you don't know, why do you look so pleased with yourself?"

Griffin flashed a lopsided grin. "Because we're going to find out."

Mr. White returned at that moment with the watchman's direction. Griffin thanked the curator and then he and Jasper swiftly took their leave, returning to their cycles and setting off to the watchman's neighborhood.

A short time later, after weaving in and out of traffic at the highest speed they could obtain and still avoid pedestrians and horses, they knocked on the door of a small, but clean and cozy little house in Shoreditch.

"Long way to travel for work," Jasper commented as they waited on the step.

Griffin shrugged. "The underground makes it much easier for Londoners to commute these days."

Jasper made a face at his mention of the subterranean railway. The cowboy didn't like tight spaces any more than Griffin did.

"No," Griff remarked with a small smile. "I don't like it, either."

The door was opened by a stocky man, shorter than Griff but easily twice as broad. Griffin consulted the card Mr. White had given him. "Mr. Angus MacFarlane?"

"Aye," the man replied, appraising Griffin's fine clothes and the pistol partially concealed by Jasper's duster. Ginger brows lowered over sharp, blue eyes. "How can I help you gentlemen?"

Griffin offered his hand. "Griffin King, Duke of Greythorne. This is my associate, Jasper Renn. We would like to talk to you about the Tussaud's robbery."

MacFarlane didn't look impressed. In fact, he looked downright wary. "Mind if I ask to see some identification, *Your Grace?*"

Jasper tried unsuccessfully to hide a chuckle. Griffin shot him a wry look as he produced one of his calling cards for the man.

The big Scot looked at the card, finely printed on the best stock and obviously decided it—and Griff—was the real deal. He stepped back from the door. "Come in."

"Thank you." Griff crossed the threshold first, followed by Jasper.

"I'd offer you a drink, but I haven't anything the likes of what you'd be used to." MacFarlane made it sound as though Griff was the one at fault. This was nothing new. With the knowledge that being a duke would open many doors for him, also came the knowledge that not everyone would like him for it.

"We have no desire to abuse your hospitality, Mr. MacFarlane," he said, all charm and smiles. "In fact, we will take as little of your time as possible. Mr. White said you did not see your attacker. Is that correct?"

"Yes, Your Grace. Snuck up behind me, the bounder did, and coshed me brainbox but good. Woke up covered in me own blood."

Griffin frowned at the man, who had no bandage, bruising or even swelling anywhere to be seen on his nearly bald skull. "You seem to have recovered remarkably well."

MacFarlane shifted uncomfortably. "That's just it, Your

Grace. A little too remarkably. 'Tis the damndest thing, pardon my French."

Still frowning, Griff asked, "Might I see where you were struck, sir?"

The Scotsman shrugged, obviously chalking this entire encounter up to aristocratic eccentricity, and turned so that Griffin had a good view of the side of his head. He could see the man's scalp through the thinning, short expanse of orange hair.

The light in the room was good, and they were near a window. Griffin took a magnifying glass from his pocket and raised it so it hovered over MacFarlane's large skull. There, just above the man's slightly cauliflowered ear. "Were you a boxer, Mr. MacFarlane?"

"Aye, Your Grace. When I was a young man. Never made much of a career of it, and all I have to show for it is me bashed-up ear. You see what you're lookin' for? Just above there."

Griffin did see it. A thin, pink line of newly healed skin just above that battered ear. It made his heart go cold. "I see it, yes."

"Now you understand why I'll be wearing a bandage when next I go to work."

Yes, he did. Anyone who saw this would think MacFarlane was either abnormal, or that he hadn't been injured at all. Griffin was surprised the man even showed him the spot.

"Were there any strange substances near the wound?" he asked, tucking the glass back into his pocket. "I realize it might have been difficult to tell with all the blood."

MacFarlane looked at him, then at Jasper and back to Griff again, as though trying to decide how much to tell them. Griffin didn't blame him, the man's story was already damn near impossible to believe. "There was oil, Your Grace. Like the kind we use to keep the museum's automatons moving smoothlike. I thought it would get into me head and make a mess of the wound, but it...it healed."

Griff schooled his features as a slow panic rose within him. "And a good thing for you, too, sir. I think you are wise to wear the bandage, and I assure you that your secret is safe with me." He smiled. "We've trespassed long enough on your hospitality. We'll see ourselves out. Good day, Mr. MacFarlane. You may keep the card, and feel free to contact me if you remember anything else."

Once they were safely outside, beneath darkening clouds that threatened rain, Jasper turned to Griffin. "That man's wound healed just like the one I had that Miss Emily put her special salve on, the stuff your grandpa found."

Griffin nodded, his mood grim as he swung his leg over the bulk of his velocycle. "The Machinist has Organites, and he's figured out a way to use them."

# Chapter 14

Emily's laboratory was like nothing Finley had ever seen before, or was likely to ever see again.

It was like some kind of macabre toy shop, or a mad inventor's lair. All around her were parts of automatons, bits of gears and machinery. Tools lay scattered over the bench that ran the entire length of one wall. The air smelled of hot metal and oil mixed with various medicinal odors. On the far wall, beakers and burners waited to be used. High shelves held differently colored liquids stored in clear bottles, while bottles of rich cobalt blue and dark amber glass contained chemicals and concoctions sensitive to light. They looked very pretty set up there—like gems of different shapes and sizes.

In one corner sat a large, gun-metal-gray cat. It looked like engravings she had seen of exotic jungle felines, only made of metal. It was beautiful and slightly…wrong, all at the same time.

On a long table near the center of the room lay a slightly

tarnished brass automaton with its front panel removed. It resembled one of those surgical engravings in the medical books Silas sold in his shop, but it was metal instead of human flesh—thankfully. The spindly machine Finley had wrecked at the circus sat on another table. Sam was right to think of her as dangerous, she thought as she saw the damage her own hands had wrought.

The waxwork of Queen Victoria was on the table closest to her, looking so lifelike it sent a chill down Finley's spine. It looked like a corpse—a poor old woman divested of her clothing, as well as her life. So realistic it was that she felt almost as though she should mourn for it, cover it with a sheet and say a brief prayer over the lifeless form.

But it was little more than a doll, she reminded herself as she came closer. Wax, not flesh, not human at all. Still, her hand hesitated a second over the form before she could actually bring herself to touch it. She poked it in the ribs, the wax was hard and unyielding. She let out a little sigh of relief.

Emily smiled at her from the other side of the table. "Were you thinkin' she might sit up and bite you?"

Finley chuckled, a little embarrassed, but not so much that she couldn't laugh at herself. "I didn't get much past the sitting-up part."

"She is unsettling. Reminds me a little bit of my nanny O'Brien."

The fond smile on Emily's face did more to squelch Finley's unsettled nerves than the knowledge that she could destroy the figure fairly easily should it do anything odd. She let her gaze roam over the statue, finally seeing it as a harmless thing.

She frowned. The thief had placed enough humanity on the figure to leave it partially dressed—to leave it with some dignity attached. Yet, it had been left in Whitechapel, a place dignity forgot.

"Why did he take the figure's gown if his only intention was to leave it on Jack's doorstep?"

"Ooh, Jack, is it?" Emily's voice was rife with teasing. "Are the two of ye intimate acquaintances now?"

Finley grinned, she couldn't help it. "You're a fine one to tease when you have both Sam and that pretty cowboy dancing attendance on you." Her gaze fell back to the wax figure, and all humor vanished. "Uh, Emily? I think I might know why he took the whole figure."

The redhead came round the side of the table, and looked where Finley pointed.

"Oh, aye. I noticed those were gone first thing."

Where the figure's glass eyes should have been were nothing but empty wax sockets.

"You can see where they were pried out," Finley said, gesturing along the lash line. God, but it was unsettling to look at. "Now, what would someone want with glass eyes?"

"Any number of things. People wear them, dolls have them. They're used in sophisticated lifelike automatons, as well."

Finley's head whipped toward her. "I've heard nasty stories about what those machines are used for."

Emily made a face. "Don't believe everything you hear. I know of several machines that are very humanoid that are treated with the greatest respect by their owners."

"Do you think The Machinist took the figure for its eyes?"

"Possibly—either for his own work or to sell. I'll send a note 'round to my supplier, ask if he's heard about anyone trying to sell a pair of Victoria-blue eyes. I would imagine they'd fetch a good price, considering they would have been made to match Her Majesty's."

Hand on her hip, Finley gazed at the smaller girl with considerable respect. "You're a very useful person, Emily O'Brien."

The Irish girl preened under the praise. "You're not so shabby yourself. *I* could never get into a boxing ring with Jasper."

"Yes, well, I reckon Jasper would have other things in mind if the two of you were in any kind of enclosed space, alone."

Pink filled Emily's cheeks. "He just likes to tease me. He doesn't mean it."

Finley rolled her eyes. "A girl as intelligent as you cannot possibly be that dense. Has he tried to kiss you?"

"No! Of course not."

Finley leaned her elbow on the table near the wax Victoria's shoulder and grinned. "How about Sam, then?"

The blush in the other girl's cheeks deepened. "Nor him."

She shook her head. "That's inexcusable. Two handsome fellows vying for your attention and you haven't kissed either of them. Of course, were I you, I'd slap that Sam for being such a brute. Kiss Jasper. He's much more charming."

"Charming with every girl he meets," Emily replied none too charitably.

Finley arched a brow. "Jealous?"

She shoved a pale hand against Finley's shoulder with enough force that Finley's upper body leaned a little. "What about you? Did you kiss Dandy?"

"No." She straightened. An image of Jack Dandy's face filled her mind. "Do you suppose he'd be a good kisser?" Before she would have blamed these thoughts on her darker nature, but now she wasn't so certain.

"I think he's had enough experience that he'd be a very fine kisser." A sly light brightened Emily's eyes. "What about Griffin?"

Finley feigned ignorance and pretended to notice something of interest on her fingernails. "What of him?"

"Has he kissed you?"

"He has not." She made a face. "Lord, I'm a charity case to him—a female whose life he feels responsible for. Nothing else."

Emily didn't look convinced. "I've seen the way he looks at you, and how you look at him. He's thought about it. Trust me."

A tiny smile flittered across Finley's lips. She leaned closer, just in case the machines could hear her, and confided, "I've thought about it, too, but I don't think it would be an intelligent thing to do—not while he's trying to help me. It would only complicate things."

"Then you might as well go back to Dandy." Emily's tone was heavy with teasing as she studied the figure's wax left hand. "I'm sure he'd be more than happy to let you practice on him. Maybe that will make Griffin realize he wants you for himself."

"No, thank you. I won't be practicing on anyone. I can't juggle two admirers like you can." But even as she spoke, Finley felt a strange confusion in her chest. She liked Griffin, and thought him very handsome, but she also felt something for Jack Dandy. Oh, the two feelings weren't nearly the same, but they were similar in the fact that she found both of them attractive in their own different ways.

She had no business thinking that way about either of them. It wasn't proper and it was just plain wrong to be thinking about kissing when obviously there was someone out there trying to ruin her life by making her look like a criminal.

"What are these?" she asked, pointing to the small grooves she had just noticed in the wax on the side of the figure's face.

Emily frowned. "I don't see anything."

It took Finley a moment to realize she wasn't imagining things, but rather she saw the "queen" the way her darker nature would see her—with preternaturally sharp eyes. "Look closer. There are marks in the wax."

Still frowning, Emily slipped her goggles over her eyes and covered both lenses with the attached magnifiers. She turned a small knob on the either side, fiddling with both as she bent slightly to study the figure's face. Still adjusting the knobs, she studied one side of the head, then the other. "They look like caliper marks. Someone was measuring Her Majesty's face."

"Could it have been someone at the museum when they made the figure?"

Emily shook her head as she gently searched the rest of the waxwork for more marks. "These figures are made by taking molds and measurements of the actual person whenever possible. The queen would have sat for all those things before they made her likeness. These, I suspect, were made by our thief."

"Again I ask, why?" Straightening, Finley folded her arms over her chest. "What is this mad bugger up to?"

"I don't know," Emily murmured, clearly as baffled as Finley. She lifted her goggles once more. "But he wanted to blame you for it, so maybe we should ask a different question."

Her gaze locked with the smaller girl's, Finley could only nod her head in grim agreement. "Who is he? And how does he know me?"

"She's trouble and no one else can see it." Sam was in a decidedly petulant mood as he sat sprawled on the sofa in Leon's apartments in Russell Street. "Scotland Yard came to the house to talk to her about the murder of the son of her former employer, and everyone's all *'poor Finley.'*" He said the last bit in a falsetto dripping with disgust and mockery.

His older friend came into the small sitting room from the small kitchen area and handed him a cup of coffee. Sam accepted the cup with thanks, wincing as the hot pottery burned his flesh. Leon's metal hand hadn't felt the heat, of course, but Sam's—even the one with metal underneath—did.

He set the mug on the low table in front of him and glanced down at the welt on his palm. It lingered for a moment, stinging and then gradually began to fade until it was little more than a slightly pink itch and then nothing at all.

"That's quite amazing," Leon remarked, seating himself in a chair beside the sofa. He looked every inch the gentleman in his immaculate silk waistcoat and brushed wool jacket. "Have you always healed so quickly?"

During one of their conversations, Sam had confided to Leon his strange strength and healing abilities, which had intensified as of late. "Not quite so quickly, no," he replied. "Usually it took some of Emily's salve to make wounds heal completely."

"Ah, yes." Leon smiled slightly. "The brilliant but Machiavellian Emily. What did she put in this 'salve' you speak of?"

Sam hesitated. It was one thing to tell his secrets, but he had sworn to Griffin that he would never divulge the truth about the Organites. "I'm not sure," he replied, looking down at his hand again so he didn't have to lie to his friend's face. "She never told me."

There was a moment's silence as Leon took a drink of the hot, strong coffee. *Café-espress* he called it. "Tell me more about this Finley person. She sounds quite extraordinary—and dangerous."

"Yes," Sam agreed wholeheartedly. "Since Griffin took her in, there's been nothing but trouble. She comes and goes as she wants, consorts with criminals, is suspected of murder, and now… Now she may be involved in a matter Griff is investigating. Even if she's not to blame, she's up to her eyes in it. I know it."

"The stalwart Duke of Greythorne." This was said with a hint of mockery. "He is just a boy, Samuel. I dare say he's infatuated with the girl and refuses to see her as anything but perfect."

Sam grunted, lifting his cup to his mouth. The coffee burned his tongue but tasted good. "He knows she's not right," he remarked. "He's seen what she's capable of, but he thinks he can fix her."

"Some people are beyond fixing." Leon set his cup on the table. "From all you've told me, I would think you would not care if the duke were made a fool of after all he's done to you." He meant, of course, what Griffin and Emily had done to him. Made him a freak. "You could simply walk away."

"They're still my friends," Sam admitted. "I don't want to see anyone injure them."

"My dear boy, if you are concerned with the safety of your friends, you have to do something about this girl."

Sam's scowl gave way to an expression of confusion. "Like what?"

Leon shrugged, making the gesture sophisticated as Sam suspected only people from the continent could. "Make them see her for what she truly is. Force her to show her true colors."

Brow furrowed, Sam thought about it. "How?"

The older man smiled patiently. "There isn't a devious bone in your body, is there? How very noble. You push her into a corner. You said this…affliction of hers tends to reveal itself when she feels threatened. Threaten her with the truth, make her tip her hand to your friends. Then they will see that you were right all along."

Sam thought about it. Leon made it sound so simple. "You're right."

"Age does have its benefits," his friend quipped with a smile.

They talked a little while longer about other things, until Leon finished his coffee and announced that he had to call their visit to an unfortunate halt. "I'm afraid I have an engagement, but we will see each other again soon, no?"

Sam rose to his full height, towering over the other man. Despite his superior size and strength he felt young and foolish next to this worldly man who had accepted the metal part of himself with grace and ease. Maybe someday Sam could do the same and not think of his new arm—of his heart—as something alien and wrong, as a betrayal by those he held so dear.

"Of course," he replied, accepting the handshake. He didn't even wince when Leon closed his chromium fingers over his, engulfing Sam's hand in both of his. The metal was warm where it had cradled the coffee cup but cold everywhere else.

"Thank you," he said as they walked to the door together. "I appreciate you taking the time to see me and offer advice."

The older man smiled. "I am here whenever you find yourself in need of a friend. I hope you always know that. You are a good man. You'll do the right thing where your friends are concerned, and they will thank you for it."

Sam smiled. How long had it been since he'd felt as though someone understood him so well? "Good day, Leon."

A brief nod of dark hair. "Samuel."

Sam left the building, clomping down the winding stairs and out into the fading afternoon. He felt happier than he had for some time. He'd return to Mayfair and he'd make the others see what Finley Jayne really was. Then they'd see that he was right and not an idiot. They'd see the truth and Finley would run straight to Jack Dandy where she belonged.

He only hoped he could get rid of her before she hurt someone.

After the museum, Jasper left to talk to some of his own contacts, agreeing to come by later that evening. Griffin returned to the house to find Emily and Finley in the cellar laboratory with the waxwork Victoria. Their eager faces made the ride down to the cellar in that tiny box of a lift almost worthwhile.

"Did you find anything?" they asked almost in unison.

"I did," he replied, glancing about the room. "Sam still gone?"

Emily nodded, worry plain in her big eyes. She looked like a waif swathed in her goggles and apron. Her clunky boots seemed too large for her feet, the goggles too big for her head. Even the ropes of her bright copper hair seemed out of proportion. Beside her, Finley looked like an Amazon warrior, with her leather corset, short-sleeved shirt and black knickers. The heels of her black leather boots looked sturdy enough to grind a man's bones to dust.

"What did you discover?" Emily asked.

Griffin turned to her, ashamed to have taken even a moment to admire Finley when he should have been concentrating on the matter at hand. "It was The Machinist. We found his oil. The night watchman got some of it on his wound and it healed him—much faster than it should have. He has Organites, and he puts them in the oil he uses on his automatons."

Emily's brow furrowed in concentration. "I don't know how the wee beasties could possibly benefit a joint lubricant, but I'll run some tests."

"Wouldn't you have found the Organites in the other samples?" Finley asked.

Emily shook her head, ropes of hair swinging around her shoulders. "They have to have something to draw energy from in order to live, plus they imitate whatever they're attached to. The sample would have to be fresh for me to detect them, otherwise they're dead and look like the very stuff suspending them."

Griffin wasn't entirely certain how much of that Finley understood. Hell, he wasn't even certain he understood and he'd grown up knowing about Organites and how they worked. "Tests sound like a good idea, Em," he said.

"Come see what we found," Emily suggested, gesturing to the wax figure.

Griffin was astounded when they pointed out the missing eyes and the supposed caliper marks. "I doubt very much you'll find those eyes have been sold. I'd say he's building an automaton."

"Of Queen Victoria?" Finley's tone was so incredulous a slight smile curved Griffin's lips.

"Yes," he replied. "He could take it to one of the jubilee celebrations, pretend it's a novelty, part of the fun and then blow it up."

"But why?" It was Emily who asked the important question. "What would be his motivation for such random violence?"

Finley shrugged. "His crimes have been pretty random so far."

"No." Griffin scowled, a million thoughts racing through his head. "They only seem random because we don't know what he's up to." He wished Cordelia were there. She was always much better at putting together puzzles than he was, but she had gone to Devon to see what, if any, damage had been done to the caverns on his estate—and find out more about this mysterious groundskeeper of his who suddenly vanished. It seemed obvious by now that it must have been The Machinist, but he needed to be certain.

"What about Dandy?" Finley asked. When Griffin looked at her, she seemed to have trouble meeting his gaze. "If this Machinist is such a criminal mastermind, surely Dandy should know *something* about him."

For a moment—and just a brief one—Griffin wondered if Sam's suspicions of Finley were correct. He really knew nothing of her. Didn't know her at all, and yet...

He couldn't bring himself to believe her a villain.

"No," he said firmly, cursing silently this time when he saw her gaze drop to the floor. "I mean..." What did he mean? He cleared his throat. "I sincerely doubt Dandy will tell us anything even if he does know. There's truth behind the saying 'honor among thieves.' It's very possible the two of them might do business together. He won't jeopardize his own standing in the underworld. He already took a big risk bringing the waxwork to us."

Finley crossed her arms over her chest. "It wouldn't hurt to ask."

Griffin's clenched his jaw all the same. He didn't want Finley anywhere near Jack Dandy, not because he was worried about her, but because he was worried Dandy's "liking" for her was reciprocated.

He swallowed the taste of jealousy building in the back of his throat. "All right," he acquiesced. "Ask him. But arrange to meet him somewhere. I don't want you going to his address alone. The Machinist knows who you are, and might still be watching you—or Dandy. I don't want to give him an opportunity to go after you."

She didn't look half as afraid of that idea as she would have when she first arrived at his house, but it was obvious that the thought hadn't crossed her mind, and that it scared her. "I will."

Emily's head suddenly jerked, as though an idea had literally slapped her in the face. "I know someone who might be able to tell us something."

"Who?" the other two chorused.

Her eyes narrowed shrewdly. "We found The Machinist's oil at other crime sites. In fact, we found it in the automaton that attacked Sam."

Griffin nodded. "That's how we theorized The Machinist was behind the metal's malfunction. But you said you didn't know what he'd done to the machine," Griffin reminded her, keeping his tone gentle so she wouldn't mistake his words for spite.

"That was before I'd realized I developed the ability to speak machine." With that, she stomped across the lab, boot soles hitting the floor with determined slaps as she headed toward the large iron vault in the top corner of the laboratory.

Griffin filled with unease. "Em, what are you doing?"

"Something I should have done long before this, but I was too much a coward." She unlocked the vault, spinning the wheel to open it. There was a hiss—the venting of steam as the gears of the vault's mechanism turned—and then a loud *click*. Emily pulled the door open.

Inside was the automaton that had attacked Sam. Seeing it almost froze Griffin's heart in his chest. It stood like a great iron man with a box-shaped body, one long arm with a large scoop of a hand, heavily treaded wheels and a small navigation dome where a head would be.

"Emily." Finley stepped forward, obviously not wanting the little Irish girl to get any closer to the abomination. It took all of Griffin's resolve to stop her instead of going after Emily himself.

"Be ready," he whispered close to Finley's ear. "Just in case."

She nodded.

"I'm going to power it up," Emily told them. "Stand clear, just in case. If anything happens, do not attack until I say so. I need a little time to make contact."

Griffin personally thought it too great a risk, but it was one he would take himself and therefore he didn't try to dissuade her. He merely stood there, silent and terrified as his wee Irish lass reached up and stuck a notched brass rod into the ignition port on the automaton's front. Every metal laborer in the city had a similar port. It was to prevent accidental power outages or ignitions, but still simple enough that a machine could be shut down quickly if necessary.

Emily turned the rod. The notches made sharp clicking sounds as they found the tumblers and moved them into the proper position. There was a hollow sounding clunk, followed almost immediately by a whirring noise and the rotation of gears. The engine began to hum, preparing to run startup procedures. The automaton shuddered as the power source—made from the ore Griffin's grandfather had discovered—worked its magic, followed by a noise that sounded like the whoosh of a heavy bellows.

The creature was coming to life.

Emily stood before it, the top of her head not even reaching three-quarters of the thing's height. Her hands looked tiny against its scarred and dirty front panel—her left had a smear of something black across the back of it.

From where he stood, Griffin could watch her as she closed her eyes, face set with determination. However she "spoke" to the metal, it wasn't with sound. If the thing were alive, he'd say it was telepathy. As it was, he had no word to describe it.

The automaton rumbled steadily, not making any movement whatsoever. Still, Griffin didn't relax and neither did Finley. He was prepared to bring the entire house down on it if he had to.

Emily's face paled with concentration, her freckles standing out against her skin. Her forehead creased, and her mouth tightened as she continued to press her hands against the metal, as though she possessed the strength to hold it at bay. How long this went on, Griffin wasn't sure, but suddenly he noticed that Emily was trembling—and that it wasn't simply the machine's vibrations running through her.

"Em?" He took a step forward. Finley glanced at him out of the corner of her eye, but didn't move. The two of them waited, holding their breath.

Locks of thick, twisted red hair fell forward as her head bowed. That moaning sound—was it from her or the machine? He couldn't be certain. He took another step. "Emily?"

He saw the blood at the same time Finley did. It ran from Emily's nose and down her face to drip on her dirty apron and the floor. Drops of it splattered on the floorboards between her boots.

Emily's knees began to buckle. Her hands left moisture prints on the grimy brass as they slid down the panel.

"Shut it down," Griffin commanded, launching forward. Finley leaped into action, as well. It was she who caught Emily as she collapsed. Griffin grabbed the ignition rod just as the automaton began to raise its one arm—parts of the other having been used to reconstruct Sam's. The whirring and rumbling whined and choked to a stop. The arm fell with a loud clunk and then everything went silent.

Chapter 15

Don't move," Finley ordered as Emily shifted in her arms. They were on the floor of the lab—her kneeling with the smaller girl's torso propped up on her legs. She used a handkerchief to wipe the blood from Emily's pale face before folding the linen into a square and using it to staunch the bright red trickling from her nose.

Bright blue-green eyes locked with hers. She could see that Emily was in pain, but there was something else—triumph.

"It spoke to me," she whispered.

"You can tell us what it said later," Finley told her. "Right now you just rest for a moment." Nothing was so important that it couldn't wait. The sight of Emily hurt had struck something deep inside her. She cared about this girl. She was the closest to a friend she'd had in such a long time, and the idea of losing that friendship terrified her.

Behind them, Finley heard the vault door creak on its hinges. She stiffened, heart hammering in her chest. Was it the machine? Then she heard the loud click of the lock followed by the turning of a wheel. Griffin had closed the vault. She closed her eyes and breathed a silent sigh of relief.

Her comfort, however, was short-lived. Just as she was about to help Emily to her feet, the door to the laboratory burst open and in stomped Sam, tails of his dark gray coat whipping out behind him. He looked around the room, and when his gaze fell on her, his eyes turned even blacker than usual.

"What the hell did you do to her?" he demanded, coming at her like a bull at a red flag.

Instinct told Finley to pass Emily to Griffin, so she did. Griffin glared at Sam, opened his mouth to speak, but was cut off by Emily. "It's only a nosebleed," she told the large boy. "I talked to the digger, Sam."

Sam's head turned to look at her, shock written plainly on his features. "You what?"

"I put my hands on the digger and it spoke to me." Emily wiped at her nose with the stained handkerchief. "I thought maybe it would tell me about The Machinist so Finley wouldn't have to ask Dandy—"

"You started up that thing," Sam cut her off as he jabbed a finger in Finley's direction. "For *her?*"

Finley mentally shook her head. Emily hadn't quite recovered from her ordeal, or she would have known better than to say anything about having "talked" to the blasted metal for Finley's benefit. She knew how much Sam thought of Emily, even if neither of them knew it themselves.

Sam came at her. She barely had time to brace herself, barely time to register that part of her wanted this seemingly unavoidable violence.

"It could have killed her," Sam raged, coming to stand in front of her, a bull ready to charge. "She wouldn't let me die, but she risked her life for *you*. You are not worth her life. You're not worth her blood."

It happened so fast then, she barely had time to realize what was happening. Big, strong—terribly strong—hands gripped her, lifted her and threw her. Finley flew through the air, dimly aware of Griffin's shout and Emily's cry. She hit the wall with a force that would have seriously injured a normal person. She crashed to the bench and then the floor, taking a pile of debris with her that included part of a velocycle frame, a clock and an assortment of tools.

Oh, God, that *hurt*. Her lungs struggled to draw breath as she lay on her belly on the floor, gasping for breath and choking on dust. She wiped her mouth with the back of her hand. Blood stained her skin; she had bitten her tongue when she struck the wall.

Slowly, she pushed herself up, assessing the damage done. The others were still far away, up by the vault. Griffin and Emily were yelling at Sam, alternating between trying to reason with him and berating him. Griffin tried to hold the goliath of a young man back, but Finley knew even Griffin couldn't keep him for long.

Sam Morgan wanted a fight, and he wanted it with her. There was no one in that room who could stop him, and she was the only one who came anywhere near being a match for him. Unless Griffin did whatever it was he did, there was no alternative but to give him that fight. She knew this with both sides of herself, so in the interest of self-preservation, she let the change happen. It didn't take much—violence always made the transition easy. This one was a little different in the fact that it hadn't taken over already. Normally she would have already lost control rather than be given the choice.

Energy raced through her, giving her strength where there had been weakness, numbness where there had been pain and anger where there had been fear. When she rose to her feet it was with a smile and she beckoned Sam with the taunting crook of a finger.

"There it is," Sam said, wiping his mouth with the back of his hand. "There's the real monster." His face ferocious, the tall, muscled young man charged at her. Finley stood her ground and let him come. Just as he was about to strike, she grabbed him by the waist of his trousers, her left hand going behind his shoulders. She used his own momentum to lift him off the ground, flip and throw him down. His back hit the floor hard—she could feel the shock of it tremble through the boards beneath her feet.

Within seconds, he arched his body and leaped to his feet with more grace than she would have expected from someone his size. She barely had time to duck the massive fist that swung at her, countering with a sharp uppercut under his chin. Pain raced up her arm as his head snapped back. Bloody hell, had Emily reinforced his skull with metal?

Shaking her hand, Finley drew back, waiting for him to make the next move. She wanted to be more aggressive. She wanted to climb him like a tree, lock her legs around him like a monkey and pound his face until he surrendered or passed out. However, that maneuver would probably hurt her more than him. And she wasn't about to be the villain in this fight. She would defend herself, but she would not attack.

Something that felt very much like the side of a carriage struck her left cheek, lifting her off her feet once more. Her side struck the table holding the waxwork Victoria, sending the queen toppling to the ground as the heavy table skidded several inches, leaving grooves in the wooden floor. She felt her ribs crack, agony shooting through her as she slumped over the tabletop. She groaned.

Gentle hands touched her arm and face. It was Griffin. "Stop this," he begged.

It hurt to breathe. Finley shook her head. "It's not my fight to stop."

He looked up. "Sam, stop it, *now*. Finley did nothing wrong."

"Idiot," Sam sneered as he stomped toward them. "You're so infatuated with her you can't see straight. Look at everything that's happened since you brought her here. She was a murder suspect. She's in league with Dandy and still you try to protect her. What does she have to do before you'll see her for what she is? Cut one of our throats?"

Finley sat up, wincing at the movement. Staying down wouldn't save her, and a part of her very much wanted to continue—fight until one of them could no longer fight. "If I cut anything of yours, you great stupid article, it will be your tongue—and then I'll make you swallow it."

He made a noise that sounded very much like a roar, picked her up by the throat as though she were a rag doll and held her above the floor as he punched her once, twice, three times. Her ears rang, her face felt hot and wet—broken. If she were normal she'd most likely be dead. But she wasn't normal and her ribs were already healing. Unfortunately, she saw that the cut on Sam's lip—no doubt from where his teeth had torn it when she punched his jaw—was almost healed, as well. Wonderful. He was bigger, stronger and healed faster than her.

The fingers around her throat tightened, cutting off her supply of air. She gasped like a beached fish, holding on to his arm so all of her weight wasn't on her neck. He was going to kill her.

"Sam!" It was Griffin's voice. Finley's vision was beginning to blur, but out of the corner of her eye she saw Griffin grab Sam's arm. "Let her go!"

It was proof of how far into his rage Sam was, because instead of letting her go, he lifted his free hand and backhanded Griffin with enough force to knock the other fellow to the floor. Emily cried out.

That was what sent Finley over the edge. As blackness swarmed the edges of her mind and vision, the sight of Griffin thrown to the floor and the sound of Emily's anguish gave her an extra shove. She opened herself up and let go of all of her fear and control, her soul reveling in a brief moment of ecstasy as the two halves of her came together.

Her vision cleared. Behind Sam she saw Griffin rising to his feet, his eyes glowing unnaturally. She'd already seen what happened when the Duke of Greythorne used his abilities, and there was no pool here to absorb the energy. She had to end this before they all died.

She looked down at Sam as she managed to pull a shallow breath into her lungs. Both of her hands tightened around his wrist and forearm. Tightening her stomach, she pulled her legs up, bent to her chest. She focused all of her strength on her lower extremities as she drew back and then snapped her legs out like a jackrabbit.

She kicked him in the chest. The heavy soles of both boots struck with all the force she could muster. She heard a sickening cracking sound as they connected. Sam grunted and dropped her, skidding backward, until he hit the wall, books raining down on him from the shelves above.

Finley knew immediately that the fight had gone too far. Whether it was that crunching noise or the look on Sam's face that told her she wasn't sure, but she knew before he slid to the floor that Sam was seriously hurt.

The fight fled from her with the swift intensity of a sneeze, leaving her twitchy and anxious in its wake. She ran across the room on shaking legs, falling to her knees beside her opponent just behind the others.

"Is he all right?" she asked, even though she didn't want the answer.

Somehow, Emily had found a stethoscope in the mess made by the fight, and placed the metal part on Sam's broad chest as she shoved the listening pods into her ears. Her face was white as she glanced at Griffin.

"His heart," Emily whispered, her hands shaking as much as her voice.

Finley swallowed hard and looked at the young man on the floor. It sounded as though he was having trouble breathing. Blood trickled from his mouth. His wide eyes sought Emily's and held them.

"Em," he whispered hoarsely, blood running down his chin. His eyes were wide and he looked like a scared little boy instead of the wild man he'd been only moments before. "I don't want to die."

Finley's throat clenched as the back of her eyes burned. She would never forgive herself for this—and neither would anyone else. How could she have lost control? Yes, she was only defending herself, but she never meant to harm Sam, only to keep him from seriously harming her.

Emily's head turned toward her. Gone was the fear and wild, wide-eyed expression. She looked calm and collected—perhaps too much so. "Pick him up," she instructed. "Take him to the infirmary."

Finley was so numb she couldn't even ask where the infirmary was. She simply did as she was told and picked Sam up. Obviously her darker half hadn't left her completely, probably because she felt so terribly guilty.

Griffin guided her to another room off the lab. It was small, but frighteningly clean and well lit. A lone table stood in the center of the room, a huge chandelier hanging overhead. It was a surgery, she realized. Quickly, she carried Sam to the table. There was a terrible pallor to his face, a light sheen of sweat over his skin.

"I'm sorry," she whispered to him, her voice cracking. "I'm so sorry."

"Open his shirt," Emily demanded, and Finley was so eager to fix her mistake she ripped the buttons off his waistcoat and tore his shirt right down the middle, the fine lawn giving away like tissue paper.

Sam's chest was broad and muscled, and it was already beginning to bruise where she kicked him—not a good sign.

"Wash your hands," Emily told her. "You're going to help me. Griffin, get the ether and Listerine out of the cabinet. Clean linen, too."

"What are you going to do?" Finley asked.

Emily glanced at her with unnervingly steady eyes. "I'm going to cut open his chest and fix his heart."

For a moment Griffin thought Finley might faint she went so pale, but then she gave her head a shake and went to wash her hands at the sink as Emily demanded.

The inside of his cheek had torn against his teeth when Sam backhanded him and he could taste blood in his mouth, see it on the front of his shirt. He wasn't even angry. At this moment all that mattered was saving Sam. Again.

If Finley hadn't done this, what would he have done? He had felt the Aether rushing to him in his anger. He would have done far more damage than this. He might have killed them all.

This was too much like the previous time they had operated on Sam. Not so much blood and carnage, but horrible all the same. He didn't want to stand there and watch Emily do what needed to be done, but he refused to leave her alone. So, he put the ether-soaked cloth over Sam's nose and mouth and watched as his friend slipped into a deep slumber before collecting the needles, pump and tubing for a transfusion. Last time Emily had operated, they discovered his blood was compatible with Sam's. Quickly, he attached the equipment, piercing the vein on the inside of Sam's large arm before doing the same with his own. Then he connected the small pump Emily had fashioned out of parts of a sewing machine. It powered up immediately, and within a few moments was producing enough steam to pull the blood from his arm into Sam's. It was much quicker than waiting for gravity to do its work.

While he'd been busy readying the transfusion machine, Emily had readied her own tools and poured Dr. Lister's "Listerine" disinfectant over her hands and Sam's torso.

Then, she raised her scalpel and quickly cut into Sam's chest. Finley handed Emily what she needed, doing what she was told quickly and without comment. Not even when she utilized that awful contraption for spreading Sam's broken ribs apart did she falter, although she grew terribly pale.

Emily frowned as she peered inside Sam's chest. "What the devil…"

"What is it?" Griffin demanded.

"Nothing that needs worrying right now," she replied curtly. "One of the intake valves is broken. Finley, hand me that one on the tray beside you."

Finley did, her eyes wide as she looked at Sam's open chest.

Emily worked quickly and efficiently, but Griff was well aware of the minutes ticking by as she clamped and removed the faulty valve. Every second brought Sam closer to death. He didn't know how long they'd been at this, but it felt like forever. He had yet to feel light-headed from blood loss, so he knew it couldn't have been that long. The transfusion pump continued its slow "breathing," inhaling Griffin's blood and exhaling it into Sam.

"Finley, I need you to hold the broken edges of his ribs together so they can knit. Otherwise they'll heal like this."

Finley swallowed hard, but she didn't hesitate to reach inside Sam's chest and do what she was told. Emily tossed the ruined valve into a bin at her feet, wiped her wet hands on a square of linen and then set about affixing the new valve. Once it was in place, she removed the clamp. Griffin held his breath. His shoulders were stiff and the entire right side of his face throbbed, but he didn't move.

Emily smiled. "It's working," she said.

No one said anything, but their collective sigh was cheer enough. As he shut down the pump and removed the needle from his arm, Griffin frowned at the brilliant Irish girl. She was still gazing inside Sam's chest, her hands paused in the act of removing the rib spreader.

"What is it, Em?" he asked, sticking a bandage in the crook of his arm and bending his elbow to stop the bleeding.

She shook her head. "I don't know, but it's amazing. Look."

Griffin wasn't a squeamish person, but it took all of his resolve to peer inside his friend. His unease was soon replaced by wonder. Tiny tendrils of blue and green wrapped around Sam's mechanical heart, framing the glowing green power crystal at its enclosed center. "Is that…?"

Emily nodded, her gaze locking with his. "The Organites. When I first opened him up, I saw that they were already trying to patch the broken valve themselves."

"How is that possible?"

She removed the spreader and Finley released the already mending ribs. "When I replaced Sam's arm, I used Organites to regrow his flesh. They replicated his cellular composition.

Obviously they spread from his shoulder into his chest. Probably the rest of his body, as well."

Griffin shook his head in wonder. "Which would explain his increased ability to heal."

Emily cast a brief glance at Finley as she began to stitch Sam's flesh together with the precision and steady hand of a seamstress merely mending a hem. "Yours, as well," she remarked. "Your father's experiments made the Organites part of you."

Griffin looked from Finley's surprised expression to Sam's peaceful face, profoundly glad that his friend was going to recover—so he could tear a strip off his hide later for being such an ass. "They looked as though they were attracted to the power core."

"Yes." Emily frowned in concentration. "I'll have to run some tests, but I've a theory brewin' about that, lad."

He grinned, he couldn't help it. Emily was one of the most soft-hearted people he knew. She cried over injured birds, but in the face of real crisis she became almost emotionless, single-minded in her purpose. It was something he admired about her, although the shock would hit her later and she'd shake like a leaf in the wind for a day or two.

When Sam was all sewn up, Emily cleaned the incision again with the Listerine, wiped it clean and then smeared a layer of her Organite-based salve to quicken the already rapid healing of Sam's body. Then she put something that looked like the flat part of a stethoscope right over where Sam's heart was. A long wire running from it was attached to a small gramophone on a nearby table. Through it, came the sound of a heart—Sam's heart—pumping.

"He'll be almost good as new when he wakes up," she told them as she went to the sink to wash her hands. She removed her stained apron and flung it in the laundry bin in the corner.

Finley, unbidden, took the surgical instruments to the sink, as well. Emily would sterilize them later. Griffin's attention turned to the girl who was still a relative stranger to them all, but had been pulled so quickly into their lives and the drama that surrounded them. She stood at the sink, her freshly washed hands gripping the white enamel. Her hunched shoulders began to shake.

"Finley?" He moved toward her.

Her sobs broke his heart. They weren't the careful tears of a gently bred young lady taught never to make a scene and never to appear ugly. These were the gut-wrenching hiccups of someone in terrible and uncontrollable pain. He and Emily exchanged a glance.

"Finley." He made his voice as gentle as possible. God only knew what she might do in this emotional state if her darker self was still lingering about, and Griffin had been battered enough for one night. So had Finley, for that matter.

She turned when he touched her shoulder, surprising him by throwing herself into his arms and sobbing against his chest. He held her for a while, stroking her hair and hushing her as Emily looked on with equal parts discomfort and concern.

"It...it's all my fault," she whispered. "I almost killed him."

What she said was truth, there was no denying that, but Griffin was hardly about to take her to task for it. "He was trying to kill you." He hated to say it, but that, too, was truth. He wasn't certain what madness had taken control of his friend, only that he must have thought Finley had harmed Emily. He had no doubt that Sam could have easily killed her in his anger.

"It's all right," Griffin told her, patting her back. "Sam's going to be fine. You're going to be fine." He was so bloody happy to be able to say that.

Finley nodded, but she didn't meet his gaze as she withdrew from his arms. The front of his shirt was damp from her tears. She sniffed and wiped at her eyes. "I'm going to go lie down for a bit."

Griffin watched helplessly as she walked away. He didn't know what to do or say. Everyone's emotions were running high at the moment; jumbled and confused. Emily stepped back to let her pass, her gaze following the other girl into the lift.

And then she was gone, leaving Griffin and Emily alone with Sam, whose heartbeat sounded out, loud and strong behind them. Regardless of how much either of them wanted to go after Finley, Sam was the one who needed their attention now, and he was the one they went to, forced to choose one friend over the other.

When Finley left the others, she went straight to her room, found a valise in the wardrobe and began stuffing as much of her belongings into it as she could. It held almost everything, as she didn't have much. She'd repay Griffin for the clothes someday.

It was her natural instinct to run whenever trouble found her, and this was no exception. It didn't matter that she liked Griffin and Emily, even Jasper. Sam had been with them longer than her and he was their real friend. If they had to choose between herself and him they would take him, and rightfully so.

But she couldn't stay there any longer knowing she'd almost killed him. If the others didn't hate her now, they would soon. Better to leave on her own than be tossed out like garbage.

She was crossing the great hall when she met Jasper Renn coming in. "You runnin'?" he asked, glancing at the luggage in her hand.

She nodded. "As fast as I can."

"I know that feelin'. You ever need somethin', don't you hesitate to find me."

Throat tight, Finley agreed. "You, as well, Jasper." She walked out the front door into the dying daylight. Evening was descending upon the city, but darkness couldn't come fast enough and end this wretched day.

The stables were open and she helped herself to the same velocycle she'd taken before. She'd have it returned to the house the next day, but for now it was the only thing that could get her out of there as quickly as she wanted to be gone.

Goggles kept the wind out of her eyes, but they were no protection for the tears that threatened. She pushed them and all thoughts aside, focusing only on her destination as she sped through the congested streets. Coach men waved their fists at her as she cut in front of them, and people shouted as she passed, but she ignored them, bent low over the steering bars as she flew through the city.

When she reached her destination, she parked the cycle on the street, disabling the starting mechanism so no one could steal it. Too bad she hadn't known how to do that the first time, she wouldn't have had to lift the bloody heavy beast onto a roof.

Then she climbed the stone steps and knocked on the door. It was the only place she could think to come. The only place where she would be accepted and not questioned.

When the door opened, she looked up into the eyes of the person standing in the threshold. "I need someplace to stay," she said. "Just for a little while."

Jack Dandy stepped back, opening the door farther so she could step inside. "Hullo, Treasure. I wondered when you'd come."

# Chapter 16

Chapter 16

She was gone.

Griffin stood in the doorway of what had been Finley's room and stared dumbly at the bed that hadn't been slept in, at the wardrobe emptied of most of its contents. He didn't fool himself into thinking she'd be back. He knew she'd taken everything she could with her.

He should have known she'd bolt after what happened yesterday. He should have talked to her, but he'd been too preoccupied with Sam and the strange discovery Emily had made while performing surgery.

Sam's body had instinctively tried to fix itself, and the Organites in his blood had strengthened that ability.

There was so much they could learn from Finley, who had been born with the Organites in her blood. And now she was gone, and he blamed himself. He should have known she'd take responsibility for the fight with Sam, even though his hotheaded friend had been the one to cross the line.

He left the empty room and walked down the corridor. He had to find Finley and bring her back. But where could she have gone. Her mother's? Griffin stopped dead in his tracks.

Jack Dandy.

He swore—long and loud—and didn't care who heard him. Of course that's where she would go. Dandy didn't make her feel judged. He accepted her as she was—or at least he accepted the darker aspect of her personality.

Finley didn't belong with a fellow like Jack Dandy, who was as morally ambiguous as a human could be. She belonged here, with him—and the others. But he couldn't think of a reason why that should be true. Oh, he wanted to help her, and knew that she would be an asset to their team, but what did she get out of the situation? A roof over her head? Someone using her for what she could do rather than appreciating her as she was?

He came to a halt in the corridor, uncertain of what to do next. He had enough money and power to do whatever he wanted but he had no idea how to tell a girl that he wanted her as part of his life, part of his family.

Jasper had come by to tell him he'd put word out with several associates. No word on The Machinist just yet, but according to gossip, the automaton attacks weren't random. They were planned.

Had the villain targeted Sam and later Finley? Or had the two of them merely gotten in the way of his plans? He didn't know—couldn't work it out—and the helplessness made him grind his teeth in frustration. He was *not* helpless.

He should go check on Sam, who had been carried up to his bed the evening before by four strapping footmen. Emily had taken first watch while Griff tried to sleep, then they switched until a surly Sam told him to get out of his room and stop hovering.

He would have to talk to his friend about what happened. It wasn't going to be easy. Part of him wanted to do a great deal of violence against Sam for attacking Finley. But as angry as he was, right now he was also profoundly relieved that his friend was alive.

Unfortunately, without something to occupy his thoughts, the journey down to the lab was a long, hellacious one.

He tugged on his cravat. The knot that had been hardly noticeable just a few moments ago now seemed to choke him. He knew it was all in his mind, but it didn't change the fact that he hated this infernal lift and the darkness that closed in on him like the brick walls on all four sides.

One hundred fifty-nine, one hundred sixty. Just a few more bricks and it would be over. He breathed deep, calling on the Aether and the runes on his body for strength and calm. He despised this cowardly aspect of himself, but he'd hated enclosed spaces ever since his parents' deaths. He'd dreamed of it—or perhaps it had been a vision—but they'd died in a carriage, trapped like animals. Ever since he took his velocle when he had to go somewhere, avoiding his steam carriage unless it was necessary, such as the visit to Finley's mother.

Finally the lift jerked to a stop. Griffin pushed the gate open and pressed the release latch for the door in front of him. He took a deep breath as he stepped into the laboratory.

"You really need to do something about that condition of yours," Emily's voice greeted him.

"I know," he replied. He pushed a hand through his hair as he walked toward her. "Tell me something I don't, Em." It was more plea than sarcasm.

"Well," she began, "I did some tests on the automaton—the one that almost killed Sam."

Griffin loved how she always worked that *almost* in there whenever she discussed the attack. The machine *had* killed

Sam. His ruined heart had stopped just before Emily gave him a new one.

"You didn't start it up again, did you?"

She scowled at him, but with her big eyes and freckles she only succeeded in looking like an annoyed pixie. "Of course not."

"What did you find?"

"Come see for yourself," she said, crossing to the workbench where she tended to do most of her mechanical work. Griffin followed after her.

"Like I said last evening, the automaton spoke to me, or rather, it spoke. I'm not sure if it was addressing me or just running something that had been told to it."

Griffin frowned. "Told to it? Or programmed into it?"

She made a face. "It's pretty much the same thing, lad, at least in this case. It told me someone messed with its thinking engine—the one where all its commands are stored. Up until now I'd been looking for defects in manufacture or an incorrect input in its operation system. But The Machinist didn't change the metal's programming, he enhanced it. The reason I didn't notice it before this is because I didn't physically look for it—I simply ran diagnostic tests. Plus, I think the tampering has become more apparent during the months the automaton has been in storage here, in the dark."

He tilted his head. "You have my attention. Show me what you found."

Emily gestured to the bench. There sat a small dome about the size of a full-grown man's skull. It was the metal shell that housed the automaton's thinking engine. It was small because most of these kind of laboring mechs had two separate engines—one for normal operations, movement, power, etc., and another for specialized commands. This smaller engine could be filled with a number of punch cards which the machine sifted through and acted upon given specific variables. Its main engine told it to dig and how to dig and what to do with the debris. The secondary, "thinking" engine housed protocol for what to do should something out of the ordinary happen, such as if the digger hit a wall, or needed to adapt for terrain, obstacles—anything that might impede it reaching its objective.

She picked the dome up and opened the latch on its back panel. The two small hatches squeaked lightly on their hinges, revealing the engine within. The gears that moved the punch cards were silent.

Griffin studied the mechanism. "What am I looking for?"

She handed him a magnifying glass. "Use this. Tell me if you see anything strange."

He took the ebony-handled glass and held it above the dome, leaning down to peer through it. What he saw made him frown. Tiny veinlike tendrils entwined with the machinery, like a young lady's hair around a finger. "Are these what I think they are?" he asked, glancing up at his pretty friend.

She nodded. "Organite pathways. Somehow they were introduced to this automaton's thinking engine. I believe it was through The Machinist's oil. The sample you gave me still had living beasties in it. They reacted when I had it near a power cell—as though it was attracted to it."

"Did they cause a malfunction?"

This time she shook her head—impatiently. Sometimes Emily forgot that not everyone was as intelligent as she—or were privy to the same information. "No. The engine works exactly as it should. If anything, the Organites made it work even better. The machine reacted to a situation without the benefit of punch cards."

"It became sentient?" There was no hiding his incredulity.

Emily's eyes brightened as she practically danced on the

balls of her feet, clad as usual in heavy boots. "Yes! Isn't that amazing?"

He arched a brow. "I suppose that's one word for it." So was *terrifying*. Metal thinking for itself? There was no telling what wonders, or disasters might occur. It made sense now, however.

The Organites lived off rock from deep inside the earth, and the ore was a result of that. One was part of the other, so when energy from the ore is released, any nearby Organites were going to be drawn to it and interact with it. In the case of the automaton, the Organites were drawn to the cell in its thinking engine and changed how the engine functioned.

"That's what happened to us!" he exclaimed. "Last night we saw what the Organites had done inside Sam's body. It was because of the power cell in his heart. We've all been exposed to power cells our entire lives. It's the combination of using the Organites and power cells that caused the leap in our genetic evolution."

He wanted to crow in victory. The mystery of the machines was solved! But then he stopped and his smile faded. Anyone out there who happened to spend much time around the ore and material that contained Organites could be "unusual." Slight traces of Organites were in the water, in the soil. The ore was used in thousands of places and items. God only knew how the people of Britain—of the world—had been altered. It was too much to even contemplate with so much else going on, but once they caught The Machinist and put a stop to whatever he had planned, it would be something for he and Emily to explore further. He'd worry about ramifications then.

"The automaton kept repeating a phrase when I interacted with it," Emily told him a few moments later when they were somewhat calm again. "*I'll set you free.* It may have been payment—a reward—for service. Or, The Machinist could see himself as a creator—giving life to machines."

Good God. "Is that even possible?"

She shrugged. "He's changed them. Whether or not they can reason remains to be seen. If I could take a look around in the train tunnels where it was working I might find a clue as to how drastically its programming was altered. It may have been given a new task—which we interrupted."

"It's been six months," he reminded her. "Any clue is probably long gone."

"But finding the spot where it dug might provide information."

She had a point, and for the first time since stumbling into this mystery, Griffin had real hope. "I'll contact the company laying the new tracks. They'll be able to tell me where the digger had been working for the months leading up to the attack."

"I wouldn't be surprised if we were close that day. The metal probably attacked Sam and those workers because it thought they were trying to stop it from doing its task."

"Bloody hell," Griffin said on a groan. "Almost torn apart because someone mucked about with a machine's engine. What I want to know is how did The Machinist know this would happen?"

She shrugged. "It could have been by accident. Could anyone who worked with your parents have talked about them?"

Now it was Griffin's turn to not have an answer. "I don't know. As far as I know they were all sworn to secrecy. Queen Victoria knows, obviously. She was the one who demanded the Organites be secret. She feared what might happen if they fell into the wrong hands."

"Like now?"

He hated not being able to find his way through this puzzle.

"Even if someone did break their vow of silence, they would have had to tell the person exactly where to locate the entrance to the cavern on my estate. It's not that easy to find."

His head snapped up as pieces of this infernal puzzle began to fall into place. "Unless they already knew."

Emily blinked. "Beg pardon?"

It all made sense now. "The gardener—the grounds-keeper—that suddenly up and quit. My steward said he got into the cavern. He even stole my stationery to cast suspicion on Finley. He did know my parents, and he knew Finley's, as well. The Machinist was involved with my parents' work, possibly even with the expedition itself."

Emily's eyes widened. "Saints preserve us."

Something sharp gnawed at Griffin's belly, stoking a fire that had burned inside him for a long, long time. It filled him with an unbearable yearning for vengeance. He lifted his head and stared straight into Emily's eyes.

"What if my parents' deaths are connected? What if The Machinist killed them and everyone else involved in their work?" Something raw bloomed darkly inside him. Was it possible that he could be so close to his parents' killer?

"You can't know that for certain," she said, a wary expression on her face. "Don't go doing anything harebrained."

Oh, he had no intention of doing anything impulsive. He had to be more careful than ever now. If The Machinist had known his parents and Finley's father, then he knew their secrets, and he knew their weaknesses. He would be hard to catch, but Griffin would catch him.

He would end this, and give his parents justice.

The black in her hair had gotten longer, more present. Finley couldn't ignore or deny it any longer, just as there was no denying what caused it. It started when she began working with Griffin on controlling her other half—when the two halves of her personality began trying to merge into one. Last night she had managed to retain some semblance of control, and her shadow had become an even larger part of her rather than something she tried to keep at bay.

She twisted her hair back and pinned it rather messily on the back of her head. She was still a little stiff and sore from her fight with Sam, but the bruises were already fading, even without the benefit of Emily's "wee beasties."

Was Sam completely recovered this morning? Griffin must have discovered her gone by now. Was he upset, or glad to be rid of her? It didn't matter. She'd made the choice to leave and now she had to go forward with it.

She slipped into her shift and an Oriental dress of violet silk with dragons embroidered upon it in gold thread. The dress was long, but had slits up the sides for ease of movement—if she got into a fight, she'd be able to use her legs. A few weeks ago she never would have thought of such a thing. She had changed so very much during her short time under the Duke of Greythorne's roof. Most of it for the better, she hoped.

Though, when she thought of how she'd used her legs against Sam, under Griffin's roof, it made her feel sick.

After attaching her stockings to her garters, she slipped into her boots and left the bedroom. She suspected this room was the one Jack used on the odd occasions he slept at his Whitechapel address. It was decorated in cherry and ebony—rich velvets and sleek silks, with a massive four-poster bed that could easily sleep four adults. It seemed a little excessive, but then Jack didn't strike her as the kind of person to do anything half-arsed.

It had been nice of him to give her his room, however. And he'd been the perfect gentleman—not a title many would assign to him. He hadn't asked any questions and she hadn't volunteered any information. How could she tell him that she'd almost caused someone's death? Yet, if anyone could understand how she felt, it was probably Jack.

She walked down the narrow hall, the heavy soles of her boots making very little noise on the richly patterned rug. The same carpet continued down the winding staircase, covering the gleaming oak with a mantle of crimson, gold and navy.

She found Jack in the library, where they had sat and talked the first night she came to visit him. It looked different in the light of day—not nearly so dangerous. Jack—she'd stopped thinking of him as "Dandy" somewhere along the way—sat on the edge of his desk, long legs crossed at the ankles of his polished black boots. He was in head-to-toe black today. Even his carelessly knotted cravat was a shimmering black silk.

His long dark hair was still damp, waving about his shoulders as he spoke into a baroque-styled telephone. He must be rich indeed to afford such a contraption. "I don't give a rat's arse about etiquette, Knobby," he growled into the mouthpiece. "If I tells you to do somefink, you does it. Is there any part of that your imbecilic brain don't understand? Good. Now, don't bother me again unless you 'ave something useful." He dropped the receiver into its cradle with a curse.

"Tsk, tsk," Finley teased from the doorway. "What would your mother say if she heard you use such language?"

Jack lifted his head. Perhaps it was vain of her, but she rather fancied his dark eyes brightened at the sight of her. "Well, if it ain't sleepin' beauty. Who do you fink taught me them words, Treasure? 'Twere me mum." He grinned. "You look heartily refreshed this morning."

So did he, but Finley knew better than to say that aloud. Jack Dandy was one of the most dangerous and attractive young men she'd ever met—bastardizing of the English language aside—and he knew it.

"Thank you," she replied. "I don't suppose you have any coffee?"

He gestured to a silver pot and cups on a tray beside him on the desk. "Freshly brewed. Ground the beans m'self just for your enjoyment."

"You are a man of many talents," she said archly as she came toward him.

"You don't know the 'alf of 'em, darling." His flirtatious tone was lightened by a smile. "Take one of them croissants, as well. You need to eat."

Her stomach rumbled at the sight of the buttery, flaky pastries that sat on a china plate also on the tray. She smiled self-consciously as he chuckled. He took one, as well.

Coffee fixed just the way she liked it, Finley took her breakfast and moved to sit on the sofa, placing her cup and plate on the low table before her. She pulled a section off the croissant—it came apart easily, still a little warm. She popped the piece into her mouth, closing her eyes in delight as the buttery flavor embraced her tongue.

"This is delicious," she said, when she finally recovered enough to speak.

Jack was watching her in a curious manner. "You could have 'em every morning if you want."

Finley stilled, another piece of croissant poised halfway to her mouth. "Pardon?"

He smiled at her, as though he found her surprise amusing. "You can stay here—with me—as long as you want." It couldn't have been coincidence that all traces of Cockney disappeared at that moment.

She wasn't certain what to say. This generosity from him wasn't totally unexpected, but she knew better than to take it as innocent. If she stayed there, eventually Jack would want something from her in return, and the idea of what he might want from her was as scary as it was strangely exciting.

"Thank you," she said at last—it seemed much safer than yes or no, especially since part of her was very tempted to say yes.

Jack shrugged his lean shoulders. "I know the minute His Grace comes for you, you'll 'ead back to Mayfair wiv him, but if ever you need somethin'..." He let the offer drift off.

Silence filled the room as they stared at one another. Finley's mouth was suddenly very dry. Good lord, what was going on?

"Last night you asked me what I knew about that Machinist bloke," he said, breaking the silence and the strange growing tension. He popped the last of a croissant in his mouth and brushed the crumbs from his long hands. "I 'aven't had dealings wiv him, but I know some who 'ave. Keeps to hisself, deals mostly in metal. My associate's 'eard of lots of thefts and anarchy believed to be The Machinist's work, but there's no proof. He knows how to keep his head down." There was a note of respect in his voice, reminding Finley that as attractive as Jack Dandy might be he was not a "good" man.

"I appreciate your help," she said sincerely. "It seems The Machinist is something of a phantom."

Jack inclined his head. "That's easy though, innit? When you get a bit o' metal to do all your dirty work."

Yes, she supposed it was. "Who do you get to do yours?" she asked before she could censure herself.

He grinned at her, flashing those straight white teeth that reminded her of a wolf. "A man's got to 'ave secrets, Treasure."

Like whether or not he killed Lord Felix—for her. The idea made her head swim. On one hand it was terribly romantic to think someone might kill for her. On the other, it was terrifying to think Jack could take a life over something so petty as a slight against her. Yes, Lord Felix had intended to do her great harm at the time, but she'd escaped relatively unscathed. He deserved to be stopped, but killed? Still, she couldn't bring herself to get the least bit upset about it. She was more tormented with the thought of finding a murderer attractive than concerned with who he might have done in.

She didn't want Jack to be a killer. There, she'd thought it, admitted it to herself. She didn't want it because she liked him, and because she didn't want to be the kind of person who could have feelings for a murderer.

A knock at the front door pulled her from her thoughts. Her head turned to gaze out into the foyer. Jack only smiled wryly into his cup. "Wonder who that could be?" he mused drily. "Do be a love and get that for me, will you?"

It was odd that he asked her to answer the knock, but since he'd been so good as to take her in when she needed it, she didn't think to refuse. Setting her cup on the table, she rose from the sofa and slowly walked out of the room, her gaze fixed on the front door.

She depressed the latch with her thumb, and swung the heavy wood inward, revealing a most unexpected surprise.

Griffin stood on the step.

Jack had predicted he would come, but she hadn't believed it, and she certainly hadn't suspected it would be this soon. And she hadn't thought for a moment that she would be so bloody happy to see him. How had he known where to find her? Had he thought the worst of her and suspected she'd run to Jack? Or did he simply know her well enough to know that she'd run to the one person who seemed to understand her as well as he did?

"Hello," he said. His voice was rough and he looked tired. He hadn't shaved and his hair was mussed beyond its usual disregard. There was an ugly bruise on his jaw where Sam had struck him. It spread up his cheek to darken his right eye and across his nose to cast a purple smear under the left eye, as well. His poor face. She wanted to touch it, but resisted the temptation, knowing how badly it must hurt.

"Hello," she echoed lamely, partially hiding behind the door frame. "How's Sam?"

"Recovering," he replied with a slight smile. "As charming as ever."

She laughed at that, more out of relief than anything else. Sam was all right, and Griffin didn't hate her.

"You didn't have to come all this way to tell me that."

He put one foot on the threshold, closing the distance between them. "I didn't."

"Oh." That was a bit of cold water in the face. She opened the door a little wider, putting herself behind it. "Did you come to see Jack? He's in the—"

"Finley." She started as his palm slapped the door frame just above her head. He leaned closer, so that their faces were only inches apart. There was a glint in his eyes she didn't understand, but it made her heart pound. "I'm not here to see Dandy, either."

"Then…" She cleared her throat. Her voice sounded like a little girl's in her ears and she cursed herself for it. "Why are you here?"

"For you."

He had to know she didn't belong at his house, with him and his friends. They wouldn't want her after yesterday. "Griffin, I…"

Suddenly he was in the doorway, looming over her in a determined fashion. Gone was sweet, patient Griffin. This was the Duke of Greythorne, one of the most powerful men in England.

"I don't care that you came to Dandy," he said, his voice

low, but sharp. "If you want to blame yourself for Sam's injury, then go ahead and be a fool. And I don't care that you could cosh my head in if you wanted. I came here to get you and if I have to, I'll toss you over my shoulder like a sack of potatoes and carry you all the way to Mayfair. I'm taking you home where you belong."

Home. How long since she'd felt like she even had one?

"Ohhh, even I 'ave goose bumps," came Jack's lightly mocking voice behind her.

Cheeks hot, Finley looked over her shoulder to see her dark savior standing there, her valise in hand. He must have run up stairs to her room and collected her things as soon as she went to answer the door. He knew she'd go if Griffin came for her.

And he wasn't giving her a choice.

"You'd better go with 'im, Treasure," he said before she could utter a word. "I don't wants 'im appearing on my step whenever he likes. I 'as a reputation to fink of." His tone was light, but she didn't believe it, not completely. And though she knew she didn't belong in his world, she was sad to leave it so soon.

"Thank you," she said, taking the bag from him. She locked her gaze with his. "For everything."

He merely inclined his head, smiling that enigmatic smile she'd come to find so charming.

She turned back to Griffin, who took her luggage.

"Take care of her," she heard Jack say, his tone more than just vaguely threatening.

Griffin shot him a hard glance. "I will."

She felt a bit like a bone between two hungry dogs.

Finley cast one last glance at Jack over her shoulder and waved goodbye. He returned the gesture with a salute and a darkly amused smile, then shut the door behind her.

Griffin's steam carriage sat in front of the building, but the ducal crest wasn't out on the door where it was normally displayed. She knew how much he disliked small spaces, so he must have given thought not only to his own privacy, but Jack's, as well. The driver wore plain black rather than Greythorne livery as he sat behind the steering wheel on his high perch.

"Would you really have carried me out of there like a sack of potatoes?" she asked.

He shot her a wicked grin before moving so quickly she scarcely had time to realize what he was doing. He came at her, bent over and scooped her off her feet as his shoulder fit against her stomach. The next thing she knew she was hanging upside down over his back, admiring the fit of his trousers across his posterior, squealing.

Griffin carried her to the carriage and hoisted her inside like she weighed no more than a child. Laughing, she fell back against the seat as he climbed inside to sit across from her. He shut the door and tapped on the roof to signal his driver to leave.

If either of them had thought to peek out the window they might have seen the man watching them—a man who wasn't Jack Dandy. A man who scowled at the sight of them together and who turned down an alley to climb into a carriage driven by an automaton.

# Chapter 17

Sam would rather eat glass than apologize to Finley, especially since the lunatic had almost killed him. But he had started the fight and tried to kill her, so he supposed that made them even.

Regardless, Emily was angry with him, as was Griffin. He was going to have to do a lot of apologizing to make up for this mess, and Finley was only the beginning.

He had to do it today, because apparently there were plans to go into the tunnels beneath the city later and he wasn't about to let the lot of them go down there without him. It didn't matter how irrationally afraid he was that an automaton would be waiting there to rip him apart once and for all. Griffin hated being underground or in enclosed spaces, and he was going. Sam wouldn't be the coward of the group. Besides, Finley would be there, and he wasn't going to leave his friends alone with her, either. It didn't matter that she wasn't the villain he thought her to be, she was still damn dangerous. Anyone who could take him down so easily was worth watching.

The incision on his chest where Emily had cut him open was healed, as though the skin there had never been touched. He pressed the flat of his palm against it, feeling the steady beating below. It felt natural, not like a machine at all.

He'd had what Griff called an epiphany then, when faced with the knowledge that his life could very well end on the floor of the laboratory. At that moment, even though he didn't like having the metal in him, he realized that it was preferable to death.

Emily had saved his life. Again. How could he ever repay her, especially when he'd been such a total arse to her?

He was fully healed and recovered from the blow Finley delivered. He might not like or trust her, but he had to hand it to her—she could fight. And she was strong. If she proved herself trustworthy, she would prove a valuable person to have around, especially if there was trouble. Emily would be safe with her around, and she could go places with Em that he and Griff and even Jasper couldn't—or wouldn't. Emily's safety meant a lot to him. She was so little and fragile, so delicate.

And yet he seemed to be the one who was always breaking and she was the one putting him back together.

Rubbing his hand absently over his chest, he threw back the covers and climbed out of bed. He bathed and shaved and dressed in a pair of brown trousers, a honey-colored waistcoat and even attempted to tie a decent knot in a cravat, despite that the blasted things made him itch. Finally he gave up, put on his boots and went downstairs to face the others. No point in delaying it any longer.

Clouds had moved in that morning and a light mist filled the afternoon air, making an outdoor meal impossible, so Sam

found the three of them in the dining room, about to have
luncheon.

There was a place set for him. The sight of it eased his anxiety a little. They couldn't despise him totally if they would
break bread with him.

They hadn't sat down yet, so they were all gathered around
the table, standing by their chairs when he entered the room.
Each and every head turned at his entrance and stared at him
in silence, waiting.

They certainly weren't going to make this easy for him,
were they? Better to get it over with as quickly as possible
then. He walked over to Finley, who looked as uncertain as
he felt. At least they had that in common—and the ability to
heal quickly given the pallor of the bruises on her face. Griffin, unfortunately, was another story. Sam actually winced
when he looked at him.

He offered Finley his hand. "I want to apologize for my
behavior yesterday. I had no right to come at you as I did. I
may not trust you, but I was wrong and I am sorry."

She arched a tawny brow. As far as apologies went, she'd no
doubt heard better, but at least his was sincere. She accepted
his handshake. "And I'm sorry for almost killing you."

Sam had to smile. He'd heard better apologies himself, but
she meant it, he could tell from the effort it took for her to
meet his gaze. Neither of them really cared for the other, but
at least they were honest with one another.

He turned to Griffin next. He didn't offer his hand this
time, and neither did his friend. "We good?" he asked.

Griffin made him sweat a moment. "I reckon so," he said
finally, with just the hint of a smile. "Though I owe you a
good thrashing."

Were it any other person, Sam would have laughed at the
idea. Physically Griffin was no match for him, but Sam had

seen some of the things his oldest friend was capable of doing, and he knew better than to underestimate him. "Sounds fair."

And then there was Emily. Dear, sweet Em. Her arms were crossed over her chest and there was a defiant brightness to her big, pretty eyes that he wasn't accustomed to, not when she looked at him. He had changed things between them, and not for the better. Her opinion of him had fallen considerably.

"Thank you," he said to her, so that all of them could hear, "for saving my life. Again. I'll try to deserve it."

That softened her up—not much, but it was a start. Her arms dropped to her sides. "You do that, lad."

They sat down then, Sam in his usual spot beside Emily and across from Finley. It wasn't the most comfortable of places to be, but he was glad to be there all the same. Griffin filled him in on some of the important discoveries they'd made as of late.

"The Machinist is responsible for your parents' deaths?" It was all he could do to keep his jaw from dropping to the table. "Are you certain?"

"As certain as I can be," Griffin replied. "I'll know more when Aunt Cordelia returns from Devon later this afternoon."

It seemed too fantastical to believe—like something out of the novels he liked to read about adventurous heroes and diabolical villains.

"We're going underground later," Griffin told him. "Back to the spot where we fought the digger. Are you able to do that?"

To be honest, Sam didn't care if it made him look weak, he'd rather rip the mechanical heart out of his own chest and stomp on it rather than go back to that dark, awful place.

"I can," he replied determinedly, absently rubbing his hand that was metal beneath the skin as he met his friend's sharp gaze. "And I will."

Conversation pretty much ceased after that. No matter that he had apologized and done what he had to, there was still tension in their party and Sam was smart enough to know it wasn't all because of him. He wondered what was going on between Griffin and Finley that made them look at one another when they thought the other wasn't looking.

And he wondered if Emily was going to look at him at all. He refused to think they could never be friends again. He would fix this rift between them if it killed him.

He started after lunch by offering to carry any equipment she might need up from the laboratory. She thanked him but told him, "Everything I need is in my satchel." She patted the leather bag slung across her front.

She wore a plain kerchief over her ropey copper hair, a leather corset over a linen shirt and knee-length trousers trimmed with lace. Her boots were scuffed brown leather and laced up to just beneath her knee. There was nothing unusual about her clothing, it was the way she usually dressed, but sometimes Sam was struck by just how pretty she was, and he felt as though he was seeing her with new eyes. This was one of those moments, and it struck him dumb as a fool.

She glanced away. Had she seen the wonder in his gaze? "You can walk out with me, though," she said softly. "If you'd like."

She may as well have called him her hero, he was so buoyed by her words. He didn't say anything, but when she turned to walk out the door, he fell into step beside her, no matter that he had to shorten his stride considerably to match hers.

They joined the others in the stables—Jasper Renn had arrived and was going to accompany them—and each climbed onto a velocycle. Griffin rode at the front and the others followed like geese. Traffic was heavy—understandable given that it was a jubilee year and they were in the vicinity of

Buckingham Palace. It took longer than it should have to reach the entrance to the underground near the north end of Vauxhall Bridge Road. Sam wasn't sure if he wanted them to get there quickly or never get there at all. He had such violent emotions about returning to that place where his blood had soaked into the ground.

Eventually, however, they reached their destination and Griffin led them down the stairwell into the dark caverns that ran beneath London's bustling streets.

At the bottom, Griff, Emily, Jasper and Sam took out their "hand torches" that Emily had built for such occasions. They were long cylindrical tubes equipped with a power cell and a bulb behind a bit of glass. They made it so much easier to see into the shadows. Unfortunately, their glow made them much more noticeable, as well.

Jasper, ever the gentleman—blast him—offered his light to Finley, who refused. "It appears that I can see very well in the dark," she informed him with a wry smile. "I seem to learn something new about myself every day."

Was there nothing she couldn't do? Sam wondered a little bitterly. He wouldn't be surprised if she sprouted wings out of her arse.

They had to squeeze through a makeshift barrier designed to keep the general public out of the work area, which was now considerably farther down the track than it had been six months ago. Somehow, seeing that change made this easier.

Emily glanced over her shoulder at him. "You all right, Sam?" she asked softly.

She referred, of course, to his emotional state, returning to the place that had been the setting for many of his nightmares. Familiar anger threatened to bloom inside him. Maybe next she could ask if he needed his nappy changed. But he knew the question came from genuine concern.

"I'm good," he said. It wasn't a total lie. His nerves felt stretched as thin and taut as a pound note being pulled between two bankers, but it wasn't unbearable. He wasn't so afraid he couldn't move, and he didn't think every shadow was another digger waiting to come for him.

Thinking of the digger made him think of his actions the day before once again. If only they'd left the vault door open, he never would have attacked Finley. He probably would have been too terrified to even think of hurting someone. What a thing to wish for! It was proof just how much he would like to go back and do things differently.

Griffin glanced back at him, as well, but he didn't speak. Sam knew his friend was checking to make certain he truly was all right, so he nodded sharply, letting him know that he was indeed up to the task at hand. Griff nodded, as well, and Sam noticed the strain around the other young man's mouth. He didn't like it down there any more than Sam did.

At last, after almost a quarter hour's walking, they found the spot. Sam recognized it before the others did. There was nothing special about it—just a small stretch along the length of a tunnel where they were laying track for a new underground train line. But he remembered that small stone section of Roman wall that had been uncovered, darkened by centuries of dirt piled on top of it. He had stared at it as his blood soaked into the ground, and the automaton fell not far away. He remembered wondering if Heaven was as pretty as that little bit of painting on that Roman wall.

He stood there, as they began to search for clues, letting his hand torch drift lazily over the area. He was looking for blood, but there was none there, thank God. It had all been cleaned up, or lost in the daily buildup of dirt. How many workmen had tracked through that crimson stain, spreading little fragments of him wherever their boots walked?

"Keep your eye out for tunnels that don't look like they should be here," Griffin told them, "or rubble that might conceal an exit. It won't be easy to find. The Machinist's too smart for that."

The Machinist. Five minutes alone with that bounder would do so much to improve his mood.

Epiphanies seemed to follow him everywhere lately, which was why it struck him as so terribly appropriate that the light of his torch should land upon a large heap of stone piled against the wall closest him. It didn't feel right. Something about it looked off.

He walked over to the debris, his heart still pounding out its anxious jig. He switched his torch to his left hand and began pulling away stone with his augmented right. Within a few seconds, he'd removed enough of the large pieces to feel a draft. The torch revealed a passage beyond—approximately six feet wide and eight feet high.

"I found it," he called over his shoulder as he resumed his clearing with renewed vigor. It made him proud to have discovered this before anyone else, made him feel useful again because he hadn't felt useful in quite some time.

Finley was the first one to his side and between the two of them they had the passage completely cleared by the time the other three joined them. Once again Griffin took point—always the leader, always in charge.

Finley was behind him, followed by Jasper, Emily and then Sam. Emily was farther back so she wouldn't get hurt if a fight broke out, or be in the way if Jasper needed to take a shot. Sam brought up the rear in case they were attacked from behind. It was the way they'd always done it, except now Griff had Finley to watch his back—or stick a knife in it. He still wasn't sure which one he thought her most likely to do.

They walked for a long time, single file, through the corridor of stone and dirt. It wasn't so narrow that he felt confined, but it was still relatively cramped. They were underground, in a secret tunnel with no light and no ready means of escape.

How was Griffin? he wondered. His friend had always been better at mastering his fears than Sam had. Someday Sam would be able to look at an automaton without thinking it might be the one to kill him.

Finally, after what felt like forever, they came to a stop. The passageway was nothing more than a dead end.

"This doesn't make sense," Emily remarked, the beam from her hand torch traveling the dirt walls. "Why dig a tunnel to nowhere?"

Griffin pointed his light at the back wall. From where he stood, Sam could see holes in the earth as though something had been driven into it. He lifted his torch at the same time Griffin did, both of them shining light up that wall to the rough ceiling above.

"I think that's a hatch," Sam said, noticing a slight incision in the stone. Those punctures in the dirt wall had been from someone—or something—climbing. "Finley, climb up on my shoulders and see if you can lift it."

The girl looked at him as though she didn't trust him. He sighed. "Fine, come here and let me climb up on yours. We can't be sure what's up there, but I can be fairly certain that, whatever it is, you and I stand the best chance of surviving it."

"Fair enough," she replied. She managed to squeeze past Jasper and Emily to get to him. The two of them flattened themselves against the wall so she could get by. There wasn't enough room for Sam to squat down, so he bent as far as he could and she climbed onto him using the wall for leverage. She was crouched on his shoulders as he slowly stood. The panel made a groaning sound as she lifted it, raining down dirt upon Sam's head. He coughed.

"I'm beneath a carpet or something," Finley told them. "I can't see…"

There was a soft thump—the sound of a rug being tossed back—and then, "Oh, my God."

"What is it?" Griffin demanded.

Sam tried to look up, but Finley blocked much of his view. He could see part of her face, however, as wherever she had popped up was well lit.

"Griffin King, is that you?" called an imperious female voice.

Griffin swore—very softly. "It is, ma'am." Then he pushed his way back to where Sam was.

"Come up here this instant," called the woman. "And, you, girl, get out of that hole."

"Be right there!" Griffin called back, agitation and mortification raising his voice an octave. "Sam," he hissed, "I need to get up there."

"Climb on up," Sam offered. Finley had done as she was told, so Griffin had a clear path.

Griffin climbed agilely onto Sam's shoulders and quickly pulled himself up through the hole.

Sam heard him talking, but his voice was low and he couldn't hear if he called the woman by name or not. He didn't hear anything at all until Griffin called down to the rest of them. "Sam, Jasper, Emily? Please come up."

Sam was beginning to feel like a stepstool, but he kept his mouth shut as he helped Emily, then Jasper up to the world above. Then, he managed to climb up a bit using the rocks jutting out of the wall to propel him a few feet up until he could get a hand on either side of the hole and pull himself up.

He emerged in a large sitting room, so richly appointed it made Greythorne House look like a humble cottage. Finley, Jasper and Emily stood huddled together, staring open-mouthed at Griffin, who was talking to an elderly woman dressed in black.

Brushing dirt from his coat, Sam ignored the wild-eyed looks the other three gave him. Surely a house like this had enough staff to clean up a little dirt?

"And who is this young man?" the old lady demanded.

Sam opened his mouth to reply, but froze when he saw just who the old woman was.

"May I present Sam Morgan, Your Highness," Griffin said.

Bloody hell. It was Queen Victoria. They'd just burrowed their way into Buckingham Palace.

"I can't believe I met the queen!" Emily gushed on the walk from the palace to where they'd left their velocycles.

"I would have liked to meet her when I didn't have dirt in my hair," Finley remarked. The horror of popping up into the queen's parlor like some kind of rodent was a humiliation she would carry with her for the rest of her days.

Still, it had been pretty amazing to meet the woman who ruled the entire British Empire. She had thought Victoria would be taller.

Griffin had been quiet during their walk. Her highness had offered them a carriage, but Griffin declined the generous offer, saying they had already imposed upon the queen enough.

Of course they'd been forced to tell her how they got there. You didn't discover a secret passage into someone's palace and not tell them everything you knew about it. Lord, Victoria could have tossed them all in gaol if she'd so chose. So Griffin had told her how they'd found the passage and what they were doing in the tunnels to begin with. The queen was very concerned, to put it lightly, especially when Griffin told her that now that they had found the passage, he was convinced it had been The Machinist who stole her hairbrush from the museum. He also asked the staff to alert him if they discovered anything missing, but in a place that size, who would notice?

By the time they left, workmen had already begun work on closing up the hole and repairing the floor. Finley didn't doubt that the tunnel would be sealed by tomorrow. That was good—The Machinist would lose his way into the palace.

Now, after talking so much to the queen, Griffin was subdued, his brow furrowed as he walked, hands deep in the pockets of his long, gray greatcoat. It was a little stained from their adventure, but nothing a skilled maid couldn't conquer. She couldn't help but wonder what it was that had his mind so occupied.

She fell back to walk with him, leaving the other three talking about the palace. They were so amazed by what had just happened that none of them seemed to remember the tension between them. Sam actually laughed at something Jasper said! And of course, Emily walked between the two of them—a kitten between two toms.

"What are you thinking?" she asked.

Griffin glanced at her, as though surprised to see her beside him. "Something I'd rather not contemplate, but has taken hold of my mind and will not let go."

In their brief acquaintance, she had never heard him speak with such gravity. Whatever plagued him, it also disturbed him very deeply.

She would have pushed further if they hadn't arrived where they'd left the velocycles. She started hers and followed the rest of them back to Mayfair. The streets were busy with aristocrats heading to Hyde Park as they did every day at five o'clock to see and be seen. They rode horses there, or drove horse-drawn carriages. It was a place to be leisurely. Modern vehicles moved too fast, and the whole point of the outing was to show yourself off.

Griffin never did such things, but then he wasn't like any other peer of the realm she'd ever met. Why didn't he go to parties and balls like other young men his age? From what she had heard of him—and seen for herself—he wasn't much for society at all. Wasn't he expected to be out and about? Someday he'd marry a woman worthy of becoming his duchess and have a family of his own. And then she, Emily, Sam and Jasper would be out on the street.

Lord, what maudlin thoughts! They served no purpose, so she pushed them to the back of her mind. She'd go off and get married herself eventually, so what did it matter? It didn't matter at all, and she certainly wasn't upset about it. It wasn't like Griffin could ever marry her. That was a joke!

By the time they arrived back at the mansion, she'd put all thoughts of Griffin and marriage out of her head. Lady Marsden had returned from Devon and wanted them all in the study. They went to her immediately, not even bothering to clean up first.

The elegant lady was waiting for them, pacing the length of the carpet, the silver chains running from ear to nose gleaming in the late-afternoon sunlight streaming through the windows. She took one look at the lot of them and her mouth fell open.

"Whatever happened to the lot of you?" she asked. She had a way of always sounding put out, even when she wasn't.

Griffin explained what had happened. His aunt didn't seem to know whether to be horrified or amused at their barging in on the queen. It didn't take long for her expression to turn grim, however, when Griffin told her that he suspected The Machinist had dug the tunnel.

"But why would he take the figure from Tussaud's?" Sam asked. "He was right there in the palace. He could have taken anything he wanted."

"It would be difficult to do that without being noticed," Finley told him. "You can't just shove a gown under your shirt or in your pocket. He might have been brazen enough to walk right into the palace, but he was careful not to get caught."

"He would be very careful not to be noticed," Lady Marsden agreed. "Because if he were, it would be highly likely Victoria would recognize him."

Griffin's head jerked up. He stared at his aunt—they all did. "You know who he is?"

"I believe so. Your steward described him to me, and it fits other accounts I've heard, but your steward mentioned one thing no else did. The Machinist has a metal hand. He lost his in a professional accident years ago—an accident I believed he blamed on your father, Griffin."

Griffin's eyes narrowed. "So he did know my father."

"He was part of the expedition," his aunt replied, holding out a photograph to him. "Leonardo Garibaldi. He was one of my brother's closest friends—and the only member of the expedition to have died whose body was never found. Obviously that was because he never actually died."

Finley peered at the photograph over Griffin's shoulder. There were his parents, looking beautiful and happy, along with several other people, one of whom she recognized as her father. Was it foolish of her to feel sad at the sight of him even though she'd never known him?

Her gaze fell upon Garibaldi. Beside her she thought she heard Sam gasp, but before she could turn her attention to him, Lady Marsden began talking again. "Garibaldi was the one who wanted to go public with the Organites. He thought they could change the world. He was furious when Victoria told them to keep it a secret. She thought there was too much potential for evil if mankind got its hands on something so miraculous."

"She was right," Griffin agreed. "It would be awful, especially now that we know the Organites are responsible for all of our special abilities. But Garibaldi already knows what they're capable of, especially their remarkable ability to replicate human tissue."

Everyone was staring at him now. "What have you discovered?" Lady Marsden demanded.

Griffin glanced at Emily. "It was Emily who discovered it, really. She saw what the Organites could do when she rebuilt Sam's arm. And recently we saw how the Organites have become part of Sam's physiology. If Garibaldi had samples of a person's skin or hair, he could conceivably construct a copy of that person. A doppelganger—at least, in the flesh. He would have to build some kind of skeleton to support it—like an automaton."

The awful truth of what he was saying finally sunk into Finley's bewildered mind. The Machinist had stolen the queen's brush, and other personal items, as well, probably. He had pieces of her, and he had Organites. And there had been caliper marks on the wax Victoria, along with those empty eye sockets.

Her gaze swung to Griffin, and she saw the truth in his expression. Her heart stopped dead in her chest. Emily's announcement solidified her fears. "He's going to replace Queen Victoria with an automaton twin."

# Chapter 18

*An automaton Victoria.*

The idea was almost too preposterous to entertain, but much too awful to ignore. There were all manner of nefarious schemes The Machinist—Leonardo Garibaldi—could get up to with a mechanical matriarch. Griffin didn't even want to try to think of them all.

If their theory was correct—and he and Emily were seldom wrong when they agreed with one another—Garibaldi was either building or had almost completed the most lifelike automaton the world had ever seen. Metal with a flesh suit and an Organite-augmented logic engine that would allow the machine to actually *think*. A sentient creature—or as sentient as Garibaldi allowed it to become. One that didn't just look like the queen from a distance, but one that would be an exact physical replica. Garibaldi would have entry anywhere and everywhere, including many of the upcoming jubilee celebrations.

"Garibaldi has to be stopped," he said. "Regardless of his intent, we cannot have a Victoria doppelganger loose in London, or anywhere else."

"Do you reckon Garibaldi would have done it if Victoria hadn't been so harsh to begin with?" Sam asked. The others turned surprised gazes on him, and he held up his hands. "It was just a question."

"Regardless of his intentions to begin with, they're no good now," Griffin informed his friend. "Let's not forget that he could very well be a murderer, as well. It was because of him that the digger attacked you and those workers. And he may be the person responsible for my parents' death, and the deaths of many of their colleagues."

Sam looked away, his jaw tight. Griffin regretted having to bring up the digger, but there could be no sympathy for The Machinist. Not now, not ever.

"Aunt Cordelia," he said. "We need to alert Buckingham Palace right away. Since my latest visit was unorthodox to say the least, may I trust you to inform Her Majesty of this unfortunate situation?"

His aunt nodded, silver chains jingling softly. "I shall go directly."

He turned to Emily next. "Em, I need you to equip us for any possibility. Find something to take down an automaton quickly and effectively."

Ginger eyebrows shot up. "You're not askin' for much, are you, lad?"

"We have to assume the worst," he replied grimly. "Garibaldi is obviously mad. There's no telling what he might do, treason could be the very least of it."

"What about me?" Jasper demanded. "Now that I'm involved in this mess, you don't expect me to just sit around, do ya? Or Miss Finley and Sam?"

As usual, Griffin found Jasper's allegiance to a country that wasn't even his humbling. "Practice," he said. "Train. I need you ready and able to control your abilities, new or otherwise." He knew Jasper was amazingly fast, he had seen it for himself. He had also been treated with Emily's Organite salve, enhancing that speed. "All we have on our side otherwise is the element of surprise. Emily's created some amazing weapons. She'll outfit you and you can practice with them."

The cowboy nodded sharply. "Will do."

Griffin turned his head. "Finley, Garibaldi knows of you. He knew your father. It stands to reason that he has some idea what you're capable of—it's imperative you learn to control yourself. I want you to work on the meditations I taught you. Later today, we'll work on it together."

He turned his head again. "Sam, you're our secret weapon. Garibaldi might know you're strong, but there's no way he can know how close to invincible you are. I need you rested, fully healed and ready to fight."

It was odd, but Griffin thought his friend's face paled. Was that guilt he saw in the larger fellow's dark eyes? Sam nodded. "I will be." It had to be paranoia, but Griffin was certain there was an extra edge to the words.

"I'm going to find out what I can about Garibaldi through the Aether," he confided. "I'll update you all later."

His companions recognized the dismissal and followed one another out of the room. Only Sam seemed to hesitate on the threshold, but Griffin ignored it—for now. He had more important things to worry about.

Left alone in the study, Griffin closed the door and immediately set to work. He removed his fine dark gray wool coat and cravat as he sipped a potion he had concocted a while back. It contained a small amount of laudanum to help relax him and lower his natural defenses so that the Aether could come more easily. He had become so good at keeping it out that sometimes it didn't always come when he tried to access it.

He didn't like to take the potion, as laudanum was derived from opium poppies—something Aether addicts were often also addicted to. It made the veil so much thinner, easier to traverse. The drug was every bit as dangerous, if not more so, than the energy it called forth.

He unbuttoned his collar and lay down on the rug in front of the fire. The warmth relaxed him and he tried to release the maelstrom of thoughts flying about his head, but there was one thing he held on to—his rage. It was deep within him, so cold he doubted his friends had even noticed it, but it was there. Festering.

He tried to let it go as he opened himself to the Aether. Warm energy rushed at him, but he held it at bay with more ease than he ever had before. He controlled how much of it filled him, and when he opened his eyes, it was as though he was within two worlds at the same time. He saw the real world as it was, and then another, secret layer on top. He was in the spirit realm, part of the Aetheric plane that didn't so much require control as it did concentration. He stood up.

He didn't have to do anything but wait and think of his parents. A few moments later they were there, standing before him, looking just as he remembered them before their deaths. His father, tall and strong with eyes exactly like Griffin's and long sideburns barely touched with gray. His mother, small and slender with thick auburn hair, green eyes and rosy cheeks. They looked so young, but they hadn't changed. Griffin was only getting older.

His mother smiled at him, even though her eyes were serious. "You shouldn't be here, dearest. It's not good for you to travel in the spirit realm."

"I won't stay long," he assured them. "I promise." Bloody hell, but it was good to see them. After they had died, he would come and visit them too often and for too long. He hadn't been able to let them go, and they had seemed so real to him. Finally he realized that he was keeping them from doing what they needed to do in the afterlife. It hadn't been easy, but he let them go. This was the first time he contacted them since.

Now, it was so strange to see them *almost* as bright and vibrant as they had been. But not quite. They weren't flesh and blood. Perhaps he noticed this because his grief for them, while still sharp, had eased somewhat.

"What is it you need, son?" his father asked. "You would not be here were it not of great importance."

"I want to know about Leonardo Garibaldi," he told them. "I believe he was responsible for your deaths. And I think he's using Organites to build an automaton doppelganger of the queen."

As he expected, his parents were shocked. Garibaldi had been their friend.

"Leonardo never forgave Victoria for commanding the Organites stay hidden," Helena remarked absently.

Edward looked at her. "And he never forgave you for marrying me."

This was news to Griffin. "And now he's directed that anger at the queen—and at me." The Machinist might have used him only to get to the Organites, but Griffin took it personally.

His father nodded. "Be careful, Griffin. Leonardo isn't mad, he's driven by righteousness. He truly believes he's doing the right thing. Those kinds of foes are always the most dangerous. Don't make the mistake of underestimating him."

"If you need to, remind him of me," Helena suggested, a

determined set to her jaw. "If he hurts you, I will haunt him to the ends of the earth."

Griffin started. He'd never heard his mother use such a tone before. Her words sent a chill down his spine because he knew she would keep that promise and drive Leonardo stark raving mad.

"Can you help me find him?" he asked.

His father shook his spectral head. "You know we can't, son. There are rules about spirits interfering in the world of the living."

"In this case I'd break them," his mother surprised him by saying. "But even so, we could only show you where Leonardo lived during our life, not now. Even the dead have their limitations. For us to locate him he would have to reach out…" She stopped, frowning.

"What is it?" Griffin demanded. A strange sensation assaulted him—like a finger of ice sliding down his back.

His parents shared a glance. "Do you feel that?" his mother asked.

Edward King nodded. "A summons."

"What sort of summons?" Griffin's gaze ricocheted between the two of them. "Why does it feel as though we are being watched?"

Ghostly eyes turned toward him, so real and yet so intangible. "Because we are. We are being summoned, as though to a séance. Whoever it is, they have something that was personal to each of us, and they're focusing on it to call us to them."

His mother's gaze was worried. "But not away from you. Griffin, you must go. You cannot be with us when—" But it was too late. The environment around Griffin changed, swirling mist replaced his study and he felt dizzy. There was nothing to hold on to as he felt himself torn away from the safety and grounding of his own home. It was all he could do to remain standing as his head swam and the mists finally began to clear, revealing a small, dark parlor.

A man sat in a wingback chair, one leg slung casually over the other. In his hand, he held an earring. Griffin recognized it instantly as belonging to his mother. She had been wearing the pair when they died. He knew this because when he saw their bodies she wore only one, the mate believed to be lost in the crash. The only way this man could have it was if he had been there. The realization that this was Leonardo Garibaldi—his parents' murderer—should have filled him with rage, but all he felt was cold inside. Dead.

Garibaldi leaned his head against the back of the chair, eyes closed in meditation. He wore some kind of strange contraption on his head—a ring of metal with prongs that seemed to dig into his skull. Small gears clicked and whirred, causing the ring to slowly undulate, pressing into different areas of the man's scalp in a careful, measured pattern. It was very similar to those used in Aether dens to summon spirits. Garibaldi had summoned his mother. Griffin and his father were there only because they had been with her at the time.

He watched as a shadow rose over Garibaldi's body—a ghost. It was the man's Aetheric self. It was a strong projection—indicating that Aether travel was not new to the villain. Unease settled in Griffin's stomach, though he knew he shouldn't be surprised. Garibaldi knew all about him, and all about his friends. He would be prepared for whatever assault any of them had to offer.

His only pleasure was seeing the surprise on Garibaldi's spectral face. He hadn't expected to get the whole family.

"Would you look at this," he commented in accented English, swarthy face breaking into a smile. "The King clan. My dear boy, you've grown since I last saw you."

Griffin's hands clenched into fists at his sides, but before he could open his mouth, his mother spoke. "What do you want, Leonardo?"

The Italian's expression changed as he turned to look at Griffin's mother—it softened. "I wanted to see you, Helena. I hoped we could talk."

Her face was hard. "Whatever could you and I have to discuss? You killed me. You killed my husband and now you endanger my son. I want nothing to do with you."

A pale hand reached out and touched her cheek. She flinched and Garibaldi recoiled as though struck. "You were not supposed to die, Helena. Never you. You always supported me and my research. I had hoped to help you recover from the loss of your husband, and perhaps take his place."

Helena paled, the translucent flesh of her cheeks going noticeably white. "I never would have married you." As if to further prove her point, she took a step back toward her husband. Garibaldi reached out and grabbed her by the arm. His ghostly fingers held fast as she tried to pull away.

Griffin's father moved forward. "Unhand her, you scoundrel."

Garibaldi held up his hand—it was metal and glowed with runes etched into its surface. There was a flash of light from his palm that zipped across the space to engulf the former duke. The glow overcame him and then collapsed into nothing but a pinpoint, leaving an empty space where Griffin's father had been.

A gasp tore from his mother's lips. Garibaldi shushed her. "Hush, my dear. He's not destroyed, merely exiled from this place."

"You shouldn't have done that," Griffin told him quietly as a familiar sensation began swirling in his chest.

Garibaldi turned that strange hand toward him. In his other, he held an object that sent a chill right down to Griff's feet. A spirit box. Such things were rare—prisons for spirits. The ghost's essence could be captured and bound to the box— and whoever owned it—forever.

The bastard was going to imprison his mother, bind her to that box and keep her as his.

"I see you recognize what this is." Garibaldi held up the box and waggled it mockingly. "You also know I have power here. Power I intend to use. Now, be a good boy or I'll use it on you."

Griffin laughed, warmth rushing through his Aetheric self. Unlike Garibaldi, he was bound to his body even in this realm. He wasn't a spirit, and no one—*no one*—had power like his. The worst Garibaldi could do to him was send him back to his body. His mother, however would become a prisoner, and even Griffin would be unable to save her then.

The villain had him and he knew it. A slow smile curved the man's lips. "Now that we understand one another, you'll run along if you ever want to see your mother again. If not, when I wake up, I start with your friends. Want to wager on whether or not I can pull their spirits from their bodies?"

He didn't think such a thing was possible, but no, he didn't want to wager the lives of his friends on it. He didn't want to lose his mother, either—not to this monster. She belonged in Heaven—the spirit realm—with his father.

The thought of his father brought Griffin's anger to the foreground. How dare Garibaldi involve his parents—hadn't he done enough to them? And how dare the man meet Griffin in this place and make threats?

He couldn't rush him, because he'd use the box on his mother. He couldn't use his own abilities against him, because his mother might get caught in the cross fire.

Glancing at Garibaldi's body in the chair, an idea occurred

to him. He turned on the villain with a smile. "Have you an effect on the tangible world in this form, sir?"

Garibaldi scowled. "Of course not." Only against other spirits did Aether travelers have form. But Griffin was not an ordinary traveler.

"I do," he said. And to prove his point, he moved—teleported, for lack of better term—to the chair and wrapped his hand around Garibaldi's throat. The spirit of the man caught his breath, his metal hand going to his throat.

Griffin looked at his mother as he squeezed harder. "Go."

She shot him a worried glance, but didn't argue. She simply disappeared, set free by Garibaldi's loss of concen-tration.

It would be a lie if Griffin were to say he wasn't tempted to end this then and there, but he was not a murderer. He would not make himself into the very thing he was so tempted to destroy at that moment. That didn't stop him from holding on just a little bit longer. Garibaldi's face began to turn blue as his spirit waned and sputtered.

A little reluctantly, Griffin let go. While the man sputtered for breath, Griffin reached down and grabbed his mother's earring from the hand made of flesh rather than metal. For now at least, Garibaldi would have no power over his parents.

His actions cost him, however. As Garibaldi's shocked body pulled his spirit back to it, his Aetheric self raised the metal hand and blasted Griffin with the same energy it had used on his father. Griffin's fingers curled around the earring just as he was sucked back into his own body in his own house.

He bolted upright on the floor of his study, the warm gold in his palm digging into his flesh. He had saved his mother, but for how long? He still had no idea where Garibaldi was hiding or of his plans for his automaton. He was exactly where he had started.

Perhaps not exactly. He knew now that Garibaldi had

power in the Aether, and he would be better prepared for that the next time around. He also knew that his mother was the villain's weak spot. He'd use that if he had to. Regardless, he would make certain he knew more about Garibaldi than the man even knew about himself. The next time they met he'd destroy that Aether oscillatory transference device he wore around his villainous head.

And he would make certain Garibaldi could never hurt his parents, or threaten his friends ever again. Even if it killed him.

When Finley met Griffin in his study early that evening before dinner, she took one look at him and gasped in dismay. "What happened to you?"

He smiled wearily at her. There were dark circles under his eyes and his skin had a slight grayish cast to it. "Headache," he explained. "Spent a little too much time in the Aether earlier and now I pay the price."

She sat down on the sofa next to him. "Are you all right?"

He nodded. "I'll be fine. I've done this before."

She wanted to believe him, but he looked so ill. "You did something you shouldn't have, didn't you?"

Another tired smile. "Let's just say I pushed the boundaries of Aetheric etiquette, and leave it at that. I didn't send for you so we could discuss how much sense I may or may not possess." He gestured to the table in front of them.

A small pot of ink sat on a stained but laundered square of linen. With it were a few other items that made it look as though Griffin was about to write a letter. But there was one thing that did not fit.

"What's that?" she asked, pointing at a wicked-looking needle-on-a–pistol contraption.

"That's a tattoo needle," he replied, taking the stopper out of the ink. "Em made it for me. I'm going to tattoo you."

She shook her head. "No, you're not."

He smiled. Oh, so her fear amused him, did it? "It won't hurt much at all. Look, I've got some." He pulled aside the collar of his shirt to show her part of a celtic knot on his chest with strange symbols around it. The ink on his flesh had a slight blue cast to it, no longer fresh and black. "I did those myself. I've some on my back, as well, that one of Pick-a-Dilly's tattooed performers was kind enough to transfer for me."

For a moment she thought to remind him that showing off his naked skin to a young woman was highly improper, but then another part of her told her to keep her mouth shut and enjoy the view, so that was what she did. This other part of her was also keenly interested in this tattooing business, so she moved closer for a better look.

"Why did you decorate yourself this way?"

"A couple are personal, but the rest come from my father's research—and my own. The runes help me control and focus my abilities, plus keep my mind and soul sharp."

"Why do you want to do it to me?"

"I want to give you a couple of runes," he told her, swabbing the needle with a medicinal smelling liquid that she remembered from Emily's laboratory. "Nothing frightening or terrible. Just something to help the two sides of you finally merge and awaken your awareness."

She watched him warily. "That sounds like more than a couple."

Another smile, this one warm and reassuring. He would make a fantastic confidence artist. "It won't take long and I'll make it as painless as possible. I'm good at this."

Judging from the ones she'd seen of his, she knew that.

"Fine. And I'm not afraid of it hurting. I'm not some silly girl."

He just kept smiling. "No. I'd never call you a silly girl." His smile faded. "Can I trust you?"

A tiny fissure of alarm tingled at the base of Finley's spine. "You can." She would never betray him, no matter what he told her.

He glanced away, fingers absently toying with the instruments on the tray. "I went into the Aether to talk to my parents."

Her eyes widened. "You can do that?" How amazing! He could commune with the dead. She couldn't help but wonder if he could somehow contact her father...

"Yes," he replied. "I can do that, and I don't know if I can contact your father."

The blood rushed from her face. "How...?"

He waved a hand. "A lucky guess, nothing more. When I was in the Aether, Garibaldi showed up. He summoned my mother's spirit and my father and I were taken along, as well. He tried to capture my mother's ghost."

Finley slumped onto the stool, disbelief practically leaking out her pores. "I didn't know such things were possible. What did you do?"

A slight smile curved his lips. "I took a tip from you and grabbed him—his physical body—by the throat. That weakened him enough so that he was forced to release my mother." The smile faded. "But he has power in the Aether—more than I'm comfortable with him having."

"What are you going to do?"

"I'm not sure. I stopped him this time, and I'm confident I can stop him again, but we need to find him and bring him to justice as soon as possible, before he tries again."

She gestured to the tray. "Will tattooing me help make that happen?"

"I hope so." Determination settled over his features, hardening them. "Yes."

"Then let's do it. What do you need me to do?"

"Just turn so that your back is to me. I'll need you to unfasten the top of your gown so I can access your skin."

Her back? Her naked back? Oh, this went against everything her mother ever taught her about being a "good" girl. Still, the darker part of her perked up at the thought of undressing for Griffin—even if it was just a little bit.

Bloody stars, if this was what it was going to be like having both halves of herself merged into one, she wasn't so certain she wanted to do it. Before everything was morally black or white, and now it was becoming alarmingly gray.

Her fingers trembling, Finley unfastened the buttons that ran on an angle from the mandarin collar on her gown to where the sleeve ended at her right shoulder. Griffin was able to peel the silk away from her back, revealing her shoulder. She shouldn't have been so alarmed. She had bared her shoulders before.

A low fire burned in the hearth a few feet away, so she wasn't the least bit chilled. In fact, as soon as his hand touched her flesh, she felt very warm indeed.

"I'm going to clean the area first," he told her. "This might be a little cold."

She jumped as the wet cloth touched her shoulder blade. "Oh!" It was more than a little cold! There was that medicinal smell again. Wonderful, she was going to smell like a surgeon's office.

"I'm going to draw the runes on you now."

She turned her head to glance up at him. "I thought you were going to tattoo them?"

"I am, but I'll draw them on first. Then I'll tattoo over them—less margin for error that way."

Her eyes narrowed. "You're not filling me with confidence toward your abilities in this area, Your Grace."

"Turn around and stop squawking, woman," he ordered, but there was too much humor in his tone for the demand to be insulting.

"I'll begin with Uruz, for strength and to banish self-doubt and weakness." Finley shivered as the tip of a quill moved ever so lightly on her shoulder. A straight line down, then a small diagonal line from the top that bent to run parallel to the first—like an awkward lowercase *n*.

"Are you cold?" Griffin asked.

"It tickled," she replied, embarrassed.

He chuckled. "Sorry. Next is Gebo for balance, then Sowilo for self-orientation and strength of will." He deftly drew each rune with the quill as he spoke—X followed by a sharp S. "Most important, is Ehwaz for partnership and Ingwas for centering and focus." Each of these symbols—M and a square diamond—were written in a single line down her shoulder blade. Her skin tingled a little.

"That's definitely more than a couple," she reminded him, once again wondering what the devil she was about allowing him to do this. She must be barking mad.

"They're small," he replied—as though that made a difference. "Hold still."

Next came the needle. Finley watched with no small amount of apprehension as he poured a small amount of ink into a reservoir on the "pistol." He was going to put marks on her—permanent marks that she would carry for the rest of her life. It was a little daunting.

"Ready?" he asked.

She knew this was the time to decline if she was going to.

He was giving her the option to run away, coward that she was. But if these markings would help her—help *them*—then there was no other choice.

"I'm ready," she replied.

She could almost see him smiling despite having her back to him. "Good girl. This might feel odd, but it won't hurt, I promise you."

There was the faint clicking of a key being turned, or a mechanism being wound. A slight buzzing noise followed, and then the needle touched her skin, following the lines of the first rune.

Griffin was right. It didn't hurt, but it wasn't exactly pleasant, either. It was somewhat annoying—like being lightly stung repeatedly by a delicate bee. However, beyond that slight annoyance there was something else—a fluttering beneath her skin, a strange sense of strength—what the rune stood for—easing through her veins. The X and angular S followed, each of which imparted a new sensation as the ink seeped into her flesh. It might have been her imagination, but she thought it felt as though something unbalanced settled inside her—as though she was a scale and both sides held the same weight.

Occasionally he would stop to wipe at her back—which was a little more uncomfortable. She turned her head to look at the cloth on the table. Amongst the blotches of black ink, were smears of blood.

"I'm bleeding?" she cried, incredulous. He never said anything about bleeding!

"It's normal," he assured her. "Just relax, Finley. I'll be done soon, and if you're a good girl, I shall give you a biscuit."

"Shortbread?" she asked. If she were going to allow herself to be bribed, it would have to be for a worthwhile prize.

"Of course. Almost done now." The last two figures were

all that remained. The needle buzzed and jabbed—annoying but still not painful. As with the others, each new mark seemed to impart its meaning, fusing the intent with her skin and her blood.

The power of the runes, Griffin explained as he worked, didn't hinge on how large the symbols were drawn, only in the intention and will behind them. That, and his blood in the ink.

"Is that why my shoulder feels hot? Because of your blood?" The thought didn't bother her as it should.

"Possibly. My connection to the Aether gives added power to the runes."

Sounded like magic, Finley thought as he wiped at her skin once more with a clean cloth and more Listerine. "I'm going to put some salve on your back to help it heal."

"Should we be using the Organites, knowing what we do about them now?" She was only slightly alarmed to feel the cool ointment on her skin as he gingerly applied it with his finger.

"They can only make us better," he told her. "In your case, since they've always been part of your blood, the Organites should make the runes part of you even faster."

His *should* was good enough for her. Besides, he was right—she already had them running through her entire body.

As if answering her silent question, there was the strangest tingling throughout her entire body. Warmth—almost like sinking into a hot bath—swept over her. It was like nothing she ever felt before, as though the bits and parts of her, everything inside was being re-sorted and arranged in a different order—the correct order.

"That's bloody *amazing!*" Griffin exclaimed above her.

"What?" she cried, holding the front of her dress as she jumped to her feet. "Why do I feel so strange?"

An expression of amazement softened Griffin's face as he held up a mirror. "Look."

Finley peered in the glass. She gasped at what she saw.

There were two strips of black in her hair now—one on either side, running down from her scalp in almost perfect symmetry, all the way to the ends, which were peeking out of the bun on the back of her head.

Lowering the mirror, she gaped at Griffin, who grinned at her with a smug I-told-you-so expression on his face.

"Looks like the runes are working already."

That night Finley found it impossible to go to sleep. The runes on her back still tingled, though not with the same intensity as before. Her skin felt sensitive, as though someone had rubbed that part of her back with a scouring pad. The black was still in her hair, and her blood was still humming, though now she felt energized rather than anxious.

She was perched on the balustrade of the small balcony off her bedroom, balanced like a bird on the plaster rail no wider than her hand. It was amazing. Before she would have been afraid to take such a precarious position, but now… Now she had faith she wouldn't fall, and if she did, she would be able to catch herself.

She didn't fool herself into thinking that Griffin and his tattoos had fixed her, but they were certainly doing something—perhaps opening her up to merging both sides of herself, easing the process. That frightened her as much as she wanted it.

When the two halves of her finally and completely merged, would one still have dominance? Would she even be aware of it? Would she be such a different person she wouldn't recognize herself? All valid fears that kept her awake this night.

But even though she was afraid, in her heart she knew this was the right thing to do.

So she breathed the night into her lungs, savoring the cool air. London didn't always smell as pretty as it did right then—like roses, damp earth and jasmine with just the faintest tint of coal, steam and metal. Around her she could hear the sound of carriage wheels on cobblestones, the whirl of a dirigible in the distant sky, its headlamps like stars, the odd whinny of a horse—though why people insisted on using horses for transport when there were steam carriages, she couldn't fathom. Poor horses.

She could also hear music coming from a nearby estate. The plaintive strains of a violin tugged at her heart. That's where Griffin ought to be, instead of trying to save the country, or what have you. He should be dancing with some insipid debutante who didn't need tattoos to be normal—who couldn't toss men around like dolls.

It was uncharitable of her to think such a way about him after he'd been so good to her, but she needed a reminder that they were from two separate worlds. It would be easier that way, and maybe put an end to this schoolgirl crush she seemed to have developed upon him.

She was thinking of the pale blue-gray of his eyes when she heard a sound to her right. She turned her head, amazed at how well her astounding vision picked out a figure on another balcony almost all the way down to the other end of the house. From the size of it, she'd say it was Sam. And when it vaulted over the side of the rail, she *knew* it was Sam. No one else but she could jump from this height and not injure themselves.

Leaning forward, she watched as he sprinted toward the stables. Where was he off to now? He'd been acting stranger than usual all day—distracted. It had started right around the time they'd had their meeting with Cordelia. She'd thought it odd after all Sam had been through and the injury he received that he seemed to pity The Machinist somewhat. He'd actually defended the villain, hadn't he? Why was that?

Her mind told her to stay put, but instinct told her to follow, and she let instinct guide her. The alternative was to sit on this bloody balcony until the sun came up.

Instead of taking the time to climb down the wall, she went over the side of the balustrade. Stealthily, she lowered herself hand over hand down one of the carved pillars until she could go no farther. Then she dropped to the grass below. Silently, she followed, careful to keep a discreet distance between them.

At the stables, she flattened herself against the wall as Sam pushed his velocycle outside. He didn't notice her—he was too intent on a quiet escape. Once he was far enough down the drive, she slipped into the stables, to the section where the cycles were kept and took the one she'd come to think of as hers. She pushed it outside, following Sam's lead.

At the road, Sam pushed the cycle a little farther before swinging a long leg over the seat and starting the engine. Finley let him get a bit of a head start before starting her own and following after him. The traffic grew thicker as she drove, past a mansion that was obviously hosting a party given all the carriages about. Sam probably wouldn't notice he was being followed, but just to be certain, she let a small, sleek steam-phaeton get in front of her. She could track him by scent and sound so long as he didn't get too far ahead. Thank God he didn't seem to share her heightened senses or he'd know she was shadowing him.

She followed him to an address in Covent Garden—nothing too posh, but not squalor, either. It looked like a normal, middle-class home. So what the devil was Sam doing knock-

ing on the front door at this hour of the night? No one re-
spectable was awake; Sam, herself and the entire aristocracy
were proof of that.

Finley parked her velocycle down the street in the shadows
where Sam wouldn't notice it, and watched as the door to the
house opened. Sam spoke to the person and then crossed the
threshold. She couldn't see who his host was, but as soon as
the door shut, she hurried toward the house—and the nearest
lit-up window. It was conveniently open, as well, so she could
hear the conversation that had already started within.

"You used me," Sam said in a voice that shook with anger
and disappointment.

"Did I?" asked a strangely accented male voice. "How so?"

"To get to the Duke of Greythorne. To get information
about us."

Finley frowned. What the devil? Slowly, she rose up on her
toes to peer in the window. Sam stood in the center of the
room, towering over his companion. A man whose left hand
was made of bright, shiny metal. She recognized the hand,
and his face. Sam was talking to Leonardo Garibaldi—The
Machinist.

"Son of a wench," she whispered. How had the big dolt
gotten himself into such a mess? It was obvious from his expression that he had been lied to and betrayed by The Machinist.

"And good information it was," Garibaldi replied. Finley
guessed his accent must be Italian. "You were a very generous
source, my friend."

"I'm not going to let you get away with it," Sam vowed,
jaw clenched. "I'm taking you to Scotland Yard."

The older man smiled sadly. "No, you're not. You underestimate me, my friend. But then you make a habit of underestimating people. It is why I like you so much. But now, like

everything else, our friendship, sadly, must die. I am sorry, Samuel. Not just for betraying you, but for leaving you with my wonderful toy, which I brought here for just such an occasion."

Finley's eyes widened as the door to the room was flung open, revealing a metal man approximately seven and a half feet tall. Its head was like a chromium skull, with lidless eyes and metal teeth set in a lifelike grimace. It moved into the room with a graceful gait, articulated limbs moving smoothly.

It was amazing. It was terrible. And it was headed right for Sam.

Garibaldi chose that moment to make his escape. "Forgive me, my friend," he said to Sam as he fled to the door, and then out.

The front door slammed. Finley saw Garibaldi flee toward a steam carriage waiting on the street. He jumped inside and the carriage began to roar away. She stepped back from the window, and ran after it, determined to catch The Machinist.

But the sound of metal hitting metal stopped her. From where she stood, she could just barely see inside the house, but what she saw was the metal man as it hit Sam in the face, knocking the large fellow into the wall. Plaster rained down. Finley swore, her gaze flitting from Sam to the disappearing carriage. She could go after Garibaldi and capture him, or she could help Sam. If she helped Sam, Garibaldi would get away and she would have to admit to letting that happen to Griffin.

But if she went after Garibaldi, there was a very good chance this brutal automaton would kill Sam—the one who thought her a villain. The one who had almost strangled her. The big lad was nigh on invincible against a human opponent, but metal didn't tire. Metal didn't give up. Metal would rip his lungs out.

Finley sighed. There really wasn't a choice, was there?

She hoped Griffin wasn't too disappointed—and that the metal didn't kill Sam and her both—as she ran full tilt toward the house and leaped through the open window.

# Chapter 19

How could he have been so stupid?

Facing the automaton with its metal grin and lidless eyes, Sam was certain he would never make it out of that house alive. And even if he did, he wasn't certain he'd deserve it.

He'd thought Leon—Leonardo—was his friend. He'd basically given their enemy every bit of information he might want to know about Griffin and Finley and the others. Griff's secret weapon indeed—he'd sold them all down the river.

And now he was going to die for it. Maybe his friends would forgive him then.

He watched the machine warily, waiting for it to strike again so he could counter and dodge. Blood from the last blow lingered on his tongue. Out of the corner of his eye, he saw something come sailing through the open window. At first he thought it was an animal, judging from the sound it made, but when it rolled to its feet not far from where he stood, he saw that it wasn't an animal at all. It was Finley.

The last person he ever expected to come to his aid. Or was she there to make sure the automaton finished its task?

But the metal man seemed as surprised to see her as Sam was. It stopped midstep and turned its torso toward her, studying the new arrival.

"Oy, scrap for brains!" Finley's voice rang out.

Sam glanced at her, not completely surprised to see that she was talking to him. "Need some help?" she asked.

The automaton turned its head, as though interested in Sam's reply. "Are you offering?" he countered.

She rolled her tawny-colored eyes. "Yes, genius."

She was as surly as he was. For a second, he almost liked Finley Jayne. "Then help would be appreciated, thank you."

Apparently picking up on the fact that it now had two opponents, the automaton made a strange whirring noise mixed with subtle clicks.

"What's it doing?" Finley asked as she moved closer to him.

Sam had been around Emily long enough to know what those sounds meant, but usually it was a person's tinkering that made it happen. "It's adapting," he replied hoarsely. "It's changing its programming to account for both of us."

Finley's lips parted in a silent gasp. Sam's jaw tightened. A bloody metal monster that could think for itself. Fear squirmed in his belly.

A panel on the thing's back opened, and two smaller, metal arms unbent from the cabinet inside. The head spun around on its jointed neck. A panel on the skull opened, as well, and a new face emerged, identical to the one on the other side. Now it could watch and fight from both sides.

"Bugger," Finley muttered, wide-eyed.

Sam couldn't agree more. "I can't see the shut-down mechanism," he ordered. "There has to be one. If you can't find it, rip apart any wires you can find."

"And electrocute myself?" she demanded, incredulous.

"You'll survive," he reminded her, and launched himself at the metal man. He thought he heard her swear before she followed after him.

Sam kicked the automaton's front panel, denting the polished metal. It buckled, making a place for him to fit his hand, but before he could reach inside, he was knocked across the room by a backhand that broke his jaw. Head spinning, he shook off the injury and jumped to his feet in time to see Finley, who had been hanging by her feet around the creature's neck, pry the panel open and reach for the wires inside. The automaton peeled her off its front like a dirty shirt and discarded her in much the same manner. She flew through the air and struck the wall just above the mantel.

Sam caught her before she fell to the ground. She shook her head, as well. She was bleeding from the head, but he couldn't see where.

"One of us is going to have to keep it busy while the other disables it," she said.

Sam nodded. "I'll distract it. You get the wires."

She glanced at him. "Are you sure?"

No. The only thing he was sure of was that his stomach jumped to his throat every time the metal turned its awful eyes in his direction. And he was fairly certain one if not both of them would die if they didn't shut this thing down soon. So he would take the beating and swallow his own fear to make that happen.

"I'm sure," he told her between clenched teeth. If he was going to die, it wouldn't be without a fight.

They charged together.

That was when the automaton changed again. It began making an awful grinding noise as its joints popped and lengthened. Its shoulders broadened, pushed open by metal gears. Within in moments it grew another foot and widened by at least two. The shields on its hands shifted, pulling back, so small spikes—like the tips of nails—slid out from its knuckles. A good hit with one of those could take out a human eye with little difficulty.

This time Finley and Sam swore together.

"We could run, you know," Finley suggested.

Sam glanced at her, not finding the suggestion cowardly. It was the smart choice. "How much would you like to wager that it will follow us?"

As though understanding his words, the metal man nodded and pointed one long, gleaming finger at Sam.

"Oh, my God," Finley breathed. It understood. The automaton understood, and it was advancing on them again.

"Get out of here," Sam told her, making a decision as he backed up, trying to put himself between Finley and the machine. "Leave me to this. Once it's killed me, it will leave. No one else has to get hurt. This is my fault."

"Reckon you folks could use some help."

Both Sam and Finley turned their heads to see Jasper sitting on the windowsill. He swung his other leg over the sill into the room. He pulled a fancy-looking pistol from the holster on his hip as Emily and Griffin burst through the door.

"Don't shoot it in the engine!" Emily cried as Jasper took aim. "We need it intact to find Garibaldi."

At the sound of her voice, the automaton turned on the new arrivals. Griffin jumped in front of Emily and the metal man picked him up in two of his hands, pinning Griffin's upper arms to his sides.

"Griffin!" Finley cried. She moved to attack the automaton, but Sam stopped her. "Wait. Griff's got a plan."

"How do you know?" she demanded.

Sam and Jasper both looked at her with bemused expressions. "Griff's always got a plan," Jasper informed her, as though it was absolute fact.

Sure enough, Griffin was able to move his arms just enough that he could raise his hands and clutch the metal arms that held him. He closed his eyes and it seemed to Sam that his friend began to glow ever so slightly. It was like he could see Griffin's power building within him.

The automaton began to tremble. The fingers on the hands holding Griffin opened and closed sporadically. The other set of limbs moved around from behind as the metal adapted once more. The hands on these arms joined the others, pinning Griffin even harder. Sam could hear his friend's groan. Griffin wasn't like him or Finley—he was much more breakable.

"Jasper!" Emily cried. "Aim for its right foot!"

Jasper's arm was a blur. One second he was holding the pistol and the next he'd fired at the automaton, but what hit the machine wasn't a bullet, it was like a small ray of energy that rippled through the air. Finley rushed in as the leg of the thing began to tremble and buckle. It freed another arm to swing at her, but she was quick enough that the metal bashed the floor instead of her, tearing through the boards like tissue paper. She leaped through the air onto the thing's shoulders, clawing at its eyes to destroy its optical receptors.

"Now, Em!" Griffin shouted.

Emily rushed in, her objective the control panel visible on the creature's open front. She was going to shut it down.

Sensing what was about to happen, the automaton released one of its arms from holding Griffin and swung it down toward the little redhead. Jasper moved faster than possible, and Sam moved faster than he ever had before. The cowboy got there first, but the machine swatted him aside like a fly. Its fist drove into the floor, splintering the boards further. The floor wasn't going to hold up under much more.

It was in that second that Sam realized Jasper had honorable feelings for Emily. Jasper should have shot the arm instead of running in, but he hadn't thought straight and he'd have the bruises to prove it if they lived through this.

Sam reached Emily just in time, putting himself between the metal and her. He seized the weakened gleaming hand with both of his own and drove it backward with a fierce shout. Gears and joints popped and snapped. A bolt flew up and struck him in the cheek just below his eye, hitting with enough force that he saw stars, but he did not let go, twisting, pushing and pulling until he had severed the mechanical hand at the wrist. He dropped it to the floor, his own hands bleeding from the struggle.

Sam turned to see if Emily was all right. She stood with her fingers on the thing's control panel, staring at him. "Sam!"

He turned around just in time to grab hold of the handless arm arching toward him. It lifted him off the floor and swung him backward toward the stone fireplace, where a handful of coals smoldered.

Sam braced himself for the impact, but it still wasn't enough. There was no way to prepare oneself for being driven through a brick wall with the ease of a finger poking through butter. The bricks shattered against his back and skull, flying outward as he was propelled into the chimney and then down toward the hearth.

Heat surrounded him. He was in the fireplace and the arm of the automaton—now strangely still—had him pinned to the coals, which blossomed into flames as they tasted his clothing.

He pushed at the arm as he kicked at the remaining brick. He had to get out or he was going to go up in flames like a Guy Fawkes effigy.

Suddenly, strong hands grabbed him. It was Finley. He shoved the arm up, clearing enough space that with her help he was able to get out of the fire. He swatted at the flames on his clothes—and then he noticed that the automaton had fallen. Emily had managed to power it down.

Only, she had done it when the machine was in the middle of flinging Sam into the fireplace, so when the hulk fell, it came down on her and Griffin. It splintered the floor around it, creating a dangerous and perilous crater.

Griffin and Emily were in that crater.

Sam barely had time to register the pain from the burns he'd suffered. There was such cold in his soul he couldn't feel them anyway. Wounds healed. He would not recover from the loss of his best friend and his—whatever Emily was—so easily. He glared at Finley for saving him when she should have saved Griffin and Emily first, but then he realized she needed his help. As strong as Finley was, she wouldn't be able to lift the metal and pull Emily and Griffin out, as well.

"I'll lift it," he informed her, already bending down to get his shoulder under the huge metal chest. He searched for secure footing, as the floor beneath him was cracked. He looked at Jasper, who was bleeding from the nose and holding his ribs but looked otherwise sound, then at Finley. "The two of you get them out."

Sam pushed with his legs, slowly straightening them as he lifted the metal man off the two most important people in his life. The broken floor groaned and shuddered in response. His mechanical heart pounded in his chest as he said a silent prayer—even though he wasn't much for praying—that Griff and Em would both be all right.

There was a wide chasm in the floor that led to the cellar beneath. In the light, Sam could barely make out the pile of debris below them—metal, dust and wood. If either Emily or

Griffin fell onto that, they would be severely injured—if they weren't already.

As he lifted, Emily's unconscious form shifted, rolling closer to the huge hole. Sam's heart stopped altogether. If he had to, he'd jump with her, to put himself between her and the death below.

But Jasper moved with that bloody impossible speed of his and saved Sam from having to choose Emily over Griffin.

It was no shock that Finley dove in to pull Griffin from the metal arms that still embraced him, or that Jasper had whisked Emily out from beneath the wreckage. Sam bore the crushing weight on his back—was it his imagination or was it getting lighter?—until everyone was free of the machine, then he began to slowly work on getting himself out from under it without it falling on him. He wasn't all that surprised when Finley appeared before him, taking some of the burden from him on her own shoulders so he could get free. Sam grabbed her hand and hauled her with him as he dove from beneath the machine. It crashed to the floor once more, the top half of it tearing through the wood like paper.

Chest rising with every heavy breath, Sam turned to the others. Griffin was already sitting up, rubbing the back of his head and coughing. He didn't seem too badly hurt, but it was Jasper who caught Sam's attention. The cowboy looked at the three of them with an expression of pale terror.

"She needs a doctor," he said.

Sam glanced down at sweet Emily, cradled in Jasper's arms. That's when he saw the blood.

A few hours later, Finley, Griffin, Jasper and Sam sat in the study, each with a small glass of whiskey in their hands. If ever there had been an excuse to have a drink, it was now.

They all looked like they had been to Hades and back.

Despite that Sam's injuries had healed completely and Finley's almost as much, they were both dirty and peppered with blood. Sam's trousers and coat had burn marks on them and were covered in soot. Both Griffin and Jasper were bruised and moving stiffly. Jasper's nose was swollen and taped—broken. Griffin had a cracked rib and his upper arms were already purple with hand-shaped bruises. Griffin had done what he could for all of them with the Organite salve, but the rest was up to time.

"Did the doctor say when Emily would be better?" Finley asked Griffin, barely able to look at him. His face was still bruised from being hit by Sam and now his left eye was swollen shut from the altercation with The Machinist's pet. The Organites would heal the eye, of course, and help with the swelling, but it took longer for the salve to permeate unbroken skin.

Griffin shook his head and took a drink from his glass. "She woke up while he was examining her and she was in a lot of pain so he gave her something to help her sleep. He said that was what she needed right now—give her time to heal."

There had been a collective sigh of relief from the four of them when they were told that, while Emily was hurt, only her left clavicle was broken. There were no internal injuries, but she would be sore and bruised for some time. That's what happened when a twenty-nine stone automaton fell on you. Of course, they had to tell the surgeon a different story. Finley couldn't remember the lie Griffin had handed the man.

Sam rubbed a dirty hand over his eyes. "This is all my fault."

"Sure appears that way," Jasper remarked casually, watching him carefully. "You aligned yourself with the wrong fella and there were consequences. Now, you can wallow in it, or you can pull that thick head of yours out of your posterior and help us figure out how to fix things."

Finley smiled ruefully and took the attention off Sam. "I should have gone after Garibaldi. If I'd had any idea that the rest of you would be there to help Sam, I would have done things differently."

"You couldn't have known," Griffin told her. "Don't ever apologize for choosing to help someone over chasing down the villain. What you did was more important than running after Garibaldi. And, Sam, Jasper's right. There's no possible benefit on dwelling on what you couldn't have foreseen. You were manipulated. We will find the bounder."

"He spends a lot of time at the Spotted Dog pub," Sam said. "That's where I met him. They knew his name." Then he frowned. "But he's too smart to return there now. How did you know where Finley and I were?"

Finley turned to look at Griffin, interested in the answer, as well. Griffin smiled. "There's a tracking device on the velocycles. We saw that you both were missing, and together. We, ah…thought there might be trouble, so we followed the signal."

For a moment, Finley thought this little revelation of suspicion—toward both her and Sam—might be the last straw, but the large fellow simply drained his glass and set it down on the coffee table. "Thank you," he said. Then he turned his head to look at Finley who sat next to him on the sofa. "And thank *you*."

She smiled. "You're welcome."

Griffin topped up Sam's glass from the whiskey bottle before raising his own. "A toast. To Finley, who officially became one of us tonight, whether she likes it or not."

The other boys raised their glasses, as well. "To Finley," they echoed.

Blushing, Finley smiled and raised her own glass.

"I don't know about you lads, but I like having a strong woman around," Griffin said with surprising good humor considering the man who had killed his parents still eluded them. "You don't have to worry about carrying everything for her, or her delicate constitution."

Finley frowned slightly. "I'm not sure if that's a compliment or not."

Griffin smiled. "It is."

They stared at each other for a moment, and just when Finley felt her cheeks begin to warm under his appreciative gaze, Jasper slapped his hands on his thighs and rose to his feet. "Time for me to head out. Thank y'all for this evening's entertainment."

As the American got up to leave, Sam turned to Griffin. "What about the metal man? Shouldn't we go collect it for Em to examine?"

"No," Griffin replied, polishing off his drink. "We're going to let The Machinist collect it and take it with him."

Sam frowned. "And why in the name of Wellington are we going to do that?"

Finley inched forward on the sofa, eager to hear what Griffin had to say in reply.

He grinned, despite his bruised face. "Because when that thing picked me up tonight, I noticed what appeared to be a homing beacon on the underside of its head. Eventually it will power up again, and when it does, I think Garibaldi will send a signal to it to come home."

"How will we know that it's powered up?" Finley asked.

"Because while it had me, I managed to slip one of Emily's tracking devices into its arm—the one Sam didn't wreck. Hopefully it will lead us to The Machinist's location."

There was a chance it wouldn't work, of course. Garibaldi was highly intelligent and crafty, but right now Finley looked at Griffin with newfound respect. No wonder he wasn't put out that Garibaldi had escaped them. "Very smart," she praised.

Still smiling, Griffin shrugged. "It's part of my charm."

Chapter 20

When Emily opened her eyes the next morning, Sam was there. Waiting. He'd been waiting for hours.

"Sam?" She blinked the sleep from her bright eyes. "What are you doing here?" She cast a glance at the bedroom door, which he had left open, as was proper.

"I wanted to make sure you're all right," he replied. "Are you?" He was anxious for her answer. There was an ugly abrasion high on her cheek and he could see awful bruising peeking out from the neckline of her nightgown.

"I'm a bit sore," she replied, wincing as she struggled to push herself up higher on the pillows with her one good arm. "Perhaps more than a bit."

Sam jumped up from the chair and carefully slid one arm behind her neck and the other beneath her legs under the blankets. Gingerly, as though she were made of glass, he lifted her so that she could sit up. Then he sat back down.

"I brought your cat up," he said, not quite meeting her

gaze, gesturing to the big mechanical animal. "I thought you might want it—in case you needed something."

Her cheeks blazed with color. "Thank you."

He glanced down at his hands. They were big, so much bigger than hers. "I want to apologize, Em. I've been a proper wanker toward you lately."

When he looked up, she was watching him, no expression on her pale face. "You were angry. I understand that, lad."

"That doesn't excuse it. I…I didn't understand why you did it, but I do now."

"You do?" She seemed slightly baffled by that.

He nodded. "Last night I realized that I would do anything to save your life, too, even let that metal man crush me."

"Don't ever trade your life for mine, Sam. I couldn't forgive you for it."

"I'd risk that." He swallowed, his throat dry. "I was stupid, Em. I let The Machinist fool me. I played right into his game."

"That's my fault," she insisted. "If I had told you everything after the surgery, you wouldn't have felt so betrayed. He wouldn't have lured you in."

"It's not your fault."

"Then it's not yours, either." Her chin was set at a defiant angle—one he'd seen too often to argue with her.

Sam smiled hesitantly, rubbing his palms against the top of his thighs. He'd wear a hole through his trousers at this rate. "Forgive me?"

"Only if you'll forgive me."

"I already have."

Her fingers closed over his, forcing them to go still. "You saved my life last night," he murmured hoarsely. "Again."

"From what I hear, you saved me and Griff, as well. Finley

said the automaton could have crushed us both but you lifted it off us, risking your own safety."

"When did you speak to Finley?" he demanded with a scowl.

"I woke up at four. She heard me and came in to help me." She blushed slightly and Sam felt his own cheeks heat. He could guess what she needed help doing and was glad Finley was there for her. God knew neither he, Jasper or Griff could have. If that barmy cowboy had come to help her, Sam would rip his arms off.

"That was good of her."

Emily arched a brow. "Does that mean you've accepted her?"

"I suppose it does. She's saved my arse a couple of times now. Let Garibaldi get away, but I can't say I'm sore about it."

She smiled at him, rubbing her thumb over his knuckles in a way that made his mouth even drier. "I'm glad you've changed your mind about her. I like Finley."

"So does Griff."

"Oh, aye. That's obvious, isn't it?" She laughed then, but stopped abruptly, grimacing.

"Do you need anything?" he asked, panicked. "Something for the pain?"

Leaning back against the pillows, she fixed him with an earnest gaze that made his heart pound and reduced the entire world to just the two of them. Her eyes said everything he needed to hear.

Sitting on the edge of the chair, his knees pressed hard against the side of her bed, he leaned closer, her hand still caught in his. When her eyelashes fluttered, his heart gave a queer little thump in his chest. Sam smiled. His heart didn't need to be real flesh and muscle to feel.

And when his lips touched Emily's, he felt so much. His

heart danced in joy. His free hand came up and cupped her cheek, stroking the soft skin with his thumb. How many times had he dreamed of doing this? It was even better than he thought it would be.

He smiled against her lips. She smiled against his, but they kept kissing. And for the first time in a long time, Sam knew true happiness.

Finley was hanging upside down on a rope, supporting her body weight by twining the fibers around one booted ankle and leg, when Griffin entered the training room. She wore the short pants she so favored, a black leather corset, sleeveless shirt and fingerless gloves.

Did she know that her stockings were mismatched? Probably, he thought with a smile.

"I say," he began as he walked toward her, arms folded across his chest. "Did you know that your face is almost the same color as a tomato? Perhaps it's time to return to an upright position?"

She curled her body upward and took hold of the rope—much like he'd seen the Pick-a-Dilly Circus trapeze artists do—and pulled herself upright.

"I like tomatoes," she quipped as she descended the rope with the agility of a monkey. Then she said, "You know, you're in very high spirits considering all that's happened."

He shrugged. He couldn't explain it, either. "I know it's odd, but just knowing the identity of my parents' murderer has lifted a great weight off my shoulders. Knowing that we're also so close to catching him pleases me."

"I imagine it would." She gave him an assessing look. When he arched a brow, she said, "What are you going to do to him when we catch him? Kill him or turn him over to the Peelers?"

It shamed him that he had to think about it. His honor demanded revenge, but knew the right thing was to let the authorities take care of it. "I don't know," he told her. "I suppose I will need my friends to help me decide."

She smiled. "Indeed, but I don't think Garibaldi's what you came in here to discuss with me."

"It is not." His good mood evaporated. "Jack Dandy telephoned a few moments ago."

She was surprised, perhaps a little more pleasantly so than Griff liked, but it was obvious she hadn't thought to hear from the criminal again.

"What did he say?"

He offered her a slip of paper where he'd jotted down Dandy's words. "That he would like you to return his call."

Finley stared at the paper for a few seconds before taking it from between his fingers. "I wonder what he wants."

"We both know what he wants," Griff replied curtly. Surely she couldn't be *that* naive? Not after all she'd been through. "He wants you."

Her head jerked up. It was probably lucky that her cheeks were flushed from her earlier exertions so he couldn't tell if she was embarrassed or not.

"I should ring him at once. It might be important."

There seemed to be a strange bitterness on Griffin's tongue, like bile. "Of course. Use my study, you'll have more privacy there."

She was at least worldly enough to look uncomfortable. "Griffin, there's nothing…romantic between Jack Dandy and me."

Was he that pathetically transparent? "It's none of my business, regardless."

She tilted her head—the perfect mockery of his gesture. "Isn't it? I am a guest in your house, and you are something of a protector of the kingdom. I would think one of your associates having ties with a notorious under lord would present certain…conflicts of interest."

Griffin's eyes narrowed. He'd not heard her speak in quite that tone before. This was part of the amalgamation of her two personalities. Challenging him was only the beginning. Oddly enough, he liked it. Frank speaking was not something he was accustomed to where young ladies were concerned.

"You have a point," he conceded. "Shall I put my foot down? How about I issue an ultimatum? It's Dandy or me. What would you say to that, Miss Jayne?"

Her honey-brown eyebrows lifted. "I would probably choose Dandy just to spite you."

"So I will keep my mouth shut and allow you to make your own choices—and mistakes."

Finley smiled at the pleasantly delivered barb. "That is very kind of you. I propose an agreement. I will tell you if I feel my association with Dandy becomes a threat to my place in this house, and you feel free to tell me if I am not seeing clearly along the way."

"Agreed, but if I think you're not taking my concerns to heart, I will toss you out on your arse. Trusting you is one thing, but I can't let you endanger my friends."

She folded her arms over her chest. "Like Sam did?"

That was a dig he hadn't expected. "Sam didn't know who he was dealing with. You do."

She gazed at him a moment, her gaze intense. "You make being a tyrant very attractive at times, Your Grace." She held up the paper. "Now, I'd best contact Mr. Dandy before he thinks I've forgotten him completely." She flashed a smile at him before practically skipping from the room.

Griffin watched her go, a reluctant smile tugging at the corners of his mouth. He wasn't really worried about Finley and Dandy—not where trust was concerned. Although, Dandy could be very charming, and girls seemed to like dangerous fellows—some foolish rot about reformed rakes making the best husbands. The idea of Finley becoming romantically involved with the criminal did bother him—more than he wanted to admit.

She'd called him a tyrant. She also called him attractive. Griffin's grin grew. One thing was for certain, since Finley Jayne appeared in it, his life had been anything but boring.

Finley took Griffin up on his offer and used his study to return Jack's telephone call. She was still agitated—in a good way, were that possible—from her conversation with Griffin and needed a few moments to collect herself first.

Griffin was jealous of Jack Dandy. She'd entertained the notion before, but not until now had she realized the truth to it. Griffin was *jealous*—over her. At that moment it didn't matter that they could never have any kind of relationship other than being friends. Right then, his overbearing attitude made her happy enough.

Still smiling, she picked up the heavily ornate silver receiver from its cradle and then requested the number Jack had left for her. A ringing sound crackled in her ear. It rang three times, then there was a click.

"'ello, Treasure."

The smile that had started at the sound of his awful Cockney froze at the sound of her name. "How did you know it was me?"

"You're the only one who has this number. I 'ope your friend the duke don't go sharin' it wiv all his Peeler friends. That would be very inconvenient for me."

Finley tightened her fingers around the paper. "He won't."

Griffin was a good person, but not so pious that he'd forget how helpful Jack had been to them.

"Got 'im wrapped around your little finger, 'ave ya?" Dandy chuckled—a faintly mocking sound echoing in her ear. "Good gel." He said gel with a hard G.

His tone annoyed Finley. "I don't have Griffin wrapped around my anything."

"Griffin, eh?"

Silence hung between them. She'd given herself away, revealed that Griffin meant something to her. For some reason she thought this was a very wrong thing to do in front of Jack Dandy.

"Why did you call me, Jack?"

"I'm not sure I like your tone, Treasure. Maybe I'll just forget what I wanted to tell you. I'm rather absentminded, you know."

She closed her eyes. Part of her wanted to apologize—beg if she had to—because she knew he wouldn't have contacted her if it weren't important. Another part wanted to hang up on him.

"Don't play games, Jack," she said in a low voice. "It doesn't become you. You didn't give Griffin your number just so we could waste time dancing around one another."

He chuckled again. "There you are. For a moment I thought you lost your backbone. I've information, Treasure. Information regarding a certain gent'lman who calls 'imself The Machinist."

Finley's heart jumped. "What is it?"

"Wot's it worth?"

She almost asked what he wanted, but then thought better of it. "My undying gratitude," she replied with mock sweetness.

"You wound me, luv." But there was humor in his voice.

"'Ow about you come 'round for dinner some night. Just the two of us."

It wasn't a good idea. Jack Dandy was dangerous and tricky. He was also very intriguing… What was that saying about keeping your enemies closer than your friends? She wasn't sure which category Jack fell into, but the notion of keeping him closer didn't bother her as much as it should.

What kind of girl was she? She was attracted to Griffin, but Griffin was way out of her sphere. She was also attracted to Jack, who was also out of her sphere, but in a much different way. But Jack also had information, which she needed.

"All right," she agreed. "I'll come to dinner. When?"

"Don't you worry nuffing about that right now. I'll let you know when. Now, you pass on to his dukeness that whispers in this part of the world say that The Machinist's plannin' something for the twenty-second."

"Planning what?"

"I don't know what," he sounded terse. "Do you know 'ow much bother it was just to find out that? The Machinist ain't exactly loquacious when it comes down to his nefarious undertakings."

There was something strange and almost lyrical about those educated words uttered in that thick Cockney. Finley shook her head. "Sorry, Jack. I was just hoping for more. I appreciate you ringing me. Honestly."

"All right then." He sounded mollified now. "If I hears anything else, I'll let you know. And, Treasure?"

"Yes, Jack?"

"Be careful, will ya? I employ a very fine cook and I 'ate for you to miss out on what will be the meal of your lifetime because you're dead."

Finley smiled—at both his words and his tone. He might have coated it with caustic wit, but she heard the genuine concern in his voice. "I would hate for that to happen, as well. Don't worry about me."

He sighed exaggeratedly. "Not sure as I 'ave much choice in the matter." Then, abruptly, "Right. I'm off then. I've a menu to plan, don't I? Let me know how things turn out."

The connection broke before Finley could say goodbye. Bemused, she hung up and then went off in search of Griffin to let him know that whatever Garibaldi had planned he was supposedly going to do it in three days.

Griffin was sifting through all information he'd managed to find in his father's notes about Garibaldi when Jasper entered his study. Not much to help them find the villain, but it provided some insight into the man's mind.

He glanced up from his father's handwriting—his father had been worried that Garibaldi might do something rash to prove to Victoria how important the Organites were to modern science. "Jas, what's wrong?"

Jasper rubbed one hand over the back of his neck. "I just wanted to tell you that whatever you need me to do to help you get this Machinist fella, I'm in."

"Thank you. I appreciate that." His acquaintance—no, friend—looked distracted. "Is there something else you'd like to discuss?"

The cowboy met his gaze. "You know, I've done some things in my life that I ain't proud of, and I haven't always been a decent sort of man. But working with you these last few days...well, I feel like I'm on the right side for a change, and I just wanted to say thank you."

Griffin couldn't have been more surprised if Jasper had shot him. "Uh...you're welcome."

Jasper shrugged. "Listen, about why I came to England..."

Whatever he was about to say was interrupted by Finley's arrival.

"Oh," she said, spotting Jasper. "I'm sorry, Griff. I thought you were alone. I'll come back later."

"No," Jasper said. "It's good, Miss Finley. I'm done." He shot one last glance at Griffin before pivoting on his heel to walk toward the door.

"We'll talk more later?" Griffin asked.

Jasper looked over his shoulder at him and shrugged. "Sure." Then he brushed past Finley and left the room.

"What was that all about?" Finley asked as she came to stand beside him. She was looking at the door as though she kept expecting Jasper to return.

"I couldn't tell you," Griffin replied with real honesty. "What do you need?" It was perhaps rude and abrupt of him, but he wasn't in the mood for patience today.

"I spoke to Dandy," Finley confided, turning toward him. "He says he heard that Garibaldi has something planned for the twenty-second."

"The twenty-second?" Griffin mulled the date for a moment. Bloody hell! He gaped at her. "That's the day of Her Majesty's jubilee procession through London."

The gravity of that realization filled Finley with dread. "It will be next to impossible to find him in that crowd. But what can he do? He can't very well walk his creation right into the throng, can he?"

"No, but he could waylay the queen at some point. If he means to make a statement, such a venue would be the perfect spot. What if he puts a bomb in the bloody thing? He could pretend to offer the automaton as a gift to Her Majesty and then detonate it. Or he could kidnap the queen and put the mech in her place. God knows what he has planned." And there was no way to find out.

"What do we do?"

"It's only three days till the procession. It's imperative at this point that we warn the queen. Hopefully he'll reclaim his toy from the house in Covent Garden and lead us to his lair. Otherwise, we're useless."

"What about that contraption of yours?" She pointed at the Aether Engine. "Can't you use that, or your powers, to find him?"

"It doesn't work that way. Don't think I haven't tried—many times."

"So we don't know what he's going to do, or how he's going to do it, but we know what date he'll do it on and that the Victoria automaton will be part of it."

Griffin's mouth tightened. "Exactly."

"Well," she said with obviously forced lightness, "that's still something, isn't it?"

Griffin raked a hand through his hair. "If we don't find him beforehand, we'll find him that day. I don't care if one of us has to hide in the boot of Her Majesty's carriage. We will prevent Garibaldi from seeing his endeavor to completion."

They had to. The fate of the monarchy—of the entire country—depended upon it.

# Chapter 21

The next two days were taken up with rigorous training and preparation. Emily worked in the lab on various weapons with the assistance of Griffin, a small automaton and her mechanized cat, since she only had the use of one hand. Sam and Finley sparred twice a day, and when she wasn't sparring with Sam, Finley worked with Griffin on controlling and completing the amalgamation of her shadow self. Jasper practiced shooting with the electro-disturbance pistols and ordinary guns, and experimented with just how fast he could be while Cordelia timed him. The cowboy misfit had become a part of their group quickly, and no one questioned his right to be there.

Warning had been delivered to Buckingham Palace that The Machinist might strike on the twenty-second and security was stepped up around Her Majesty, who sent along her hope that Garibaldi would be arrested prior to that so that "We may continue with our plans."

All this activity did nothing to take Griffin's mind off the fact that they were essentially waiting. Waiting for The Machinist to reveal his hand so they could make a preemptive strike.

On the eve of the twenty-second, as Griffin left Emily to her devices in the laboratory so that he might confer with his aunt, the small apparatus in his jacket pocket began to click and clank. His heart kicked against his ribs as he freed the contraption and looked at it. It was to power on once the mechanism the remote portion was attached to began to move—Emily called it "motion sensitive." Once it came on, it would stay on until it was shut down. The rectangular device in Griff's hand had a built-in compass that pointed in the right direction and the audio signal emitted by the tracker became louder the closer you got to the tracker. The alarm meant that The Machinist had powered up the automaton left behind in Covent Garden. It was moving.

Elation rushed over him. It didn't matter that he was in the dreaded lift still below ground, but climbing. He stopped counting bricks and shouted with glee, "Got you! Garibaldi, you bounder, I've got you!"

He pulled his pocket telegraph from his coat and sent a message to Emily to come to the surface as soon as possible and to bring her equipment. Then he sent a message to Sam. One more went to Jasper, whom he directed to fetch Finley. He really should have Emily make one of these gadgets for Finley, as well, blast it. The last message was to Cordelia, who was at Buckingham Palace, scanning the minds of staff and guests to make certain Garibaldi didn't have an accomplice on the inside. The tunnel beneath the palace had been sealed, so there would be no one using it to sneak in or out.

When he finally exited the lift, Sam was there, eyes wide. "Is it him?" he asked, with bloodthirsty exuberance.

Griffin nodded and clapped him on the shoulder. "I believe so, my friend. Help Emily bring up the equipment. Jas and Finley should be here directly."

His large friend saluted him. "Give me a couple of minutes' head start then send the lift down after me."

Griffin's stomach turned. He hated when his friend did what he was about to do, but in the interest of time, he decided not to argue. He watched, slightly nauseated as Sam maneuvered his considerable bulk around the side of the lift. Then, using the caging as a handhold, he eased himself down into the shaft. A few seconds later, there was a zipping sound, that quickly faded into nothingness as Sam slid down the cables to the laboratory far below.

Griffin sent up a silent prayer that his friend wouldn't fall, or that if he did, he healed quickly, and then closed the gate and sent the lift downward so they could load it with what they needed.

He stopped by his study, where he poured a glass of water from the crystal pitcher on the sideboard and took a small cobalt bottle from the locked drawer in his desk. It was a new version of his Aether potion—one that wouldn't tire him. He removed the top and poured a small amount into the water. He stared at it for a moment before lifting it into his mouth and downing it all in one swift, bitter swallow. No turning back now.

A photograph of him with his mother and father, taken when he was thirteen, lay on the bottom of the drawer. Griffin picked it up and studied the smiling faces of the adults standing behind him, their hands on each of his shoulders. His mother was so pretty and young. His father so tall and noble-looking. He knew he resembled his father in many ways, but he fancied he had his mother's smile.

"Soon," he said to their likeness. "Leonardo Garibaldi will

answer for what he did to you." Then he dropped the photograph back into the drawer, which he shut and locked, slipping the key into his waistcoat pocket.

Straightening his cuffs, he left the study to run upstairs so he could change clothes. Anticipation sang in his veins.

Soon, he would have justice.

They assembled in the foyer within twenty minutes of Griffin's summons. Finley wore her usual uniform of short-knickers, stockings and boots. But this time she wore a long black coat over her corset. Snug, with a mandarin collar and long sleeves, it would keep her warm, but the dearth of buttons below the waist gave her freedom of movement. The fellows wore their usual clothing paired with heavy, thick-soled boots. The only deviance from this was Griffin, who joined them dressed entirely in black and without his usual cravat. He looked vaguely like a pirate, Finley thought, enjoying the sight of him.

But Emily was the biggest surprise. She wore her usual short trousers and corset-vest over a short-sleeved top. Her jacket was a military style—a mossy green color that complemented her pale skin. It wasn't her clothing, however, that caught Finley's attention—it was the great cat sitting at her feet. Finley had never seen it operational before this, and it hadn't looked like this even then. Easily three feet tall, its head was the size of a human's and its paws sported razor-sharp claws. Its engraved coat was the flat gray of gunmetal, and all-too-real-looking feline eyes stared from inside iron sockets. It was beautiful and scary at the same time. Finley didn't know if she should pet it or stay as far away from it as possible.

"You finally finished it," Griffin commented, stroking a hand over the cat's smooth head. "She's beautiful, Em."

Emily beamed under the praise. "I know. I made a few changes in her design to aid in our adventure."

"Equipment's loaded," Sam informed Griffin. "We're all set."

Griffin looked around them, meeting each and every one of their gazes. "I don't have to tell you how much danger we're putting ourselves in. Garibaldi will undoubtedly have more than one automaton sentinel at his workshop. Stay focused, stay sharp and, for God's sake, stay *together*. Understood?"

They all nodded. Finley's heart was like a thundering train in her chest. She opened and clenched her fists, experimenting with the feel of the brass knuckles Emily had made for her. They anchored with a bracelet around each wrist and a ring around each finger. Thin but strong chains crisscrossed over the back of her hands and fingers, attached to curved metal shields over each of her knuckles. She'd be able to hit that much harder now.

They filed out into the night. It was dry and cool, not the faintest hint of rain in the air. In the stables, they each climbed onto their velocycles.

Emily's cycle was different from the others. It had two back wheels instead of one. Spaced about three feet apart, they gave more stability to her vehicle, which was needed because she had a small storage area built into the back of the cycle to store weapons and equipment. Her cat sat atop this bin. Powerful magnets insured that the cat wouldn't fall off during travel.

It was at that moment, that even though she'd thought it before, Finley realized that Emily was a bloody genius.

Griffin started up his cycle and the others followed suit. Within moments they were speeding through Mayfair, toward their as yet unknown destination. Griffin had the tracking device, so they followed his lead, occasionally slowing or stopping so that he could get a better fix on the direction.

Eventually they arrived on the docks east of Victoria Embankment. It was darker here, the buildings throwing shadows where there wasn't much light to be found. Here the smells of the Thames were strong and unpleasant, rife with the salty scent of fish and the much more pungent odors of human waste. Finley's keen sense of smell rebelled and she shuddered at the overpowering smells. It was awful.

"Here." It was Emily. She smeared a tiny bit of some kind of waxy ointment underneath Finley's nose. Suddenly, all she could smell was lavender—not a scent she liked normally, but it was better than the rot of the harbor.

"We'll go the rest of the way on foot," Griffin explained as they gathered in one of the many darkened sections. The shadows hid their velocycles from view should anyone pass by the area. "Gather your gear and let's go."

Emily's cat stood by her side as she opened the compartment on her cycle. "There are chest guards in here for everyone. Jasper, I have ammunition and the mechanical disruptor pistol. There's a setting for engines and one for moving parts. I think you'll find it works better than the old one. I want everyone to take one of these little gizmos, as well." She held up a tiny bell-shaped metal doodad and slipped it into her right ear. "They amplify speech, so we'll be able to hear one another regardless of pitch or situation."

Finley stared at her. "You really are brilliant."

Emily grinned at her. "Yes. Yes, I am." Then softly, just for Finley's ears, "Though I'd gladly give up just a little of my intelligence to fight like you."

A slow smile curved Finley's lips. "I'll teach you if you teach me." It was more than an offer between friends—it was a promise to make it out of this confrontation alive.

"Agreed." Emily took the earpiece from her and slipped it into Finley's right ear. "How's that?" she whispered.

Finley's eyes widened. It sounded as though Emily had spoken at her normal volume. "Perfect."

"Good. Do you need a chest guard or are you wearing the corset I made you?"

"Corset," Finley replied, feeling more than a little smart herself for having thought of it.

"Excellent." Then Emily walked away to check on one of the other fellows.

Griffin appeared at Finley's side. "You all right?" he asked.

"Yes," she replied, surprised to realize it was true. "I'm anxious to get it over with."

"Me, too," he confided. "Then, let's do this. Stay safe, Fin."

*Fin.* She had a nickname, like Em and Jas. She was one of them. The realization warmed and centered her in a way she never thought possible. At that moment, it didn't matter if she lived or died, only that she would put her life at risk with friends, and if she perished, it would not be in vain.

They moved as a unit behind Griffin as he followed the tracker's signal. A few minutes later they stood in front of an old warehouse that looked as though it had been around since London was a baby. That it was still standing was a miracle.

"This is The Machinist's lair?" Jasper whispered, incredulous. "Not very impressive."

"This is just a smoke screen," Griffin replied just as softly, his words amplified by the earpieces. "The real den is inside, or beneath." He disabled the tracker and slid it into his jacket. "Sam, you take point."

Sam's large shadow passed over them as he took the lead. If there were any traps waiting on the other side of the warehouse door, they'd hit him—the one who could heal from just about anything.

Sam opened the door. There seemed to be nothing on the other side of it but darkness. But then there was a soft *click* and a twanging sound. Sam pivoted out of the way and narrowly avoided an ax blade in the throat. The weapon embedded itself deep into the door frame, the handle vibrating under the force of impact.

Emily jumped, and Finley reached down and took her hand. What had scared the petite girl wasn't the ax so much as where it would have struck Sam. Even he couldn't recover from decapitation.

When Sam went to press on, seemingly unfazed by his close call, Emily stopped him and pointed at her mechanical cat. Griffin gave her the thumbs-up. Emily pushed up her left sleeve to reveal a long, leather cuff covered by metal panel that curved around her forearm. It opened like a locket to reveal the controls for the cat. She made a few adjustments, turned a few knobs, and when she was done, the metal feline took over Sam's position as point. Any more traps and it would be the one to set them off.

Torches, similar to the handheld devices Emily had made, burned from within the cat's eyes, lighting their path and enabling all of them to keep their hands free. They moved quietly through the desolate interior. It was obvious that this space hadn't been used in some time, but footprints in the dust on the floor told another story. Finley frowned, realizing that someone had tried to conceal the tracks. Emily toyed with the controls on her arm again and the cat crouched, exhaling a fine puff of air that lifted the "new" dust to reveal boot prints pressed into the layers beneath. Whoever made the tracks—no doubt Garibaldi—had stepped in oil or something, and the dust stuck to the floorboard where he'd trod.

*Bloody brilliant. Genius,* Finley thought rather caustically. Garibaldi might be smart, but she was convinced he was no match for Emily.

The tracks led to a door, well concealed toward the back of

the warehouse. The cat sat and waited for Sam to open it—
and they all pressed themselves against the wall so if anything
came flying out it would miss them. Nothing happened, and
the cat slowly descended the stairs within. The metal beast
was as quiet and stealthy as its wild counterpart.

Single file, they made their way down into the dirt and wet.
A faint whiff of fish clung to the air, and there was something
else she smelled over the lavender. Finley sniffed again. "Machine oil," she whispered, alerting the others that they were
on the right path.

The cat reached the bottom of the stairs. Finley watched as
its right front "paw" struck something on the floor. Suddenly,
the space filled with lights, the gas jets in the sconces on the
wall igniting with such brightness it was almost blinding.

When her eyes adjusted, she saw Jasper had both pistols
drawn, but there didn't seem to be any immediate danger.

Well, at least not *yet*.

Standing like an army waiting for orders was row after row
of silent automatons. Some looked like the metal man they'd
fought before, and sure enough, there was the one they had
fought there in the far corner. Others were small, like dolls
or children. They were the most disturbing to Finley because
of their garish, painted faces that looked nothing like the innocence of childhood. Not even the spiderlike creature with a
doll's head unsettled her quite so much. Others were nothing
more than bits of rubbish put together. Some had feet, some
had wheels. Some had faces and some didn't have anything
resembling a face. But one thing was for certain, they were
metal, and they were strong.

But this mechanical army paled in comparison to their
general.

Standing at the front of the ranks was an old woman, plump

with a bit of a jowly look to her, dressed all in black, her white-and-gray hair back in a severe bun.

It was Queen Victoria. Not an automaton simply painted to look like her—it was the very image of Her Majesty right down to the flesh that glowed with vitality.

"Mary and Joseph," Emily whispered on a breath. As though compelled, she moved closer to the…*thing,* her good hand outstretched. No one seemed capable of moving to stop her, they were so in shock.

If Emily was a genius, what the devil was Garibaldi to have conceived and built such a thing? No one, not even the queen's own children would look at this figure and think it anything but their mother.

Emily's fingers touched the thing's face and then snatched back, as though burned. "It's skin," she whispered. "Real skin. He managed to do it. He's made an organic automaton."

Finley wasn't quite sure what that was, but she knew it wasn't good. She also knew it wasn't good when "Victoria's" eyes snapped open.

"Intruders," it said in a perfect imitation of the queen's voice. "We are *not* amused."

"Well, well, well," came a voice from the far end of the room. Finley turned her attention toward that voice, keeping the automaton in her peripheral vision. There, just inside an open door, was a dark and swarthy man of about average height and build. "Look who set off the imperceptible auditory alarm. Sam! How lovely to see you still alive."

Beside Finley, Sam said nothing, but she could see the muscles in his jaw clench.

"This isn't going to work, Garibaldi," Griffin said in a firm, clear voice. Finley mentally cheered for him, knowing how hard it must be for him to keep his emotions under control.

"I think it will," Garibaldi taunted. "I've worked long and

hard to get here, Your Grace. I'm not about to let a bunch of children stop me now." Finley jumped as his cold dark gaze met hers. "Much of this started with your father, you know. It was my carriage he tried to steal that night. He came to me, begging for help and as his friend I tried to help him, but then he changed right before my very eyes. He attacked me, otherwise I never would have shot him. That's when I knew the Organites had to be revealed to the world. No more secret experiments left to go so drastically wrong."

Rage, somehow both hot and cold, swept over Finley. Darkness flooded her and she let it, but instead of giving into it, she let it trip through her veins, drawing strength from it. Garibaldi spoke as though he had done the right thing—as though he had committed a service for her father rather than killing him without mercy and in cold blood.

"Do you mean that?" she asked calmly. "Or were you just put out that Greystone trusted my father with the experiments and not you?"

Garibaldi's face flushed so dark, she could see it from where she stood. She'd struck a nerve.

"Edward went to Thomas Sheppard because Sheppard wasn't bound by any promise to the queen. Edward knew that if Sheppard was caught there was little way to link his experiments to our discovery. How highly do you think of the heroic late Duke of Greythorne now?"

Finley glanced at Griffin, whose cheeks were also dark. He hadn't known this about his father. She turned back to Garibaldi. "It doesn't appear that you kept your promise to keep the Organites secret, either, sir. The duke tried to help my father. He was a true friend, which is more than you did for him."

"My dear girl, it was self-defense. Your father was in such a feral state I feared for my life, as your friends should fear for theirs with you under the same roof. By the way, I must apologize for that incident at Pick-a-Dilly. The server automaton was not supposed to attack you or anyone else. You certainly made short work of the poor thing. Perhaps you have your father's murderous tendencies."

Heat rushed up from Finley's feet to her face, but she didn't look away. She would not be ashamed of herself. "You talk a lot."

Garibaldi smiled. "Quite right. A flaw, to be sure. I will be quiet now, and let my children talk for me." He threw a large switch on the wall. "Wake up, my dearests!"

The floor beneath her feet seemed to hum and vibrate as clockwork gears clicked into place beneath the machines. Suddenly every automaton raised its head, the room filled with a dull roar as each and every one of them was brought to life—even Victoria. He had put start mechanisms in the bottom of them, making it difficult to shut them down.

Finley moved first, followed by the cat and then Sam. She did exactly as Emily had told her to do; the first machine she grabbed had a headlike attachment lit from within. She tore that from the metal shoulders and threw it to the floor where Sam stomped it with his heavy boot, crushing it like a vegetable tin. Then, she reached into the chest cavity, grabbed hold of as many wires and guts as she could and pulled. The light in the thing's chest sputtered and died as the machine fell to the floor.

One down. Twenty-five to go. Around her she watched as Sam ripped some of the lesser automatons apart with his bare hands. Griffin took on some of the smaller ones, as well, and helped Emily shut down others with her abilities as Jasper used the augmented guns Emily made him to cripple the machines. Finley and Sam double-teamed the larger ones.

Griffin kept going. Finley's gaze skipped to the back of the space, where she saw Garibaldi throwing things into a valise. He was going to try to escape while the rest of them were fighting. A noise to her left caught her eye and she spied the Victoria automaton also moving toward Garibaldi, presumably to follow him. Another mech moved closer, as well—man-size and intent on Griffin.

Garibaldi saw Griffin coming and pulled a pistol from his coat, aiming it at Griff. "One more step and you'll be with your parents for eternity—your father, I mean."

Griffin hesitated, but only for a moment. It seemed as though his eyes were changing—like they were lit from within. He was beautiful.

Out of the corner of her eye, Finley saw an opportunity and took it. She ran and jumped, grabbing hold of a chain that hung from the ceiling, she swung herself at Garibaldi, managing to land a solid kick to his shoulder as she sailed by. Then, she whipped herself around and landed on the shoulders of a large metal man. As she had with the others, she seized the thing by the skull, twisted and pulled. The head came off like the lid of a jar. She tossed it to the floor and then somersaulted off the wide metal shoulders. She landed, both feet on the automaton head, feeling it crumple beneath her boots. Then she pivoted and shoved her hand into the panel on the chest, grasping and ripping at wires. The machine fell.

They were making short work of The Machinist's army. Only a handful of automatons left. Finley was nigh-on victorious. And then a hail of bullets cut the air just above her head. She hit the floor with enough force the air rushed from her lungs. She looked up to see two plump arms, the hands of which had flipped back on macabre hinges to reveal smoking gun barrels within.

Queen Victoria had joined the fight.

Jasper rolled to his back not far from her. With one hand,

he used his disruptor pistol to stun one of the last automatons long enough so Emily could shut it down. His other hand moved so fast Finley wasn't sure if he switched pistols or not, but two shots rang out. Victoria's arms jerked. When the smoke cleared, Jasper held a regular pistol in his hand—and Victoria's arm-rifles were still, though scorched around the wrists. He'd destroyed both by shooting into the barrels.

Finley would have looked at him in sufficient awe if her attention was not stolen by Garibaldi. The Machinist cried out in rage at the damage to his precious machine. Victoria's hands flipped back into place, now with black marks up the arms, and moved closer to her master. She even moved like an elderly but regal person; slowly, but with grace. And silent. Not a whir or click to be heard as she walked.

Finley launched herself then, coming up into a crouch and then jumping straight at the Victoria machine. She landed on its shoulders just in time to see Sam take down the last of the other machines. She seized the queen's head as the useless gun arms came up and began beating at her. It hurt—every blow like being struck with a sack full of pennies—but she did not let go. She grunted, squeezing and turning with all her strength. Finally, she felt the neck give way, heard the metal inside grinding and snapping. She pulled and the head came off in her hands.

She dropped it to the floor with a cry. It looked too real—and Garibaldi had added veins to the flesh "suit" the automaton wore. Finley had blood on her hands. For a second, she thought she had actually killed a person.

She'd froze only for a second, but it was all the automaton needed. The headless Victoria whirled, striking her across the back and the ribs with enough force to send her into the wall hard and she crashed to the floor, but she was on her feet again as soon as she caught her breath.

When she managed to get to her feet, she saw Jasper fire the disruptor pistol at the headless queen as she ran toward him, spritzing blood from the stump of her neck. The blast jerked the automaton backward, but didn't stop her. Jasper slapped his hand against the side of the gun.

The blast should have stopped the machine, if only for a moment. But the pistol's malfunction had turned the metal's attention to Jasper and now he was defenseless.

Emily ran in front of him, reaching the machine as Jasper tossed the useless weapon aside and pulled another. She slapped both of her palms against the headless queen's chest, sweat running down her brow.

The automaton twitched and jerked. Suddenly, there was a flash—like an explosion—that sent Emily sailing backward. Finley moved quick and managed to catch her, both of them falling to the floor.

They were surrounded by broken automatons—smoking and steaming in ruin, scattering the floor like bizarre metal corpses. Blood from "Victoria" sprinkled them, casting a gruesome pall over the wreckage.

Beside her Emily lay as still as death.

# Chapter 22

Garibaldi spat a mouthful of blood on the dirty floor near where Griffin lay. "Just admit defeat, boy."

Slowly, painfully, Griffin rose to his knees. "No." He glanced toward his friends and saw them in the midst of destroying the Victoria automaton. He saw Emily and Finley hit the floor and prayed they were both all right. "It's over, Garibaldi."

The Italian glanced where Griffin had and saw what had become of his invention. His face contorted into a mask of rage and he lashed out, landing a savage kick to Griffin's chest. "You've ruined everything!"

The guard protected Griffin from the worst of the blow, but it still knocked the breath out of him. He fell to his side on the floor, gasping. He didn't have time to recover before he was grasped by the lapels of his coat, pulled to his feet by the infuriated madman.

"I'm going to rip your heart out," Garibaldi seethed, spit

flying as he finally went completely mad. His obsession with proving the usefulness of Organites finally broke his mind as he saw all his work in ruins. "I'm going to send you to your mommy and daddy in *pieces*."

It was the thought of his parents that cleared Griffin's mind. He thought of them and how much he'd loved them, how much he wanted to make them proud. It was almost as though he could see them, standing there behind Garibaldi.

Wait. They were there. He really could see them.

Griffin glanced around. The Aether. He was accessing the Aether without consciously reaching for it. It was all around him, like beautiful shimmering light. And there, attached to his parents by an ugly, pulsing black cord of energy, was Leonardo Garibaldi. He couldn't stand that taint touching his parents. The cord extended to him as well, thicker and blacker. There was no goodness in Garibaldi anymore—no lightness or purity of soul. He had been corrupted by his own righteousness and was something dark and nasty now—so much so that he glowed with it.

"What are you staring at?" Garibaldi demanded, shaking him. He punched him again.

Griffin tasted blood in his mouth. He shook his head to clear it. "My parents," he replied. "They're here."

Garibaldi sneered at him, his expression nothing but murderous hatred. "Give them my regards." The air around them shimmered, and Griffin saw the runes on the villain's metal hand begin to glow. It made sense for him to have the ancient symbols, having been a part of Griff's parents' team before he betrayed them. For a moment their forms dimmed—all but disappeared—and he felt his own defenses slip.

Something sharp and hot thrust into his side just as he reached out for more power and let the Aether fill him again.

Garibaldi held him with one hand now and Griff looked down to see what was causing that awful fire in his gut.

The handle of a dagger protruded from just beneath the edge of his chest guard. A few inches higher and Garibaldi wouldn't have that triumphant sneer on his face. If Griffin had only been better prepared, stronger, he would have sensed the danger before it happened. The villain had bested him. "See you in hell, Your Grace." Garibaldi shoved him aside.

Griffin staggered, but he didn't fall, despite the numbness spreading through his lower limbs. There was more blood in his mouth. The Aether closed around him, like an embrace and he thought he could feel the warm arms of his mother, welcoming him.

He was dying.

"No," he said hoarsely. "You won't see me there, you son of a bitch." It would not end this way. Garibaldi would imprison his mother if Griff couldn't defeat him.

Griffin closed his eyes and mentally opened a door in his mind, in his soul. With joyful abandon, he let the Aether in. He let it fill him until he could feel it seeping into his veins. He couldn't take much more.

The entire warehouse shuddered, bits of debris falling from the ceiling.

"Griffin!" It was Finley's voice through his earpiece that pulled him back. He heard her anguished cry and realized that he didn't want to leave his friends. He didn't want to leave her. And if he let go now, they would perish with him. With every last ounce of his strength, he pulled the Aether to him, coiling it, gathering it. He had never done this before—never felt like he had some control over the great rush of power. It had always felt as though it controlled him, but at this moment, he wasn't afraid of it.

He looked down and saw the most beautiful glow surrounding his body. It was his aura, bright with power. He had taken so much of the energy into him he burned like a candle in the Aetheric plane.

He flung out his hand, sending a bolt of energy into Garibaldi's chest. The villain flew back, hitting the floor. More Aether wanted to pour out, as well, but he stopped it.

Garibaldi must be wearing some sort of armor, too, for he recovered from the blast quickly. He pointed his metal hand toward Griff and it began to glow, light dancing along the fingers like lightning in the sky. He had put on that odd crownlike device from their previous encounter.

An Aether generator. Some of the more expensive Aether dens had the machines rather than using mediums and spiritualists. The machines could access the Aetheric plane and gather energy, but they were often unstable and could explode if they absorbed too much—the Aether was not constant.

Suddenly light flew from Garibaldi's metal fingers straight at Griffin. It hit him just below the chest guard—his opponent knowing exactly where to strike. But instead of knocking him down, the energy joined his own and filled him, stretching his skin until he thought he might burst into a million pieces.

He had to let it out, but the Aether was the only thing keeping him on his feet. Griffin placed one hand on the wall to support himself, the other he pointed at Garibaldi to direct the dark energy that filled him like life itself.

Then he let it go.

The blast sent his nemesis skidding across the floor until he crashed into the remains of several of his own machines. Energy skipped over the automatons, making them jerk even though they had been powered down. Garibaldi's limbs twitched and he cried out in torment.

At that moment, Griffin knew he could kill the man if he so desired. He could destroy him just as Garibaldi had destroyed his parents. But killing him would give him greater access to the Aether—and Griffin's mother.

The decision was easier than he thought. He lowered his hand, breaking the flow between himself and The Machinist. Garibaldi continued to writhe on the floor, the Aether still swarming him despite Griffin's release.

Griffin closed his eyes, and could feel heat behind his eyelids. He had never absorbed so much before. He placed both palms on the wall now, and mentally pushed. Aether drained from him into the wall and spread through the beams of the building.

Plaster began to rain from the ceiling and the entire warehouse began to tremble, then shudder.

Griffin sagged, but someone caught him. It was Sam. "Hold it together, my friend," Sam said. "Just till I get you out of here."

Griffin nodded, afraid that if he opened his mouth the Aether would pour out and kill them all.

Sam picked him up like a child, mindful of the dagger sticking out of him. Griffin's vision was narrowing, become nothing more than light, but he saw Finley run over to Garibaldi and kick him—hard. Then she ran after the rest of them and took Emily's limp frame from Jasper. They picked up speed then, Emily's cat leading the way up the stairs and out of the trembling warehouse.

Once outside, Griffin struck his hand against Sam's chest, gesturing to the ground. Thankfully, his surly friend didn't argue. He set Griffin on his feet, keeping his big hands close in case Griff fell.

The numbness in his limbs was spreading. Soon, he'd lose consciousness. Griffin placed both palms on the rough outer wall of the warehouse and pushed once more with his mind— his soul—letting go of the Aether inside him.

The building shuddered once and then imploded with a loud cracking noise. The warehouse collapsed, wood splintering as if it was nothing more than substantial than toothpicks beneath a giant boot. The force of it was so strong it knocked Griffin to the ground, where the pain in his gut came rushing back and he gasped, writhing with the agony.

His parents hovered over him, their ghostly faces etched with worry. They reached for him, and he felt his soul lift as though to join them.

Then everything went black.

There wasn't time to get Griffin home. Emily was also still unconscious and they had to get both her and Griffin somewhere safe, fast. Already they could hear the sirens of approaching Peelers. There was no hope that someone wouldn't report a collapsing warehouse, even at this time of night. The noise it made, people probably thought London was being invaded.

"Whitechapel," Finley said, making a decision she hoped was the right one. She got Sam to put Griffin on her cycle while Jasper took Emily on hers—along with the cat. Sam held Emily while a quick as lightning Jasper hitched his cycle to Emily's and Griffin's to Sam's.

She led the way, tearing through the city streets at full speed as much as she could. When she arrived at the familiar Whitechapel address, she was relieved to see a light from one of the windows. Good thing, because she'd been prepared to kick the door in if no one was there.

As it was, she had to have Jasper knock on the door for her because she had Griffin in her arms. Sam now held Emily, the big mechanical cat at his side. It was like a real-life pet, determined not to leave its mistress's side.

Jack Dandy opened the door, his usual cocky grin on his

face when he spotted Finley, but that grin faded when he saw Griffin and Emily. He simply stood back and held the door for them to come in.

Finley took Griffin upstairs and the rest followed.

"First on the right," Dandy said to Sam at the top of the stairs. Finley had already taken Griffin into the room she'd slept in her one night under this roof. She had Emily's medical bag over her shoulder, and as soon as she put Griffin on the bed, she tore open the satchel with shaking hands.

Jack was immediately beside her. One of his long, strong hands closed over hers. "I've seen worse, Treasure. It don't look as though the blade is positioned properly to have hit anyfin' important."

"How do you know?" Finley demanded, trying very hard not to cry.

Jack squeezed her hands. "I've 'ad me some experience with knives and the like. Got a scar on me own hip very much like the one 'is Grace is going to have. Now, what do you 'ave in there for stitchin' 'im up?"

When it came down to it, Finley trusted Jack—perhaps not with her virtue, but certainly with Griffin's life. Jack was smart enough to know having a duke in his debt could only be a good thing.

She helped, holding Griffin as Jack removed the blade, keeping pressure on the wound as it bled. He used the Listerine from Emily's bag to clean the wound, which eased Finley's mind greatly. If he knew to do what Emily would, then he must indeed know what he was doing. His stitches were small, quick and perfect.

Afterward, Jack gathered up the bloodstained linens. "Stay as long as you like," he told her. "I'll be 'eading out soon. Business and all that."

Finley didn't want to know, but she went to the tall, lanky

young man and wrapped her arms around his waist, hugging him. "Thank you," she said, tears leaking out of her eyes. "Thank you so much."

A gentle and hesitant hand came down on her back. "Don't cry, Treasure. You'll get me all wet and then I'll melt. I'm made of sugar, don't you know."

She laughed at that and released him, swiping at her eyes with the backs of her wrists—the only parts of her hands that weren't bloodstained. "I forgot," she said.

Jack smiled crookedly at her, his dark eyes bright with something she didn't want to identify. "I'm thinking that's going to be a five-course dinner," he informed her. "It could take the better part of the evening."

Finley nodded, feeling so much better she didn't care that he was extorting more time out of her. It was worth it. "Sounds fair," she replied.

With that, Jack tipped an imaginary hat to her and left the room. Once he was gone, Finley took the atomizer of Organites from Emily's bag, peeled back the bandage on Griffin's side and applied a generous amount of the earthy smelling spray to Griffin's wound. She even made herself pull at the sides of the wound so some could trickle between the stitches and raw flesh.

Now, all she could do was wait. She pulled a blanket from the foot of the bed over him and sat down on the edge of the mattress to watch him. The bruises on his face were finally beginning to fade, leaving a faint greenish-yellow cast to his skin.

Picking up his left hand, she held it in hers, ignoring the blood under her fingernails. It was his blood. She tried to concentrate solely on him, not on the horror of the evening, or the relief of knowing it was over. She didn't want to picture that horrifying automaton Queen Victoria bleeding, or how she'd felt as though the world had ended when she saw Griffin with the blade sticking out of him.

He had brought an entire building down with his power. He'd buried the automaton queen and all her minions. He'd undoubtedly killed and buried Leonardo Garibaldi, as well. Though, no one in their right mind would call it murder.

Then again, no one would ever know the truth of what had happened there. It would be months, even years before they discovered what was left of The Machinist and his plans underneath the warehouse floor.

Why had Garibaldi done it? Just because Victoria hadn't thought the world should know about the Organites? Because Griffin's parents—and her father—had agreed? Or was it for revenge because those three people continued their work with Organites while he could not? Maybe it was because of his lost hand. Or, perhaps it was all of the above. Garibaldi had obviously gone mad a long time ago. Who knew his true reasoning?

She was glad it was done, and now their lives didn't have to revolve around solving this mystery or stopping the villain. Right now all that mattered was Emily and Griffin being all right. Everything else was just frosting on the cake.

She just hoped Jack was right and that Griffin would heal. Because she didn't know what she would do if the only person who ever demanded her complete trust, and offered his in return, died.

It was Sam who thought to send word to Cordelia that they had defeated Garibaldi. He didn't tell her about Griffin's injury or where they were, the former because he didn't want to worry her and the latter because, despite the fact that he was nothing more than a common criminal, Jack Dandy had taken them in and helped them when they most needed it. A good turn was a good turn as far as Sam was concerned.

He was sitting at Emily's bedside, trying to stay awake by reading one of the dime novels he loved so much about cowboys in the American West. Odd that he found that culture so amazing yet could cheerfully strangle Jasper, though the cowboy had proven himself a friend, as well.

His eyelids were beginning to droop. He was so bloody tired. Now that the battle was over he felt as though he could sleep for a week. All he needed was to know that Emily and Griffin were fine, then he could sleep.

"Sam?"

His eyes snapped up and he pitched forward in his chair, suddenly very much awake.

"Em." She looked like an angel against the stark white sheets, though it was doubtful an angel would ever step foot in Jack Dandy's house. Her ropey hair was spread out around her, and her eyes as bright as jewels gazed up at him, clear and free of pain.

"How do you feel?" he asked.

"Like an elephant stepped on me," she replied with a smile. "It's not so bad, but my head..." She frowned. "My head feels so strange."

He inched forward on the chair. "Do you need me to call for a surgeon?"

She shook her head, stopping him from getting up by grasping his hand in hers. "I don't need a surgeon."

"How do you know?"

She lifted her gaze to his. "I just...know. Sam, I think interacting with the Victoria automaton's advanced engine might have changed me, made me think faster—better."

"Bloody hell," he whispered. "I couldn't keep up with you

before. You're not going to want to talk to me at all if you're even smarter now."

She smiled at him, and squeezed his hand. "I think that's one of the nicest and dumbest things you've ever said to me. Of course I want to talk to you. There's no one I'd rather talk to than you, Sam."

It was like someone lit a candle inside him, a small flickering flame that warmed him from the inside out. "Not even Griffin?"

"Especially not him. Faith, he thinks *he's* smarter than everyone else."

They chuckled over that and she looked around the room, realizing that they were not at home. "Where are we?"

"You'll never believe it." He leaned forward to whisper, "Finley brought us to Jack Dandy's."

And then Sam heard a voice in his ear, "I can hear you, you big dolt." It was Finley, and of course she could hear him, she had the ears of…well, he didn't know what. And he could hear her because he still had his earpiece in.

"Stop listening," he hissed, and pulled the little metal device from his ear. He would have crushed it had Emily not made it.

"How's Griffin?" Emily asked, still smiling over his exchange with Finley. "Did he defeat Garibaldi?"

Sam swallowed. "He did, but Garibaldi stabbed him. It was pretty bad. Dandy and Finley fixed him up. She remembered to use your 'beasties' on him, as well—not in front of Dandy, though."

Emily pushed herself up against the pillows. "How bad?"

He shook his head. "I don't know. He's still out. He brought the whole building down, Em. I wish you could have seen it. He brought it down like it was made of toothpicks, or sand."

"I would have liked to see that." Her brow puckered. "Was Garibaldi inside?"

Sam nodded.

"Good." Her face took on a tight expression. "I never thought I'd ever say that there was a person who the world would be better off without, but The Machinist's one of 'em. Though, if I know Griffin, he's bound to carry some guilt for it."

Before Sam could agree with her, there was a knock against the open door frame. Sam turned to see Jasper standing on the threshold. Of course he would show up, just as he was about to tell Emily how glad he was that she was unhurt, that he didn't know what he would do without her.

"Miss Emily, you are a sight for sore eyes," he told her, and tipped his cowboy hat. "I'm glad to see you awake."

"Thank you, Jasper. It does me good to see you upright and looking none the worse for wear, as well."

Sam frowned. "Did you want something, Renn, or are you just going to stand there all night?" Emily pinched him—hard. He flashed a glance at her, she did not look impressed.

Jasper shrugged. "Just thought y'all might like to know that Griffin's awake." Then he turned on his heel and left.

"You're so mean to him," Emily scolded lightly.

Sam made a face, but he didn't say anything. He especially did not apologize. "You want to go see Griff?"

She nodded and he stood and helped her out of bed. She had all her clothes on so she didn't need to stop for anything. They walked down the hall to the other bedroom where Finley and Jasper sat on the side of the bed and Griffin lay against the pillows, pale but awake.

"It's good to see you all," he said, his voice hoarse. "I thought I might not ever have that pleasure again. Even your ugly mug looks pretty to me, Sam."

Sam grinned. "Who do you think lugged you out of there, Your Grace?"

"Thank you." Griffin was serious this time. "All of you. Thank you for helping me fight, and thank you for saving my life."

"It's what you'd do for us," Jasper reminded him.

"It's enough that you're alive," Finley told him. Sam noticed that the girl was holding Griffin's hand in her own and his friend didn't seem to mind.

"Yes," Griff agreed. "I hear I have Mr. Dandy to thank for that. Is he here?"

Finley told him that Dandy had left some time ago, but that he'd told them to stay for as long as they needed. Griffin seemed oddly relieved that their host was missing, Sam thought. Kind of like how he felt whenever Jasper Renn *wasn't* around. Jealousy, that's what it was. He never would have thought Griffin capable of such emotion, not when he was born to a position in life that meant he could pretty much have whatever he wanted.

Although, the human heart didn't come with a price on it.

Two days later, a fully recovered Griffin came down to breakfast to find his friends and aunt gathering. Cordelia poured him a cup of coffee, fluttering over him like a mother hen. She even tried to fix him a plate of food, but he convinced her he could get his own. When he found out whomever it was who told her how badly he'd been hurt, he'd string them up by their toes.

"I just received a note from the Director," Cordelia told them all once they settled down to eat. "They've searched the warehouse. Twenty automatons were accounted for, but Garibaldi and the remains of the Victoria automaton were missing."

Griffin froze, a knot of dread forming in his chest. "You mean, Garibaldi may still be alive?" He hadn't wanted to kill him because that would give him better access to the Aether, but hearing the villain might still be alive chilled him.

"It's unlikely," Cordelia replied in one of her more soothing tones. "The Director believes Garibaldi had an accomplice, who went into the wreckage shortly after the collapse and got both man and machine out of there. I suspect one of his automatons was still operational and pulled Garibaldi's body from the building. There's no way he could have survived what you did to the building, Griffin."

Griffin shook his head. "Without a body, no one can say for certain The Machinist is dead." He might come back.

Obviously Cordelia sensed his unease because he soon heard her voice in his head, "Garibaldi is gone, Griffin. He could never have survived what you did to that place You must believe me."

He smiled at her to show that he did. Of course he believed her. It was just that he'd feel so much better if they had proof. If he could go to the funeral and see Garibaldi in the casket with his own two eyes.

He'd gotten justice for his parents, but it didn't feel as satisfying as he thought it would, and not just because Garibaldi was missing, but because no matter what he did, he couldn't bring his parents back. As wealthy and powerful as he was, he was still as helpless as any man.

*"And,"* Cordelia began, smiling around the table at them as she interrupted his maudlin thoughts, "Her Majesty would like for you all to come to tea at the palace next Wednesday so she can personally thank each and every one of you for sabotaging The Machinist's plot to replace and possibly kill her."

"Are we certain that's what he wanted to do?" Griffin

asked. He wasn't as flabbergasted by the queen's invitation as the others. "Kill her?"

His aunt nodded. "My friend found bits of notes amongst the papers and blueprints in the warehouse—all of which are on your desk, by the way—that seem to indicate Garibaldi's plan was to kill the real Victoria and replace her with his metal doppelganger. With his machine in place, he would effectively rule the country, and his revenge for what he considered his monarch's betrayal would be complete. He had plans to take away the Devonshire mines from Greythorne and make them his own."

"All of this for the Organites," Griffin muttered. "So many dead for those strange little creatures." He would have liked to see Garibaldi just *try* to take his home away.

"Her Majesty was right to want them kept secret." Finley turned to him. "Look what they did to Garibaldi."

"Well, he's gone now," Sam said, slathering a thick slice of toast with jam. "And I say good riddance."

Griffin raised his coffee cup. "Hear, hear." When everyone went back to talking amongst themselves, he directed his attention at Finley. "Would you care to take a walk with me later? I thought we might go to Hyde Park." Where they had first met, though he didn't say that aloud. He also pretended not to notice that everyone at the table was listening with interest, waiting to hear Finley's reply.

She smiled. "I'd like that. Jasper's going to teach me more kung fu later, and Emily and I have plans to discuss Da Vinci, but I'm free around two."

He grinned. Most girls he knew would cancel those other things to conform to his whim, not tell him to wait. He liked it. "Two it is." He then glanced at Jasper, who had become something of a regular fixture around his house as of late. In fact, they hadn't continued that conversation Jasper began in his study before Finley interrupted.

They were just finishing up breakfast when a knock sounded upon the front door. A few moments later, Mrs. Dodsworth bustled in, four rough-looking men behind her.

"I told them to wait, Your Grace, but they refused!"

Griffin calmly rose to his feet. "Who are you and what are you doing in my house?"

One of the men stepped forward and tipped his hat. "Morning, Your Grace. Sorry to barge in on you like this, but my associates and I are here to arrest Jasper Renn and take him New York City."

A collective gasp of surprise rose from those around the table.

"What?" Griffin scowled at the man. "On what charges?"

"Murder," the man replied, his gaze darting from Griffin to Jasper and back again. He offered Griffin a folded and tattered piece of brownish paper. "We don't want no trouble."

Griffin opened the paper. It was a Wanted poster, and on it was a good likeness of Jasper, along with the promise of a $5000 reward for whoever brought him in. It looked official.

"America's laws aren't law here," he told the man, thrusting the poster into his hand. "Please leave."

The man hitched up his gun belt. "I don't think you understand. We're not leaving without Renn."

"Oh, yes, you are," Finley said, rising to her feet. Sam and Emily stood, as well.

The man laughed and pulled a gun from the holster around his hips. "I got six bullets right here that say we're taking the boy with us and you're gonna let us."

Since the night at the warehouse, the Aether came readily to Griffin—almost too readily. It didn't overwhelm him as it had when he was younger, but it always seemed to be there, just waiting for his call. Right now he was going to call it to knock this yokel on his dirty arse.

"I'll go."

All heads turned. Jasper stood and faced the men with an expression Griffin could only term resigned. It was that expression that told him that this was what Jasper had wanted to talk about. He was in trouble and Griffin had been too caught up in his own affairs to see that.

"Griff, don't do anything." Jasper moved toward the Americans, eyeing them with an unflinching gaze. "I'll go willingly, just put the gun away."

The man hesitated for a moment, then relented. "Get the cuffs on him."

Griffin couldn't allow his friend to be taken from his house like a criminal, but Jasper shot him a look that told him to stay out of it. It was also a look of remorse. Rather than endanger his friends, he was going to allow these ruffians to take him back to America where he'd stand trial—if he lived that long—for murder.

Griffin swallowed, hard. It was difficult for him not to try to take control of this situation, not to order the men out of his house. Very, very difficult to allow Jasper to make his own decisions. Even the others didn't want that. Finley was one of the more vocal as they clapped irons around Jasper's wrists.

"You can't let them do this!" Finley cried at him.

Griffin looked at her. "It's Jasper's choice, not ours."

Voices rose again, arguing with him, but it was Jasper's that cut through the cacophony. "Stop!"

They all looked at him.

"Y'all have been real good to me—the best friends I've ever had—but a man can outrun his past only for so long before he's got to pay for his sins." His gaze locked with Griffin's. "Thank you…for everything. Goodbye." The last was addressed to all of them, though the cowboy's gaze lingered just an extra half second on Emily, who had tears in her big eyes. Finley, too. Even Cordelia looked saddened.

Griff inclined his head. "Goodbye, Jas."

They stood in silence as the men led Jasper out of the room, sandwiched between the four of them. It wasn't until they heard the door shut that everyone turned on him, demanded to know why he hadn't done something, and what were they going to do now? They couldn't just let Jasper hang.

"No, we can't," Griffin agreed, silencing them. They gaped at him like fish in a bowl. "And we're not going to." Lifting his coffee cup, he drained the rest of it, set it down and then began to walk across the room.

"Where are you going?" Sam demanded. Even Sam didn't want to see Jasper go. That was a pleasant surprise.

"To pack," Griffin replied. He flashed a grin at Finley, who was staring at him as though he were mad. "How do you feel about taking that walk in New York City?"

★ ★ ★ ★ ★

# *Acknowledgments*

An author rarely writes a book all on his/her own. There's usually a put-upon friend who sits and listens while we drone on about our "fascinating" plot, or a spouse who eats takeout more often than either he/she wants. In my case, there are several people who seriously need to be thanked for this book ever finding its way into your fabulous little hands. First of all I need to thank Krista Stroever, editor extraordinaire. When I told Krista I wanted to write *League of Extraordinary Gentlemen* meets teen *X-Men* she replied, "Steampunk. Cool." She treats me like a rock star and I love her to bits for it. I'm just waiting for her to get a restraining order!

Also, I have to give a shout-out to three fabulous writer friends who held my hand through this process and provided much need pep talks and rational thinking when I'd lost all of mine. So Jesse Petersen, Colleen Gleason and Sophie Jordan—you are the best girlfriends I could ask for. I just wish I could see more of you.

Thanks to Nancy Yost for selling this book and for years of invaluable guidance. Miriam Kriss, thanks for being your rockin' self and not laughing at my Yoda backpack. The Force is strong in you.

More thanks have to go out to my friends for understanding when I can't come out to play, or when I'm crazier than usual. Thank you to my family for being more incredible characters than I could ever create (I'm looking at you, Weezie). And thank you to Sarah Rose for reading this book in the early stages and giving me ideas for T-shirts.

Last, but certainly never least, I have to point the spotlight at my husband, Steve, without whom I quite literally could not have written this book. Thank you for your research, your brains, your enthusiasm and tireless support. I don't have enough words to explain what a huge part you played in this project, which is good because if I did have the words, I'm sure you'd never let me forget them. Most of all, thanks for just being your fabulous self because there's no one else I'd rather spend the rest of my life laughing with than you.

Oh, and I would be remiss if I didn't acknowledge those awkward years I spent between the ages of thirteen and eighteen. I wouldn't go back to you for any amount of money, but I wouldn't change you, either. Though, I wouldn't mind giving you a good slap or two.

# Coming soon... Book one in the new
# Blood of Eden series

In a future world, vampires reign.
Humans are blood cattle.
And one girl will search for the key
to save humanity.

Allison Sekemoto survives in the Fringe, the
outermost circle of a vampire city. Until one night
she is attacked—and given the ultimate choice.
Die...or become one of the monsters.

www.miraink.co.uk

Join us at facebook.com/miraink

M253_TIR

# Read Me. Love Me. Share Me.

Did you love this book? Want to read other amazing teen books for free online and have your voice heard as a reviewer, trend-spotter and all-round expert?

Then join us at **facebook.com/MIRAink** and chat with authors, watch trailers, WIN books, share reviews and help us to create the kind of books that you'll want to carry on reading forever!

Romance. Horror. Paranormal. Dystopia. Fantasy.

**Whatever you're in the mood for, we've got it covered.**

Don't miss a single word

 twitter.com/MIRAink

let's be friends

 facebook.com/MIRAink

Scan me with your smart phone

 to go straight to our facebook page